John Mortimer

RUMPOLE

Selected and introduced
by the author

Illustrations by
Paul Cox

The Folio Society
London 1994

1995

Contents

Introduction

About eighteen years ago I thought I needed a character, like Maigret or Sherlock Holmes, to keep me alive in my old age. I wanted a sort of detective, who could be the hero of a number of stories but whose personality and approach to life were more important than the crimes with which he was concerned. He would have to be a comic character, as well as being courageous and more than usually astute, because I believe life to be best portrayed as comedy.

I spent most of my life following two professions. I was first and last a writer, an inventor of stories. I also practised as a lawyer and I defended many people accused of crimes at the Old Bailey, London's Central Criminal Court. There I was concerned with stories, many of which were too fantastic and improbable for even the most gifted writer to persuade his readers to believe. An English criminal trial is a very theatrical occasion – the barristers and judges wear wigs and gowns, some of the judges are in scarlet and ermine and, on state occasions, carry bunches of flowers (once necessary to protect their noses from prison stench). I often left court to go to a rehearsal of a play I had written and felt I had left the world of fantasy and make-believe at the Old Bailey for the harsh reality of the world of art.

So, when I looked for a character to be my detective I found him very near at hand. I thought of all the old defenders in criminal trials I had known – rumpled, untidy men, fond of claret and steak and kidney pie, who often called the most unattractive judges and the most hardened bank robbers 'old darling' but never called their wives 'old darling'. I thought of my father, who was also a barrister, and his costume which was rather like that which Mr Churchill used to wear in the war: a black jacket and waistcoat across which stretched a gold watch-chain, often smothered in cigar ash, a stand-up collar and a bow-tie. My father also had Rumpole's habit of quoting poetry at very inapposite moments. When I was about four when he saw me he would say, 'Is execution done on Cawdor?' which, when you're four, is a pretty tough question to have to answer. Barristers are meant to be polite to solicitors, who bring them work, but when he was displeased with one of them my father often said, 'The devil damn thee black, thou cream-faced loon,' thinking they'd be glad of another quotation from *Macbeth*.

So, from a collection of characters, Horace Rumpole was born. He is very unlike me, being a far more stoic and single-minded person than I am. However, he has this great advantage – he does say a good many of the things I think and if I said them they might sound rather leftish and off-putting, but when given voice by Rumpole they become crusty, conservative and much more appealing. He is, after all, the great defender of muddled and sinful humanity, the man who believes in never pleading guilty. He is, in its most admirable form, the archetypal Old Bailey hack.

Although the defence in a criminal case has a number of rights, many judges tend to favour the prosecution, and old defenders such as Rumpole are often treated as though they were criminals themselves. Some judges do this with great subtlety; others, like Rumpole's old enemy Judge Bullingham, are given to head-on confrontations. When summing up, judges are bound to remind the jury of the defence case, but there are various ways of doing this. An Australian judge is said to have held his nose and pulled an imaginary lavatory chain after reading out the evidence given on behalf of the accused. His Honour Judge Bullingham and his like content themselves with sighing heavily, raising their eyes to heaven and saying, 'Of course you can believe that if you want to, Members of the Jury. It's a matter entirely for you.' Over the years Rumpole has learnt to fight this snorting and purple-faced member of the judiciary with the skill of a toreador, sometimes emerging with a figurative ear or a tail. But such days in court are hard for Rumpole.

He also has a number of fights on his hands in his Chambers, where his total lack of respect for authority gets him into perpetual trouble with the more pompous legal hacks. Throughout these stories I have been anxious to make it clear that judges and lawyers are not all wise, infallible and trustworthy but as vain, insecure, sometimes as prejudiced, and often as foolish as the rest of us.

And then there is Rumpole's home life, which I wanted to make as testing an experience for him as his days in court. The particular term of endearment he uses for the formidable Hilda – 'She Who Must Be Obeyed' – comes from *She* by Rider Haggard, a book Rumpole remembers having read as a boy. The 'She' in that story was kept alive in a cave for about a thousand years and may have even once been Queen Cleopatra. Hilda simply calls her husband 'Rumpole', but their adversarial relationship springs from a deep mutual need. Although the Rumpoles sometimes feel they can't stand living together they couldn't, I'm sure, contemplate living apart. Their differences may come from the fact that Hilda might not mind a bit of sex but Rumpole's amorous experiences wouldn't fill one wet weekend in Weston-super-Mare. In writing about them I have found that any incident in married life, between a large assortment of people, fits easily into the mansion flat in the Gloucester Road where the Rumpoles argue their various causes.

I wrote the first Rumpole story as a one-off *Play For Today* on BBC television. When I had written it I looked around for an actor to play Rumpole and I thought of the magnificent Alastair Sim. However Mr Sim was dead and unable to take on the part. In a happy moment Leo McKern was approached and in an even happier moment he agreed to play the role. He is a superb actor of endless invention and instinctive taste. He brought Rumpole wholly and wonderfully to life, and it would now be impossible to think of anyone else playing the part. After our one-off play the BBC was a little slow to commission the series so we went off to commercial television, for which I have written about thirty-six Rumpole stories. After the initial play, Rumpole's Chambers filled with characters – the opera-loving and susceptible Claude Erskine-Brown; the beautiful Phillida Erskine-Brown, née Trant, the 'Portia of our Chambers'; the accident-prone Guthrie Featherstone, QC, MP, soon to become one of Her Majesty's most haunted judges; Uncle Tom, the briefless old barrister who practises putting in the clerk's room and has a head full of legal anecdotes and music-hall songs; Mizz Liz Probert, the fearless young radical lawyer; Henry the clerk and the intolerably pompous Sam Ballard, QC, leading light of the Lawyers As Christians Society and well-trained husband of the ex-matron at the Old Bailey. It has been a great pleasure to weave their stories in with the crimes and the trials and the Rumpoles' domestic life, but doing so has meant that every Rumpole story has had to have at least three plots, so I must have invented well over a hundred stories. I hope this makes them more enjoyable to read, although it doesn't make them any easier to write.

The first Rumpole on the BBC was fairly well received, but nothing prepared me for his long life or, indeed, for his popularity abroad. He is as resolutely English as boiled beef and carrots and yet perhaps his greatest success has been in America and Australia. In the vast Gas and Electricity Building in San Francisco the ever-growing Rumpole Society holds its meetings. Californian judges in 'She Who Must Be Obeyed' T-shirts serve out Château Thames Embankment in a mock-up of Pommeroy's Wine Bar. There is a character in the stories called Dodo Mackintosh who makes 'cheesy bits' for the Chambers' parties; the proceedings in San Francisco start with a blind tasting of Dodo's cheesy bits. They also include such events as a Hilda Rumpole look-alike competition and the compilation of a Rumpole cookbook. As I write the stories quite fast, my hero's address in Froxbury Mansions has appeared in somewhat different forms. This gives the Rumpolians much to speculate about and discuss. Apart from having a number of societies to his name, Rumpole has several pubs, an office building and an excellent restaurant in Brisbane which, however, serves none of his favourite food.

He also has to suffer the indignity of having me mistaken for him. Criminals I defended often said, 'That Mr Rumpole could have got me off this one, I don't know why you couldn't.' Passing through Australian airports, I am often greeted with cries of 'G'day Rumpole!' When I did my last case, which happened to be in Singapore, I staggered into the robing-room of that country's Central Court, jet lagged, hung-over, with no clear idea of what the case was all about, in the usual position of a leading counsel at the beginning of an important criminal trial. This particular oriental robing-room was presided over by an elderly Chinese woman who was busy brewing up Nescafé and pouring out cough mixture for barristers with sore throats. At the sight of me, she called out gleefully, 'Ah, there you are, Lumpore of the Bairey!' I knew I didn't want to spend my declining years trudging around the Far East being called Lumpore, so I gave up my legal practice. All the same, I am not at all ashamed of having been mistaken for the great man.

It is said that Conan Doyle grew tired of his creation and, for that reason, arranged for him to be pushed off the Reichenbach Falls, although he had to bring him back to life by popular request. I have never felt tempted to push Rumpole under a train at the Temple station. Although I can imagine an author tiring of Holmes's dry and ascetic character, Rumpole stories have the great advantage, for me, of moving with the times. Whatever's happening in the world, and needs mocking – the power of social workers, the fallibility of judges, euthanasia, political correctness and the ghastliness of our penal system – can all be dealt with in a Rumpole story. So each one doesn't only need three plots, it also needs a theme, a basic idea and something, I hope something unsettling, to think about while you laugh.

And in creating Rumpole I did have another purpose in mind. On the whole, lawyers are as unpopular as income tax collectors and traffic wardens. People think they tell lies and make a great deal of money. In fact, old criminal defenders like Rumpole don't make much money and they stand up for our great legal principles – free speech, the idea that people are innocent until someone proves them guilty to the satisfaction of ten ordinary members of a jury, and the proposition that the police should not invent more of the evidence than is absolutely necessary. They protect the rights for which we have fought and struggled over the centuries, and do so at a time when jury trials and the rights of an accused person to silence are under constant attack from the Government. So Rumpole has always been popular with lawyers, although it's embarrassing to go into the wine bars round the Old Bailey and see a lot of fat, elderly barristers with cigar ash on their watch-chains drinking bad claret and pretending to be the original Rumpole. Writing Rumpole plays had another great advantage for me when I worked in the courts: if the judge did something especially silly I could always write him into a Rumpole.

In this book I have chosen ten of my favourite Rumpole stories. They are the stories I have enjoyed writing most, those which made me laugh a little when I was writing them (the only reliable test of a successful piece of work), and which drew some laughter from the actors when they read through the television versions. 'Rumpole and the Younger Generation' was the story which became the first play in the first television series. 'Rumpole and the Showfolk' illustrated the make-believe world of law courts and the serious reality of theatres. 'Rumpole and the Tap End' had some basis in an actual case and shows that the end which a judge occupies, when taking a bath with his wife, may influence his view of a case. 'Rumpole and the Bubble Reputation' deals with the ever-fascinating question of libel and the absurd monetary value placed on persons of the most doubtful repute.

I wrote 'Rumpole and the Old Boy Net' about the old school tie which still, unfortunately, joins judges to barristers and, occasionally, those who find themselves in the dock. I dreamt up a couple who were extremely respectable brothel keepers, catering for old public-school boys in search of a rare moment of pleasure. To my delight they were acted, impeccably, by Michael Denison and Dulcie Gray in the television version of the story. I wrote 'Rumpole and the Bright Seraphim' about a court martial in the British army in Germany, and writing it led to a curious incident in which fiction became fact in a somewhat unnerving manner.

I had never appeared in a court martial when I was a barrister, so I went to Germany to find out the procedure. I watched the trial of a young soldier accused of smoking cannabis, the only evidence against him being that he said that was what his cigarette contained. Was he lying, or boasting vainly, or could his word be relied on? After I had discovered how court martials worked I came home and wrote 'Rumpole and the Bright Seraphim', which starts when a sergeant is found outside a disco bar in a small German town wearing a woman's red evening dress and stabbed through the heart. The story became a television play. A couple of years later I was invited to dinner by a Guards regiment in Germany and I went for a drink in the sergeants' mess. There I was asked if I'd ever visited the army in Germany before. I said I had and that I'd come out to attend the court martial of a young soldier accused of smoking a cannabis cigarette. 'Oh, no you didn't,' one of the sergeants corrected me, 'you came out because of that murder we had here a few years ago. The one where they found an NCO outside a disco stabbed through the heart and wearing a woman's dress.' It was with a mixture of excitement and fear that I felt I had exceeded a writer's powers and invented a story which had become history.

'Rumpole and the Family Pride' was a story I wrote because I wanted to gratify Hilda's longing for social success and Rumpole's instinctive mistrust of the upper classes.

'Rumpole à la Carte' is a mystery which takes place among the octagonal plates and silver domes that conceal the minute portions of food in snooty restaurants run by egomaniac chefs. It is designed to show Rumpole's dislike of such places and his contempt for *nouvelle cuisine*. 'Rumpole and the Children of the Devil' is a comedy about a diabolically obsessed social worker (I don't think there is any subject you should not write a comedy about). 'Rumpole on Trial' is the latest of the long sequence of Rumpole stories; in it Rumpole is in grave danger of being pushed off the Reichenbach Falls. Does our hero survive to fight another case? That is something, I'm afraid, which you will have to find out for yourselves.

JOHN MORTIMER

Rumpole and the Younger Generation

I, Horace Rumpole, barrister at law, sixty-eight next birthday, Old Bailey hack, husband to Mrs Hilda Rumpole (known to me only as She Who Must Be Obeyed) and father to Nicholas Rumpole (lecturer in social studies at the University of Baltimore, I have always been extremely proud of Nick); I, who have a mind full of old murders, legal anecdotes and memorable fragments of the *Oxford Book of English Verse* (Sir Arthur Quiller-Couch's edition) together with a dependable knowledge of bloodstains, blood groups, fingerprints, and forgery by typewriter; I, who am now the oldest member of my Chambers, take up my pen at this advanced age during a lull in business (there's not much crime about – all the best villains seem to be off on holiday in the Costa Brava), in order to write my reconstructions of some of my recent triumphs (including a number of recent disasters) in the Courts of Law, hoping thereby to turn a bob or two which won't be immediately grabbed by the taxman, or my clerk Henry, or by She Who Must Be Obeyed, and perhaps give some sort of entertainment to those who, like myself, have found in British justice a life-long subject of harmless fun.

When I first considered putting pen to paper in this matter of my life, I thought I must begin with the great cases of my comparative youth, the 'Penge Bungalow Murder', where I gained an acquittal alone and without a leader, or the 'Great Brighton Benefit Club Forgery', which I contrived to win by reason of my exhaustive study of typewriters. In these cases I was, for a brief moment, in the public eye, or at least my name seemed almost a permanent feature of the *News of the World*, but when I come to look back on that period of my life at the Bar it all seems to have happened to another Rumpole, an eager young barrister whom I can scarcely recognise and whom I am not at all sure I would like, at least not enough to spend a whole book with him.

I am not a public figure now, so much has to be admitted; but some of the cases I shall describe, the wretched business of the Honourable Member, for instance, or the charge of murder brought against the youngest, and barmiest, of the appalling Delgardo brothers, did put me back on the front page of the *News of the World* (and even got me a few inches in *The Times*). But I suppose I have become pretty well known, if not something of a legend, round the Old Bailey, in Pommeroy's Wine Bar in Fleet Street, in the robing-room at London Sessions and in the cells at Brixton Prison. They know me there for never pleading guilty, for chain-smoking small cigars, and for quoting Wordsworth when they least expect it. Such notoriety will not long survive my not-to-be-delayed trip to Golders Green Crematorium. Barristers' speeches vanish quicker than Chinese dinners, and even the greatest victory in Court rarely survives longer than the next Sunday's papers.

To understand the full effect on my family life, however, of that case which I have called 'Rumpole and the Younger Generation', it is necessary to know a little of my past and the long years that led up to my successful defence of Jim Timson, the sixteen-year-old sprig, the young hopeful, and apple of the eye of the Timsons, a huge and industrious family of South London villains. As this case was, by and large, a family matter, it is important that you should understand my family.

My father, the Reverend Wilfred Rumpole, was a Church of England clergyman who, in early middle age, came reluctantly to the conclusion that he no longer believed any one of the Thirty-nine Articles. As he was not fitted by character or training for any other profession, however, he had to soldier on in his living in Croydon and by a good deal of scraping and saving he was able to send me as a boarder to a minor public school on the Norfolk coast. I later went to Keble College, Oxford, where I achieved a dubious third in law – you will discover during the course of these memoirs that, although I only feel truly alive and happy in Law Courts, I have a singular distaste for the law. My father's example, and the number of theological students I met at Keble, gave me an early mistrust of clergymen whom I have always found to be most unsatisfactory witnesses. If you call a clergyman in mitigation, the old darling can be guaranteed to add at least a year to the sentence.

When I first went to the Bar, I entered the Chambers of C. H.

Wystan. Wystan had a moderate practice, acquired rather by industry than talent, and a strong disinclination to look at the photographs in murder cases, being particularly squeamish on the fascinating subject of blood. He also had a daughter, Hilda Wystan as was, now Mrs Hilda Rumpole and She Who Must Be Obeyed. I was ambitious in those days. I did my best to cultivate Wystan's clerk Albert, and I started to get a good deal of criminal work. I did what was expected of me and spent happy hours round the Bailey and Sessions and my fame grew in criminal circles; at the end of the day I would take Albert for a drink in Pommeroy's Wine Bar. We got on extremely well and he would always recommend 'his Mr Rumpole' if a solicitor rang up with a particularly tricky indecent assault or a nasty case of receiving stolen property.

There is no point in writing your memoirs unless you are prepared to be completely candid, and I must confess that, in the course of a long life, I have been in love on several occasions. I am sure that I loved Miss Porter, the shy and nervous, but at times liberated daughter of Septimus Porter, my Oxford tutor in Roman Law. In fact we were engaged to be married, but the engagement had to be broken off because of Miss Porter's early death. I often think about her, and of the different course my home life might have taken, for Miss Porter was in no way a girl born to command, or expect, implicit obedience. During my service with the ground staff of the RAF I undoubtedly became helplessly smitten with the charms of an extremely warm-hearted and gallant officer in the WAAFs by the name of Miss Bobby O'Keefe, but I was no match for the wings of a pilot officer, as appeared on the chest of a certain Sam 'Three-Fingers' Dogherty. During my conduct of a case, I once again felt a hopeless and almost feverish stirring of passion for a young woman who was determined to talk her way into Holloway Prison. My relationship with Hilda Wystan was rather different.

To begin with, she seemed part of life in Chambers. She was always interested in the law and ambitious, first for her widowed father, and then, when he proved himself unlikely Lord Chancellor material, for me. She often dropped in for tea on her way home from shopping, and Wystan used to invite me in for a cup. One year I was detailed off to be her partner at an Inns of Court ball. There it became clear to me that I was expected to marry Hilda; it seemed a step in my career like getting a brief in the Court of Appeal, or doing a murder. When she proposed to me, as she did over a glass of claret cup after an energetic waltz, Hilda made it clear that, when old Wystan finally retired, she expected to see me Head of Chambers. I, who have never felt at a loss for a word in Court, found absolutely nothing to say. In that silence the matter was concluded.

So now you must picture Hilda and me twenty-five years later, with a son at that same east coast public school which I just managed to afford from the fruits of crime, in our matrimonial home at 25B Froxbury Court, Gloucester Road. (A mansion flat is a misleading description of that cavernous and underheated area which Hilda devotes so much of her energy to keeping shipshape, not to say Bristol fashion.) We were having breakfast, and, between bites of toast, I was reading my brief for that day, an Old Bailey trial of the sixteen-year-old Jim Timson charged with robbery with violence, he having allegedly taken part in a wage snatch on a couple of elderly butchers: an escapade planned in the playground of the local comprehensive. As so often happens, the poet Wordsworth, that old sheep of the Lake District, sprang immediately to mind, and I gave tongue to his lines, well knowing that they must only serve to irritate She Who Must Be Obeyed.

> *'Trailing clouds of glory do we come*
> *From God, who is our home;*
> *Heaven lies about us in our infancy!'*

I looked at Hilda. She was impassively demolishing a boiled egg. I also noticed that she was wearing a hat, as if prepared to set out upon some expedition. I decided to give her a little more Wordsworth, prompted by my reading the story of the boy Timson.

> *'Shades of the prison house begin to close*
> *Upon the growing boy.'*

Hilda spoke at last.

'Rumpole, you're not talking about your son, I hope. You're never referring to Nick . . . '

' "Shades of the prison house begin to close?" Not round our son, of course. Not round Nick. Shades of the public school have grown round him, the thousand-quid-a-year remand home.'

Hilda always thought it indelicate to refer to the subject of school fees, as if being at Mulstead were a kind of unsolicited honour for Nick. She became increasingly business-like.

'He's breaking up this morning.'

'Shades of the prison house begin to open up for the holidays.'

'Nick has to be met at 11.15 at Liverpool Street and given lunch. When he went back to school you promised him a show. You haven't forgotten?'

Hilda was clearing away the plates rapidly. To tell the truth I had forgotten the date of Nick's holidays; but I let her assume I had a long-planned treat laid on for him.

'Of course I haven't forgotten. The only show I can offer him is a robbery with violence in Number 2 Court at the Old Bailey. I wish I could lay on a murder. Nick's always so enjoyed my murders.'

It was true. On one distant half term Nick had sat in on the 'Peckham Billiard Hall Stabbing', and enjoyed it a great deal more than *Treasure Island.*

'I must fly! Daddy gets so crotchety if anyone's late. And he does love his visits.'

Hilda removed my half-empty coffee cup.

'Our father which art in Horsham. Give my respects to the old sweetheart.'

It had also slipped my mind that old C. H. Wystan was laid up with a dicky ticker in Horsham General Hospital. The hat was, no doubt, a clue I should have followed. Hilda usually goes shopping in a head-scarf. By now she was at the door, and looking disapproving.

' "Old sweetheart" is hardly how you used to talk of the Head of your Chambers.'

'Somehow I can never remember to call the Head of my Chambers "Daddy".'

The door was open. Hilda was making a slow and effective exit.

'Tell Nick I'll be back in good time to get his supper.'

'Your wish is my command!' I muttered in my best imitation of a slave out of *Chou Chin Chow*. She chose to ignore it.

'And try not to leave the kitchen looking as though it's been hit by a bomb.'

'I hear, O Master of the Blue Horizons.' I said this with a little more confidence, as she had by now started off on her errand of mercy, and I added, for good measure, 'She Who Must Be Obeyed'.

I had finished my breakfast, and was already thinking how much easier life with the Old Bailey judge than marriage.

Soon after I finished my breakfast with Hilda, and made plans to meet my son at the start of his holidays from school, Fred Timson, star of a dozen Court appearances, was seeing *his* son in the cells under the Old Bailey as the result of a specially arranged visit. I know he brought the boy his best jacket, which his mother had taken spe-

cially to the cleaners, and insisted on his putting on a tie. I imagine he told him that they had the best 'brief' in the business to defend him, Mr Rumpole having always done wonders for the Timson family. I know that Fred told young Jim to stand up straight in the witness box and remember to call the judge 'my Lord' and not show his ignorance by coming out with any gaffe such as 'your Honour', or 'Sir'. The world, that day, was full of fathers showing appropriate and paternal concern.

The robbery with which Jim Timson was

charged was an exceedingly simple one. At about 7 p.m. one Friday evening, the date being 16 September, the two elder Brixton butchers, Mr Cadwallader and Mr Lewis Stein, closed their shop in Bombay Road and walked with their week's takings round the corner to a narrow alley-way known as Green's Passage, where their grey Austin van was parked. When they got to the van they found that the front tyres had been deflated. They stooped to inspect the wheels and, as they did so, they were attacked by a number of boys, some armed with knives and one flourishing a cricket stump. Luckily, neither of the butchers was hurt, but the attaché case containing their money was snatched.

Chief Inspector 'Persil' White, the old darling in whose territory this outrage had been committed, arrested Jim Timson. All the other boys got clean away, but no doubt because he came from a family well known, indeed almost embarrassingly familiar, to the chief inspector, and because of certain rumours in the school playground, he was charged and put on an identity parade. The butchers totally failed to identify him; but, when he was in the remand centre, young Jim, according to the evidence, had boasted to another boy of having 'done the butchers'.

As I thought about this case on my way to the Temple that morning, it occurred to me that Jim Timson was a year younger than my son, but that he had got a step further than Nick in following his father's profession. I had always hoped Nick would go into the law, and, as I say, he seemed to thoroughly enjoy my murders.

In the clerk's room in Chambers Albert was handing out the work for the day: rather as a trainer sends his string of horses out on the gallops. I looked round the familiar faces, my friend George Frobisher, who is an old sweetheart but an absolutely hopeless advocate (he can't ask for costs without writing down what he's going to say), was being fobbed off with a nuisance at Kingston County Court. Young Erskine-Brown, who wears striped shirts and what I believe are known as 'Chelsea Boots', was turning up his well-bred nose at an indecent assault at Lambeth (a job I'd have bought Albert a double claret in Pommeroy's for at his age) and saying he would prefer a little civil work, adding that he was so sick to death of crime.

I have very little patience with Erskine-Brown.

'A person who is tired of crime', I told him quite candidly, 'is tired of life.'

'Your Dangerous and Careless at Clerkenwell is on the mantelpiece, Mr Hoskins,' Albert said.

Hoskins is a gloomy fellow with four daughters; he's always lurking about our clerk's room looking for cheques. As I've told him often enough crime doesn't pay, or at any rate not for a very long time.

When a young man called MacLay had asked in vain for a brief I invited him to take a note for me down at the Old Bailey. At least he'd get a wig on and not spend a miserable day unemployed in Chambers. Our oldest member, Uncle Tom (very few of us remember that his name is T. C. Rowley) also asked Albert if there were any briefs for him, not in the least expecting to find one. To my certain knowledge, Uncle Tom hasn't appeared in Court for fifteen years, when he managed to lose an undefended divorce case, but, as he lives with a widowed sister, a lady of such reputed ferocity that she makes She Who Must Be Obeyed sound like Mrs Tiggywinkle, he spends most of his time in Chambers. He looked remarkably well for seventy-eight.

'You aren't actually *expecting* a brief, Uncle Tom, are you?' Erskine-Brown asked. I can't like Erskine-Brown.

'Time was,' Uncle Tom started one of his reminiscences of life in our Chambers. 'Time was when I had more briefs in my corner of the mantelpiece, Erskine-Brown, than you've seen in the whole of your short career at the Bar. Now', he was opening a brown envelope, 'I only get invitations to insure my life. It's a little late for that.'

Albert told me that the robbery was not before 11.30 before Mr Justice Everglade in Number 1 Court. He also told me who was prosecuting, none other than the tall, elegant figure with the silk handkerchief and gold wristwatch, leaning against the mantelpiece and negligently reading a large cheque from the Director of Public Prosecutions, Guthrie Featherstone, MP. He removed the silk handkerchief, dabbed the end of his nose and his small moustache and asked in that voice which comes over so charmingly, saying nothing much about any important topic of the day in 'World at One',

'Agin me Rumpole? Are you agin me?' He covered a slight yawn with the handkerchief before returning it to his breast-pocket. 'Just come from an all-night sitting down at the House. I don't suppose your robbery'll be much of a worry.'

'Only, possibly, to young Jim Timson,' I told him, and then gave Albert his orders for the day. 'Mrs Rumpole's gone down to see her father in Horsham.'

'How is Wystan? No better, is he?' Uncle Tom sounded as gently pleased as all old men do when they hear news of illness in others.

'Much the same, Uncle Tom, thank you. And Young Nick. My son . . .'

'Master Nick?' Albert had always been fond of Nick, and looked forward to putting him through his paces when the time came for him to join our stable in Chambers.

'He's breaking up today. So he'll need meeting at Liverpool Street. Then he can watch a bit of the robbery.'

'We're going to have your son in the audience? I'd better be brilliant.' Guthrie Featherstone now moved from the fireplace.

'You needn't bother, old darling. It's his dad he comes to see.'

'Oh, *touché*, Rumpole! *Distinctement touché!*'

Featherstone talks like that. Then he invited me to walk down to the Bailey with him. Apparently he was still capable of movement and didn't need a stretcher, even after a sleepless night with the Gas Mains Enabling Bill, or whatever it was.

We walked together down Fleet Street and into Ludgate Circus, Featherstone wearing his overcoat with the velvet collar and little round bowler hat, I puffing a small cigar and with my old mac flapping in the wind; I discovered that the gentleman beside me was quietly quizzing me about my career at the Bar.

'You've been at this game a long while, Rumpole,' Featherstone announced. I didn't disagree with him, and then he went on.

'You never thought of taking silk?'

'Rumpole, QC?' I almost burst out laughing. 'Not on your Nelly. Rumpole "Queer Customer". That's what they'd be bound to call me.'

'I'm sure you could, with your seniority.' I had no idea then, of exactly what this Featherstone was after. I gave him my view of QCs in general.

'Perhaps, if I played golf with the right judges, or put up for Parliament, they might make me an artificial silk, or, at any rate, a nylon.' It was at that point I realised I had put up a bit of a black. 'Sorry. I forgot. You *did* put up for Parliament.'

'Yes. You never thought of Rumpole, QC?' Featherstone had apparently taken no offence.

'Never,' I told him. 'I have the honour to be an Old Bailey hack! That's quite enough for me.'

At which point we turned up into Newgate Street and there it was in all its glory, touched by a hint of early spring sunshine, the Old Bailey, a stately Law Court, decreed by the City Fathers, an Edwardian palace, with an extensive modern extension to deal with the increase in human fallibility. There was the dome and the blindfold lady. Well, it's much better she doesn't see *all* that's going on. That, in fact, was our English version of the Palais de Justice, complete with murals, marble statues and underground accommodation for some of the choicest villains in London.

Terrible things go on down the Bailey – horrifying things. Why is it I never go in the revolving door without a thrill of pleasure, a slight tremble of excitement? Why does it seem a much *jollier* place than my place in Gloucester Road under the strict rule of She Who Must Be Obeyed? These are questions which may only be partly answered in the course of these memoirs.

At the time when I was waving a cheerful umbrella at Harry, the policeman in the revolving door of the Old Bailey extension, my wife Hilda was at her daddy's bedside at the Horsham General arranging her dozen early daffs and gently probing, so she told me that evening, on the subject of his future, and mine.

'I'll have to give up, you know. I can't go on forever. Crocked up, I'm afraid,' said Wystan.

'Nonsense, Daddy. You'll go on for years.'

I imagine Hilda did her best to sound bracing, whilst putting the daffs firmly in their place.

'No, Hilda. No. They'll have to start looking for another Head of Chambers.'

This gave Hilda her opportunity. 'Rumpole's the senior man. Apart from Uncle Tom and he doesn't really practise nowadays.'

'Your husband the senior man.' Wystan looked back on a singularly uneventful life. 'How time flies! I recall when he was the junior man. My pupil.'

'You said he was the best youngster on bloodstains you'd ever known.' Hilda was doing her best for me.

'Rumpole! Yes, your husband was pretty good on bloodstains. Shaky, though, on the law of landlord and tenant. What sort of practice has Rumpole now?'

'I believe . . . Today it's the Old Bailey.' Hilda was plumping pillows, doing her best to sound casual. And her father showed no particular enthusiasm for my place of work.

'It's always the Old Bailey, isn't it?'

'Most of the time. Yes. I suppose so.'

'Not a frightfully good *address*, the Old Bailey. Not exactly the SW1 of the legal profession.'

Sensing that Daddy would have thought better of me if I'd been in the Court of Appeal or the Chancery division, Hilda told me she thought of a master stroke.

'Oh, Rumpole only went down to the Bailey because it's a family he knows. It seems they've got a young boy in trouble.'

This appealed to Daddy, he gave one of his bleak smiles which amount to no more than a brief withdrawal of lips from the dentures.

'Son gone wrong?' he said. 'Very sad that. Especially if he comes of a really good family.'

That really good family, the Timsons, was out in force and waiting outside Number 1 Court by the time I had got on the fancy dress, yellowing horsehair wig, gown become more than a trifle tattered over the years, and bands round the neck that Albert ought to have sent to the laundry after last week's death by dangerous driving. As I looked at the Timson clan assembled, I thought the best thing about them was the amount of work of a criminal nature they had brought into Chambers. They were all dressed for the occasion, the men in dark blazers, suede shoes and grey flannels; the ladies in tight-fitting suits, high heels and elaborately piled hairdos. I had never seen so many ex-clients together at one time.

'Mr Rumpole.'

'Ah, Bernard! You're instructing me.'

Mr Bernard, the solicitor, was a thirtyish, perpetually smiling man in a pinstriped suit. He regarded criminals with something of the naïve fervour with which young girls think of popular entertainers. Had I known the expression at the time, I would have called him a grafters' 'groupie'.

'I'm always your instructing solicitor in a Timson case, Mr Rumpole.' Mr Bernard beamed and Fred Timson, a kindly man and most innocent robber, stepped out of the ranks to do the honours.

'Nothing but the best for the Timsons, best solicitor and best barrister going. You know my wife Vi?'

Young Jim's mother seemed full of confidence. As I took her hand, I remembered I had got Vi off on a handling charge after the Croydon bank raid. Well, there was really no evidence.

'Uncle Cyril.' Fred introduced the plumpish uncle with the small moustache whom I was sure I remembered. What was *his* last outing exactly? Carrying house-breaking instruments by night?

'Uncle Dennis. You remember Den, surely, Mr Rumpole?'

I did. Den's last little matter was an alleged conspiracy to forge log books.

'And Den's Doris.'

Aunty Doris came at me in a blur of hennaed hair and darkish perfume. What was Doris's last indiscretion? Could it have been receiving a vast quantity of stolen scampi? Acquitted by a majority, at least I was sure of that.

'And yours truly. Frederick Timson. The boy's father.'

Regrettable, but we had a slip-up with Fred's last spot of bother. I was away with flu, George Frobisher took it over, and he got three years. He must've only just got out.

'So, Mr Rumpole. You know the whole family.'

A family to breed from, the Timsons. Must almost keep the Old Bailey going single-handed.

'You're going to do your best for our young Jim, I'm sure, Mr Rumpole.'

I didn't find the simple faith of the Timsons that I could secure acquittals in the most unlikely circumstances especially encouraging. But then Jim's mother said something which I was to long remember.

'He's a good boy. He was ever so good to me while Dad was away.'

So that was Jimbo's life. Head of the family at fourteen, when Dad was off on one of his regular visits to Her Majesty.

'It's young Jim's first appearance, like. At the Old Bailey.' Fred couldn't conceal a note of pride. It was Jim boy's Bar Mitzvah, his first Communion.

So we chatted a little about how all the other boys got clean away, which I told them was a bit of luck as none of them would go into the witness-box and implicate Jim, and Bernard pointed out that the identification by the butchers was pretty hopeless. Well, what did he expect? Would you have a photographic impression of the young hopeful who struck you a smart blow on the back of the head with a cricket stump? We talked with that curious suppressed excitement there always is before a trial, however disastrous the outcome may be, and I told them the only thing we had to worry about, as if that were not enough, was Jim's confession to the boy in the remand centre, a youth who rejoiced in the name of Peanuts Molloy.

'Peanuts Molloy! Little grass.' Fred Timson spoke with a deep contempt.

'Old "Persil" White fitted him up with that one, didn't he?' Uncle Cyril said it as if it were the most natural thing in the world, and only to be expected.

'Chief Detective Inspector White,' Bernard explained.

'Why should the chief inspector want to fit up your Jimbo?' It was a question to which I should have known what their answer would be.

'Because he's a Timson, that's why!' said Fred.

'Because he's the apple of our eye, like,' Uncle Den told me, and the boy's mother added:

'Being as he's the baby of the family.'

'Old Persil'd fit up his mother if it'd get him a smile from his super.' As Fred said this the chief inspector himself, grey-haired and avuncular, walked by in plain clothes, with a plain-clothes sergeant.

'Morning, Chief Inspector,' Fred carried on without drawing breath.

'Morning, Fred. Morning, Mrs Timson.' The chief inspector greeted the family with casual politeness; after all they were part of his daily work, and Vi sniffed back a 'Good morning, Chief Inspector.'

'Mr Timson. We'll shift our ground. Remove good friends.'

Like Hamlet, after seeing the ghost, I thought it was better to continue our conference in private. So we went and sat round a table in
the canteen, and, when we had sorted out who took how many lumps,
and which of them could do with a choc roll or a cheese sandwich, the
family gave me the lowdown on the chief prosecution witness.

'The chief inspector put that little grass Peanuts Molloy into Jim's
painting class at the remand centre.' Fred had no doubt about it.

'Jim apparently poured out his soul to Peanuts.' The evidence
sounded, to my old ears, completely convincing, and Bernard read us
a snatch from his file.

'We planned to do the old blokes from the butcher's and grab the
wages . . .'

'That', I reminded the assembled company, 'is what Peanuts will
say Jim told him.'

'You think I'd bring Jim up to talk in the nick like that? The Timsons ain't stupid!' Fred was outraged, and Vi, pursing her lips in a
sour gesture of wounded respectability added, 'His dad always told
him. Never say a word to anyone you're banged up with – bound to
be a grass.'

One by one, Aunty Doris, Uncle Den and Uncle Cyril added their support.

'That's right. Fred's always brought the boy up proper. Like the way he should be. He'd never speak about the crime, not to anyone he was banged up with.'

' 'Specially not to one of the Molloys!'

'The Molloys!' Vi spoke for the Timsons, and with deep hatred. 'Noted grasses. That family always has been.'

'The Molloys is beyond the pale. Well known for it.' Aunty Doris nodded her hennaed topknot wisely.

'Peanuts's grandad shopped my old father in the "Streatham Co-op Robbery". Pre-war, that was.'

I had a vague memory then of what Fred Timson was talking about. The Streatham Co-op case, one of my better briefs – a long case with not much honour shown among thieves, as far as I could remember.

'Then you can understand, Mr Rumpole. No Timson would ever speak to a Molloy.'

'So you're sure Jimbo never said anything to Peanuts?' I was wondering exactly how I could explain the deep, but not particularly creditable, origins of this family hostility to the jury.

'I give you my word, Mr Rumpole. Ain't that enough for you? No Timson would ever speak to a Molloy. Not under any circumstances.'

There were not many matters on which I would take Fred Timson's word, but the history of the Streatham Co-op case came back to me, and this was one of them.

It's part of the life of an Old Bailey hack to spend a good deal of his time down in the cells, in the basement area, where they keep the old door of Newgate, kicked and scarred, through which generations of villains were sent to the treadmill, the gallows or the whip. You pass this venerable door and ring a bell, you're let in and your name's taken by one of the warders who bring the prisoners from Brixton. There's a perpetual smell of cooking and the warders are snatching odd snacks of six inches of cheese butties and a gallon of tea. Lunch is being got ready, and the cells under the Bailey have a high reputation as one of the best caffs in London. By the door the screws have their pin-ups and comic cartoons of judges. You are taken to a waiting-room, three steel chairs and a table, and you meet the client. Perhaps he is a novice, making his first appearance, like Jim Timson. Perhaps he's an old hand asking anxiously which judge he's got, knowing their form as accurately as a betting-shop proprietor. Whoever he is, the client will be nervously excited, keyed up for his great day, full of absurd hope.

The worst part of a barrister's life at the Old Bailey is going back to the cells after a guilty verdict to say 'goodbye'. There's no purpose in it, but, as a point of honour, it has to be done. Even then the barrister probably gets the best reaction, and almost never any blame. The client is stunned, knocked out by his sentence. Only in a couple of weeks' time, when the reality of being banged up with the sour smell of stone walls and his own chamber-pot for company becomes apparent, does the convict start to weep. He is then drugged with sedatives, and Agatha Christies from the prison library.

When I saw the youngest Timson before his trial that morning, I couldn't help noticing how much smaller, and how much more experienced, he looked than my Nick. In his clean sports jacket and carefully knotted tie he was well dressed for the dock, and he showed all the carefully suppressed excitement of a young lad about to step into the limelight of Number 1 with an old judge, twelve jurors and a mixed bag of lawyers waiting to give him their undivided attention.

'Me speak to Peanuts? No Timson don't ever speak to a Molloy. It's a point of honour, like,' Jim added his voice to the family chorus.

'Since the raid on the Streatham Co-op. Your grandfather?'

'Dad told you about that, did he?'

'Yes. Dad told me.'

'Well, Dad wouldn't let me speak to no Molloy. He wouldn't put up with it, like.'

I stood up, grinding out the stub end of my small cigar in the old Oxo tin thoughtfully provided by HM's Government. It was, I thought, about time I called the meeting to order.

'So Jim,' I asked him, 'what's the defence?'

Little Jim knitted his brows and came out with his contribution. 'Well. I didn't do it.'

'That's an interesting defence. Somewhat novel – so far as the Timsons are concerned.'

'I've got my alibi, ain't I?'

Jim looked at me accusingly, as at an insensitive visitor to a garden who has failed to notice the remarkable display of gladioli.

'Oh, yes. Your alibi.' I'm afraid I didn't sound overwhelmed with enthusiasm.

'Dad reckoned it was pretty good.'

Mr Bernard had his invaluable file open and was reading from that less-than-inspiring document, our Notice of Alibi.

'Straight from school on that Friday September the 2nd, I went up to tea at my Aunt Doris's and arrived there at exactly 5.30. At 6 p.m. my Uncle Den came home from work accompanied by my Uncle Cyril. At 7 p.m. when this alleged crime was taking place I was sat round the television with my aunty and two uncles. I well remember we was watching *The Newcomers*.'

All very neat and workmanlike. Well, that was it. The family gave young Jim an alibi, clubbed together for it, like a new bicycle. However, I had to disappoint Mr Bernard about the bright shining alibi and we went through the swing doors on our way into Court.

'We can't use that alibi.'

'We can't?' Mr Bernard looked wounded, as if I'd just insulted his favourite child.

'Think about it Bernard. Don't be blinded by the glamour of the criminal classes. Call the uncles and aunties? Let them all be cross-examined about their records? The jury'll realise our Jimbo comes from a family of villains who keep a cupboard full of alibis for all occasions.'

Mr Bernard was forced to agree, but I went into my old place in Court (nearest to the jury, furthest from the witness-box) thinking that the devilish thing about that impossible alibi was that it might even be true.

So there I was, sitting in my favourite seat in Court, down in the firing line, and there was Jim boy, undersized for a prisoner, just peeping over the edge of the dock, guarded in case he ran amok and started attacking the judge, by a huge dock officer. There was the jury, solid and grey, listening impassionately as Guthrie Featherstone spread out his glittering mass of incriminating facts before them. I don't know why it is that juries all look the same; take twelve good men and women off the street and they all look middle-aged, anonymous, slightly stunned, an average jury, of average people trying an average case. Perhaps being a jury has become a special profession for specially average people. 'What do you want to do when you grow up my boy?' 'Be a jury man, Daddy.' 'Well done my boy. You can work a five-hour day for reasonable expenses and occasionally send people to chokey.'

So, as the carefully chosen words of Guthrie Featherstone passed over our heads like expensive hair oil, and as the enthusiastic young MacLay noted it all down, and the Rumpole Supporters Club, the Timsons, sat and pursed their lips and now and then whispered, 'Lies. All lies' to each other, I sat watching the judge rather as a noted toreador watches the bull from the barrier during the preliminary stages of the corrida, and remembered what I knew of Mr Justice Everglade, known to his few friends as 'Florrie'. Everglade's father was Lord Chancellor about the time when Jim's grandfather was doing over the Streatham Co-op. Educated at Winchester and Balliol, he always cracked *The Times* crossword in the opening of an egg. He was most happy with International Trust companies suing each other on nice points of law, and was only there for a fortnight's slumming down the Old Bailey. I wondered exactly what he was going to make of Peanuts Molloy.

'Members of the jury, it's right that you should know that it is alleged that Timson took part in this attack with a number of other youths, none of whom have been arrested,' Featherstone was purring to a halt.

' "The boy stood on the burning deck whence all but he had fled," ' I muttered, but the judge was busy congratulating learned counsel for Her Majesty the Queen who was engaged that morning in prosecuting the pride of the Timsons.

'It is quite right you should tell the jury that, Mr Featherstone. Perfectly right and proper.'

'If your Lordship pleases.' Featherstone was now bowing slightly, and my hackles began to rise. What was this? The old chums' league? Fellow members of the Athenaeum?

'I am most grateful to your Lordship for that indication.' Featherstone did his well-known butler passing the sherry act again. I wondered why the old darling didn't crawl up on the bench with Mr Justice Everglade and black his boots for him.

'So I imagine this young man's defence is – he wasn't *ejusdem generis* with the other lads?' The judge was now holding a private conversation, a mutual admiration society with my learned friend. I decided to break it up, and levered myself to my feet.

'I'm sorry. Your Lordship was asking about the defence?'

The judge turned an unfriendly eye on me and fumbled for my name. I told you he was a stranger to the Old Bailey, where the name of Rumpole is, I think, tolerably well known.

'Yes, Mr . . . er . . . ' The clerk of the Court handed him up a note on which the defender's name was inscribed. 'Rumpole.'

'I am reluctant to intrude on your Lordship's confidential conversation with my learned friend. But your Lordship was asking about the defence.'

'You are appearing for the young man . . . Timson?'

'I have that honour.'

At which point the doors of the Court swung open and Albert came in with Nick, a boy in a blazer and a school-tie who passed the boy in the dock with only a glance of curiosity. I always thank God, when I consider the remote politeness with which I was treated by the Reverend Wilfred Rumpole, that I get on extremely well with Nick. We understand each other, my boy and I, and have, when he's at home, formed a strong but silent alliance against the almost invincible rule of She Who Must Be Obeyed. He is as fond as I am of the Sherlock Holmes tales, and when we walked together in Hyde Park and Kensington Gardens, young Nick often played the part of Holmes whilst I trudged beside him as Watson, trying to deduce the secret lives of those we passed by the way they shined their shoes, or kept their handkerchiefs in their sleeves. So I gave a particularly welcoming smile to Nick before I gave my attention back to Florrie.

'And, as Jim Timson's counsel,' I told his Lordship, 'I might know a little more about his case than counsel for the prosecution.'

To which Mr Justice Everglade trotted out his favourite bit of Latin. 'I imagine', he said loftily, 'your client says he was not *ejusdem generis* with the other lads.'

'*Ejusdem generis?* Oh yes, my Lord. He's always saying that. *Ejusdem generis* is a phrase in constant use in his particular part of Brixton.'

I had hit a minor jackpot, and was rewarded with a tinkle of laughter from the Timsons, and a smile of genuine congratulation from Nick.

Mr Justice Everglade was inexperienced down the Bailey, he gave us a bare hour for lunch and Nick and I had it in the canteen. There is one thing you can say against crime, the catering facilities aren't up to much. Nick told me about school, and freely confessed, as I'm sure he wouldn't have done to his mother, that he'd been in some sort of trouble that term. There was an old deserted vicarage opposite Schoolhouse (my old house and Nick's) and he and his friends had apparently broken in the scullery window and assembled there for poker parties and the consumption of cherry brandy. I was horrified as I drew up the indictment which seemed to me to contain charges of burglary at common law, housebreaking under the Forcible Entries Act, contravening the Betting, Gaming, Lotteries Act and Serving Alcohol on Unlicensed Premises.

'Crabtree actually invited a couple of girls from the village,' Nick continued his confession. 'But Bagnold never got to hear of that.'

Bagnold was Nick's headmaster, the school equivalent of 'Persil' White. I cheered up a little at the last piece of information.

'Then there's no evidence of girls. As far as your case goes there's no reason to suppose the girls ever existed. As for the other charges, which are serious . . .'

'Yes, yes, I suppose they are rather.'

'I imagine you were walking past the house on Sunday evening and, attracted by the noise . . . You went to investigate?'

'Dad. Bagnold came in and found us – playing poker.'

Nick wasn't exactly being helpful. I tried another line.

'I know, "My Lord. My client was only playing poker in order not to look too pious whilst he lectured his fellow sixth formers on the evils of gambling and cherry brandy." '

'Dad. Be serious.'

'I am serious. Don't you want me to defend you?'

'No. Bagnold's not going to tell the police or anything like that.'

I was amazed. 'He isn't? What's he going to do?'

'Well . . . I'll miss next term's exeat. Do extra work. I thought I should tell you before you got a letter.'

'Thank you, Nick. Thank you. I'm glad you told me. So there's no question of . . . the police?'

'The police?' Nick was laughing. 'Of course not. Bagnold doesn't want any trouble. After all, we're still at school.'

I watched Nick as he finished his fish and chips, and then turned my thoughts to Jim Timson, who had also been at school; but with no kindly Bagnold to protect him.

Back in Court I was cross-examining that notable grass, Peanuts Molloy, a skinnier, more furtive edition of Jim Timson. The cross-examination was being greatly enjoyed by the Timsons and Nick, but not much by Featherstone or Chief Detective Inspector 'Persil' White who sat at the table in front of me. I also thought that Mr Justice 'Florrie' Everglade was thinking that he would have been happier snoozing in the Athenaeum, or working on his *grospoint* in Egerton Terrace, than listening to me bowling fast in-swingers at the juvenile chief witness for the prosecution.

'You don't speak. The Molloys and the Timsons are like the Montagues and the Capulets,' I put it to Peanuts.

'What did you say they were?' The judge had, of course, given me my opportunity. I smacked him through the slips for a crafty single. 'Not *ejusdem generis*, my Lord,' I said.

Nick joined in the laughter and even the ranks of Featherstone had to stifle a smile. The usher called 'Silence'. We were back to the business in hand.

'Tell me, Peanuts . . . How would you describe yourself?'

'Is that a proper question?' Featherstone uncoiled himself gracefully. I ignored the interruption.

'I mean artistically. Are you a latter-day Impressionist? Do all your oils in little dots, do you? Abstract painter? White squares on a white background? Do you indulge in watches melting in the desert like dear old Salvador Dali?'

'I don't know what you're talking about.' Peanuts played a blocking shot and Featherstone tried a weary smile to the judge.

'My Lord, neither, I must confess, do I.'

'Sit quietly, Featherstone,' I muttered to him. 'All will be revealed to you.' I turned my attention back to Peanuts. 'Are you a dedicated artist? The Rembrandt of the remand centre?'

'I hadn't done no art before.' Peanuts confirmed my suspicions.

'So we are to understand that this occasion, when Jim poured out his heart to you, was the first painting lesson you'd ever been to?'

Peanuts admitted it.

'You'd been at the remand centre how long?'

'Couple of months. I was done for a bit of an affray.'

'I didn't ask you that. And I'm sure the reason you were on remand was entirely creditable. What I want to know is, what inspired you with this sudden fascination for the arts?'

'Well, the chief screw. He suggested it.'

Now we were beginning to get to the truth of the matter. Like his old grandfather in the Streatham Co-op days, Jim had been banged up with a notable grass.

'You were suddenly told to join the painting class, weren't you . . . and put yourself next to Jim?'

'Something like that, yeah.'

'What did he say?' Florrie frowned. It was all very strange to him and yet he was starting to get the hint of something that wasn't quite cricket.

'Something like that, my Lord,' I repeated slowly, giving the judge a chance to make a note. 'And you were sent there, not in the pursuit of art, Peanuts, but in the pursuit of evidence! You knew that and you supplied your masters with just what they wanted to hear – even though Jim Timson didn't say a word to you!'

Everyone in Court, including Nick, looked impressed. D. I. White bit hard on a polo mint and Featherstone oozed to his feet in a rescue bid.

'That's great, Dad!'

'Thanks, Nick. Sorry it's not a murder.'

'I don't know quite what my learned friend is saying. Is he suggesting that the police . . . '

'Oh, it's an old trick,' I said, staring hard at the chief inspector. 'Bang the suspect up with a notable grass when you're really pushed for evidence. They do it with grown-ups often enough. Now they're trying it with children!'

'Mr Rumpole,' the judge sighed, 'you are speaking a language which is totally foreign to me.'

'Let me try and make myself clear, my Lord. I was suggesting that Peanuts was put there as a deliberate trap.'

By now, even the judge had the point. 'You are suggesting that Mr Molloy was not a genuine "amateur painter"?'

'No, my Lord. Merely an amateur witness.'

'Yes.' I actually got a faint smile. 'I see. Please go on, Mr Rumpole.'

Another day or so of this, I felt, and I'd get invited to tea at the Athenaeum.

'What did you say first to Jim? As you drew your easel alongside?'

'Don't remember.'

'Don't you?'

'I think we was speaking about the Stones.'

'What "stones" are these?' The judge's ignorance of the life around him seemed to be causing him some sort of wild panic. Remember this was 1965, and I was in a similar state of confusion until Nick, whispering from behind me, gave me the clue.

'The Rolling Stones, my Lord.' The information meant nothing to him.

'I'm afraid a great deal of this case seems to be taking place in a foreign tongue, Mr Rumpole.'

'Jazz musicians, as I understand it, my Lord, of some notoriety.' By courtesy of Nick, I filled his Lordship in on 'the scene'.

'Well, the notoriety hasn't reached me!' said the judge, providing the obedient Featherstone with the laugh of the year, if not the century. When the learned prosecuting counsel had recovered his solemnity, Peanuts went rambling on.

'We was talking about the Stones concert at the Hammersmith Odeon. We'd both been to it, like. And, well . . . we talked about that. And then he said . . . Jim said . . . Well, he said as how he and the other blokes had done the butchers.'

The conversation had now taken a nasty turn. I saw that the judge was writing industriously. 'Jim said . . . that he and the other blokes . . . had done the butchers.' Florrie was plying his pencil. Then he looked up at me, 'Well, Mr Rumpole, is that a convenient moment to adjourn?'

It was a very convenient moment for the prosecution, as the evidence against us would be the last thing the jury heard before sloping off to their homes and loved ones. It was also a convenient moment for Peanuts. He would have his second wind by the morning. So there was nothing for it but to take Nick for a cup of tea and a pile of crumpets in the ABC, and so home to She Who Must Be Obeyed.

So picture us three that evening, finishing dinner and a bottle of claret, celebrating the return of the young master at Hack Hall, Counsel's Castle, Rumpole Manor, or 25B Froxbury Court, Gloucester Road. Hilda had told Nick that his grandpa had sent his love and expected a letter, and also dropped me the encouraging news that old C. H. Wystan was retiring and quite appreciated that I was the senior man. Nick asked me if I was really going to be Head of Chambers, seeming to look at me with a new respect, and we drank a glass of claret to the future, whatever it might be. Then Nick asked me if I really thought Peanuts Molloy was lying.

'If he's not, he's giving a damn good imitation.' Then I told Hilda as she started to clear away, 'Nick enjoyed the case. Even though it was only a robbery. Oh, Nick . . . I wish you'd been there to hear me cross-examine about the bloodstains in the "Penge Bungalow Murder".'

'Nick wasn't born, when you did the "Penge Bungalow Murder".'

My wife is always something of a wet blanket. I commiserated with my son. 'Bad luck, old boy.'

'You were great with that judge!'

I think Nick had really enjoyed himself.

'There was this extraordinary judge who was always talking Latin and Dad was teasing him.'

'You want to be careful,' Hilda was imposing her will on the pudding plates. 'How you tease judges. If you're to be Head of Chambers.' On which line she departed, leaving Nick and I to our claret and conversation. I began to discuss with Nick the horrifying adventure of 'The Speckled Band'.

'You're still reading those tales, are you?' I asked Nick.

'Well . . . not lately.'

'But you remember. I used to read them to you, didn't I? After She had ordered you to bed.'

'When you weren't too busy. Noting up your murders.'

'And remember we were Holmes and Watson? When we went for walks in Hyde Park.'

'I remember *one* walk.'

That was odd, as I recall it had been our custom ever at a weekend, before Nick went away to boarding school. I lit a small cigar and looked at the great detective through the smoke.

'Tell me, Holmes. What did you think was the most remarkable piece of evidence given by the witness Peanuts Molloy?'

'When he said they talked about the Rolling Stones.'

'Holmes, you astonish me.'

'You see, Watson. We were led to believe they were such enemies I mean, the families were. They'd never spoken.'

'I see what you're driving at. Have another glass of claret – stimulates the detective ability.' I opened another bottle, a clatter from the kitchen telling me that the lady was not about to join us.

'And there they were chatting about a pop concert. Didn't that strike you as strange, my dear Watson?'

'It struck me as bloody rum, if you want to know the truth, Holmes.' I was delighted to see Nick taking over the case.

'They'd both been to the concert . . . Well, that doesn't mean anything. Not necessarily . . . I mean, *I* was at that concert.'

'Were you indeed?'

'It was at the end of the summer holidays.'

'I don't remember you mentioning it.'

'I said I was going to the Festival Hall.'

I found this confidence pleasing, knowing that it wasn't to be shared with Hilda.

'Very wise. Your mother no doubt feels that at the Hammersmith Odeon they re-enact some of the worst excesses of the Roman Empire. You didn't catch sight of Peanuts and young Jimbo, did you?'

'There were about two thousand fans – all screaming.'

'I don't know if it helps . . . '

'No.'

'If they were old mates, I mean. Jim might really have confided in him. All the same, Peanuts is lying. And *you* noticed it! You've got the

instinct, Nick. You've got a nose for the evidence! Your career at the Bar is bound to be brilliant.' I raised my glass to Nick. 'When are you taking silk?'

Shortly after this She entered with news that Nick had a dentist's appointment the next day, which would prevent his re-appearance down the Bailey. All the same, he had given me a great deal of help and before I went to bed I telephoned Bernard the solicitor, tore him away from his fireside and instructed him to undertake some pretty immediate research.

Next morning, Albert told me that he'd had a letter from old C. H. Wystan, Hilda's Daddy, mentioning his decision to retire.

'I think we'll manage pretty well, with you, Mr Rumpole, as Head of Chambers,' Albert told me. 'There's not much you and I won't be able to sort out, sir, over a glass or two in Pommeroy's Wine Bar . . . And soon we'll be welcoming Master Nick in Chambers?'

'Nick? Well, yes.' I had to admit it. 'He is showing a certain legal aptitude.'

'It'll be a real family affair, Mr Rumpole . . . Like father, like son, if you want my opinion.'

I remembered Albert's words when I saw Fred Timson waiting for me outside the Court. But before I had time to brood on family tradition, Bernard came up with the rolled-up poster for a pop concert. I grabbed it from him and carried it as unobtrusively as possible into Court.

'When Jim told you he'd done up the butchers . . . He didn't tell you the date that that had happened?' Peanuts was back, facing the bowling, and Featherstone was up to his usual tricks, rising to interrupt.

'My Lord, the date is set out quite clearly in the indictment.'

The time had come, quite obviously, for a burst of righteous indignation.

'My Lord, I am cross-examining on behalf of a sixteen-year-old boy on an extremely serious charge. I'd be grateful if my learned friend didn't supply information which all of us in Court know – except for the witness.'

'Very well. Do carry on, Mr Rumpole.' I was almost beginning to like Mr Justice Everglade.

'No. He never told me when, like. I thought it was sometime in the summer.' Peanuts tried to sound co-operative.

'Sometime in the summer? Are you a fan of the Rolling Stones, Peanuts?'

'Yes.'

'Remind me . . . they were . . . ' Still vaguely puzzled the judge was hunting back through his notes.

Sleek as a butler with a dish of peas, Featherstone supplied the information. 'The musicians, my Lord.'

'And so was Jim a fan?' I ploughed on, ignoring the gentleman's gentleman.

'He was. Yes.'

'You had discussed music, before you met in the remand centre?'

'Before the nick. Oh yes.' Peanuts was following me obediently down the garden path.

'You used to talk about it at school?'

'Yes.'

'In quite a friendly way?' I was conscious of a startled Fred Timson looking at his son, and of Jim in the dock looking, for the first time, ashamed.

'We was all right. Yes.'

'Did you ever go to a concert with Jimbo? Please think carefully.'

'We went to one or two concerts together.' Peanuts conceded.

'In the evening?'

'Yes.'

'What would you do? . . . Call at his home and collect him?'

'You're joking!'

'Oh no, Peanuts. In this case I'm not joking at all!' No harm, I thought, at that stage, in underlining the seriousness of the occasion.

'Course I wouldn't call at his home!'

'Your families don't speak. You wouldn't be welcomed in each other's houses?'

'The Montagues and the Capulets, Mr Rumpole?' The old sweetheart on the bench had finally got the message. I gave him a bow, to show my true love and affection.

'If your Lordship pleases . . . Your Lordship puts it extremely aptly.' I turned back to Peanuts. 'So what would you do, if you were going to a concert?'

'We'd leave school together, like – and then hang around the caffs.'

'Hang around the caffs?'

'Cafays, Mr Rumpole?' Mr Justice Everglade was enjoying himself, translating the answer.

'Yes, of course, the cafays. Until it was time to go up West? If my Lord would allow me, up to the "West End of London" together?'

'Yes.'

'So you wouldn't be separated on these evenings you went to concerts together?' It was one of those questions after which you hold your breath. There can be so many wrong answers.

'No. We hung around together.'

Rumpole breathed a little more easily, but still had the final question, the great gamble, with all Jim Timson's chips firmly piled on the red. *Faites vos jeux, m'sieurs et mesdames* of the Old Bailey jury. I spun the wheel.

'And did that happen . . . When you went to the Rolling Stones at the Hammersmith Odeon?'

A nasty silence. Then the ball rattled into the hole.

Peanuts said, 'Yes.'

'That was this summer, wasn't it?' We were into the straight now, cantering home.

'In the summer, yeah.'

'You left school together?'

'And hung around the caffs, like. Then we went up the Odeon.'

'Together . . . All the time?'

'I told you – didn't I?' Peanuts looked bored, and then amazed as I unrolled the poster Bernard had brought, rushed by taxi from Hammersmith, with the date clearly printed across the bottom.

'My Lord. My learned friend might be interested to know the date of the only Rolling Stones concert at the Hammersmith Odeon this year.' I gave Featherstone an unwelcome eyeful of the poster.

'He might like to compare it with the date so conveniently set out in the indictment.'

When the subsequent formalities were over, I went down to the cells. This was not a visit of commiseration, no time for a 'sorry old sweetheart, but . . . ' and a deep consciousness of having asked one too many questions. All the same, I was in no gentle mood, in fact, it would be fair to say that I was bloody angry with Jimbo.

'You had an alibi! You had a proper, reasonable, truthful alibi, and, joy of joys, it came from the prosecution! Why the hell didn't you tell me?'

Jim, who seemed to have little notion of the peril he had passed, answered me quite calmly, 'Dad wouldn't have liked it.'

'Dad! What's Dad got to do with it?' I was astonished.

'He wouldn't've liked it, Mr Rumpole. Not me going out with Peanuts.'

'So you were quite ready to be found guilty, to be convicted of robbery, just because your dad wouldn't like you going out with Peanuts Molloy?'

'Dad got the family to alibi me.' Jim clearly felt that the Timsons had done their best for him.

'Keep it in the family!' Though it was heavily laid on, the irony was lost on Jim. He smiled politely and stood up, eager to join the clan upstairs.

'Well, anyway. Thanks a lot, Mr Rumpole. Dad said I could rely on you. To win the day, like. I'd better collect me things.'

If Jim thought I was going to let him get away as easily as that, he was mistaken. Rumpole rose in his crumpled gown, doing his best to represent the majesty of the law. 'No! Wait a minute. I didn't win the day. It was luck. The purest fluke. It won't happen again!'

'You're joking, Mr Rumpole.' Jim thought I was being modest. 'Dad told me about you . . . He says you never let the Timsons down.'

I had a sudden vision of my role in life, from young Jim's point of view and I gave him the voice of outrage which I use frequently in Court. I had a message of importance for Jim Timson.

'Do you think that's what I'm here for? To help you along in a career like your dad's?' Jim was still smiling, maddeningly. 'My God! I shouldn't have asked those questions! I shouldn't have found out the date of the concert! Then you'd really be happy, wouldn't you? You could follow in Dad's footsteps all your life! Sharp spell of borstal training to teach you the mysteries of housebreaking, and then a steady life in the nick. You might really do well! You might end up in Parkhurst, maximum security wing, doing a glamorous twenty years and a hero to the screws.'

At which the door opened and a happy screw entered, for the purpose of springing young Jim – until the inevitable next time.

'We've got his things at the gate, Mr Rumpole. Come on Jim. You can't stay here all night.'

'I've got to go,' Jim agreed. 'I don't know how to face Dad, really. Me being so friendly with Peanuts.'

'Jim,' I tried a last appeal. 'If you're at all grateful for what I did . . .'

'Oh I am, Mr Rumpole, I'm quite satisfied.' Generous of him.

'Then you can perhaps repay me.'

'Why – aren't you on Legal Aid?'

'It's not that! Leave him! Leave your dad.'

Jim frowned, for a moment he seemed to think it over. Then he said, 'I don't know as how I can.'

'You don't know?'

'Mum depends on me, you see. Like when Dad goes away. She depends on me then, as head of the family.'

So he left me, and went up to temporary freedom and his new responsibilities.

★

My mouth was dry and I felt about ninety years old, so I took the lift up to that luxurious eatery, the Old Bailey canteen, for a cup of tea and a Penguin biscuit. And, pushing his tray along past the urns, I met a philosophic Chief Inspector 'Persil' White. He noticed my somewhat lugubrious expression and tried a cheering 'Don't look so miserable, Mr Rumpole. You won didn't you?'

'Nobody won, the truth emerges sometimes, Inspector, even down the Old Bailey.' I must have sounded less than gracious. The wily old copper smiled tolerantly.

'He's a Timson. It runs in the family. We'll get him sooner or later!'

'Yes. Yes. I suppose you will.'

At a table in a corner, I found certain members of my Chambers, George Frobisher, Percy Hoskins, and young Tony MacLay, now resting from their labours, their wigs lying among cups of Old Bailey tea, buns and choccy bics. I joined them. Wordsworth entered my head, and I gave him an airing . . . ' "Trailing clouds of glory do we come." '

'Marvellous win, that. I was telling them.' Young MacLay thought I was announcing my triumph.

'Yes, Rumpole. I hear you've had a splendid win.' Old George, ever generous, smiled, genuinely pleased.

'It'll be *years* before you get the cheque,' Hoskins grumbled.

> *'Not in entire forgetfulness and not in utter nakedness,*
> *But trailing clouds of glory do we come*
> *From God who is our home . . . '*

I was thinking of Jim, trying to sort out his situation with the help of Wordsworth.

'You don't get paid for years at the Old Bailey. I try to tell my grocer that. If you had to wait as long to be paid for a pound of sugar, I tell him, as we do for an armed robbery . . . ' Hoskins was warming to a well-loved theme, but George, dear old George was smiling at me.

'Albert tells me he's had a letter from Wystan. I just wanted to say, I'm sure we'd all like to say, you'll make a splendid Head of Chambers, Rumpole.'

> *'Heaven lies about us in our infancy,*
> *Shades of the prison house begin to close*
> *Upon the growing boy . . .*
> *But he beholds the light, and whence it flows,*
> *He sees it in his joy.'*

I gave them another brief glimpse of immortality. George looked quite proud of me and told MacLay, 'Rumpole quotes poetry. He does it quite often.'

'But does the growing boy behold the light?' I wondered. 'Or was the old sheep of the Lake District being unduly optimistic?'

'It'll be refreshing for us all, to have a Head of Chambers who quotes poetry,' George went on, at which point Percy Hoskins produced a newspaper which turned out to contain an item of news for us all.

'Have you seen *The Times*, Rumpole?'

'No, I haven't had time for the crossword.'

'Guthrie Featherstone. He's taken silk.'

It was the apotheosis, the great day for the Labour-Conservative Member for wherever it was, one time unsuccessful prosecutor of Jim Timson and now one of Her Majesty's Counsel, called within the Bar, and he went down to the House of Lords tailored out in his new silk gown, a lace jabot, knee breeches with *diamanté* buckles, patent shoes, black silk stockings, lace cuffs and a full-bottomed wig that made him look like a pedigree, but not over-bright, spaniel. However, Guthrie Featherstone was a tall man, with a good calf in a silk stocking, and he took with him Marigold, his lady wife, who was young enough, and I suppose pretty enough, for Henry our junior clerk to eye wistfully, although she had the sort of voice that puts me instantly in mind of headscarves and gymkhanas, that high pitched nasal whining which a girl learns from too much contact with the saddle when young, and too little with the Timsons of this world in later life. The couple were escorted by Albert, who'd raided Moss Bros for a top hat and morning coat for the occasion and when the Lord Chancellor had welcomed Guthrie to that special club of Queen's Counsel (on whose advice the Queen, luckily for her, never has to rely for a moment) they came back to Chambers where champagne (the NV cooking variety, bulk bought from Pommeroy's Wine Bar) was served by Henry and old Miss Patterson our typist, in Wystan's big room looking out over Temple Gardens. C. H. Wystan, our retiring head, was not among those present as the party began, and I took an early opportunity to get stuck into the beaded bubbles.

After the fourth glass I felt able to relax a bit and wandered to where Featherstone, in all his finery, was holding forth to Erskine-Brown about the problems of appearing *en travestie*. I arrived just as he was saying, 'It's the stockings that're the problem.'

'Oh yes. They would be.' I did my best to sound interested.

'Keeping them up.'

'I do understand.'

'Well, Marigold. My wife Marigold . . . ' I looked across to where Mrs Q C was tinkling with laughter at some old legal anecdote of Uncle Tom's. It was a laugh that seemed in some slight danger of breaking the wine glasses.

'*That* Marigold?'

'Her sister's a nurse, you know . . . and she put me in touch with this shop which supplies suspender belts to nurses . . . among other things.'

'Really?' This conversation seemed to arouse some dormant sexual interest in Erskine-Brown.

'Yards of elastic, for the larger ward sister. But it works miraculously.'

'You're wearing a suspender belt?' Erskine-Brown was frankly fascinated. 'You sexy devil!'

'I hadn't realised the full implications', I told the Q C, 'of rising to the heights of the legal profession.'

I wandered off to where Uncle Tom was giving Marigold a brief history of life in our Chambers over the last half-century. Percy Hoskins was in attendance, and George.

'It's some time since we had champagne in Chambers.' Uncle Tom accepted a refill from Albert.

'It's some time since we had a silk in Chambers,' Hoskins smiled at Marigold who flashed a row of well-groomed teeth back at him.

'I recall we had a man in Chambers once called Drinkwater – oh, before you were born, Hoskins. And some fellow came and paid Drinkwater a hundred guineas – for six months' pupillage. And you know what this Drinkwater fellow did? Bought us all champagne – and the next day he ran off to Calais with his junior clerk. We never saw hide nor hair of either of them again.' He paused. Marigold looked puzzled, not quite sure if this was the punch line.

'Of course, you could get a lot further in those days – on a hundred guineas,' Uncle Tom ended on a sad note, and Marigold laughed heartily.

'Your husband's star has risen so quickly, Mrs Featherstone. Only ten years call and he's an MP *and* leading counsel.' Hoskins was clearly so excited by the whole business he had stopped worrying about his cheques for half an hour.

'Oh, it's the PR you know. Guthrie's frightfully good at the PR.'

I felt like Everglade. Marigold was speaking a strange and incomprehensible language.

'Guthrie always says the most important thing at the Bar is to be polite to your instructing solicitor. Don't you find that, Mr Rumpole?'

'Polite to solicitors? It's never occurred to me.'

'Guthrie admires you so, Mr Rumpole. He admires your style of advocacy.'

I had just sunk another glass of the beaded bubbles as passed by Albert, and I felt a joyous release from my usual strong sense of tact and discretion.

'I suppose it makes a change from bowing three times and offering to black the judge's boots for him.'

Marigold's smile didn't waver. 'He says you're most amusing out of Court, too. Don't you quote poetry?'

'Only in moments of great sadness, Madam. Or extreme elation.'

'Guthrie's so looking forward to leading you. In his next big case.'

This was an eventuality which I should have taken into account as soon as I saw Guthrie in silk stockings; as a matter of fact it had never occurred to me.

'Leading *me*? Did you say, *leading* me?'

'Well, he has to have a junior now . . . doesn't he? Naturally he wants the best junior available.'

'Now he's a leader?'

'Now he's left the Junior Bar.'

I raised my glass and gave Marigold a version of Browning. 'Just for a pair of knee breeches he left us . . . Just for an elastic suspender belt, as supplied to the nursing profession . . . ' At which the QC himself bore down on us in a rustle of silk and drew me into a corner.

'I just wanted to say, I don't see why recent events should make the slightest difference to the situation in Chambers. You *are* the senior man in practice, Rumpole.'

Henry was passing with the fizzing bottle. I held out my glass and the tide ran foaming in it.

'"You wrong me, Brutus,"' I told Featherstone. '"You said an older soldier, not a better."'

'A quotation! *Touché*, very apt.'

'Is it?'

'I mean, all this will make absolutely no difference. I'll still support you Rumpole, as the right candidate for Head of Chambers.'

I didn't know about being a candidate, having thought of the matter as settled and not being much of a political animal. But before I had time to reflect on whatever the Honourable Member was up to, the door opened letting in a formidable draught and the Head of Chambers. C. H. Wystan, She's Daddy, wearing a tweed suit, extremely pale, supported by Albert on one side and a stick on the other, made the sort of formidable entrance that the ghost of Banquo stages at dinner with the Macbeths. Wystan was installed in an armchair, from which he gave us all the sort of wintry smile which seemed designed to indicate that all flesh is as the grass, or something to that effect.

'Albert wrote to me about this little celebration. I was determined to be with you. And the doctor has given permission, for no more than one glass of champagne.' Wystan held out a transparent hand into which Albert inserted a glass of non vintage. Wystan lifted this with some apparent effort, and gave us a toast.

'To the great change in Chambers! Now we have a silk. Guthrie Featherstone, QC, MP!'

I had a large refill to that. Wystan absorbed a few bubbles, wiped his mouth on a clean, folded handkerchief, and proceeded to the oration. Wystan was never a great speech maker, but I claimed another refill and gave him my ears.

'You, Featherstone, have brought a great distinction to Chambers.'

'Isn't that nice, Guthrie?' Marigold proprietorially squeezed her master's fingers.

'You know, when I was a young man. You remember when we were young men, Uncle Tom? We used to hang around in Chambers for weeks on end.' Wystan had gone on about these distant hard times at every Chambers meeting. 'I well recall we used to occupy ourselves with an old golf ball and mashie niblick, trying to get chip shots into the waste-paper baskets. Albert was a boy then.'

'A mere child, Mr Wystan,' Albert looked suitably demure.

'And we used to pray for work. *Any* sort of work, didn't we, Uncle Tom?'

'We were tempted to crime. Only way we could get into Court.' Uncle Tom took the feed line like a professional. Moderate laughter, except for Rumpole who was busy drinking. And then I heard Wystan rambling on.

'But as you grow older at the Bar you discover it's not having any work that matters. It's the *quality* that counts!'

'Here, here! I'm always saying we ought to do more civil.' This was the dutiful Erskine-Brown, inserting his oar.

'Now Guthrie Featherstone, QC, MP, will, of course, command briefs in all divisions – planning, contract,' Wystan's voice sank to a note of awe, 'even Chancery! I was so afraid, after I've gone, that this Chambers might become known as merely a criminal set.' Wystan's voice now sank in a sort of horror. 'And, of course, there's no doubt about it, too much criminal work does rather lower the standing of a Chambers.'

'Couldn't you install pithead baths?' I hadn't actually meant to say it aloud, but it came out very loud indeed.

'Ah, Horace.' Wystan turned his pale eyes on me for the first time.

'So we could have a good scrub down after we get back from the Old Bailey?'

'Now, Horace Rumpole. And I mean no disrespect whatever to my son-in-law.' Wystan returned to the oration. From far away I heard myself say, 'Daddy!' as I raised the hard-working glass. 'Horace does practise almost exclusively in the Criminal Courts!'

'One doesn't get the really fascinating points of *law*. Not in criminal work,' Erskine-Brown was adding unwanted support to the motion. 'I've often thought we should try and attract some really lucrative tax cases into Chambers.'

That, I'm afraid, did it. Just as if I were in Court I moved slightly to the centre and began my speech.

'Tax cases?' I saw them all smiling encouragement at me. 'Marvellous! Tax cases make the world go round. Compared to the wonderful world of tax, crime is totally trivial. What does it matter? If some boy loses a year, a couple of years, of his life? It's totally unimportant! Anyway, he'll grow up to be banged up for a good five, shut up with his own chamber-pot in some convenient hole we all prefer not to think about.' There was a deafening silence, which came loudest from Marigold Featherstone. Then Wystan tried to reach a settlement.

'Now then, Horace. Your practice no doubt requires a good deal of skill.'

'Skill? Who said "skill"?' I glared round at the learned friends. 'Any fool could do it! It's only a matter of life and death. That's all it is. Crime? It's a sort of a game. How can you compare it to the real world of Off Shore Securities. And Deductible Expenses?'

'All you young men in Chambers can learn an enormous amount from Horace Rumpole, when it comes to crime.' Wystan now seemed to be the only one who was still smiling. I turned on him.

'You make me sound just like Fred Timson!'

'Really? Whoever's Fred Timson?' I told you Wystan never had much of a practice at the Bar, consequently he had never met the Timsons. Erskine-Brown supplied the information.

'The Timsons are Rumpole's favourite family.'

'An industrious clan of South London criminals, aren't they, Rumpole,' Hoskins added.

Wystan looked particularly pained. 'South London criminals?'

'I mean, do we want people like the Timsons forever hanging about in our waiting-room? I merely ask the question.' He was not bad, this Erskine-Brown, with a big future in the nastier sort of Breach of Trust cases.

'Do you? Do you merely ask it?' I heard the pained bellow of a distant Rumpole.

'The Timsons . . . and their like, are no doubt grist to Rumpole's mill,' Wystan was starting on the summing up. 'But it's the balance that *counts*. Now, you'll be looking for a new Head of Chambers.'

'Are we still looking?' My friend George Frobisher had the decency to ask. And Wystan told him, 'I'd like you all to think it over carefully. And put your views to me in writing. We should all try and remember. It's the good of the Chambers that matters. Not the feelings, however deep they may be, of any particular person.'

He then called on Albert's assistance to raise him to his feet, lifted his glass with an effort of pure will and offered us a toast to the good of Chambers. I joined in, and drank deep, it having been a good thirty seconds since I had had a glass to my lips. As the bubbles exploded against the tongue I noticed that the Featherstones were holding hands, and the brand new artificial silk was looking particularly delighted. Something, and perhaps not only his suspender belt, seemed to be giving him special pleasure.

Some weeks later, when I gave Hilda the news, she was deeply shocked.

'*Guthrie Featherstone!* Head of Chambers!' We were at breakfast. In fact Nick was due back at school that day. He was neglecting his cornflakes and reading a book.

'By general acclaim.'

'I'm sorry.' Hilda looked at me, as if she'd just discovered that I'd contracted an incurable disease.

'He can have the headaches – working out Albert's extraordinary book-keeping system.' I thought for a moment, yes, I'd like to have been Head of Chambers, and then put the thought from me.

'If only you could have become a Q C.' She was now pouring me an unsolicited cup of coffee.

'Q C? C T. That's enough to keep me busy.'

'C T? Whatever's C T?'

'Counsel for the Timsons!' I tried to say it as proudly as I could. Then I reminded Nick that I'd promised to see him off at Liverpool Street, finished my cooling coffee, stood up and took a glance at the book that was absorbing him, expecting it to be, perhaps, that spine-chilling adventure relating to the footprints of an enormous hound. To my amazement the shocker in question was entitled simply *Studies in Sociology*.

'It's interesting,' Nick sounded apologetic.

'You astonish me.'

'Old Bagnold was talking about what I should read if I get into Oxford.'

'Of course you're going to read law, Nick. We're going to keep it in the family.' Hilda the barrister's daughter was clearing away deafeningly.

'I thought perhaps PPE and then go on to Sociology.' Nick sounded curiously confident. Before Hilda could get in another word I made my position clear.

'PPE, that's very good, Nick! That's very good indeed! For God's sake. Let's stop keeping things in the family!'

Later, as we walked across the barren stretches of Liverpool Street Station, with my son in his school uniform and me in my old striped trousers and black jacket, I tried to explain what I meant.

'That's what's wrong, Nick. That's the devil of it! They're being born around us all the time. Little Mr Justice Everglades . . . Little Timsons . . . Little Guthrie Featherstones. All being set off . . . to follow in father's footsteps.' We were at the barrier, shaking hands awkwardly. 'Let's have no more of that! No more following in father's footsteps. No more.'

Nick smiled, although I have no idea if he understood what I was trying to say. I'm not totally sure that I understood it either. Then the train removed him from me. I waved for a little, but he didn't wave back. That sort of thing is embarrassing for a boy. I lit a small cigar and went by tube to the Bailey. I was doing a long firm fraud then; a particularly nasty business, out of which I got a certain amount of harmless fun.

Rumpole and the Showfolk

I have written elsewhere of my old clerk Albert Handyside who served me very well for a long term of years, being adept at flattering solicitors' clerks, buying them glasses of Guinness and enquiring tenderly after their tomato plants, with the result that the old darlings were inclined to come across with the odd Dangerous and Careless, Indecent Assault, or Take and Drive Away which Albert was inclined to slip in Rumpole's direction. All this led to higher things such as Robbery, Unlawful Wounding and even Murder; and in general for that body of assorted crimes on which my reputation is founded. I first knew Albert when he was a nervous office boy in the Chambers of C. H. Wystan, my learned father-in-law; and when he grew to be a head clerk of magisterial dimensions we remained firm friends and often had a jar together in Pommeroy's Wine Bar in the evenings, on which relaxed occasions I would tell Albert my celebrated anecdotes of Bench and Bar and, unlike She Who Must Be Obeyed, he was always kind enough to laugh no matter how often he had heard them before.

Dear old Albert had one slight failing, a weakness which occurs among the healthiest of constitutions. He was apt to get into a terrible flurry over the petty cash. I never enquired into his book-keeping system; but I believe it might have been improved by the invention of the abacus, or a monthly check-up by a primary-school child well versed in simple addition. It is also indubitably true that you can't pour drink down the throats of solicitors' managing clerks without some form of subsidy, and I'm sure Albert dipped liberally into the petty cash for this purpose as well as to keep himself in the large Bells and sodas, two or three of which sufficed for his simple lunch. Personally I never begrudged Albert any of this grant in aid, but ugly words such as embezzlement were uttered by Erskine-Brown and others, and, spurred on by our second clerk Harry who clearly thirsted for promotion, my learned friends were induced to part with Albert Handyside. I missed him very much. Our new clerk Henry goes to Pommeroy's with our typist Dianne, and tells her about his exploits when on holiday with the *Club Méditerranée* in Corfu. I do not think either of them would laugh at my legal anecdotes.

After he left us Albert shook the dust of London from his shoes and went up North, to some God-lost place called Grimble, and there joined a firm of solicitors as managing clerk. No doubt northerly barristers' clerks bought him Guinness and either he had no control of the petty cash or the matter was not subjected to too close an inspection. From time to time he sent me a Christmas card on which was inscribed among the bells and holly 'Compliments of the Season, Mr Rumpole, sir. And I'm going to bring you up here for a nice little murder just as soon as I get the opportunity. Yours respectfully, A. Handyside.' At long last a brief did arrive. Mr Rumpole was asked to appear at the Grimble Assizes, to be held before Mr Justice Skelton in the Law Courts, Grimble: the title of the piece being the Queen (she does keep enormously busy prosecuting people) versus Margaret Hartley. The only item on the programme was 'Wilful Murder'.

Now you may have noticed that certain theatrical phrases have crept into the foregoing paragraphs. This is not as inappropriate as it may sound, for the brief I was going up to Grimble for on the Intercity train (a journey about as costly as a trip across the Atlantic) concerned a murder which took place in the Theatre Royal, East Grimble, a place of entertainment leased by the 'Frere-Hartley Players': the victim was one G. P. Frere, the leading actor, and my client was his wife known as 'Maggie Hartley', co-star and joint director of the company. And as I read on into *R.* v. *Hartley* it became clear that the case was like too many of Rumpole's, a born loser: that is to say that unless we drew a drunken prosecutor or a jury of anarchists there seemed no reasonable way in which it might be won.

One night after the performance, Albert's instructions told me, the stage-door keeper, a Mr Croft, heard the sound of raised voices and quarrelling from the dressing-room shared by G. P. Frere and his wife Maggie Hartley. Mr Croft was having a late cup of tea in his cubby-hole with a Miss Christine Hope, a young actress in the company, and they heard two shots fired in quick succession. Mr Croft went along the passage to investigate and opened the dressing-room door. The scene that met his eyes was, to say the least, dramatic.

It appeared from Mr Croft's evidence that the dressing-room was in a state of considerable confusion. Clothes were scattered round the room, and chairs overturned. The long mirror which ran down the length of the wall was shattered at the end furthest from the door. Near the door Mr G. P. Frere, wearing a silk dressing-gown, was sitting slumped in a chair, bleeding profusely and already dead. My client was standing half-way down the room still wearing the long white evening-dress she had worn on the stage that night. Her make-up was smudged and in her right hand she held a well-oiled service revolver. A bullet had left this weapon and entered Mr Frere's body between the third and fourth metacarpal. In order to make quite sure that her learned counsel didn't have things too easy, Maggie Hartley had then opened her mouth and spoken, so said Croft, the following unforgettable words, here transcribed without punctuation:

'I killed him what could I do with him help me.'

In all subsequent interviews the actress said that she remembered nothing about the quarrel in the dressing-room, the dreadful climax had been blotted from her mind. She was no doubt, and still remained, in a state of shock.

I was brooding on this hopeless defence when an elderly guard acting the part of an air hostess whispered excitedly into the intercom. 'We are now arriving at Grimble Central. Grimble Central. Please collect your hand baggage.' I merged into a place which seemed to be nestling somewhere within the Arctic Circle, the air bit sharply, it was bloody cold, and a blue-nosed Albert was there to meet me.

'After I left your Chambers in disgrace, Mr Rumpole . . . '

'After a misunderstanding, shall we say.'

'My then wife told me she was disgusted with me. She packed her bags and went to live with her married sister in Enfield.'

Albert was smiling contentedly, and that was something I could understand. I had just had, *à côté de* Chez Albert Handyside, a meal which his handsome, still youngish second wife referred to as tea, but which had all the appurtenances of an excellent cold luncheon with the addition of hot scones, Dundee cake and strawberry jam.

'Bit of luck then really, you getting the petty cash so "confused".'

'All the same. I do miss the old days clerking for you in the Temple, sir. How are things down South, Mr Rumpole?'

'Down South? Much as usual. Barristers lounging about in the sun. Munching grapes to the lazy sounds of plucked guitars.'

Mrs Handyside the Second returned to the room with another huge pot of dark brown Indian tea. She replenished the Rumpole cup and Albert and I fell to discussing the tea-table subject of murder and sudden death.

'Of course it's not the Penge Bungalow Job.' Albert was referring to my most notable murder and greatest triumph, a case I did at Lewes Assizes alone and without the so-called aid of leading counsel. 'But it's quite a decent little case, sir, in its way. A murder among the showfolk, as they terms them.'

'The showfolk, yes. Definitely worth the detour. There is, of course, one little fly in the otherwise interesting ointment.'

Albert, knowing me as he did, knew quite well what manner of insect I was referring to. I have never taken silk. I remain, at my advanced age, a 'junior' barrister. The brief in *R*. v. *Hartley* had only one drawback, it announced that I was to be 'led' by a local silk, Mr Jarvis Allen, QC. I hated the prospect of this obscure North Country Queen's Counsel getting all the fun.

'I told my senior partner, sir. I told him straight. Mr Rumpole's quite capable of doing this one on his own.' Albert was suitably apologetic.

'Reminded him, did you? I did the Penge Bungalow Murders alone and without a leader.'

'The senior partner did seem to feel . . . '

'I know. I'm not on the Lord Chancellor's guest list. I never get invited to breakfast in knee breeches. It's not Rumpole, QC. Just Rumpole, Queer Customer . . . '

'Oo I'm sure you're not.' Mrs Handyside the Second poured me another comforting cup of concentrated tannin.

'It's a murder, sir. That's attracted quite a lot of local attention.'

'And silks go with murder like steak goes with kidney! This Jarvis Allen, QC . . . Pretty competent sort of man, is he?'

'I've only seen him on the Bench . . . '

'On the what?'

The Bench seemed no sort of a place to see dedicated defenders.

'Sits as recorder here. Gave a young tearaway in our office three years for a punch-up at the Grimble United Ground.'

'There's no particular *art* involved in getting people into prison, Albert,' I said severely. 'How is he at keeping them out?'

After tea we had a conference fixed up with my leader and client in prison. There was no women's prison at Grimble, so our client was lodged in a room converted from an unused dispensary in the hospital wing of the masculine nick. She seemed older than I had expected as she sat looking composed, almost detached, surrounded by her legal advisers. It was, at that first conference, as though the case concerned someone else, and had not yet engaged her full attention.

'Mrs Frere.' Jarvis Allen, the learned QC started off. He was a thin, methodical man with rimless glasses and a general rimless appearance. He had made a voluminous note in red, green and blue Biro: it didn't seem to have given him much cause for hope.

'Our client is known as Maggie Hartley, sir,' Albert reminded him. 'In the profession.'

'I think she'd better be known as Mrs Frere. In Court,' Allen said firmly. 'Now, Mrs Frere. Tommy Pierce is prosecuting and of course I know him well . . . and if we went to see the judge, Skelton's a perfectly reasonable fellow. I think there's a sporting chance . . . I'm making no promises, mind you, there's a sporting chance they might let us plead to manslaughter!'

He brought the last sentence out triumphantly, like a Christmas present. Jarvis Allen was exercising his remarkable talent for getting people locked up. I lit a small cigar, and said nothing.

'Of course, we'd have to accept manslaughter. I'm sure Mr Rumpole agrees. You agree, don't you, Rumpole?' My leader turned to me for support. I gave him little comfort.

'Much more agreeable doing ten years for manslaughter than ten years for murder,' I said. 'Is that the choice you're offering?'

'I don't know if you've read the evidence . . . Our client was found with the gun in her hand.' Allen was beginning to get tetchy.

I thought this over and said, 'Stupid place to have it. If she'd actually *planned* a murder.'

'All the same. It leaves us without a defence.'

'Really? Do you think so? I was looking at the statement of Alan Copeland. He is . . . ' I ferreted among the depositions.

'What they call the "juvenile", I believe, Mr Rumpole,' Albert reminded me.

'The "juvenile", yes.' I read from Mr Copeland's statement. 'I've worked with G. P. Frere for three seasons . . . G.P. drank a good deal. Always interested in some girl in the cast. A new one every year . . . '

'Jealousy might be a powerful motive, for our client. That's a two-edged sword, Rumpole.' Allen was determined to look on the dreary side.

'Two-edged, yes. Most swords are.' I went on reading. 'He quarrelled violently with his wife, Maggie Hartley. On one occasion, after the dress rehearsal of *The Master Builder*, he threw a glass of milk stout in her face in front of the entire company . . . '

'She had a good deal of provocation, we can put that to the judge. That merely reduces it to manslaughter.' I was getting bored with my leader's chatter of manslaughter.

I gave my bundle of depositions to Albert and stood up, looking at our client to see if she would fit the part I had in mind.

'What you need in a murder is an unlikeable corpse . . . Then if you can find a likeable defendant . . . you're off to the races! Who knows? We might even reduce the crime to innocence.'

'Rumpole.' Allen had clearly had enough of my hopeless optimism.

'As I've had to tell Mrs Frere very frankly. There is a clear admission of guilt – which is not disputed.'

'What she said to the stage-door man, Mr . . . '

'Croft.' Albert supplied the name.

'I killed him, what could I do with him? Help me.' Allen repeated the most damning evidence with great satisfaction. 'You've read that, at least?'

'Yes, I've read it. That's the trouble.'

'What *do* you mean?'

'I mean, the trouble is, I read it. I didn't *hear* it. None of us did. And I don't suppose Mr Croft had it spelled out to him, with all the punctuation.'

'Really, Rumpole. I suppose they make jokes about murder cases in London.'

I ignored this bit of impertinence and went on to give the QC some unmerited assistance. 'Suppose she said . . . Suppose our client said, "I killed him" and then,' I paused for breath, ' "What could I do with him? Help me!"?'

I saw our client look at me, for the first time. When she spoke her voice, like Cordelia's, was ever soft, gentle and low, an excellent thing in woman.

'That's the reading,' she said. I must admit I was puzzled, and asked for an explanation.

'What?'

'The reading of the line. You can tell them. That's exactly how I said it.'

At last, it seemed, we had found *something* she remembered. I thought it an encouraging sign; but it wasn't really my business.

'I'm afraid, dear lady,' I gave her a small bow, 'I shan't be able to tell them anything. Who am I, after all, but the ageing juvenile? The reading of the line, as you call it, will have to come from your QC, Mr Jarvis Allen, who is playing the lead at the moment.'

After the conference I gave Albert strict instructions as to how our client was to dress for her starring appearance in the Grimble Assize Court (plain black suit, white blouse, no make-up, hair neat, voice gentle but audible to any OAP with a National Health deaf-aid sitting in the back row of the jury, absolutely no reaction during the prosecution case except for a well-controlled sigh of grief at the mention of her deceased husband) and then I suggested we met later for a visit to the scene of the crime. Her Majesty's Counsel for the defence had to rush home to write an urgent, and no doubt profitable, opinion on the planning of the new Grimble Gas Works and so was unfortunately unable to join us.

'You go if you like, Rumpole,' he said as he vanished into a funereal Austin Princess. 'I can't see how it's going to be of the slightest assistance.'

The Theatre Royal, an ornate but crumbling Edwardian Music Hall, which might once have housed George Formby and Rob Wilton, was bolted and barred. Albert and I stood in the rain and read a torn poster.

A cat was rubbing itself against the poster. We heard the North Country voice of an elderly man calling 'Puss . . . Puss . . . Bedtime, pussy.'

The cat went and we followed, round to the corner where the stage-door man, Mr Croft, no doubt, was opening his door and offering a saucer of milk. We made ourselves known as a couple of lawyers and asked for a look at the scene.

'Mr Derwent's round the front of the house. First door on the right.'

I moved up the corridor to a door and, opening it, had the unnerving experience of standing on a dimly lit stage. Behind me flapped a canvas balcony, and a view of the Mediterranean. As I wandered forward a voice called me out of the gloom.

'Who is it? Down here, I'm in the Stalls Bar.'

There was a light somewhere, a long way off. I went down some steps that led to the stalls and felt my way towards the light with Albert blundering after me. At last we reached the open glass door of a small bar, its dark-red walls hung with photographs of the company, and we were in the presence of a little gnome-like man, wearing a bow tie and a double-breasted suit, and that cheerily smiling but really quite expressionless apple-cheeked sort of face you see on some ventriloquist's dolls. His boot-black hair looked as if it had been dyed. He admitted to Albert that he was Daniel Derwent and at the moment in charge of the Frere-Hartley Players.

'Or what's left of them. Decimated, that's what we've been! If you've come with a two-hander for a couple of rather untalented juveniles, I'd be delighted to put it on. I suppose you *are* in the business.'

'The business?' I wondered what business he meant. But I didn't wonder long.

'Show business. The profession.'

'No . . . Another . . . profession altogether.'

I saw he had been working at a table in the empty bar, which was smothered with papers, bills and receipts.

'Our old manager left us in a state of total confusion,' Derwent said. 'And my ear's out to *here* answering the telephone.

'The vultures can't hear of an actor shot in East Grimble but half the character men in *Spotlight* are after me for the job. Well, I've told everyone. Nothing's going to be decided till after Maggie's trial. We're not re-opening till then. It wouldn't seem right, somehow. *What* other profession?'

'We're lawyers, Mr Derwent,' Albert told him. 'Defending.'

'Maggie's case?' Derwent didn't stop smiling.

'My name's Handyside of Instructing Solicitors. This is Mr Rumpole from London, junior counsel for the defence.'

'A London barrister. In the sticks!' The little Thespian seemed to find it amusing. 'Well, Grimble's hardly a number one touring date. All the same, I suppose murder's a draw. Anywhere . . . Care for a tiny rum?'

'That's very kind.' It was bitter cold, the unused theatre seemed to be saving on central heating and I was somewhat sick at heart at the prospect of our defence. A rum would do me no harm at all.

'Drop of orange in it? Or as she comes?'

'As she comes, thank you.'

'I always take a tiny rum, for the chords. Well, we depend on the chords, don't we, in our professions.'

Apart from a taste for rum, I didn't see then what I had in common, professionally or otherwise, with Mr Derwent. I wandered off with my drink in my hand to look at the photographs of the Frere-Hartley Players. As I did so I could hear the theatre-manager chattering to Albert.

'We could have done a bomb tonight. The money we've turned away. You couldn't buy publicity like it,' Derwent was saying.

'No . . . No, I don't suppose you could.'

'Week after week all we get in the *Grimble Argus* is a little para. "Maggie Hartley took her part well." And now we're all over the front page. And we can't play. It breaks your heart. It does really.' I heard him freshen his rum with another slug from the bottle. 'Poor old G.P. could have drawn more money dead than he ever could when he was alive. Well, at least he's sober tonight, wherever he is.'

'The late Mr G. P. Frere was fond of a drink occasionally?' Albert made use of the probing understatement.

'Not that his performance suffered. He didn't act any worse when he was drunk.'

I was looking at a glossy photograph of the late Mr G. P. Frere, taken about ten years ago I should imagine: it showed a man with grey sideburns and an open-necked shirt with a silk scarf round his neck and eyes that were self-consciously quizzical. A man who, despite the passage of the years, was still determined to go on saying 'Who's for tennis?'

'What I admired about old G.P.', I heard Derwent say, 'was his selfless concern for others! Never left you with the sole responsibility of entertaining the audience. He'd try to help by upstaging you. Or moving on your laugh line. He once tore up a newspaper all through my long speech in *Waiting for Godot* . . . Now you wouldn't do that, would you, Mr Rumpole? Not in anyone's long speech. Well, of course not.'

He had moved, for his last remarks, to a point rather below, but still too close to, my left ear. I was looking at the photographs of a moderately pretty young girl, wearing a seafaring sweater, whose lips were parted as if to suck in a quick draft of ozone when out for a day with the local dinghy club.

'Miss Christine Hope?' I asked.

'Miss Christine Hopeless I called her.' This Derwent didn't seem to have a particularly high opinion of his troupe. 'God knows what G.P. saw in her. She did that audition speech from *Saint Joan*. All breathless and excited . . . as if she'd just run up four flights of stairs because the angel voices were calling her about a little part in *Crossroads*. "We could *do* something with her," G.P. said. "I know what," I told him. "Burn her at the stake." '

I had come to a wall on which there were big photographs of various characters, a comic charlady, a beautiful woman in a white evening-dress, a duchess in a tiara, a neat secretary in glasses, and a tattered siren who might have been Sadie Thompson in *Rain* if my theatrical memory served me right. All the faces were different, and they were all the faces of Maggie Hartley.

'Your client. My leading lady. I suppose *both* our shows depend on her.' Derwent was looking at the photographs with a rapt smile of appreciation. 'No doubt about it. She's good. Maggie's good.'

I turned to look at him, found him much too close and retreated a step. 'What do you mean', I asked him, 'by good exactly?'

'There is a quality. Of perfect truthfulness. Absolute reality.'

'Truthfulness?' This was about the first encouraging thing we'd heard about Maggie Hartley.

'It's very rare.'

'Excuse me, sir. Would you be prepared to say that in Court?' Albert seemed to be about to take a statement. I moved tactfully away.

'Is that what you came here for?' Derwent asked me nervously.

I thought it over, and decided there was no point in turning a friendly source of information into a hostile witness.

'No. We wanted to see . . . the scene of the crime.'

At which Mr Derwent, apparently reassured, smiled again. 'The Last Act,' he said, and led us to the dressing-room, typical of a provincial rep. 'I'll unlock it for you.'

The dressing-room had been tidied up, the cupboards and drawers were empty. Otherwise it looked like the sort of room that would have been condemned as unfit for human habitation by any decent local authority. I stood in the doorway, and made sure that the mirror which went all along one side of the room was shattered in the corner furthest away from me.

'Any help to you, is it?'

'It might be. It's what we lawyers call the *locus in quo*.'

Mr Derwent was positively giggling then.

'Do you? How frightfully camp of you. It's what we actors call a dressing-room.'

So I went back to the Majestic Hotel, a building which seemed rather less welcoming than Her Majesty's Prison, Grimble. And when I was breaking my fast on their mixed grill consisting of cold greasy bacon, a stunted tomato and a sausage that would have looked ungenerous on a cocktail stick, Albert rang me with the unexpected news that at one bound put the Theatre Royal killing up beside the Penge Bungalow Murders in the pantheon of Rumpole's forensic triumphs. I was laughing when I came back from the telephone, and I was still laughing when I returned to spread, on a slice of blackened toast, that part of margarine which the management of the Majestic were apparently unable to tell from butter.

Two hours later we were in the judges' room at the Law Courts discussing, in the hushed tones of relatives after a funeral, the unfortunate event which had occurred. Those present were Tommy Pierce, QC, counsel for the prosecution, and his junior Roach, the learned judge, my learned leader and my learned self.

'Of course these people don't really live in the real world at all,' Jarvis Allen, QC, was saying. 'It's all make-believe for them. Dressing up in fancy costumes . . . '

He himself was wearing a wig, a tailed coat with braided cuffs and a silk gown. His opponent, also bewigged, had a huge stomach from which a gold watch-chain and seal dangled. He also took snuff and blew his nose in a red spotted handkerchief. That kind and, on the whole, gentle figure Skelton J. was fishing in the folds of his scarlet gown for a bitten pipe and an old leather pouch. I didn't think we were exactly the ones to talk about dressing up.

'You don't think she appreciates the seriousness,' the judge was clearly worried.

'I'm afraid not, Judge. Still, if she wants to sack me . . . Of course it puts Rumpole in an embarrassing position.'

'Are you embarrassed, Rumpole?' His Lordship asked me.

As a matter of fact I was filled with a deeper inner joy, for Albert's call at breakfast had been to the effect that our client had chosen to dismiss her leading counsel and put her future entirely in the hands of Horace Rumpole, BA, that timeless member of the Junior Bar.

'Oh yes. Dreadfully embarrassed, Judge.' I did my best to look suitably modest. 'But it seems that the lady's mind is quite made up.'

'Very embarrassing for you. For you both.' The judge was understanding. 'Does she give any reason for dispensing with her leading counsel, Jarvis?'

'She said . . . ' I turned a grin into a cough. I too remembered what Albert had told us. 'She said she thought Rumpole was "better casting".'

' "Better casting"? Whatever can she mean by that?'

'Better in the part, Judge,' I translated.

'Oh dear.' The judge looked distressed. 'Is she very actressy?'

'She's an actress,' I admitted, but would go no further.

'Yes. Yes, I suppose she is.' The judge lit his pipe. 'Do you have any views about this, Tommy?'

'No, Judge. When Jarvis was instructed we were going to ask your views on a plea to manslaughter.'

The portly Pierce twinkled a lot and talked in a rich North Country accent. I could see we were in for a prosecution of homely fun, like one of the comic plays of J. B. Priestley.

'Manslaughter, eh? Do you want to discuss manslaughter, Rumpole?' I appeared to give the matter some courteous consideration.

'No, Judge, I don't believe I do.'

'If you'd like an adjournment you shall certainly have it. Your client may want to think about manslaughter . . . Or consider another leader. She should have leading counsel. In a case of this . . . ' the judge puffed out smoke . . . 'seriousness.'

'Oh, I don't think there's much point in considering another leader.'

'You don't?'

'You see,' I was doing my best not to look at Allen, 'I don't honestly think anyone else would get the part.'

When we got out of the judges' room, and were crossing the imposing Victorian Gothic hallway that led to the Court, my learned ex-leader, who had preserved an expression of amused detachment up to that point, turned on me with considerable hurt.

'I must say I take an extremely dim view of that.'

'Really?'

'An extremely dim view. On this circuit we have a tradition of loyalty to our leaders.'

'It's a local custom?'

'Certainly it is.' Allen stood still and pronounced solemnly. 'I can't imagine anyone on this circuit carrying on with a case after his leader has been sacked. It's not in the best traditions of the Bar.'

'Loyalty to one's leader. Yes, of course, that is extremely important . . . ' I thought about it. 'But we must consider the other great legal maxim, mustn't we?'

'Legal maxim? What legal maxim?'

' "The show must go on." Excuse me. I see Albert. Nice chatting to you but . . . Things to do, old darling. Quite a number of things to do . . . ' So I hurried away from the fired legal eagle to where my old clerk was standing, looking distinctly anxious, at the entrance of the Court. He asked me hopefully if the judge had seen fit to grant an adjournment, so that he could persuade our client to try another silk, a course on which Albert's senior partner was particularly keen.

'Oh dear,' I had to disappoint him. 'I begged the judge, Albert. I almost went down on my knees to him. But would he grant me an adjournment? I'm afraid not. No, Rumpole, he told me, the show must go on.' I put a comforting hand on Albert's shoulder. 'Cheer up, old darling. There's only one thing you need say to your senior partner.'

'What's that, sir?'

'The Penge Bungalow Murders.'

I sounded supremely confident of course; but as I went into Court I suddenly remembered that without a leader I would have absolutely no one to blame but myself when things went wrong.

'I don't know if any of you ladies and gentlemen have actually attended *performances* at the Theatre Royal . . . ' Tommy Pierce, QC, opening the case for the prosecution, chuckled as though to say 'Most of us have got better things to do, haven't we, Members of the jury?' 'But we all have passed it going up the Makins Road in a trolley-bus on the way to Grimble Football Ground. You'll know where it is, Members of the jury. Past the Snellsham roundabout, on the corner opposite the Old Britannia Hotel, where we've all celebrated many a win by Grimble United . . . '

I didn't know why he didn't just tell them: 'The prisoner's repres- ented by Rumpole of the Bailey, a smart-alecky lawyer from London, who's never ever heard of Grimble United, let alone the Old Britan- nia Hotel.' I shut my eyes and looked uninterested as Tommy rum- bled on, switching, now, to portentous seriousness.

'In this case, Members of the jury, we enter an alien world. The world of the showfolk! They live a strange life, you may think. A life of make-believe. On the surface everyone loves each other. "You were wonderful, darling!" said to men and women alike . . . '

I seriously considered heaving myself to my hind legs to protest against this rubbish, but decided to sit still and continue the look of bored indifference.

'But underneath all the good companionship,' Pierce was now

trying to make the flesh creep, 'run deep tides of jealousy and passion which welled up, in this particular case, Members of the jury, into brutal and, say the Crown, quite cold-blooded murder . . . '

As he went on I thought that Derwent, the little gnome from the theatre, whom I could now see in the back of the pit, somewhere near the dock, was perfectly right. Murder *is* a draw. All the local nobs were in Court including the judge's wife Lady Skelton, in the front row of the stalls, wearing her special matinée hat. I also saw the sheriff of the county, in his fancy dress, wearing lace ruffles and a sword which stuck rather inconveniently between his legs, and Mrs Sheriff of the county, searching in her handbag for something which might well have been her opera glasses. And then, behind me, the star of the show, my client, looking as I told her to look. Ordinary.

'This is not a case which depends on complicated evidence, members of the jury, or points of law. Let me tell you the facts.'

The facts were not such that I wanted the jury to hear them too clearly, at least not in my learned friend's version. I slowly, and quite noisily, took a page out of my notebook. I was grateful to see that some of the members of the jury glanced in my direction.

'It simply amounts to this. The murder weapon, a Smith and Wesson revolver, was found in the defendant's hand as she stood over her husband's dead body. A bullet from the very weapon had entered between the third and fourth metacarpal!'

I didn't like Pierce's note of triumph as he said this. Accordingly I began to tear my piece of paper into very small strips. More members of the jury looked in my direction.

'Ladies and Gentlemen. The defendant, as you will see on your abstract of indictment, was charged as "Maggie Hartley". It seems she prefers to be known by her maiden name, and that may give you some idea of the woman's attitude to her husband of some twenty years, the deceased in this case, the late Gerald Patrick Frere . . . '

At which point, gazing round the Court, I saw Daniel Derwent. He actually winked, and I realised that he thought he recognised my paper tearing as an old ham actor's trick. I stopped doing it immediately.

'It were a mess. A right mess. Glass broken, blood. He was sprawled in the chair. I thought he were drunk for a moment, but he weren't. And she had this pistol, like, in her hand.' Mr Croft, the stage-doorman was standing in the witness-box in his best blue suit. The jury clearly liked him, just as they disliked the picture he was painting.

'Can you remember what she said?' The learned prosecutor prompted him gently.

'Not too fast . . . ' Mr Justice Skelton was, worse luck, preparing himself to write it all down.

'Just follow his Lordship's pencil . . . ' said Pierce, and the judicial pencil prepared to follow Mr Croft.

'She said, "I killed him, what could I do with him?" '

'What did you understand that to mean?'

I did hoist myself to my hind legs then, and registered a determined objection. 'It isn't what this witness understood it to mean. It's what the jury understands it to mean . . . '

'My learned friend's quite wrong. The witness was there. He could form his own conclusion . . . '

'Please, gentlemen. Let's try and have no disagreements, at least not before luncheon,' said the judge sweetly, and added, less charmingly, 'I think Mr Croft may answer the question.'

'I understood her to say she was so fed up with him, she didn't know what else to do . . . '

'But to kill him . . . ?' Only the judge could have supplied that and he did it with another charming smile.

'Yes, my Lord.'

'Did she say anything else? That you remember?'

'I think she said, "Help me." '

'Yes. Just wait there, will you? In case Mr Rumpole has some questions.'

'Just a few . . . ' I rose to my feet. Here was an extremely dangerous witness whom the jury liked. It was no good making a head-on attack. The only way was to lure Mr Croft politely into my parlour. I gave the matter some thought and then tried a line on which I thought we might reach agreement.

'When you saw the deceased, Frere, slumped in the chair, your first thought was that he was drunk?'

'Yes.'

'Had you seen him slumped in a chair drunk in his dressing-room on many occasions?'

'A few.' Mr Croft answered with a knowing smile, and I felt encouraged.

'On most nights?'

'Some nights.'

'Were there some nights when he *wasn't* the worse for drink? Did he ever celebrate, with an evening of sobriety?'

I got my first smile from the jury, and the Joker for the prosecution arose in full solemnity.

'My Lord . . . '

Before Tommy Pierce could interrupt the proceedings with a speech I bowled the next question.

'Mr Croft. When you came into the dressing-room, the deceased Frere was nearest the door . . . '

'Yes. Only a couple of feet from me . . . I saw . . . '

'You saw my client was standing half-way down the room?' I asked, putting a stop to further painful details. 'Holding the gun.'

Pierce gave the jury a meaningful stare, emphasising the evidence.

'The dressing-room mirror stretches all the way along the wall. And it was broken at the far end, away from the door?'

'Yes.'

'So to have fired the bullet that broke that end of the glass, my client would have had to turn away from the deceased and shoot behind her back . . . ' I swung round, by way of demonstration, and made a gesture, firing behind me. Of course I couldn't do that without bringing the full might of the prosecution to its feet.

'Surely that's a question for the jury to decide.'

'The witness was there. He can form his own conclusions.' I quoted the wisdom of my learned friend. 'What's the answer?'

'I suppose she would,' Croft said thoughtfully and the jury looked interested.

The judge cleared his throat and leaned forward, smiling politely, and being as it turned out, surprisingly unhelpful.

'Wouldn't that depend, Mr Rumpole, on where the deceased was at the time that particular shot was fired . . . ?'

Pierce glowed in triumph and muttered 'Exactly!' I did a polite bow and went quickly on to the next question.

'Perhaps we could turn now to the little matter of what she said when you went into the room.'

'I can remember that perfectly.'

'The words, yes. It's the reading that matters.'

'The *what*, Mr Rumpole?' said the judge, betraying theatrical ignorance.

'The stress, my Lord. The intonation . . . It's an expression used in show business.'

'Perhaps we could confine ourselves to expressions used in Law Courts, Mr Rumpole.'

'Certainly, my Lord.' I re-addressed the witness. 'She said she'd killed him. And then, after a pause, "What could I do with him. Help me." '

Mr Croft frowned. 'I . . . That is, yes.'

'Meaning. What could I do with his dead body, and asking for your help . . . ?'

'My Lord. That's surely . . . ' Tommy Pierce was on his hind legs, and I gave him another quotation from himself.

'He was there!' I leant forward and smiled at Croft trying to make him feel that I was a friend he could trust.

'She never meant that she had killed him because she didn't know what to do with him?'

There was a long silence. Counsel for the prosecution let out a deep breath and subsided like a balloon slowly settling. The judge nudged the witness gently. 'Well. What's the answer, Mr Croft? Did she . . . ?'

'I . . . I can't be sure how she said it, my Lord.'

And there, on a happy note of reasonable doubt, I left it. As I came out of Court and crossed the entrance hall on my way to the cells I was accosted by the beaming Mr Daniel Derwent, who was, it seemed, anxious to congratulate me.

'What a performance, Mr Rumpole. Knock-out! You were

wonderful! What I admired so was the timing. The pause, before you started the cross-examination.'

'Pause?'

'You took a beat of nine seconds. I counted.'

'Did I really?'

'Built-up tension, of course. I could see what you were after.' He put a hand on my sleeve, a red hand with big rings and polished fingernails. 'You really must let me know. If ever you want a job in rep.'

I dislodged my fan club and went down the narrow staircase to the cells. The time had clearly come for my client to start remembering.

Maggie Hartley smiled at me over her untouched tray of vegetable pie. She even asked me how I was; but I had no time for small talk. It was zero hour, the last moment I had to get some reasonable instructions.

'Listen to me. Whatever you do or don't remember . . . it's just impossible for you to have stood there and fired the first shot.'

'The first shot?' She frowned, as if at some distant memory.

'The one that *didn't* kill him. The one that went behind you. He must have fired that. He *must* . . . '

'Yes.' She nodded her head. That was encouraging. So far as it went.

'Why the hell . . . why in the name of sanity didn't you tell us that before?'

'I waited. Until there was someone I could trust.'

'Me?'

'Yes. You, Mr Rumpole.'

There's nothing more flattering than to be trusted, even by a confirmed and hopeless villain (which is why I find it hard to dislike a client), and I was convinced Maggie Hartley wasn't that. I sat down beside her in the cell and, with Albert taking notes, she started to talk. What she said was disjointed, sometimes incoherent, and God knows how it was going to sound in the witness-box, but given a few more breaks in the prosecution case, and a following wind I was beginning to get the sniff of a defence.

One, two, three, four . . .

Mr Alan Copeland, the juvenile lead, had just given his evidence-in-chief for the prosecution. He seemed a pleasant enough young man, wearing a tie and a dark suit (good witness-box clothing) and his evidence hadn't done us any particular harm. All the same I was trying what the director Derwent had admired as the devastating pause.

Seven . . . eight . . . nine . . .

'Have you any questions, Mr Rumpole?' The judge sounded as if he was getting a little impatient with 'the timing'. I launched the cross-examination.

'Mr Alan . . . Copeland. You know the deceased man owned a Smith and Wesson revolver? Do you know where he got it?'

'He was in a spy film and it was one of the props. He bought it.'

'But it was more than a bit of scenery. It was a real revolver.'

'Unfortunately, yes.'

'And he had a licence for it . . . ?'

'Oh yes. He joined the Grimble Rifle and Pistol Club and used to shoot at targets. I think he fancied himself as James Bond or something.'

'As James who . . . ?' I knew that Mr Justice Skelton wouldn't be able to resist playing the part of a mystified judge, so I explained carefully.

'A character in fiction, my Lord. A person licensed to kill. He also spends a great deal of his time sleeping with air hostesses.' To Tommy Pierce's irritation I got a little giggle out of the ladies and gentlemen of the jury.

'Mr Rumpole. We have quite enough to do in this case dealing with questions of *fact*. I suggest we leave the world of fiction . . . outside the Court, with our overcoats.'

The jury subsided into serious attention, and I addressed myself to the work in hand. 'Where did Mr Frere keep his revolver?'

'Usually in a locker. At the Rifle Club.'

'Usually?'

'A few weeks ago he asked me to bring it back to the theatre for him.'

'He asked *you*?'

'I'm a member of the club myself.'

'Really, Mr Copeland.' The judge was interested. 'And what's your weapon?'

'A shotgun, my Lord. I do some clay pigeon shooting.'

'Did Frere say *why* he wanted his gun brought back to the theatre?' I gave the jury a puzzled look.

'There'd been some burglaries. I imagine he wanted to scare any intruder . . .'

I had established that it was Frere's gun, and certainly not brought to the scene of the crime by Maggie. I broached another topic. 'Now you have spoken of some quarrels between Frere and his wife.'

'Yes, sir. He once threw a drink in her face.'

'During their quarrels, did you see my client retaliate in any way?'

'No. No, I never did. May I say something, my Lord . . .'

'Certainly, Mr Copeland.'

I held my breath. I didn't like free-ranging witnesses, but at his answer I sat down gratefully.

'Miss Hartley, as we knew her, was an exceptionally gentle person.'

I saw the jury look at the dock, at the quiet almost motionless woman sitting there.

'Mr Copeland. You've told us you shot clay pigeons at the Rifle Club.' The prosecution was up and beaming.

'Yes, sir.'

'Nothing much to eat on a clay pigeon, I suppose.'

The jury greeted this alleged quip with total silence. The local comic had died the death in Grimble. Pierce went on and didn't improve his case.

'And Frere asked for this pistol to be brought back to the theatre. Did his wife know that, do you think . . . ?'

'I certainly didn't tell her.'

'May I ask why not?'

'I think it would have made her very nervous. I certainly was.'

'Nervous of what, exactly?'

Tommy Pierce had broken the first rule of advocacy. Never ask your witness a question unless you're quite sure of the answer.

'Well . . . I was always afraid G.P.'d get drunk and loose it off at someone . . .'

The beauty of that answer was that it came from a witness for the prosecution, a detached observer who'd only been called to identify the gun as belonging to the late-lamented G. P. Frere. None too soon for the health of his case Tommy Pierce let Mr Copeland leave the box. I saw him cross the Court and sit next to Daniel Derwent, who gave him a little smile, as if of congratulation.

In the course of my legal career I have had occasion to make some study of firearms; not so intensive, of course, as my researches into the subject of blood, but I certainly know more about revolvers than I do about the law of landlord and tenant. I held the fatal weapon in a fairly expert hand as I cross-examined the inspector who had re-

covered it from the scene of the crime.

'It's clear, is it not, Inspector, that two chambers had been fired?'

'Yes.'

'One bullet was found in the corner of the mirror, and another in the body of the deceased, Frere?'

'That is so.'

'Now. If the person who fired the shot into the mirror pulled back this hammer', I pulled it back, 'to fire a second shot . . . the gun is now in a condition to go off with a far lighter pressure on the trigger?'

'That is so. Yes.'

'Thank you.'

I put down the gun and as I did so allowed my thumb to accidentally press the trigger. I looked at it, surprised, as it clicked. It was a moderately effective move, and I thought the score was fifteen-love to Rumpole. Tommy Pierce rose to serve.

'Inspector. Whether the hammer was pulled back or not, a woman would have no difficulty in firing the pistol?'

'Certainly not, my Lord.'

'Yes. Thank *you*, Inspector.' The prosecution sat down smiling. Fifteen-all.

The last witness of the day was Miss Christine Hope who turned her large *ingénue* eyes on the jury and whispered her evidence at a sound level which must have made her unintelligible to the audiences at the Theatre Royal. I had decided to cross-examine her more in sorrow than in anger.

'Miss Hope. Why were you waiting at the stage door?'

'Somehow I can never bear to leave. After the show's over . . . I can never bear to go.' She gave the jury a 'silly me' look of girlish enthusiasm. 'I suppose I'm just in love with the theatre.'

'And I suppose you were also "just in love with G. P. Frere"?'

At which Miss Hope looked helplessly at the rail of the witness-box, and fiddled with the Holy Bible.

'You waited for him every night, didn't you? He left his wife at the stage door and took you home.'

'Sometimes . . . '

'You're dropping your voice, Miss Hope.' The judge was leaning forward, straining to hear.

'Sometimes, my Lord,' she repeated a decibel louder.

'Every night?'

'Most nights. Yes.'

'Thank you, Miss Hope.'

Pierce, wisely, didn't re-examine and *la belle* Christine left the box to looks of disapproval from certain ladies on the jury.

I didn't sleep well that night. Whether it was the Majestic mattress, which appeared to be stuffed with firewood, or the sounds, as of a giant suffering from indigestion, which reverberated from the central heating, or mere anxiety about the case, I don't know. At any rate Albert and I were down in the cells as soon as they opened, taking a critical look at the client I was about to expose to the perils of the witness-box. As I had instructed her she was wearing no make-up, and a simple dark dress which struck exactly the right note.

'I'm glad you like it,' Maggie said. 'I wore it in *Time and the Conways*.'

'Listen to the questions, answer them as shortly as you can.' I gave her her final orders. 'Every word to the North Country comedian is giving him a present. Just stick to the facts. Not a word of criticism of the dear departed.'

'You want *them* to like me?'

'They shouldn't find it too difficult.' I looked at her, and lit a small cigar.

'Do I have to swear on . . . the Bible?'

'It's customary.'

'I'd rather affirm.'

'You don't believe in God?' I didn't want an obscure point of theology adding unnecessary difficulties to our case.

'I suppose He's a possibility. He just doesn't seem to be a very frequent visitor to the East Grimble Rep.'

'I know a Grimble jury,' Albert clearly shared my fears. 'If you *could* swear on the Bible?'

'The audience might like it?' Maggie smiled gently.

'The jury,' I corrected her firmly.

'They're not too keen on agnostic actresses. Is that your opinion?'

'I suppose that puts it in a nutshell.'

'All right for the West End, is that it? No good in Grimble.'

'Of course I want you to be *yourself* . . . ' I really hoped she wasn't going to be difficult about the oath.

'No you don't. You don't want me to be myself at all. You want me to be an ordinary North Country housewife. Spending just another ordinary day on trial for murder.' For a moment her voice had hardened. I looked at her and tried to sound as calm as possible as I pulled out my watch. It was nearly time for the curtain to go up on the evidence for the defence.

'Naturally you're nervous. Time to go.'

'Bloody sick to the stomach. Every time I go on.' Her voice was gentle again, and she was smiling ruefully.

'Good luck.'

'We never say "good luck". It's bad luck to say "good luck". We say "break a leg" . . . '

'Break a leg!' I smiled back at her and went upstairs to make my entrance.

Calling your client, I always think, is the worst part of any case. When you're cross-examining, or making a final speech, you're in control. Put your client in the witness-box and there the old darling is, exposed to the world, out of your protection, and all you can do is ask the questions and hope to God the answers don't blow up in your face.

With Maggie everything was going well. We were like a couple of ballroom dancers, expertly gyrating to Victor Sylvester and certain to walk away with the cup. She seemed to sense my next question, and had her answer ready, but not too fast. She looked at the jury, made herself audible to the judge, and gave an impression, a small, dark figure in the witness-box, of courage in the face of adversity. The Court was so quiet and attentive that, as she started to describe that final quarrel, I felt we were alone, two old friends, talking intimately of some dreadful event that took place a long time ago.

'He told me . . . he was very much in love with Christine.'

'With Miss Hope?'

'Yes. With Christine Hope. That he wanted her to play Amanda.'

'That is . . . the leading lady? And what was to happen to you?'

'He wanted me to leave the company. To go to London. He never wanted to see me again.'

'What did you say to that?'

'I said I was terribly unhappy about Christine, naturally.'

'Just tell the ladies and gentlemen of the jury what happened next.'

'He said it didn't matter what I said. He was going to get rid of me. He opened the drawer of the dressing-table.'

'Was he standing then?'

'I would say, staggering.'

'Yes, and then . . . ?'

'He took out the . . . the revolver.'

'This one . . . ?'

I handed the gun to the usher, who took it to Maggie. She glanced at it and shuddered.

'I . . . I think so.'

'What effect did it have on you when you first saw it?'

'I was terrified.'

'Did you know it was there?'

'No. I had no idea.'

'And then . . . ?'

'Then. He seemed to be getting ready to fire the gun.'

'You mean he pulled back the hammer . . . ?'

'My Lord . . . ' Pierce stirred his vast bulk and the judge was inclined to agree. He said:

'Yes. Please don't lead, Mr Rumpole.'

'I think that's what he did,' Maggie continued without assistance. 'I didn't look carefully. Naturally I was terrified. He was waving the gun. He didn't seem to be able to hold it straight. Then there was a terrible explosion. I remember glass, and dust, everywhere.'

'Who fired that shot, Mrs Frere?'

'My husband. I think . . . '

'Yes?'

'I think he was trying to kill me.' She said it very quietly, but the jury heard, and remembered. She gave it a marked pause and then went on. 'After that first shot, I saw him getting ready to fire again.'

'Was he pulling . . . '

'Please don't lead, Mr Rumpole.' The trouble with the great comedian was that he couldn't sit still in anyone else's act.

'He was pulling back . . . That thing.' Maggie went on without any help.

Then I asked the judge if we could have a demonstration and the usher went up into the witness-box to play the scene with Maggie. At my suggestion he took the revolver.

'We are all quite sure that thing isn't loaded?' The judge sounded nervous.

'Quite sure, my Lord. Of course, we don't want *another* fatal *accident*!'

'Really, my Lord. That was quite improper!' Pierce rose furiously. 'My learned friend called it an accident.'

I apologised profusely, the point having been made. Then Maggie quietly positioned the usher. He raised the gun as she asked him. It was pointed murderously at her. And then Maggie grabbed at the gun in his hand, and forced it back, struggling desperately, against the usher's chest.

'I was trying to stop him. I got hold of his hand to push the gun away . . . I pushed it back . . . I think . . . I think I must have forced back his finger on the trigger.' We heard the hammer click, and now Maggie was struggling to hold back her tears. 'There was another terrible noise . . . I never meant . . . '

'Yes. Thank you, Usher.'

The usher went back to the well of the Court. Maggie was calm again when I asked her:

'When Mr Croft came you said you had killed your husband?'

'Yes . . . I had . . . By accident.'

'What else did you say?'

'I think I said . . . What could I do with him? I meant, how could I help him, of course.'

'And you asked Mr Croft to help you?'

'Yes.'

It was time for the curtain line.

'Mrs Frere. Did you ever at any time have any intention of killing your husband?'

'Never . . . ! Never . . . ! Never . . . !' Now my questions were finished she was crying, her face and shoulders shaking. The judge leaned forward kindly.

'Don't distress yourself. Usher, a glass of water?'

Her cheeks hot with genuine tears, Maggie looked up bravely.

'Thank you, my Lord.'

'Bloody play-acting!' I heard the cynical Tommy Pierce mutter ungraciously to his junior, Roach.

If she was good in chief Maggie was superb in cross-examination. She answered the questions courteously, shortly, but as if she were genuinely trying to help Tommy clear up any doubt about her innocence that may have lingered in his mind. At the end he lost his nerve and almost shouted at her:

'So according to you, you did nothing wrong?'

'Oh yes,' she said. 'I did something terribly wrong.'

'Tell us. What?'

'I loved him too much. Otherwise I should have left him. Before he tried to kill me.'

During Tommy's final speech there was some coughing from the jury. He tried a joke or two about actors, lost heart and sat down upon reminding the jury that they must not let sympathy for my client affect their judgment.

'I agree entirely with my learned friend,' I started my speech. 'Put all sympathy out of your mind. The mere fact that my client clung faithfully to a drunken, adulterous husband, hoping vainly for the love he denied her; the terrible circumstance that she escaped death at his hands only to face the terrible ordeal of a trial for murder; none of these things should influence you in the least . . . ' and I ended with my well-tried peroration. 'In an hour or two this case will be over. You will go home and put the kettle on and forget all about this little theatre, and the angry, drunken actor and his wretched infidelities. This case has only been a few days out of your lives. But for this lady I have the honour to represent . . . ' I pointed to the dock, '*all* her life hangs in the balance. Is that life to be broken and is she to go down in darkness and disgrace, or can she go back into the glowing light of her world, to bring us all joy and entertainment and laughter once again? Ask yourselves that question, Members of the jury. And when you ask it, you know there can only be one answer.'

I sank back into my seat exhausted, pushing back my wig and mopping my brow with a large silk handkerchief. Looking round the Court I saw Derwent. He seemed about to applaud, until he was restrained by Mr Alan Copeland.

There is nothing I hate more than waiting for a jury to come back. You smoke too much and drink too many cups of coffee, your hands sweat and you can't do or think of anything else. All you can do is to pay a courtesy visit to the cells to prepare for the worst. Albert Handyside had to go off and do a touch of Dangerous Driving in the Court next door, so I was alone when I went to call on the waiting Maggie.

She was standing in her cell, totally calm.

'This is the bad part, isn't it? Like waiting for the notices.'

I sat down at the table with my notebook, unscrewed my fountain pen.

'I had better think of what to say if they find you guilty of manslaughter. I think I've got the facts for mitigation, but I'd just like to get the history clear. You'd started this theatrical company together?'

'It was my money. Every bloody penny of it.' I looked up in some surprise. The hard, tough note was there in her voice; her face was set in a look which was something like hatred.

'I don't think we need go into the financial side.' I tried to stop her, but she went on:

'Do you know what that idiotic manager we had then did? He gave G.P. a contract worth fifty per cent of the profits: for an investment of nothing and a talent which stopped short of being able to pour out a drink and say a line at the same time. Anyway I never paid his percentage.' She smiled then, it was quite humourless. 'Won't need to say that, will we?'

'No.' I said firmly.

'Fifty per cent of ten years' work! He reckoned he was owed around twenty thousand pounds. He was going to sue us and bankrupt the company . . . '

'I don't think you need to tell me any more.' I screwed the top back on my fountain pen. Perhaps she had told me too much already.

'So don't feel too badly, will you? If we're not a hit.'

I stood up and pulled out my watch. Suddenly I felt an urgent need to get out of the cell.

'They should be back soon now.'

'It's all a game to you, isn't it?' She sounded unaccountably bitter. 'All a wonderful game of "let's pretend". The costume. The bows. The little jokes. The onion at the end.'

'The onion?'

'An old music-hall expression. For what makes the audience cry. Oh, I was quite prepared to go along with it. To wear the make-up.'

'You didn't wear any make-up.'

'I know, that was brilliant of you. You're a marvellous performer, Mr Rumpole. Don't let anyone tell you different.'

'It's not a question of performance.' I couldn't have that.

'Isn't it?'

'Of course it isn't! The jury are now weighing the facts. Doing their best to discover where the truth lies.' I looked at her. Her face gave nothing away.

'Or at least deciding if the prosecution has proved its case.'

Suddenly, quite unexpectedly, she yawned, she moved away from me, as though I bored her.

'Oh, I'm tired. Worn out. With so much *acting*. I tell you, in the theatre we haven't got time for all that. We've got our livings to get.'

The woman prison officer came in.

'I think they want you upstairs now. Ready, dear?'

When Maggie spoke again her voice was low, gentle and wonderfully polite.

'Yes thanks, Elsie. I'm quite ready now.'

★

'Will your foreman please stand? Mr Foreman. Have you reached a verdict on which you are all agreed?'

'Not guilty, my Lord.'

Four words that usually set the Rumpole ears tingling with delight and the chest to swell with pleasure. Why was it, that at the end of what was no doubt a remarkable win, a famous victory even, I felt such doubt and depression? I told myself that I was not the judge of fact, that the jury had clearly not been satisfied and that the prosecution had not proved its case. I did the well-known shift of responsibility which is the advocate's perpetual comfort, but I went out of Court unelated. In the entrance hall I saw Maggie leaving; she didn't turn back to speak to me, and I saw that she was holding the hand of Mr Alan Copeland. Such congratulations as I received came from the diminutive Derwent.

'Triumph. My dear, a total triumph.'

'You told me she was truthful . . . ' I looked at him.

'I meant her acting. That's quite truthful. Not to be faulted. That's all I meant.'

At which he made his exit and my learned friend for the prosecution came sailing up, beaming with the joy of reconciliation.

'Well. Congratulations, Rumpole. That was a bloody good win!'

'Was it? I hope so.'

'Coming to the Circuit dinner tonight?'

'Tonight?'

'You'll enjoy it! We've got some pretty decent claret in the mess.'

If my judgement hadn't been weakened by exhaustion I would never have agreed to the Circuit dinner which took place, as I feared, in a private room at the Majestic Hotel. All the gang were there, Skelton J., Pierce, Roach and my one-time leader Jarvis Allen, QC. The food was indifferent, the claret was bad, and when the port was passed an elderly silk whom they called 'Mr Senior' in deference to his position as Leader of the Circuit, banged the table with the handle of his knife and addressed young Roach at the other end of the table.

'Mr Junior, in the matter of Rumpole.'

'Mr Senior,' Roach produced a scribble on a menu. 'I will read the indictment.'

I realised then that I had been tricked, ambushed, made to give myself up to the tender mercies of this savage northerly Circuit. Rumpole was on trial, there was nothing to do but drink all the available port and put up with it.

'Count One,' Roach read it out. 'Deserting his learned leader in his hour of need. That is to say on the occasion of his leader having been given the sack. Particulars of Offence . . . '

'Mr Senior. Have five minutes elapsed?' Allen asked.

'Five minutes having elapsed since the loyal toast, you may now smoke.'

Tommy Pierce lit a large cigar. I lit a small one. Mr Junior Roach continued to intone.

'The said Rumpole did add considerably to the seriousness of the offence by proceeding to win in the absence of his learned leader.'

'Mr Junior. Has Rumpole anything to say by way of mitigation?'

'Rumpole.' Roach took out his watch, clearly there was a time-limit in speeches. I rose to express my deepest thoughts, loosened by the gentle action of the port.

'The show had to go on!'

'What? What did Rumpole say?' Mr Justice Skelton seemed to have some difficulty in hearing.

'Sometimes. I must admit, sometimes . . . I wonder why.' I went on, 'What sort of show is it exactly? Have you considered what we are *doing* to our clients?'

'Has that port got stuck to the table?' Allen sounded plaintive and the port moved towards him.

'What are we *doing* to them?' I warmed to my work. 'Seeing they wear ties, and hats, keep their hands out of their pockets, keep their voices up, call the judge "my Lord". Generally behave like grocers at a funeral. Whoever they may be.'

'One minute,' said Roach, the timekeeper.

'What do we tell them? Look respectable! Look suitably serious! Swear on the Bible! Say nothing which might upset a jury of lay-preachers, look enormously grateful for the trouble everyone's taking before they bang you up in the nick! What do we find out about our clients in all these trials; do we ever get a fleeting glimpse of the truth? Do we . . . ? Or do we put a hat on the truth. And a tie. And a serious expression. To please the jury and my Lord the Judge?' I looked round the table. 'Do you ever worry about that at all? Do you *ever*?'

'Time's up!' said Roach, and I sat down heavily.

'All right. Quite all right. The performance is over.'

Mr Senior swigged down port and proceeded to judgment.

'Rumpole's mitigation has, of course, merely added to the gravity of the offence. Rumpole, at your age and with your experience at the Bar you should have been proud to get the sack, and your further conduct in winning shows a total disregard for the feelings of an extremely sensitive silk. The least sentence I can pass is a fine of twelve bottles of claret. Have you a cheque-book on you?'

So I had no choice but to pull out a cheque-book and start to write. The penalty, apparently, was worth thirty-six quid.

'Members of the Mess will now entertain the company in song,' Roach announced to a rattle of applause.

'Tommy!' Allen shouted.

'No. Really . . . ' The learned prosecutor was modest but was prevailed upon by cries of 'Come along, Tommy! Let's have it. "The Road to Mandalay" . . . etc., etc.'

'I'm looking forward to this,' said Mr Justice Skelton, who was apparently easily entertained. As I gave my cheque to young Roach, the stout leading counsel for the Crown rose and started in a light baritone.

> 'On the Road to Mandalay . . .
> Where the old Flotilla lay . . .
> And the dawn came up like thunder
> Out of China 'cross the Bay!'

Or words to the like effect. I was not really listening. I'd had quite enough of show business.

Rumpole and the Old Boy Net

To call the public school where I spent some of the worst years of my life 'minor' would be to flatter it. It was a small, poorly run penal colony on the Norfolk coast where the water habitually froze in the bogs and, on one remarkable occasion, we all believed, turned the glass of Milton, which contained the headmaster's teeth, into a solid block of ice. Such education as was on offer had to be wrung out of reluctant masters whose own ambition was to rush from the class-room and huddle round the common-room fire. It's true that Jimmie Jameson, a somewhat primitive type of Scottish Circuit judge, had been to Linklaters, as, for a short spell when his parents were abroad, had old Keith from the Lord Chancellor's office. Apart from having once been asked to organise the Old Linklaters at the Bar, I have never had much to do with my old school acquaintances, and having possessed the Old Linklater tie (I used it to secure a bulky set of books I was taking by train to a case in Chester about thirty years ago and haven't seen it since) has never helped me in the slightest degree on my way through life. Say 'I'm an Old Linklater' to most men of power and influence in this world, and their answer is most likely to be 'Mine's a Scotch.'

It is not so, of course, with the great public schools such as Eton, Harrow, Winchester and Lawnhurst. Having 'swung, swung together, with their bodies between their knees' at school, the ex-pupils of such places are liable to stick to each other for the rest of their natural lives. No sooner have they left school, but they meet up again in the Cabinet, or the House of Lords, or on the board of the United Metropolitan Bank, or perhaps at an address in Barnardine Square which, as you may or may not know, is not a million miles from Victoria Station.

But I am going too fast. I should watch his Lordship's pencil, or my rapidly fading biro. All I wished to bring to your attention at the moment is the remarkable loyalty, as some would say, or the unspeakable clannishness, as others would hold, of the English public school system. Now I would ask you to turn, as my wife Hilda did on that gusty March morning at breakfast time in our mansion flat at 25B Froxbury Court, to the news pages of the *Daily Telegraph*. Hilda takes the *Telegraph*, although I prefer the obituaries and the crossword in *The Times*. The *Telegraph* gives Hilda much that she needs, including detailed coverage of many scandalous events. On that particular morning the stories on offer in Hilda's favourite journal included one entitled, 'London Vice House Catered for Top People', and described the committal at the Central Criminal Court of a couple named Lee, on charges of blackmail and keeping a disorderly house.

'Can you understand it, Rumpole?'

'Understand what, Hilda?' I was spreading butter on my toast and couldn't see that the news item presented any form of intellectual challenge.

'These members of the aristocracy, top civil servants, and a vicar! Well really, haven't they got wives?' No doubt she was referring to the patrons of the Lee house in Barnardine Square.

'Life at the top isn't all roses, Hilda. Is that the marmalade gone to ground under your *Daily Telegraph*?'

'Well! Surely a wife's enough for anyone.'

'Quite enough,' I said, munching toast and Oxford marmalade.

'So why – run after other women?' Hilda seemed genuinely puzzled.

'I must confess, I'm baffled.' It was, I suppose, decidedly rum. I stood up, finishing my toast. Hilda looked at me critically, apparently finding that I might come last in any contest for the best-dressed barrister.

'Rumpole,' she said, 'come here. You've got marmalade on your waistcoat!' She fetched a damp teacloth from the kitchen sink and started to dab at me in a violent manner.

'I quite like marmalade on it,' I protested.

'You've got to be careful of your appearance now Guthrie Featherstone's been made a judge.'

'Out of respect to the dead?' I wasn't following her drift.

'Because you're going to take your rightful place, now Guthrie's gone, as Head of Chambers! Well, they said they'd come to a final decision, didn't they, when you got back from the jungle?'

'It wasn't the jungle, Hilda. It was the High Court of Neranga. Chief Justice Sir Worthington Banzana presiding.'

Hilda, however, pursued her own train of thought and disregarded the connection. 'There isn't another QC to take Guthrie's place. You're the only candidate! I shall ask my friend Dodo Mackintosh to take on the catering at your first Chambers party. Marigold Featherstone will never have put on a do like it.'

I sighed. 'Those occasions are quite grim enough without Dodo's rock cakes.'

'Nonsense. Dodo's pastry's as light as a feather.' She stood back, apparently noticing some sartorial improvement in my good self. 'There now. You look more like a Head of Chambers! Someone fit to take the place Daddy once occupied!'

I beat it hastily to the door. Hilda hadn't noticed that, for the sake of greater comfort after my return from Africa, I had taken to wearing a delightful old pair of brown suede shoes with the dark blue suit I wore when I wasn't actually engaged in any of Her Majesty's Courts of Justice. Whilst I was working in Chambers I hoped that the Sovereign wouldn't notice my feet.

About an hour later I put my head round the door of the clerk's room in Equity Court and saw Henry checking the diary and Dianne busily decorating her fingernails with some preparation that smelled of model aeroplanes.

> *'This be the verse you grave for me:*
> *"Here he lies where he longed to be;*
> *Home is the sailor, home from the sea,*
> *And the hunter home from the hill!"' '*

I announced.

'You're back then, Mr Rumpole.' Henry scarcely lifted his eyes from the diary.

'And not much thanks to you, Henry,' I said. 'That idiotic cable you sent me to Africa! I was almost dragged off to execution.'

'It was my duty to keep you informed, sir, about your position at the Old Bailey.'

'They thought I was going to *do* a murder. Not appear in one.'

'Oh really!' Dianne gave one of her silvery laughs. 'How dreadful!'

'Anyway,' said Henry, who didn't seem to appreciate the dire effects of his message. 'That murder's gone off. It won't be this term.'

'I came back ready for anything. Are you trying to tell me there's no work, Henry?' I started to open the various bills and circulars which had been awaiting my return.

'Oh, it's not as bad as that, sir. Mr Staines rang. He wanted a *con.* today, in the bawdy house case, *R.* v. *Lee.*'

My heart leapt up at the sight of what might be said to be a bit of a *cause célèbre*.

'Keep thy foot out of brothels, Henry! Such places are no doubt more entertaining to litigate about than to visit. Tell Stainey that I'm ready for him.' I did a quick sorting job on my correspondence. 'On Her Majesty's Service! Hasn't our gracious Queen anything better to do than to keep writing me letters?' I shed a pile of expendable mail and opened another envelope. 'What's this? A communication from LAC! "Lawyers As Churchgoers – Moral Purpose in the Law – A Call to Witness for all Believing Barristers"!' I let that one follow the circulars. 'Brothel case, eh? Not much danger of finding a moral purpose in that, I suppose.'

At this point Claude Erskine-Brown came into our clerk's room, started to collect his letters, and looked up to see the traveller returned.

'Rumpole! We thought you'd gone native. We pictured you ruling some primitive tribe under a bong tree!'

'Most amusing, Erskine-Brown!' I gave him a rapidly disappearing smile. 'Well, now I suppose I've got to take over the extremely primitive tribe in these Chambers?'

I realised that She Who Must Be Obeyed would never let me hear the last of it if I didn't claim my rightful place as Head, now that Guthrie Featherstone had been translated.

'We're deciding the Head of Chambers problem at the end of the month. When we have our meeting.' Erskine-Brown was always a stickler for formality.

'And after that I'll have to shoulder the cares of office. No one in Mr Justice Featherstone's old room, is there, Henry?'

'I don't think so, but . . . '

I had left him and was going up to take possession of the captain's quarters before he could finish his sentence. However, as I was mounting the stairs, Erskine-Brown came panting after me; apparently he had something to communicate in the deepest confidence.

'Horace. I think I should let you know. I've done it!'

'Then your only course is to plead guilty.' I gave him sound legal advice, but the fellow looked distinctly miffed.

'I have applied for silk, Rumpole,' he said with dignity. 'I think I've got a reasonable chance. Philly's right behind me.'

'I can't see her.' I looked behind him in vain.

'I mean', he said, with some impatience, 'my wife is right behind me in my application for silk. "Claude Erskine-Brown, QC." How do you think it sounds?'

'Pretty encouraging, if you happen to be on the other side.' He looked displeased at that, so I went on brightly, 'Tell me, Claude. When is this QC business likely to happen?'

'In about six weeks' time.'

'*After* the decision as to Head of Chambers?'

'Yes. I suppose so. After that.'

'Well, that's all right then. Best of British luck.'

I gave the man a reassuring slap on the shoulder. Of course, if he were to acquire a silk gown before the Chambers meeting, Claude would be entitled to that position which Hilda had set her heart on for me. As it was, I could see no way of stopping the 'Rumpole for Head of Chambers' bandwagon. I entered into my inheritance, Guthrie Featherstone's old room, and heard the sound of a woman in tears.

The woman in question was, in fact, no more than a mere slip of a girl. She was wearing dark clothes, had longish dark hair and, from what I could see of her face, she was extremely personable. At that moment she was in clear distress; her eyes were pinkish, she was dabbing at them with a small handkerchief which she had wound into a ball, and an occasional sob escaped her.

'I'm sorry.' I didn't quite know why I was apologising; perhaps it was because I had intruded on private grief. 'Can I help at all?'

She looked up at me guiltily, as though I had caught her doing something wrong. 'I thought it was all right to come in here,' she excused herself. 'Doesn't this room belong to a judge who doesn't come here any more?'

'Bare ruin'd choirs, where late old Guthrie sang. Yes that's right.' I was overcome by curiosity. 'What's the trouble? Shoplifting? You look too young for a divorce.'

'I'm a b . . . b . . . barrister.' She sobbed again.

'Oh, bad luck!' I was sorry it seemed to be causing her such distress, and I offered her a large red and white spotted handkerchief as a back-up to the sodden ball of lace she was clutching.

'I'm Mrs Erskine-Brown's pupil. Thanks.' She dabbed her eyes again.

'Mrs Erskine-Brown, Phillida Trant that was, the Portia of our Chambers? Miss Trant now has a pupil? How time flies!' Much had happened, it seemed, during my absence in the tropics.

'She left me in a case after lunch at Tower Bridge. Well, there was a terrible argument about the evidence and I said I couldn't do it without my learned leader, Miss Trant, who was in a difficulty.'

'You should have plunged in – taken your chance,' I told her.

'And the magistrate said, "What sort of difficulty?" and I said, "I think she's still at the hairdresser." '

I could understand our Portia's irritation with her tactless and inexperienced pupil. 'You forgot the most important lesson at the Bar,' I told her. 'Protect the private life of your learned pupil master – *or* mistress.'

'Now Mrs Erskine-Brown says I'm wet behind the ears and I'd

better get a nice job in the glove department at Harrods. She says that they probably won't want another woman in Chambers anyway.' She gave one final sniff, and handed me back my handkerchief.

'Got a name, I suppose?' I asked her.

'Fiona Allways.'

'Well, it's not your fault,' I comforted her.

'It's all I've ever wanted to *be*,' Fiona Allways explained. 'When the girls at school wanted to ride show-jumpers, I just stood in front of the mirror and made speeches in murder cases!'

I looked at her, made a decision and went to sit behind Feather-stone's old desk.

'I've got a conference later. You could take a note of it, if you'd like to. Make yourself useful. No particular objection to prostitution, have you?' To my dismay she seemed to be about to cry again. 'Well, what on earth's the matter now?'

Miss Allways looked at me, fighting back her tears, and said, 'I sup-pose that's all you think I'm fit for!'

The police had been keeping observation on the Lees' large Victorian house in Barnardine Square for weeks. They had chronicled, in boring detail, the visits of a large number of middle-aged men of respectable appearance to that address and had seen girls arrive in the morning and leave at night.

On the day of the arrest, a particularly respectable middle-aged man arrived on the doorstep, rang the bell, and was heard to say in to the door speaker, 'I'm a caller. Come to visit a friendly house.' He was a man who would subsequently become unknown to the world as 'Mr X'. As the door was opened, police officers invaded the house and flushed out a large number of distinguished citizens in positions of unusual friendliness with certain youngish ladies. Mr X was asked for his name and address and subsequently gave a lengthy statement to the police. Both Mr Napier Lee, the owner of the premises, and his wife, Mrs Lorraine Lee, were present when the police raided. Mr Lee protested and said that an Englishman's home was, after all, his castle. Mrs Lee asked if the matter couldn't be dealt with in a civilised manner, and invited the officers to take a nice cup of Earl Grey tea. Now Mr and Mrs Lee were in conference with my learned self; also present were Mr Staines, our solicitor, and Miss Fiona Allways, who had so far recovered her spirits as to be able to take a note.

'Apart from the little matter of keeping a disorderly house,' I reminded the assembled company, 'there's an extremely unpleasant charge of blackmail.'

'Demanding money with menaces. I have explained that to the clients,' said Mr Staines.

'Neither Napier nor I can understand anyone saying that about us, can we, Nappy?' Mrs Lee sounded deeply hurt. 'All our clients are such awfully decent people. Public school, of course, and I do think that makes *such* a difference.'

This madame, I thought, would appear to be the most appalling old snob. I looked at my visitors. Mr and Mrs Lee were the sort of genteel, greying couple you might meet any day at the Chelsea Flower Show. He was wearing an elderly tweed suit, meticulously polished shoes, and what I later assumed to be an Old Lawnhurst tie. Mrs Lee was in a twinset and pearls, with a tweed skirt and brogues. Only Mr Staines, the solicitor, who affected striped suits and a number of rings, looked anything like a ponce.

'All our visitors are thoroughly good sorts, Mr Rumpole,' Mr Lee assured me. 'All out of the absolutely top drawer, not a four-letter man among them! And I'll tell you something else my lady and I have noticed, haven't we, Lorraine?'

'What's that, Nappy?' His wife smiled vaguely.

'Absolutely no side. I mean, they come into our home and behave just like one of us.'

'I'm sure they do,' I murmured.

'Napier was at Lawnhurst,' Mrs Lee told me proudly. 'Down for it from birth, weren't you, Nappy?'

'Oh yes. The guv'nor put me down for Lawnhurst at birth.'

We had had enough, I thought, of childhood reminiscences, and I spoke a little sharply. 'Mrs Lorraine Lee, Mr Napier Lee, it may be all very pleasant to sit here, over a cup of tea, and discuss the merits of the public school system, but you are charged with obtaining money by threats from a certain . . . '

'Please, Mr Rumpole!' Mrs Lee held up her hand in a call for discretion.

'There's no need to name names, is there?' Mr Napier Lee asked anxiously.

'Not when it comes to a man in his position.' Mrs Lee was referring, deferentially, to the future 'Mr X'.

'Lawnhurst, New College Oxford, the Brigade of Guards and then the Ministry.' Mr Lee gave the man's curriculum vitae.

'Napier was destined for the Foreign Office if his guv'nor hadn't had a bit of bad luck in the City, weren't you Nappy?' Mrs Lee was now positively glowing with pride.

'Well, dear. I never had the "parlez-vous" for the Foreign Office.'

Mr Lee smiled at his wife modestly. I was anxious to return to the case and picked up a couple of accounts from the brief.

'This gentleman in question seems, from time to time, to have paid your gas bills,' I reminded them.

'When business was slack, I'm not denying it, he helped us out, Mr Rumpole.' Mrs Lee smiled with extreme candour.

'And did you threaten to publish his little secret?' It was the sixty-four-thousand-dollar question, but the Lees rejected the suggestion with disdain.

'Oh no. He knew we'd never have done that. Didn't he, Nappy?' Mrs Lee appealed to her husband.

'Of course he knew. That would have been against the code, wouldn't it?'

'Sneaking! One does not sneak, does one?' Mrs Lee gathered up her handbag, as though to bring the proceedings to an end. 'Well Nappy,' she said, 'I really think that's all we can tell Mr Rumpole.'

'No, it's not,' I said firmly. 'You can tell me something else. How did you get into this business?' I asked Mrs Lee. 'Looking at you, a small cardigan shop in Cheltenham Spa might have seemed more appropriate.'

'Napier had a bit of bad luck in the City. Also his health wasn't quite up to it after the war.'

'Ticker a bit dicky. You know the sort of thing.'

'It was Nappy's war service.'

'Four years playing a long innings against Brother Boche.'

'And Napier had a dicky ticker.'

'Then I happened to run into a friend. Quite by chance,' Mr Lee told me. 'Well, we discussed the possibilities of a business along the lines of the one we're running now.'

'A friendly house!' Mrs Lee smiled. 'For the nicer sort of customer. People Nappy got to know on the "Old Boy Net".'

'And this fellow very decently came up with a spot of capital.'

'And was this helpful friend someone you'd known for a long time?'

'Oh yes. An old "mate", you understand. From way back. Of course, we'd drifted apart a bit, over the years.'

'An old school friend, perhaps?' I suggested.

'Oh, Napier couldn't possibly tell you that.' Mrs Lee pursed her lips.

'No. I couldn't tell you that,' Napier agreed.

'Against the code?' I wondered.

'The unwritten law,' Napier said. 'The sort of thing that just isn't done. It would be as unthinkable as . . . ' He searched for some suitable enormity. 'Well, as wearing brown suede shoes with a blue suit, for instance.' Then he looked down at my feet.

'Don't worry,' I said. 'I wasn't at Lawnhurst, you know.'

When the conference was over, I went into the clerk's room to say good-night to the workers. There Henry told me, somewhat puzzled, that he had just had a telephone call from She Who Must Be Obeyed.

'Did she want me?' I wondered what I had done amiss.

'She seemed to want to speak to *me*, sir. On the subject of snacks.'

'*Snacks*, Henry?'

'Sausage rolls. Rolled-up asparagus. She said her friend, Mrs Mackintosh, would provide us with little cheesy things, sir. I told her we weren't having the Chambers party until after the meeting, and then we'd be able to welcome our new Head of Chambers.'

'Head of Chambers! She Who Must Be Obeyed has set her heart on it. She won't take no for an answer. You follow me?' I looked hard and long at Henry. I wanted to be sure that the man was on my side in my bid for the leadership.

It was a sunny morning on the day the Lees' trial started, and I decided to take a slightly longer walk along the Embankment down to the Bailey. As the wind sent small white clouds chasing each other across the sky, and the seagulls came swooping in over Temple Gardens, I was put in mind of certain lines by the old sheep of the Lake District:

> *Earth has not anything to show more fair:*
> *Dull would he be of soul who would pass by*
> *A sight so touching in its majesty . . .*

A sight not quite so touching in its majesty was likely to be his Honour Judge Bullingham. The Mad Bull had been picked by some practical joker on the Bailey staff to try the case of the frightfully nice bawdy-house keepers. Did the Bull go to a public school? I wondered. I couldn't remember. Probably he went to some establishment where they played soccer with a cannon ball and learning to read was an optional extra.

I passed Ludgate Circus and turned up towards the dome of the Old Bailey. I was just about to cross the road and dive in through the swing doors, when I heard a panting sound at my elbow, and Hoskins, a fairly unmemorable barrister in our Chambers was at my side.

'Rumpole,' said Hoskins, 'you've got back from Africa!'

'No, Hoskins. I'm still there, dispensing tribal justice in a loin cloth and a top hat. What're you talking about?'

'Just to let you know that I'm against you in the brothel case. Sam Ballard's leading me.'

'Who?' The name was unknown to me.

'Sam Ballard. The Q C from the North-East Circuit. You know, the one who's coming to practise in London. Haven't you been told?'

'Yes. You've just told me.' I was glad Hoskins was on the other side in our case and not helping me. His mind seemed to be wandering.

'But you haven't been told anything else about him?' Hoskins looked surprisingly embarrassed.

'No. What is there to tell?'

'You'll get on with him like a house on fire,' Hoskins assured me. 'He's Chairman of L A C, you know – "Lawyers As Churchgoers".'

Having climbed laboriously into the wig and gown (did I detect, still hanging in the horsehair, the dry scented smell of Africa?), I made my way to Judge Bullingham's Court attended by my small retinue consisting of Miss Fiona Allways and Mr Staines.

When I got to the courtroom door, I found a tall, somewhat stooping figure waiting for me. He was, I supposed, younger than he looked. He seemed the sort of man who had felt the weight of heavy responsibilities in the nursery: his brow was furrowed by a look of anxiety and his mouth was drawn down in an expression of almost permanent disapproval. He wore his black Court coat and striped trousers like a suit of mourning and, in all the circumstances, his silk QC's gown seemed something of a frivolity. His face was pale, and when he spoke his tone was slow and sepulchral. I suppose you could sum the matter up by saying that he was a character who might have been quite nice looking, when he was alive.

'Are you Horace Rumpole?' The question seemed to contain a lurking accusation.

'I suppose I must be.'

'Sam Ballard.' He introduced himself. 'I'm leading for the Crown. In "Lee". By the way, I passed Chambers this morning. In fact I dropped something in your tray.'

'Did you, Bollard?' I said airily. 'Can't say I noticed.'

'It was about a meeting of LAC.' He pronounced it as one word, like the place Sir Lancelot came from. 'I do hope you can find time to join us. We *should* value your contribution.'

' "Lawyers As Churchgoers"? I may have to give that a miss, Bollard. My doctor has advised me to avoid all excitement.'

'Ballard.'

'Yes, of course. I imagine your little get-together might put considerable strain on the ticker. Where do you meet? Pentonville Women's Institute? The whole orgy topped up by barn dancing and silent prayer?'

'Henry warned me about you, Rumpole.' The man was unsmiling.

'Henry?' I wondered why Henry had discussed my character with this lay reader.

'Henry the clerk. He said you had a sense of humour.'

'Only a mild one, Bollard. Nothing fatal. You've managed to keep free of it? What do you do? Jog a lot, I imagine.' He looked at me in silence for a long time and then said, more in sorrow than in anger, 'Some of our keenest members scoffed at the outset.'

'I dare say they did.' Fascinating as this conversation was, duty called. I had to tear myself away, and moved towards the door of the Court. As I did so, I uttered a pious thought. 'Well, all I hope is that this little prosecution will be conducted in a thoroughly Christian spirit.'

'You can rely on me for that.'

I was almost through the door as I said, 'Perhaps you'll show a certain reluctance about casting the first stone.'

*

Far from showing any reluctance in the stone-throwing department, the lugubrious Ballard fired off a volley of moderately lethal rocks in the course of his opening speech to the jury.

There I sat facing Judge Bullingham, who glowered like a larger white (or rather purplish) Sir Worthington Banzana, and I looked round the Court to which I had come home from my travels. I saw the Lees, sitting calmly in the dock as though they had just been asked to drop in for a cup of tea. I glanced at the Press box which was more than usually full, *R*. v. *Lee* being, it seemed, a bit of a draw and likely to fill the Sunday papers for the next couple of weeks. Prominent among the journalists I saw a youngish girl in a boiler suit and glasses, who wore a button bearing the legend HOME COUNTIES TELEVISION. I thought that she was smiling at me and I smiled back, somewhat flattered, until I saw that the message was being beamed at Fiona Allways, who was sitting beside me, industriously writing down Ballard's rubbish. Then I closed my eyes, hoping to indicate to the jury that nothing the prosecution said could possibly be of the slightest interest. Steadily, remorselessly, the voice of the Ballard droned on.

'Decent men, family men, men who had earned the respect of the community and were placed in positions of trust, found themselves tempted by this house, 66 Barnardine Square, Victoria. Some of you may know Victoria, Members of the jury, you may know its brightly lit streets and British Railway Terminal. I'm sure none of you know the darker streets, where the market is in human flesh. Men left that particular house, Members of the jury, with their consciences burdened with guilt and their wallets lightened. In the case of one of the witnesses I am about to call, the financial gain to those who exercised this appalling trade was considerably more. This is the subject of Count Two of the indictment, my Lord.'

I opened my eyes as the judge weighed in with, 'Yes, Mr Ballard. I am sure the jury understand. The *blackmail!*' The Bull looked at the jury to remind them that this was a very grave charge indeed and then glowered at me as though it were all my fault.

I smiled back at Bullingham in a friendly fashion.

'Among the many respectable figures who fell to the temptations of 66 Barnardine Square . . .' Ballard went on, and I began to speculate, in a random sort of way, as to who the many respectable figures might be. Doctors? Politicians? Police officers? Lawyers? *Lawyers? Judges!* I looked at his Honour Judge Roger Bullingham with a wild surmise. I thought I must ask my clients. Of course, they'd never tell me. But a Bull in a knocking shop! The idea was almost too good to be true. I couldn't suppress a momentary gasp of merriment.

'Did you say something, Mr Rumpole?' The Bull cast a scowl in my direction.

'Nothing at all, my Lord!' I rose slightly and then sank into silence.

'I should remind everyone in Court that this is a most serious case.' The judge made a pronouncement. 'The charges are extremely grave, and if the evidence as outlined by Mr Ballard is true . . . Of course, I haven't begun to make up my mind about it yet.'

'Haven't you, Bull?' I muttered to myself in the most *sotto* of possible *voces* as his Lordship continued.

'Then all I can say is that the activities at this property in Victoria were very wicked indeed. So we will have no laughter from anywhere in this Court.' After a meaningful look at counsel for the defence, the judge smiled on the prosecution. 'Yes, Mr Ballard.'

'If your Lordship pleases.' My opponent bobbed a small bow to the learned Bull and then carried on with his work. 'Members of the jury,' he said. 'A suitable motto to be written up over the door of 66 Barnardine Square is that which Dante chose for his inferno . . . ' I didn't think much of that for a legal reference. His Lordship probably thought that Dante was someone who did conjuring tricks on television, but Ballard soldiered on with: ' "Abandon hope all ye who enter here." Because, of course, once he was in the door, and once the spiders got to know who he was, a fact which they took great pains to find out, the fly was trapped. He couldn't get away, and if he was a man who enjoyed a high and responsible position, he would pay anything, you may think, to buy the silence of this brazen woman and her procuring husband . . . '

The jury looked at the couple in the dock. Napier Lee had his hand cupped over his ear and a gently pained expression as a result of what he was able to hear. At which point Ballard announced that he would call his first witness. I noticed that this announcement was not accompanied by any name, and then the usher went out of Court and returned, after a longer lapse of time than usual, with a tall, distinguished-looking, grey-haired man wearing a dark suit, a striped shirt with a stiff white collar, and a Guards tie. He walked across the Court with the stiff-upper-lipped expression of an officer and gentleman marching out to face a firing squad. Once in the box he lifted the Bible, raised his eyes to heaven and repeated the oath as though it were his last will and testament. When he had finished he put the Good Book down carefully on the ledge in front of him, and turned to face the fusillade of Ballard's questions. Before he did so, I gave vent to a loud mutter of 'Name please.'

Triggered off by this perfectly normal request, Ballard made an application to the learned judge.

'My Lord,' he started confidently, 'I would like to make the usual application in a blackmail case. I ask that this witness should be known simply as Mr X and that your Lordship directs that the ladies and gentlemen of the Press should not repeat his name under any circumstances.'

I glanced at the Press box and saw the young lady television reporter look up from her notebook, and stare hard at the man in the witness-box. Meanwhile, the judge was nodding his agreement. 'That seems to be a very proper order to make, in view of this gentleman's position,' he said. 'I imagine you have no objection, Mr Rumpole?'

I rose slowly to my feet, glowing with helpfulness.

'I would have no objection, my Lord, provided a similar concession is made for the benefit of my clients.'

'My Lord.' My words had clearly alarmed my learned friend. 'Perhaps we should continue with this in the absence of the jury, if there is to be an argument.' Well, he could bet his old hair shirt there was going to be an argument.

'Very well. Members of the jury.' Bullingham smiled in an ingratiating manner at the twelve good men and women and true. 'Unfortunately, legal matters arise from time to time which have to be resolved. Would you go to your room? We shouldn't have to detain you long.'

The jury filed out, grateful for a smoke and a cup of Old Bailey coffee. The boiler-suited girl in the Press box was writing furiously in her notebook. As the door closed on the last jury member the Bull fixed me with a malevolent eye.

'Now, Mr Rumpole,' he said. 'Did I hear a somewhat unusual argument with regard to the defendants in this case?'

'That they should be known as Mr and Mrs Y? Why not, my

Lord?' I asked innocently. 'My learned friend talks about embarrassment. Mr and Mrs Napier Lee have been spattered over the front pages of every newspaper in England. "Alleged Vice Queen Arrested"; "The Darby and Joan who owned the House of Shame"; "Charged with being the Top People's Madame" ... and so on. They have had to submit to a barrage of prejudicial publicity whilst this client of theirs can creep into Court under cover of a letter of the alphabet and preserve his precious respectability intact!'

'Mr Rumpole. There is no charge against this gentleman. He is innocent of any crime!' His Lordship seemed to be turning a darker shade of purple.

'So are my clients innocent!' I did my bit to match the judge's outrage. 'Until they're proven guilty. Or doesn't that rule still apply in your Lordship's Court?' I was regarded with a look of admiration from Miss Fiona Allways and the boiler-suited television lady, and a trumpet of indignation from the Bench.

'Mr Rumpole! This Court is entitled to some respect.'

'I am so full of respect to this Court, my Lord, that I give it credit for still applying the law of England – or has that been changed while I was out of the country? I merely ask for information.' I tried a charming smile, which was about as calming as a red rag to the Bull. He came charging to judgment. 'Your application that your clients' names should not be published is refused, Mr Rumpole,' he said. 'This case can be reported in full so far as they are concerned.'

'And they will no doubt be delighted to contribute to the pleasures of the great British breakfast.' I bowed with great courtesy and sat. 'If your Lordship pleases.'

'Now, Mr Ballard.' The judge turned to the more congenial matter of dealing with the prosecution. 'Your application for this witness to remain anonymous is made on good authority?'

'Certainly, my Lord. The Contempt of Court Act gives your Lordship power to order that the witness's name should never be published.'

'In perpetuity?' I grumbled from a seated position.

'My learned friend says, "In perpetuity?" and the answer would be "yes",' Ballard answered without hesitation.

'I suppose your argument would be,' the judge suggested helpfully, 'that if this witness's secrets are exposed to the public, then in effect the blackmail threat would have been successful. Is that your argument, Mr Ballard?' Of course it was, once the judge had told him.

'Yes, it is, my Lord. And your Lordship puts it so much better than

I can.' At least Ballard's religious integrity didn't prevent a little grov-elling on occasions.

'What's your answer to *that*, Mr Rumpole?' His Lordship turned to the defence.

'What blackmail?' I rose with apparent reluctance. 'What black-mail is your Lordship referring to? I merely ask for information.'

'We all know what this case is about,' Bullingham rumbled.

I responded with another burst of carefully simulated outrage. 'There hasn't yet been a word of evidence about blackmail,' I said. 'Nothing has been proved. Nothing! In my submission your Lord-ship cannot make a decision based on unproven allegations. And one more thing . . . '

'Yes, Mr Rumpole.' The judge looked pointedly at the clock and sighed.

'One more principle of which this Court should be reminded. British justice is meant to take place in public. Justice is not to be seen cowering behind an initial.'

'Is that all, Mr Rumpole?' His Lordship sighed again.

It was all that was fit for mixed company, so I bowed with elaborate courtesy. 'If your Lordship pleases. With the greatest respect.' I bowed again. 'I think your Lordship has my argument.' I did a final gesture of mock subservience and sat down.

'Yes, Mr Rumpole. I think I have. I see it's nearly one o'clock, but I'll give judgment on this point now, so that the witness may have his lunch with some degree of peace of mind.' The judge smiled at the silent figure in the witness-box, and continued. 'The defendants, through their counsel, seem particularly anxious that this gentleman's patronage of their alleged house of ill repute should become widely known to the public.'

Turning round I saw Mrs Lee, deeply wounded, shake her head. Bullingham continued with grim determination. 'If that were allowed it would be a blackmailer's charter. No victim would ever dare to go to the police. I am determined that this witness's high reputation shall be protected. He will give his evidence to the jury as "Mr X" *after* luncheon. Thank you, Mr Ballard.'

The usher called us to our feet and the judge left us. I told Stainey to inform the Lee family that I would visit them in the cells shortly and gathered up my papers. When I got outside the Court I saw Fiona Allways, my learned note-taker, in close conversation with the lady from the Press box. When she saw me, Fiona said to her, 'See you, Izzy. See you here after lunch,' and joined me on my journey to the lifts.

'Who was that?' I asked by way of idle chatter.

'Isobel Vincent. She was a prefect when I was at Benenden. I hero-worshipped her rather,' Miss Allways admitted.

'Do girls have an "Old Boy Net" too?'

'Izzy works for Home Counties News.' Fiona Allways sounded deeply impressed. 'She's tremendously into Women's Liberation.'

'So am I!' I said as we waited for the lift.

'You?'

'All for Women's Liberation. Particularly the liberation of Mrs Lorraine Lee.'

The lift arrived and we stepped into it and sank towards the cells. As we did so Miss Allways was looking at me with the sort of admiration she had previously reserved for Izzy, the fearless television reporter.

'I say, Rumpole. You *were* splendid. Really fighting.'

'Let's say – going through the motions towards a graceful defeat.'

'Well, I think it's *jolly* unfair. Keeping his name a secret.'

'Do you, Fiona?'

She spoke with a passion which I found unexpected. 'I mean, those sort of places wouldn't exist at all, would they, if it weren't for the Mr Xs?' She looked at the papers I was clutching. 'The name's in your brief, isn't it? I suppose *you* know what his name is?'

'He signed his deposition. I know it, yes,' I admitted.

'So you could tell anybody . . . ?'

'Contempt of Court, Fiona,' I told her, 'should be a silent exercise, like meditation.'

The lift stopped and we got out in the basement. We passed the carefully preserved door of Old Newgate prison, rang for a screw and were finally admitted to the dungeon department of the Central Criminal Court.

'We don't want his name splashed around the papers, Mr Rumpole. We wouldn't want that.' I don't know what it was about Mrs Lorraine Lee, but she could make the dreary little interview room, with its plastic table and old tin which did for an ashtray, seem somehow cosy and refined. Both of the Lees were looking at me, more in sorrow than in anger. I was taking exercise, walking up and down the confined space as I smoked a small cigar, and Fiona was sitting at the table nonchalantly turning the pages of my brief.

'Damned painful for him to be asked to give his name, in *his* position,' Napier Lee agreed with his good lady.

'We abide by the code, you see,' Mrs Lee said. 'The unwritten law. All the chaps who come to our house know they can trust us.'

'The "Old Boy Net"!' I said with some asperity. 'Look, he's "sneaked" on you. Why not return the compliment?'

'That's not how it works, I'm afraid.' Mr Lee shook his head. 'Whatever he's done, we've got to do the decent thing.'

'We think the judge is a perfect gentleman, don't we, Nappy?' Mrs Lee amazed me by saying.

'He understands the code, you see,' her husband agreed.

'He didn't want the poor fellow's name mentioned. That would've been terribly embarrassing.'

'And it would be terribly embarrassing, Mrs Lorraine Lee, if you and your husband got five years for blackmail!' I suggested. 'I mean, you might be as snug as bugs in the nick, but what's going to happen to me? I just can't afford to lose cases, not at this particular point in my career. I'm just about to be elected to high office in my Chambers.' Then I turned on her and asked, 'Why just the gas bill?'

'What?' Lorraine seemed confused.

'Use a lot of gas, did you, at Barnardine Square?' I pressed my enquiries.

'Not particularly,' Napier Lee said. 'The bills used to lie out on the hall table and, well, he offered to pay one or two – out of kindness, really.'

'Just a tremendously decent gesture,' his wife agreed. 'It was over and above the call of duty.'

'*How* did he pay them, exactly?'

'Oh, he used to give us a cheque,' Mrs Lee told me.

'A cheque!' I was astonished. 'In a house of ill repute? Mr X is either very naïve or . . . '

'Or what?' Napier Lee was puzzled, as though the point had never occurred to him before.

'I don't know. And we may never have a chance to find out.' I stubbed out the cigar end and was preparing to leave them, when Mr Lee uttered a mild rebuke. 'We don't like it called a house of ill repute, Mr Rumpole. We call it a friendly house.'

My usual luncheon, when engaged on a case down the Bailey, consisted of a quickly snatched sandwich and a glass of stout in the pub opposite if I was in a hurry, or a steak pie washed down with *vin* extremely *ordinaire* in the same resort. Our visit to the cells had left us so little time, however, that Fiona Allways and I took the lift up to the Bar Mess, the eatery on the top floor. This is a place I habitually avoid. It is always full of barristers telling each other of the brilliant way they dealt with discovery of documents, or the coup they brought off in some hire-purchase claim in Luton. The large room was resonant with the sort of buzz and clatter that usually accompanies school dinners, and there was a marked absence of cheerful atmosphere.

My reluctance to mingle freely with the learned friends at the trough was justified by the fact that, when Fiona and I put down our ham salads at the long table, we found ourselves sitting opposite the lugubrious Ballard, who was peeling himself a chocolate biscuit.

'Hello, Ballard,' I said, making the best of things. 'Enjoyed the sermon.'

'Did you, Rumpole?' A shadow of a smile flitted across his face, and was promptly dismissed.

'Haven't had such a good time since our old school parson gave us three quarters of an hour on hell fire,' I assured him. 'Always eat here, do you?'

'Don't you use the Bar Mess?' Ballard seemed puzzled.

'As a matter of fact, no. I prefer the pub – you get the chance of rubbing shoulders with a few decent criminals.'

To my surprise, the Ballard smile returned, and his tone was unexpectedly friendly. 'Perhaps you'll take me to your pub sometime. I mean, we should get rather better acquainted,' he said.

'Should we?' I could see no pressing reason for this bizarre suggestion.

'Well, we're going to have to spend a good deal of time together.'

'Why? This case isn't going to go on for ever, is it? Talking of which . . . '

'Yes?'

'Sam. I might come along to one of those churchgoers' meetings of yours . . . ' I, too, was having a go at the friendly approach.

'Really?' The man seemed gratified.

'I mean, there is a great deal to be said for introducing a little more Christian spirit into the law . . . '

'I'm so glad you think so.' Those who had seen St Paul on the road to Damascus no doubt looked a little like Ballard, QC, peering at Rumpole.

'Oh, I do,' I assured him. 'There is more joy in heaven, as I understand it, old darling, over one sinner that repenteth, and all that sort of thing.'

'That sort of thing, yes,' Ballard agreed.

'And if two sinners repenteth,' I was getting nearer to the nub, the heart of this unusual conversation. 'I mean, repent to the tune of pleading guilty to keeping a disorderly house, wilt thou not drop the blackmail charges, old cock?'

'No.' All smiles were discontinued. Ballard closed his teeth firmly on his chocolate biscuit.

'Did I hear you aright?' I said, with a good deal of sorrow.

'I said, "No." It's quite impossible.'

'Look here.' I wrestled patiently for the man's soul. 'Is that an entirely Christian attitude? Forgive them their trespasses, unto seventy times seven! Well, there's only one little count of blackmail.'

'No doubt they may be forgiven eventually. After a suitable period of confinement.' Ballard masticated unmercifully.

'The Mad Bull is quite capable of giving them five years for blackmail.' I pointed out the brutal facts of the matter.

'Is *that* what you call the learned judge?' Ballard looked at me severely. 'I had thought in terms of seven, for blackmail. And the top sentence for keeping a disorderly house is six months. Is that the reasoning behind your appeal to Christian principles, Rumpole?'

'You show a remarkably cynical attitude, for a churchgoer.' It pained me to find the man so worldly.

'As a churchgoer, I have a duty to protect public decency. I don't know what your particular morality is.'

'It mainly consists of getting unfortunate sinners out of trouble. You don't learn about that, apparently, in your scripture lessons.'

'Blessed are the blackmailers, for they shall walk out without a stain on their characters.' A hint of the smile returned. 'Is that your version of the Sermon on the Mount, Rumpole?'

' "Prisons are built with stones of law, brothels with bricks of religion." That's William Blake, not me. And I'll give you another quotation: "I come not to call the righteous, but the sinners to repentance." Matthew 8, verse 13.'

'How do *you* know that?' Ballard was clearly surprised.

'My old father was a cleric. And I'll tell you something. He hated Bible classes.'

A silence fell between us. Ballard was rolling the silver-paper wrapping of his chocolate biscuit between his fingers. 'It's a pretty odd sort of story, isn't it, for blackmail?' I said.

'It seems a painfully usual one to me.'

'Does it? If you were in a brothel, would you write out a couple of cheques on the NatWest, and sign them with your real name? Particularly if you're such a shy, retiring violet as your precious witness Mr X.'

Ballard looked at his watch. 'The judge'll be coming back,' he said firmly.

The theological debate was over. Ballard left us and Fiona Allways looked at me in evident distress. 'Five years!' she said. 'They'd really get five years?'

I finished my Bar Mess light ale and gave her my learned opinion. 'You know what we need in this case? A witness who knows something about Mr X. No one's going to come rushing to our aid while his name's kept a deadly secret. There, Fiona old girl, is the rub.'

The gentleman in the Guards tie gave his damning evidence of blackmail to an attentive jury and an appreciative Bull, and it wasn't until later in the afternoon that I rose to cross-examine.

'You won't mind me calling you Mr X?' I started politely.

'No.'

'I thought you wouldn't. For how long were you a *habitué* of this house of ill repute?'

'Really, Mr Rumpole,' the judge protested. 'Does that make the slightest difference?'

'Please answer the question.' I kept my eye on the witness. 'Unless my Lord rules against it, on a point of law.' My Lord didn't.

'I had been visiting there for about five years.'

'On your way home from directing the nation's affairs?' The question had the desired effect on his Lordship, who uttered a loud rebuke. 'Mr Rumpole!'

'Very well,' I said in my usual conciliatory fashion. 'On your way home from work. Before you got lost in the bosom of your family, it was your practice to visit 66 Barnardine Square?'

'Yes,' Mr X answered reluctantly.

'How did you first hear of this place of resort?'

'Hear of it?' The witness seemed puzzled by the question.

'Yes. Bit of gossip at the club, was it? Or an advertisement in *The Times* personal column?'

There was a welcome little patter of laughter in Court. The judge didn't join in. It took some time for Mr X to answer.

'I heard about it from a friend.'

'An *old* friend? I don't mean in years, but a friend of long standing?'

'Yes.'

'I really can't imagine what the relevance of these questions is.' Ballard rose to protest, and the judge came to his assistance.

'Mr Rumpole. What *has* this got to do with it?' he asked wearily.

'My Lord.' I decided to go into a bit of an aria. 'I'm fighting this case in the dark, with my hands tied behind my back, against a prosecution witness who has chosen to shelter behind anonymity. I must be allowed to cross-examine him as I think fit. After all, it would greatly add to the costs of this case if it had to be reconsidered . . . elsewhere.'

His Honour Judge Bullingham was no fool. He got the clear reference to the Court of Appeal, where his interventions might not look so attractive on the transcript of evidence as they sounded in the flesh. He thought briefly and then came out, in judicial tones, with 'I think we may allow Mr Rumpole to pursue his line, Mr Ballard.' Then he turned to me and said, 'It remains to be seen, of course, Mr Rumpole, if these questions will do your clients any good, in the eyes of the jury.'

So, having registered a sort of minor and equivocal success, I turned back to the witness. 'Was it a friend you had known from your schooldays, by any chance?' For that I got a reluctant agreement.

'You had kept up with him?' I went on.

'No. We met again after an interval of a good many years.'

'Where did you meet?'

'In a public house.'

'In the Victoria area?' I took a gamble and asked.

'Somewhere near there. Yes.'

'Meet a nice type of girl in that public house, do you?'

'Mr Rumpole!' The Bull was growing restive again and had to be dealt with.

'My Lord. I withdraw the question. What did your friend tell you?' I asked the witness.

'He told me that he'd been ill. And that he'd had a bit of bad luck in business. He said he had a house near Victoria Station and his wife and he were starting a business there.'

'A business . . . in agreeable ladies?'

We were then treated to a long pause before Mr X said, 'Yes.'

So, with a good deal of the preparatory work done, I decided to be daring and ask a question to which I didn't know the answer – always a considerable risk in cross-examination.

'Did you offer to put a little much-needed capital into this business? I mean, the Court has kept your name a secret because you are so respectable, Mr X. Were you in fact an investor in a bawdy house?'

The jury looked so interested in the answer that Ballard rose to make an objection. 'My Lord,' he said. 'The witness should be warned.'

'I *do* know my job, Mr Ballard.' For the first time, Bullingham sounded a little testy with the prosecution. Then he turned to the witness and said, 'I should warn you that you are not bound to answer any question that might incriminate you. Now, do you wish to answer Mr Rumpole's question or would you prefer not to?'

There was a long pause during which perhaps Mr X's whole life flashed before his eyes, in slow motion. At long last he said, in the nicest possible way, 'I would prefer not to, my Lord.'

I looked hard at the jury, raised an eyebrow or two, and repeated, 'You would prefer not to?' As no answer came from the witness-box I tried another question. 'Can you answer this? How long ago was the meeting in the public house in Victoria?'

'About five years ago.' Mr X appeared to be back in answering mood.

'And was the public house the Barnardine Arms?'

'Yes.'

'And was the old school friend in question by any chance Mr Napier Lee, the male defendant in this case?' He had only to say, 'No,' politely, and I would have had to sit down with egg all over my silly face. However, my luck stayed in, and Mr X gave us a very quiet, 'Yes.'

'Speak up, Mr X,' I said.

'Yes, my Lord, it was. Mr Napier Lee.'

For some obscure reason, best known to Himself, God seemed to be on my side that day.

'So you met Mr Lee some five years ago,' I continued the cross-examination. 'And his wife, Mrs Lorraine Lee?'

'I met her shortly afterwards.'

'When you started to patronise their business?'

'Yes.'

'So ever since he was an inky school boy in the fourth form at Lawnhurst, Mr Napier Lee has known exactly who you were.'

'We met in Lower Five actually.'

'In Lower Five. Oh yes. I stand corrected. So he has had at least five years to blackmail you, if he wanted to.'

Mr X gave a puzzled look at the jury, but they looked as if they saw the point perfectly well. Then he answered, 'Yes.'

'And neither he nor his wife made any suggestion of this sort until six months ago?'

'That is right,' Mr X admitted.

'When you were asked to pay a couple of trivial little gas and electricity bills.' I opened my brief then, not a thing I find I have to do too often, and fished out copies of the documents in question. 'Bills for £45 and £37.53.' Mr X agreed. He seemed to have something of a head for figures.

'And you paid these bills for the Lees by cheque?'

'Yes.'

'Why on earth . . . ?' My eyebrows went up again, and I turned to the jury.

'Because, as I have told you, Mr Rumpole, they threatened to tell my employers about my visits to their . . . house unless I did so.'

'I don't mean *that*.' I showed a little well-calculated impatience. 'I mean why pay by *cheque*?'

'I . . . I don't know exactly . . . ' Mr X faltered. The point seemed not to have occurred to him.

'Did you ever pay by cheque when you visited this house on any other occasion?'

'No.'

'Always in cash?'

'Of course.'

'Yes. Of course,' I agreed. 'Because you didn't want to leave a record of your name in connection with the Lees' "business".' I paused as meaningfully as I could, and then asked, 'But on the occasion of this alleged blackmail you *did* want to leave a record?'

'I told you . . . I don't know why I paid them by cheque.' Mr X was looking to Ballard for help. None was immediately forthcoming.

'Was it because you wanted evidence on which to base this unfounded allegation of blackmail against my clients?' I suggested.

'No!' Mr X protested vehemently, and then added, weakly, 'I suppose I just didn't think about it.'

'Thank you, Mr X!' I gave the jury a last meaningful look and then sat down with the feeling of a job well done. His Lordship leant forward and, in a quiet and reassuring tone of voice, did his best to repair the damage.

'Mr X. I suppose you paid the . . . "girls" at this establishment in cash?' Bullingham's smile said, 'We're all men of the world here, now aren't we?'

'Yes, my Lord. I did,' Mr X answered, encouraged.

'Did it strike you as a different matter when you were paying the Gas Board and the Electricity Board?'

'Yes, my Lord.' The witness took the hint gratefully.

'You saw no particular harm in paying those two great authorities by cheque?' Bullingham suggested gently.

'No harm at all, my Lord.' Mr X was clearly feeling better.

'Very well, we'll rise now.' The judge smiled at the jury, conscious of a job pretty well done. 'Shall we say, 10.30 tomorrow morning?'

That night Hilda and I were sitting at leisure in the living room of our 'mansion' flat at 25B Froxbury Court in Gloucester Road. She Who Must Be Obeyed was knitting some garment. I have no idea what it was, except that it was long and pink and was no doubt destined for her old school friend Dodo Mackintosh, and I was smoking a small cigar, watching the tide go down in a glass of Pommeroy's very ordinary, when She asked me, not with the air of anyone who intended to listen too closely to the answer, 'Went the day well?' or words to that effect.

'You could describe it as a nightmare,' I confided in her, blowing out smoke.

'You mean it's not going well?'

'Well.' I gave one of my mirthless laughs. 'We've got a prosecutor who wears a hair shirt and seems to have done his pupillage with the Inquisition. The Mad Bull is madder than ever. The chief witness has this in common with the late Lohengrin – no one must ever ask him his name. And my clients think it's in the best public-school tradition to get convicted of blackmail. There we are, all together at the Old Bailey,

> 'Rolled round in earth's diurnal course,
> With rocks, and stones, and trees . . .

It's making my head ache.'

My glass seemed to have drained itself during this monologue. I rose to refresh it from the bottle.

'I mean in Chambers. The *Headship*, Rumpole! Is it going to be ours?' Hilda asked with some impatience.

'You have great legal ambitions, Hilda. I'm sorry, I can't bring you back the Lord Chief Justice's chain of office with a bottle of Pommeroy's Château Plonkenheim.' I raised my glass to her, in recognition of her fighting spirit, and drank.

'I'm not looking for Lord Chancellor, Rumpole,' Hilda told me patiently. 'Just Head of Daddy's old Chambers. Of course, I was brought up in the law.' There was a pause. She looked at me with some suspicion, her knitting needles clicked, and then she asked, 'There's no one more senior than you, is there? No one else they might appoint?'

'No one who has been longer in the bottle as an Old Bailey hack, no,' I reassured her.

'And no silks?' For a moment, Hilda stopped knitting, as though her fingers were frozen in suspense. I gave her encouraging news. 'Not as yet. Erskine-Brown's application doesn't come up till after the meeting.'

'Then it's in the bag, isn't it?' Hilda breathed a sigh of relief, and her knitting needles clicked again.

'Fear not, Hilda. So far as I can see, your election is assured.' I poured another glass to drink to her success. I must say, She Who Must Be Obeyed smiled with some satisfaction.

'Dodo's agreed to help me out at the party,' she told me. 'She does all sorts of dips.'

'Damned versatile, old Dodo,' I agreed, and then with a mind to see what, if anything, was going on in the world outside Froxbury Court, I switched on the small and misty television set we hire from Mr Mehta who keeps a shop full of electrical appliances on our corner of the Gloucester Road. Thanks to the wonders of science, I was immediately rewarded by the sight of Fiona Allways's friend Isobel Vincent, who was clutching a microphone, wearing her boiler suit, standing under the dome of the Old Bailey, and giving a waiting world much too much news of the events that had occurred in Court during that eventful day.

'The Top People's Disorderly House Case,' said Izzy. 'Home Counties News can reveal the fact that Mr X is in fact the very senior civil servant at the Foreign Office, Sir Cuthbert Pericles. He is just one of the men, highly placed in public life, who are believed to have visited the house in Barnardine Square. This is Isobel Vincent, Home Counties News, at the Old Bailey.'

I switched off the set, Isobel Vincent shrank to a small point of light and vanished, unhappily not off the face of the earth. I looked at Hilda, appalled. 'My God,' I said. 'What a disaster!'

'Whatever is it, Rumpole?' Hilda sighed. Again she was not over-interested.

'You were nearest the window, Hilda. Didn't you hear a loud noise', I asked her, 'coming from Kensington?'

'What sort of noise?'

'His Honour Judge Bullingham', I suggested, 'blowing up?'

The next day, his Honour was still in one piece, although sitting on
the Bench breathing heavily and a darker purple than ever. I began to
fear that we were about to witness one of the few recorded cases of
spontaneous combustion. He was delivering a pretty decided judgment on Miss Isobel Vincent, who stood, still defiantly boiler suited,
in the well of the Court in front of him, about as apologetic as Saint
Joan when called on to answer a nasty heresy charge before the
Inquisition.

'In almost half a
century's experience
at the Bar and on the
Bench, I have never
known such a flagrant,
wicked and inexcusable
Contempt of Court!'
Bullingham boomed. I
must say I wasn't giv-
ing him my full atten-
tion. I was turning to
the door hoping that at
any minute Mr Staines,
my instructing solici-
tor, might come into
Court with the news I
was hoping and pray-
ing for.

Meanwhile Isobel
was still looking noble,
Fiona Allways was try-
ing to look at no one in
particular, and the judge was still carrying on. 'I have heard that your
employers, Home Counties Television, had no idea that you were
disobeying a Court Order. That will be investigated. If anyone who
has been in this Court, anyone at all, had anything to do with this
matter . . .' At this point his Lordship could be seen glaring at Horace
Rumpole. 'They will be sought out and punished.'

And then the miracle happened. Old Stainey filtered back into
Court and whispered the news that the man I was waiting for was
without, and he wanted to know if I would call him first.

'Of course I'll call him first,' I whispered back. 'It shouldn't be long now. The Bull's running out of steam.'

'I will send the papers to the proper quarter in order that it may be decided what action shall be taken against this most foolish and wicked young woman . . . ' The judge dismissed Isobel then, and she left the Court with her head held high and a look at Fiona which caused that young lady to blush slightly. Shortly thereafter the show was on the road again, and I was on my hind legs opening our defence to the jury.

'Members of the jury. It is my duty to outline to you the evidence the defence is going to call. I'm going to call a witness . . . ' – well, I hoped to God I was going to call a witness – 'who may be able to pen-etrate the pall of secrecy which has fallen over this case. Someone, perhaps, may have the bad manners and rotten taste to tell us the truth about the evidence. Someone may be able to cast aside the "Old Boy Net" and let the secret out. Ladies and Gentlemen of the jury, I will now call . . . ' I paused long enough to stoop and whisper to old Staines, who was sitting in front of me, 'Whom the hell will I now call, Stainey?'

'Mr Stephen Lucas,' Mr Staines whispered back.

'I will now call Mr Simon . . . ' I started.

'Stephen!' Another whisper from Stainey.

'Mr Stephen Lucas.' I was confident at last.

'Very well, Mr Rumpole.' The judge picked up his pencil with an air of resignation, and prepared to make a few jottings. And then a man came into Court, entered the witness-box as though he had a day full of far better things to do, and promised to tell us the truth, the whole truth and nothing but the truth. He was a smaller, fatter, more jovial type of person than Mr X, but when he spoke it was with the impatient confidence of someone who had spent many years in a trusted position in the corridors of power. He gave his name as Stephen Lucas.

'Are you a member of the Foreign Office legal department?' I asked him.

'Yes, I am.'

'And do you know the witness we have called "Mr X"? I have asked him to remain in Court so that you may identify him.'

The witness looked down at the man who was sitting in front of Ballard with as much detachment as if Mr X were something that had just arrived in his in-tray.

'Yes, I do,' he said.

'Are you a friend of his?'

'We meet, of course, in the Foreign Office,' Lucas said cautiously. 'I would say I've known him fairly well, and over a long period.'

'Of course. Do you remember having lunch with him at his club about a year ago? Was that at his invitation?'

'Yes, it was.'

'What did he discuss, do you remember?'

'Well, we discussed a number of things, the work of my department and so on, and then he asked me some questions about the recent Contempt of Court Act. He seemed to want my opinion about it, as a lawyer. It's not really my subject, but I told him what I knew.'

'What aspect of the Act was our "Mr X" particularly interested in?'

'In the Court's power to order that the name of a witness in a blackmail case should be kept secret, perhaps for ever.' The witness paused. The jury were looking at him with interest and the Bull, I was pleased to see, was writing busily. Then Lucas went on with his story. 'I remember his saying that if you didn't want your name to come out in a particular scandal or something of that sort, all you would have to do would be to accuse someone of blackmail.'

'Mr Lucas, what made you remember this conversation?' I asked, to pre-empt a bit of Ballard's cross-examination.

'It was last night, when I heard Mr X's name on the television news. I thought it might have some bearing on this case.'

The judge frowned, and I went on quickly to prevent any unfriendly comment from the Bench. 'Tell us, Mr Lucas. You say you've known Mr X for a long time. You weren't at school together, by any chance?'

'No. I wasn't at Lawnhurst,' Lucas admitted.

'Or at any public school?'

'No.'

Thank God, I thought, or we'd never have got a word out of him. I sat down and Ballard was up with his long black silk gown flapping with indignation.

'So, Mr Lucas, you would never have come here to give evidence if there hadn't been a flagrant Contempt of Court and Mr X's name had not appeared on the television news.'

'That's right.' Lucas seemed to be not in the least worried by the course of events.

'It's most unfortunate, I agree, Mr Ballard.' The judge looked sadly at the prosecutor. 'But I don't see what I can do about it. I can't exclude this evidence.'

'Oh no, my Lord. But it *is* most unfortunate.' Ballard seemed to be regretting some huge historical disaster, like the decline and fall of the Roman Empire.

'Of course it is.' The judge cast a meaningful glance at the Rumpole faction. 'But the harm's been done.' Whether it was harm or good, of course, depended on which side you were sitting.

Well, in due course the Lees gave evidence and denied the blackmail in a pained sort of way, and answered Ballard's passionate denunciations with excessively polite murmurs of dissent, as though they were regretfully declining the offer of more bread and butter. Later in the proceedings, my learned opponent gave the jury another two-hour sermon, during the course of which I was delighted to see them getting somewhat restive. And then, almost before I knew it, final speech time was round again.

'Mr X couldn't give up his visits to the friendly house in Barnardine Square, Members of the jury,' I told them. 'But he was always terrified that the place might be raided and his name would come out in the ensuing scandal. So he hit on this somewhat over-ingenious device: a couple of cheques, a sure proof that he had paid money to the Lees, could lay the basis for a trumped-up blackmail charge that would keep his name a secret for ever! It was an elaborate plan, complicated, expensive and entirely futile. Just the sort of plan, you may think, that would occur to someone high in the government of our country. Why was it futile? Because Mr X need have had no fear. The Lees would never have betrayed his pathetic little secrets. You see, it was for them, as it never was for him, a question of morality. They had their code.'

At the end of it all the judge summed up with surprising moderation. The jury stayed out for three hours, and mugs of tea were being served in the cells when we got down to discuss the result with Mr and Mrs Napier Lee.

'A great win on the blackmail, Mr Rumpole.' Mr Staines, at least, could always be relied on to say the right thing.

'Wasn't it, Stainey! Six months for the disorderly house, I'm afraid,' I said regretfully.

'I just hope "Custard" doesn't think we sneaked on him.' Mr Lee looked extremely worried.

'He knows we'd never do a thing like that!' Mrs Lorraine Lee was consoling him.

'Who the hell's "Custard"?' I felt I was losing my grip.

'Pericles. His name's Cuthbert, so we called him "Custard" at school.'

'I suppose that follows,' I admitted.

'*We* know we didn't break the code, Nappy. We've got that to comfort us,' Lorraine told her husband. And I thought that I'd add my own two pennyworth of consolation for them both.

'They'll probably send you to an open nick,' I said. 'You might meet some of the chaps from school.'

'I never went to Lawnhurst,' Mrs Lee said regretfully.

'By Jove, that's a point.' Napier seemed suddenly depressed.

'Daddy had set his heart on Roedean for me. But it was a question of the readies,' Mrs Lee explained.

But Napier seemed to realise quite suddenly that he was about to be separated from his wife. 'It's boys only where I'm going, I suppose?' he said.

'I'm afraid so. No co-education.' I had to break it to him.

'Sorry, old girl. We'll be separated.' He held out his hand to his wife, and she took it.

'Not for long, Nappy,' she said. 'And we've had a marvellous offer for the freehold.'

'Not to mention the good will!'

'Then you've just got to bear it for six months,' I said as I moved to the door, the rest of the legal team following behind me.

'When a chap's been to Lawnhurst, Mr Rumpole,' Napier said, 'he can't really feel afraid of prison.'

When we left them, they were still holding hands.

Walking back to Chambers with Miss Fiona Allways, I could feel her deep embarrassment and fear of the subject which I knew perfectly well I would have to mention. There was a fine rain falling over Fleet Street then. The buses were roaring beside us, no one could hear what I had to say and, I hoped to goodness, no one had guessed Miss Allways's secret; otherwise hers might have been one of the shortest careers in the history of the legal profession.

'You'd better learn something quickly, Fiona,' I told her. 'If you want to be a barrister, keep the rules!'

'I don't know what you mean . . .' she started unconvincingly, and then blushed beneath her headscarf.

'Don't you?' I looked at her. 'Don't worry. I don't imagine Mizz Isobel Vincent is going to reveal her sources. She's all out for glorious martyrdom, and I bet she doesn't want to share her publicity with anyone.' We were turning into the Temple entrance, and I stopped, faced her, and said with all the power I could command, 'But you have to keep the rules! You can swear at them, argue your way round them, do your damnedest to change them, but if you break the rules yourself, how the hell are you going to help the other idiots out of trouble?'

Miss Allways looked at me for a long time, and I hoped to God I wasn't going to see her in tears ever again. 'I'll never get a place in Chambers now,' she said.

'I don't know. Perhaps you will. Perhaps you won't,' I said briskly and started to walk into our place of work. 'You can help me out on another little cause or matter.'

'Can I?' Miss Allways trotted behind me eagerly. I told her what I had in mind. 'Look up the cases on Contempt of Court, why don't you?' I suggested. 'We may be having to cope with the defence of Mizz Vincent, and we've got to keep the good Mizz out of chokey. Martyrs make me exceedingly nervous.'

When I got into the clerk's room, Henry told me that a Chambers meeting was about to take place – a forum, I instantly realised, for preliminary discussions on the Headship, at which the way would be smoothed for the Rumpole take-over at Number 3 Equity Court. So, in the shortest possible time, the ambitions of She Who Must Be Obeyed might be fulfilled. Before I went upstairs, Henry handed me a letter which, he said, had been delivered by hand as a matter of urgency. I stuffed it into my pocket and went upstairs to what had been Guthrie Featherstone's room, and would now, I thought, be my room in perpetuity.

As I got to the head of the stairs, I heard the buzz of voices and, for a moment, I was puzzled that the meeting should have started without my good self as the natural chairperson and Master of Ceremonies. Then I supposed that they were merely chattering about the splendours and miseries of their days in various Courts. I advanced a couple of steps, threw open the door, entered the room, and then, it is no exaggeration to say, I was frozen in horror and dismay.

Of all the nasty moments in Macbeth's life, and they certainly came to him thick and fast after his encounter with the witches, I have always thought that by far the worst must have come when he went to take his old place at the dinner party and found that the ghost of Banquo had got there before him, and was glowering at the poor old Thane in a blood-bolter'd and accusing sort of way. So it was for me on the occasion of that Chambers meeting, only the person in the chair behind Guthrie's old desk, the man in the seat of honour directing the proceedings, was not Banquo but Sam Ballard, one of Her Majesty's Counsel and founder member of the Lawyers As Churchgoers Society.

'Come along, Rumpole, you're late.' This spectre spoke. 'And would you mind shutting the door.'

'Bollard.' I looked around the room which contained Claude Erskine-Brown, Hoskins, Uncle Tom (our oldest inhabitant) and five or six other assorted barristers. Mrs Phillida Erskine-Brown, our Portia, was apparently away doing a long firm fraud in York.

'What's this?' I asked Ballard. 'A prayer meeting or something? What on earth are you doing here?'

'Hasn't anyone told you?' The man, Ballard, seemed genuinely puzzled. 'Featherstone J. said he'd written you a note as soon as he knew you were back from Africa.'

I pulled the letter Henry had given me from my pocket, and saw it was embossed with the insignia of the Royal Courts of Justice. I have kept the Featherstone letter in my Black Museum to this day, together with other criminally used instruments of murder and mayhem, so I can now give it to you verbatim. All you will miss is Guthrie's haphazard and occasionally illegible handwriting.

'Dear old Horace, old boy,' the letter ran. 'Just a brief note to introduce Sam Ballard, who was, in fact, my fag master at Marlborough, and is now a silk with an excellent practice in the Midlands.' As I read this I felt a faint hope: perhaps the wretched Bollard would stay in the Midlands. 'But,' the letter went on, 'Sam came to us looking for a

London home. All the other fellows agreed and, as you were off in the jungle, we knew you'd have no objection. Someone'll have to take over as Head of Chambers as I'm detained "During Her Majesty's Pleasure". And Sam Ballard is clearly a likely candidate. But I don't want to interfere, at this distance, with the democratic process of my old set. Marigold joins me in sending all our best wishes to you and Hilda. May you soldier on for many years yet, old fellow. Guthrie Featherstone.'

'Glad you could make it to the meeting, Rumpole.' Hoskins was smiling at me.

'Are you?' I took a seat by the door.

'We thought Roger Bullingham might have put you in chokey, Horace, on a little matter of Contempt of Court!' Claude was having his little joke.

'Oh, Erskine-Brown, you're so amusing!'

'Well. Now we're all assembled . . . ' The Bollard throat was being cleared in an ecclesiastical manner.

'Dearly beloved brethren,' I muttered.

'I suppose we should decide who is going to approach the Inn, as the new Head of this Chambers,' Ballard ploughed on regardless. 'Now I don't suppose it's a matter we should want to discuss in a public meeting.'

'What do you suggest we do, Bollard?' I asked. 'Go into a session of silent prayer, and then send puffs of smoke up from the clerk's room? Let's have it out, for God's sake.'

'Speaking for myself, I have been in these Chambers for a good many years,' Erskine-Brown weighed in.

'Not half as long as Rumpole!' Uncle Tom made the first pro-me remark. I thanked him for it silently.

'Rumpole's been here since the year dot, as far as I can remember,' Uncle Tom added, less helpfully.

'And although I've not yet been able to put on the knee-breeches and silk gown, as you have, Ballard,' Erskine-Brown gave a modest grin, 'my application is in to the Lord Chancellor's office and I can't imagine there'll be any difficulty.'

'Don't count your chickens, old darling,' I warned him.

'Why? Have you heard anything?' I was relieved to see a look of anxiety on the Erskine-Brown face.

'There's many a slip', I improvised, 'between the knee-breeches and the hip.' This managed to get a lone chuckle from Uncle Tom.

'Of course, I'm a complete newcomer here,' Ballard started off again, very seriously.

'Yes, you are,' I agreed. 'They just dropped you in with today's *Times*.'

'But whoever heads these Chambers will, I hope, be able to take the position seriously.' Ballard gave me an aloof sort of look.

'Here endeth the first lesson,' I said.

'It's also terribly important that whoever heads us should be a barrister entirely *sans reproche*,' Claude suggested.

'Oh, *absolument*, Erskine-Brown,' I said.

'Our Chambers is riding high at the moment. One of our number has just been made up to the High Court Bench,' Claude went on.

'Oh, I agree.' Hoskins always agreed. 'We should remember that this election is caused because Guthrie Featherstone has been made a judge.'

'The age of miracles is not dead.' I did a bit of agreeing myself.

'We must be careful to keep our high reputation,' Erskine-Brown said. 'It would be most unfortunate if we had a Head who could possibly be accused of sharp practice.' He gave a casual glance in my direction, and I asked him, 'What do you mean exactly, Erskine-Brown?'

'I don't think there should be any speculation arising out of the recent case at the Old Bailey,' Ballard was delighted to say. 'It's true a question of Contempt of Court *did* arise, but that issue still has to be decided. There has been no finding as to how the information was "leaked". Of course,' he also gave me a look, 'one hopes that the "leak" didn't come from any member of the legal profession.'

'Does one really hope that?' I asked, but Ballard ignored the question.

'So I would ask you all to put the regrettable matter of a flagrant Contempt out of your minds for the purposes of this decision. Wouldn't you agree that that is the fair approach?'

'Oh, Bollard,' I thought. 'How very clever!'

'Well now. Rumpole, as an old member of this set . . . '

'Of course he's old. Rumpole can't help being old!' Uncle Tom explained to the meeting.

'Have you anything to say?' Ballard asked.

'Why sentence of death should not be passed against me?' I said, and then addressed them all. 'Only this. Don't forget the claims of someone who has been associated with these Chambers for far, far longer than any of you, who grew up in these fly-blown rooms and on this dusty staircase, who doesn't aspire to silk, or judicial office, or even to appearing before the Uxbridge Magistrates, one whose whole ambition is centred on that meaningless title, "Head of Chambers"!'

'What's Rumpole talking about?' Uncle Tom asked no one in particular.

'He means himself,' said Claude.

'No, Erskine-Brown,' I assured him. 'I don't mean me.'

I was thinking, of course, of She Who Must Be Obeyed, whose ambition to be married to the Head of her father's old chambers was, thinking again of the old Scottish Tragedy, much like Lady Macbeth's bizarre longing to see her husband tricked out in Duncan's crown. When I got home to our mansion flat, She was ambling round a hot stove, and once again She asked me how it went.

'Half and half,' I told her.

'What?'

'The Lees got off the blackmail. Six months apiece on the disorderly house.'

'I don't mean in Court! I mean in *Chambers*.'

'Well, it's in Court that things happen, Hilda. People don't get sent to prison in Chambers. Well, not yet, anyway.'

'Oh, don't be so tiresome, Rumpole. I mean in the Chambers meeting! Has it been decided yet?'

It was time to attack an evening bottle of the ordinary claret with a corkscrew, and I did so without delay. Someone had to celebrate something.

'Well. Not finally,' I told her.

'But in principle, Rumpole. I mean, it's been decided in principle?'

'Yes. Yes, I think so.'

'The Chambers party's on the 29th. That's when they'll announce the decision, isn't it?'

'I shouldn't bother to go to that, Hilda.' I poured her a generous slurp. 'They're pretty grim occasions.'

'This won't be grim!' She assured me. 'It'll be a triumph, Rumpole. And nothing on earth is going to keep me away!'

★

Until the day of the Chambers party dawned, I avoided discussing the subject further with Hilda, and She remained determined to join in what she felt sure would be the jollifications. Not long before the party, our assorted barristers voted on the question of leadership, but for one reason or another I didn't bring home to Hilda the result of their decision. On the day in question, several large cardboard boxes, filled, so it seemed, with 'cocktail snacks', were brought by Hilda's friend, Dodo Mackintosh, round to the mansion flat, and I had to ferry them down to Chambers by taxi.

So, at the end of the day, we all assembled in the former Feather-stone room, where Henry and Dianne had set up a bar on the desk, and had Dodo's delicacies set out on plates ready for handing round. Hilda was there, resplendent in what seemed to be a new rig-out, and there were a few other wives and girlfriends, although Mrs Phillida Erskine-Brown, whose practice seemed to be growing to gigantic proportions, was now away doing an arson in Swansea.

I hovered around, keeping within pouring distance of the bar, and I heard my wife in close conversation with the blasted Bal-lard. She seemed to be giving him a guided tour of Dodo's cookery, which he was consuming steadily without interrupting her flow of words.

'These are cheese-and-oniony, and those are the little sausage arrangements, if that's what you'd prefer,' I heard Hilda telling him. 'Of course, I'll be looking after these parties now. Marigold Feather-stone was a sweet person, wasn't she? But I don't think she took a great interest in the canapés.' The same could not be said of Ballard. He took another couple of items from a plate, and Hilda went on talk-ing. 'That's a little prawny sort of vol-au-vent arrangement. Fright-fully light, isn't it? I do want these evenings to be a success for Rumpole!'

There was a scatter of applause then for Henry, who requested silence by bumping a glass on the desk, and Uncle Tom was called on to say a few moderately ill-chosen words.

'It falls to me', he started, 'as the oldest member of Chambers, in the matter of years, to do honours here tonight.'

'Uncle Tom!' Hilda called out to him in high excitement. He stopped and gave her a look of some surprise. 'Mrs Rumpole?'

'Carry on then, Uncle Tom,' Hilda gave her permission gracefully.

'Thank you. I remember Number 3 Equity Court years ago, when old C. H. Wystan was Head of Chambers.'

'Uncle Tom remembers Daddy!' Hilda announced to the world in general.

'Exactly. And Horace Rumpole and I used to hang about waiting for work. I used to practise approach shots with an old mashie niblick! It seemed my one legal ambition was to get my balls into the waste-paper basket in the clerk's room.'

This last sentence caused Miss Fiona Allways to choke on an asparagus roll, and have to be slapped on the back by Henry. Uncle Tom went on with his past history of Equity Court.

'Then the present Mr Justice Featherstone came to head us. Of course, he was then plain Guthrie Featherstone, QC, MP. And now another chapter opens in our history . . . '

'Hear, hear!' Hilda applauded loudly.

'The man I have to introduce as our new Head, agreed on by a comfortable majority, is well known, not only in legal circles but in the Church . . . ' Uncle Tom said, and in this puzzled She Who Must Be Obeyed. She looked at me, startled, and murmured, 'Rumpole religious?'

'He is a man deeply concerned with problems of morality,' Uncle Tom continued, warming to his work. 'I happened to be taking dinner with old Tuppy Timpson, ex-Canon of Southwark Cathedral, and he said, "Little bird told me about your new Head of Chambers. You've got a sound man there. And one who walketh in the ways of righteousness, even through the Valley of the Central Criminal Court." '

'The ways of righteousness!' Hilda was laughing. 'You ought to see him at breakfast, particularly when he's in a nasty temper!'

'Hilda!' I whispered to her, begging her to stop.

'Not much of the ways of righteousness then, Uncle Tom,' She said, but the oldest inhabitant was into his peroration.

'So let us raise a glass, ladies and gentlemen, to our new Head of Chambers. I give you our dear old Chambers, Number 3 Equity Court, coupled with the name . . . '

'Rumpole!' Hilda said loudly, but Uncle Tom was louder when he announced, 'The name of Sam Ballard, one of Her Majesty's Counsel. Long may he reign over us!'

They were all drinking to the Bollard health and all I could say was, 'Amen.' Then I turned to Hilda, and there were tears in her eyes.

'I'm sorry old girl.' I felt I should comfort her.

'You never told me!'

'I funked it.' It was perfectly true.

'Passed over again!' She dabbed her eyes with her handkerchief, sniffed and looked extremely bleak.

'Cheer up,' I said. 'It's not the end of the world. You know you're

still a great advocate. Terrific in argument. Who cares about being
Head of Chambers?'

Henry had found a bottle of Pommeroy's special offer champagne
to toast our new leader, and I got my fingers round it. Hilda looked at
me coldly, and then pronounced judgment.

'You're a failure, Rumpole!' she said.

'Then take a slurp of champagne, why don't you?' I filled our
glasses. 'Let's drink to failure!'

But Hilda was looking across to where Ballard stood masticating.

'He's eating *all* Dodo's little cheesy bits. The *cheek* of it!' she said.
She sounded furious and I knew, with considerable relief, that She
Who Must Be Obeyed was herself again.

Rumpole and the Bright Seraphim

I know little of army life. It's true that I was able to serve my country during the last war (sometimes it seems only yesterday, the years rush by with such extraordinary speed) in the RAF at Dungeness (ground staff, they never sent me up in the air). It was there that I met Bobby O'Keefe in the Women's Auxiliary Air Force, and was a little dashed in spirits when she was finally hitched to a pilot officer, 'Three-Fingers Dogherty' – events which I have described elsewhere. Those years, in turn exciting, boring, alarming and uncomfortable, gave me no insight whatever into life in a 'good' cavalry regiment. I knew nothing of the traditions of the officers' mess, and I had never even appeared at a court martial until the extraordinary discovery of the body of Sergeant Jumbo Wilson in the 37th and 39th Lancers, clad in women's attire outside the Rosenkavalier bar and discotheque in Badweisheim, West Germany, and the subsequent prosecution of Trooper Boyne for murder. It is a case which had its points of interest, notably in my cross-examination of an inexpert expert witness as to the time of death and the strange solution at which I arrived by an unaided process of deduction.

When we had any minor cause for celebration, or when the East wind was not blowing and conversation flowed freely between us, it was the practice of myself and She Who Must Be Obeyed to call in at the Old Gloucester pub (Good Food Reasonably Priced, Waitress Service and Bar Snacks), which is but the toss of a glass from our so-called 'mansion' flat at Froxbury Court. It was there we made the acquaintance of a major, recently retired and in his forties, named Johnnie Pageant, who had taken a flat in the Gloucester Road area, and who spent his days writing to various golf clubs, of which he would have liked to become secretary. I found him a most amiable fellow, an excellent listener to my fund of anecdotes concerning life at the Bailey, and never slow to stand his round consisting, invariably, of a large claret for me and jumbo-sized gin and tonics for himself and She.

One evening in the Old Gloucester I was holding forth as usual about the murderers and other friends I had made down the Bailey, explaining that those accused of homicide were usually less tiresome and ruthless customers than parties in divorce cases, and, having often killed the one person they found intolerable, they were mostly grateful for anything you could do for them. 'You've done a lot of murders?' the ex-major wondered.

'More, perhaps, than you've had hot dinners.'

'Try not to show off, Rumpole,' She Who Must Be Obeyed warned.

'My nephew Sandy Ransom's got a bit of a murder in his regiment in Germany. Young trooper out there in a spot of bother.'

'Murder, in the regiment, do you say?'

'Mention the word "murder" and you can see Rumpole pricking up his ears.' My wife, Hilda, of course, knew me of old. 'Murder's mother's milk to Rumpole.'

'Who's this young lad supposed to have murdered?' I wanted further and better particulars.

'His troop sergeant, apparently.'

'Murdered his sergeant; isn't that justifiable homicide?' I asked, being ignorant of army law.

'You should know. You've done a court martial or two, I suppose. Perhaps even more than I've had hot dinners,' Johnnie Pageant laughed.

'Court martials? Of course!' Then I thought it better to qualify the claim. 'Perhaps not more than you've had gin and tonics . . .'

'Point taken, Horace! Hilda, the other half?'

'Well. Just perhaps the tiniest, weeniest, Johnnie.' So, ex-Major Johnnie wandered off to the bar, and Hilda turned on me. 'What *are* you talking about, Rumpole? You've never done a court martial in your life.'

'Mum's the word, Hilda,' I warned her. 'I thought I could sniff, for a moment, the odour of a distant brief.'

And I was right. A week or so later, when I went into our clerk's room, Henry handed me the brief in a court martial in Germany, the charge being one of murder. I asked if there were any sort of rank attached: Lieutenant-Colonel or Major-General Rumpole? Henry said no, but there was a cheque under the tape and a first-class air ticket to Badweisheim. 'First class?' Well, it seemed only right and proper; an officer and a gent couldn't huddle with other ranks in steerage.

'The solicitors said it was a heavy sort of case and at first I thought they wanted a silk, Mr Ballard, perhaps, to lead you,' Henry said, as I thought tactlessly.

'Bollard to lead? He'd be following far behind.'

'But then they said no. What they wanted was just an ordinary barrister.'

'An *ordinary* barrister.' I was, I confess, somewhat irked. 'Then they've come to the wrong fellow!'

'Shall I return the brief then, Mr Rumpole?'

'No, Henry. We do not return briefs. When we are called to the colours, we do not hesitate. And if the army needs me. Company ... Atten—shun! *Present Arms!*' So I marched out of the clerk's room with my umbrella over my shoulder, chanting, 'Boots, boots, boots, boots movin' up and down again. There's no discharge in the war!' much to the consternation of Bollard and that grey barrister, Hoskins, who had just come in and no doubt thought that 'Old Rumpole' had taken leave of his senses.

The 37th and 39th Lancers, the Duke of Clarence's Own, familiarly known as the Bright Seraphim because of the sky-blue plumes they still wore, in a somewhat diminished version, in their headgear, had been a crack cavalry regiment with a list of battle honours stretching back to the Restoration. Even now, when they were encased in rattling sardine tins and not mounted on horses, the regiment was hugely proud of its reputation. Its officers ran to hunters, country estates and private incomes, its mess silver and portraits were some of the most valuable, and its soldiers the best looked-after in the British forces stationed in Germany. Should one of the Bright Seraphim stray from the paths of righteousness, I learnt early in my preparation for the court martial, the whole regiment would close ranks to protect the boy in trouble and the high reputation of the Duke of Clarence's Own.

The scandalous circumstances surrounding the death of Sergeant James 'Jumbo' Wilson were therefore particularly unwelcome. Military police touring the streets of Badweisheim, the German town close to the Bright Seraphim's barracks, searched, as a result of a telephone call received at 3.45 a.m., an alleyway which ran by the side of the Rosenkavalier disco-bar. It was at 4 a.m. that they then found Sergeant Wilson's body. His short haircut, florid face and moustache indicated his military occupation; the scarlet, low-cut frock he wore did not. He had received a stab wound in the stomach which had penetrated the aorta, but the time of his death was a matter which would become the subject of some controversy. One other matter – the sergeant was an extremely unpopular NCO and few of those who came under his immediate command seemed to have much reason to love him.

One wing of the barracks at Badweisheim consisted of married quarters for the non-commissioned officers and men; on the whole the officers lived in various houses in the town. Sergeant Wilson and his wife – they were a childless couple – occupied a flat up a short, iron staircase at one end of the wing. Next door, but on a lower level, lived Danny Boyne, a good-looking Glasgow Irish trooper in his early twenties, with his wife and baby son.

Trooper Boyne had, unusually for anyone in the regiment, married a German girl, and he was noted for his quick temper and his deep hatred of Sergeant Wilson, who, so many witnesses had noticed, lost no opportunity of picking on Danny and putting him on charges for a number of offences, many trivial but some more serious. Witnesses had also been found who had heard Danny threaten to cut the sergeant up. He was, undoubtedly, present at the disco on the night the sergeant died; and when the shirt he wore on that occasion was examined, a bloodstain of Sergeant Wilson's group was found on the cuff. For these cogent reasons, he was put under arrest and now had to face a general court martial with Horace Rumpole called to the colours to undertake his defence.

When I came out into the glass and concrete concourse of Badweisheim airport, a crisp, cheerful and thoroughly English voice called out to me, 'Horace Rumpole? Consider yourself under arrest, sir. The charge is smuggling an old wig through customs.'

The jokester concerned turned out to be a youngish, fair-haired captain, with a sky-blue cockade of the Seraphim in his beret and a lurcher at his heels. 'Very funny!' I hadn't smiled.

'Oh, do you think so? I can do much better than that. Sandy Ransom. I think you know my old uncle Johnnie?'

'Captain Ransom.' I didn't know if I should attempt a salute.

'I'm the defending officer.'

'Oh, really? I thought I was doing the defending.'

'Of course, you are. You're O C defence. I'm just your fag. Anything you want I'll run and get it. I'm the prisoner's friend. We are all the friends of any trooper in trouble. It's a question of regimental honour.'

'I see,' I said, although I didn't entirely, at the time.

'You'll need a porter, won't you?' He whistled to a man and said in what was, as far as I could tell, an impeccable German accent, *'Träger! Bitte nehmen sie das Gepäck.'* He also whistled to his obedient lurcher and led me to the jeep in which he was to drive me to the barracks. 'I told my Uncle Johnnie we were looking for an ordinary sort of barrister,' he told me when we were *en route.*

'Ordinary!' Again it seemed a most inadequate description of Rumpole's talents.

'The court-martial officers will be from other regiments,' Sandy Ransom explained. 'Pay Corps. That sort of rubbish. Very downmarket. They're all highly suspicious of the cavalry. Think we're all far too well-off, which is luckily quite true. Parade a flashy QC and they'd convict Danny Boy before he got his hat off. Just to teach the cavalry a lesson. Anyway, old Uncle Johnnie said you'd done loads of court martials.'

'Oh, yes, loads.' Well, we were far from home and no one, I hoped, would know any different.

At last we drew in at a gate-house manned by a sergeant who saluted Sandy and got a brief acknowledgement, and then we were in a huge square surrounded by brick buildings erected, I learned, for the *Wehrmacht.* In the square there was a large collection of military vehicles – cars, jeeps, lorries and even tanks – and we passed various groups of the Duke of Clarence's Own, all of whom saluted us smartly. Some lines from the *Ancient Mariner* floated into my mind:

This seraph-band, each waved his hand:
It was a heavenly sight!
They stood as signals to the land,
Each one a lovely light.

This seraph-band, each waved his hand,
No voice did they impart -
No voice; but oh! the silence sank
Like music on my heart.

And I felt my own hand rising, irresistibly, to the brim of my hat.

'Steady on, sir,' Sandy told me. 'There's no need for you to return their salutes.'

That evening the candlelight gleamed on the silver and the paintings of long-gone generals and colonels wearing wigs and scarlet coats, three-cornered hats, swords and sashes, posed against gunmetal skies or on rearing horses. The few officers dining with us in the mess that night wore elderly tweed suits as though they were guests in some rather grand country house, with the exception of a young lieutenant in uniform. Sandy Ransom introduced me to a shortish, quietly spoken, amused and intelligent-looking man – considerably younger than me – as the colonel of the regiment, Lieutenant-Colonel Hugh Undershaft, a high-flier at military college from whom even greater things were apparently expected. The colonel performed the other introductions.

'Sandy you know, of course. And this is Major Graham Sykes.' A greying, rather sad-looking man who, I had been told, wouldn't rise higher in the service, nodded a greeting. 'And Lieutenants Tony Ross and Alan Hammick. Alan's duty officer, which is why he's all togged up. Is that all of us?'

'All we could rustle up, sir,' Sandy told him. The lurcher was also among those present, and was lapping up a bowl of water before going to sleep under the table.

'Can't lure many people into the mess nowadays,' the colonel admitted. 'They prefer to be at home with their wives or girlfriends. We felt we'd better turn out.'

'Very decent of you, Colonel.'

'I told Borrow to bring up some of the regimental Bollinger in honour of your visit. That suit you?' The elderly white-coated mess attendant handed round the champagne, which suited me admirably. I raised my glass and said, 'Well, here's to crime!'

'I think we'd prefer to drink to the regiment . . . ' the colonel said quietly and the other officers muttered 'the regiment', as they raised their glasses. 'The boy had to go to a court martial, of course. But we rely on you to get him off, Rumpole. It's a question of the honour of the regiment.' It was not the first time I had been told this, and I looked at a gilded coat of arms and list of battle honours hanging on the wall: Malplaquet, Blenheim, Waterloo, Balaclava, Mons, El Alamein, I read and the regiment's motto 'For the sake of honour'.

'Well, we can't have it said that we had a murderer in our ranks, can we?' the colonel asked.

'Certainly not!' I found the courage to say. 'Not after you've killed so many people.' There was an uncomfortable silence, and then Sandy laughed. 'I say, you know. That was rather funny!'

'Was it really?' I asked him to reassure me.

'Oh yes. Distinctly humorous. Bit of a joker aren't you, sir, in your quiet way?' The colonel looked at me and emptied his glass. 'Shall we start dinner,' he said. 'We heard you were a claret man, Rumpole.'

There was absolutely nothing wrong with the 1971 Margaux, and when the Cockburn 1960 was circulating, I was able to tell the assembled officers that I had done the State some service under battle conditions in the RAF, Dungeness. 'Ground staff merely,' I admitted, 'but that's not to say that we didn't have some pretty hairy nights.'

'Don't tell me' – Sandy was laughing – 'a bomb fell on the NAAFI?'

'Well, as a matter of fact it did.' I was a little put out. 'Not a very laughable experience.'

'Of course not,' the colonel rebuked Sandy mildly. 'The port seems to have stuck to the table . . . '

'I don't know exactly how many of you gentlemen served through the Second World War?' I was still a little stung by Sandy's joke.

'Too young for it, I'm afraid,' even Major Sykes admitted.

'I wasn't even a glint in my father's eye,' this from young Captain Sandy Ransom.

'*My* father was in Burma,' Lieutenant Ross boasted. 'He's inclined to be a terrible bore about it.'

'I suppose I was about one when it ended. Hardly in a position to join the regiment,' the colonel told me. 'And somehow we never even got invited to the Falklands . . . '

'Soldiers of the Queen,' I discovered. 'Born too late for a war.'

'Do you honestly think it's too late?' The colonel looked at me; he was smiling gently.

'Too late for your sort of war, anyway,' I told him. 'Too late for Blenheim and Balaclava and the Thin Red Line, and hats off to you

fuzzy-wuzzies 'cos you broke a British square. Even too late for Pas-
schendaele and Tobruk . . . Next time some boffin will press a button, and good-night all. "Farewell the plumed troop and the big
wars/That make ambition virtue!" ' I was getting into my stride:

> '*O, farewell!*
> *Farewell the neighing steed and the shrill trump,*
> *The spirit-stirring drum, the ear-piercing fife,*
> *The royal banner, and all quality,*
> *Pride, pomp, and circumstance of glorious war! . . .*
> *Farewell! The colonel's occupation's gone.*'

I looked round at their slightly puzzled faces and said, 'Nowadays,
let's face it, you're only playing at soldiers, aren't you?'

'Perhaps you're right,' the colonel admitted. 'But while we're here,
we may as well play the game as well as possible; it would be exceedingly boring if we didn't. And we have to do our best for the
regiment.'

'Oh, yes. Yes, of course.' I raised my glass. 'The regiment!'

'It's not customary to drink to the regiment after dinner,' Major
Sykes corrected me quietly. 'Except on formal evenings in the mess.'

So I drank, but not to the regiment, and the colonel got up and
went to a small grand piano in the corner of the mess. He sat on the
piano stool, gently massaging his fingers and, as this was more as I
expected an evening among soldiers would be, I started to sing 'Roll
out the Barrel' just as we had sung it during the late war:

> '*Roll out the barrel,*
> *We'll have a barrel of fun*
> *Drink to the barrel*
> *We've got the blues on the run . . .* '

And then I fell silent, feeling exceedingly foolish as Colonel
Undershaft began to play what even I could recognise as Beet-
hoven's *Moonlight Sonata*. Over a soft passage he spoke to no one in
particular: 'Perhaps we are all practising idiotically for a war
which would begin by obliterating us all. But we're still responsible,
aren't we? Responsible for our soldiers. Boys like Danny Boy. We
pick them out of a back-street in Glasgow and give them clean boots
and a haircut. We feed them and water them and teach them to kill
people in all sorts of ingenious ways, and then we can't even offer
them a proper soldier's war to do it in. Can we expect them to turn
into nice, quiet members of the Salvation Army? We're responsible

for Danny Boy' –
he stopped playing
and looked at me – 'which is
why we've got to take all possible steps to see that he's acquitted.'

'I'm sorry,' I said in the ensuing silence.

'Why?' the colonel asked.

'Sorry about that "Roll out the Barrel" business. It seems that I got things rather wrong.'

Later Sandy took me across the square to a comfortable guest-room with a bathroom attached. On the way I asked him to show me the married quarters. I saw the late sergeant's flat up a short, iron staircase at the foot of which two or three large dustbins stood against a wall; and, on ground level, I saw Trooper Danny's small accom-modation. There were lights on up and below the outside staircase. Two wives, parted from their husbands, were, it seemed, unable to sleep. When we got to my room, Sandy said we would see Danny in the morning and asked if I had all the 'paperwork' I needed.

'Oh yes. An interesting little brief, especially the post-mortem pho-tographs. Quite a lot to be learned from them.'

'What about?' Captain Sandy Ransom didn't sound particularly interested.

'About the time of death. It's the hypostasis, you see, the post-mortem staining of the body that shows the time when the blood settles down to the lowest level.'

'Time of death? I shouldn't have thought it was the time that mattered. It's *who* dunnit.'

'Or it's *when* dunnit?' I suggested. 'Perhaps that's what makes this case interesting.'

The next morning I found myself alone at breakfast-time in the mess with Major Sykes, who was now in uniform and methodically consuming eggs, bacon and sausages. 'Sandy told us you were brilliant at murders,' he said, an accusation to which I had to plead guilty.

'Of course Sandy's a great one for jokes, usually of the practical variety.'

'I can imagine that.'

'Oh yes.' The major gave me an instance: 'We had some sort of man from the Ministry out here – Under-Secretary at defence, something like that. And Sandy turned up in the mess pretending to be a visiting German officer. He'd got hold of the uniform somewhere. God knows where. Of course Sandy speaks German. About the only one of us who does. Anyway, he started doing Nazi salutes and singing the "Horst Wessel". Nearly scared the fellow from the Ministry out of his few remaining wits.'

'Does your colonel allow that sort of thing?' I wondered.

'Oh, Hugh was away that night, somewhere at Brigade HQ. But no one can really be angry with Sandy. He's a sort of licensed jester. Puts on the panto, you know. *Aladdin* last year. I was the Dame.' He turned and nodded to one of the many framed regimental photographs on the wall behind him. It showed Major Sykes with other members of the pantomime cast.

'You have hidden talents, Major,' I had to admit my surprise.

'Oh, it's Sandy brought it out in me. He's such a wonderful "producer" – is that the word for it? He can get the best out of everyone. Tell me. How do you find the UK?'

'Go out of that door, turn west and keep straight on.' I shouldn't have done it and the major didn't smile.

'You're a joker, aren't you?' he said. 'Like Sandy. I only asked because I'm retiring next year. Got to. Back to live with my sister in Surrey. I never married – not to anyone except the regiment.'

'Now you've got to divorce?'

'It'll be a bit of a wrench, although I wasn't born into it. I'm not like Sandy; his father was a colonel, of course, and his grandfather a lieutenant-general. Sandy was born into the cavalry.'

'With a silver bit in his mouth?'

'Oh, he's got plenty of money. But generous with it. He's paying for you, you know . . .'

'For *me*? No. I didn't know that.' It came as a surprise, and I didn't know whether I wanted to feel so much indebted to the young defending officer.

'When anyone's in trouble, like this young Trooper Boyne' – the Major explained the situation – 'Sandy'll always come to their rescue. He'd do anything for the regiment.'

'Even making you a Dame?' At which point Major Sykes folded his arms and did a surprising Dame's North Country accent.

'Where's that naughty boy Aladdin now?' he crowed, and then added, in his own voice, 'Yes. He'd even do that.'

After breakfast Sandy Ransom, an officer so popular, I later discovered, that it seemed inevit-
able that Trooper Danny
Boyne should choose him for
his defence, and I sat in a small
office set aside in the guard
room and interviewed our
client. He seemed shy, indeed
nervous, of me, and directed many of his answers
to Captain Sandy Ransom,
who perched on a small upright chair beneath which slept
his favourite lurcher.

'You said Sergeant Jumbo
Wilson picked on you,' I
started at the beginning. 'Why
do you think that was?'

'I don't know.'

'No idea?'

'I don't know, I told you.'
And then he turned to Sandy
as if to explain, 'I told him.'

'Mr Rumpole's here to help you. Trust him.' It was, I supposed, an order from a superior officer, but it didn't seem to have a great deal of effect. I picked up Danny's statement and went on to one of the most damaging parts of the evidence.

'Did you ever say you'd carve him up?'

'That was a long time ago.'

'About three weeks, apparently, before he died.'

'Jumbo Wilson came into the disco, throwing his weight about like he always did' – the Trooper started to talk more easily – 'shouting, so people'd notice him. I may have said that to some boys by the bar.'

'Some boys who're coming to give evidence!' I reminded him.

'Witnesses from another regiment,' Sandy said as though that disposed of the matter. 'Of course,' I remembered, 'Seraphs wouldn't give evidence against each other – but you admit you said it?' I asked Danny.

'Like you'd say about anyone that picked on you: "I'll carve him up." It's like a common saying.'

'Danny comes from Glasgow.' Sandy supplied what must have seemed to him an obvious explanation. 'Is that going to be our defence?' Not if I had anything to do with it, I thought. I came on to the fatal occasion. 'On that evening, Saturday November the 22nd . . . '

'We were practising for the panto Captain Ransom puts on at Christmas.' Danny now seemed more confident.

'I can confirm that.' Sandy confirmed it.

'Until when?'

'It was about nine o'clock.'

'Or 21.00 exactly.' I wasn't sure whether I was getting the answers from the client or the defending officer.

'I went back to the married quarters block. I changed and went out again. I was meeting my mates in the square. Just in front of my quarters.'

'Where?'

'Just on the square. In front of the quarters.'

'And there you met . . . ?'

'Finchie and Goldie.'

'Troopers Finch and Goldsmith,' Sandy gave me the names and added, for good measure, 'I can confirm that too. I happened to see them. I stayed on a little while after the rehearsal and then I saw the three men when I came out.'

'Where did you three go to?'

'The disco.'

'The Rosenkavalier?'

'Got there about 21.30, didn't you?' Sandy asked, and Danny Boy said, 'About that. Yes, sir.'

'Did you see Sergeant Wilson?' I asked.

'He was there, yes. In a corner.'

'Your statement says the place was dark and very crowded. Are you sure you recognised the sergeant?'

'I could tell that bastard anywhere.' At least he was sure about that, but I thought he could do with a little training as a witness. 'When you give your evidence, Trooper Boyne,' I told him, 'please try not to call the dear departed a bastard. It won't exactly endear you to the tribunal. How was the sergeant dressed?'

'Casual – a sports jacket, I think. A shirt without a tie.'

'Not in a frock?'

'Not when I saw him.' He seemed a little puzzled, but when I asked, 'And then you saw this other man?', he answered with quiet conviction, 'I saw this German.'

'How did you know he was German?'

'He was speaking Kraut to the girl by the door. Then he spotted Wilson and went over to his table.'

'A man in a black leather jacket. With spiky hair . . . ' I read from the statement our client had made to the investigating officer.

'This punk.' Danny spoke with a good deal of dislike. Basically, I thought, he was a very conventional young man.

'Did the sergeant speak to him at all?'

'Just "Helmut". We heard him call out, "Helmut".'

'What else?'

'We didn't hear what they said. They sat together in the corner; they were still there when we left.'

'Which was at, approximately?'

'01.00 hours, wasn't it, Danny?' Again Captain Sandy Ransom supplied the time and our client nodded his head.

'And you never saw Sergeant Jumbo Wilson alive again?'

'Never!'

'And you got back into the barracks over the back wall?'

'We don't bother about booking in and out at the guard room.'

'Especially as you were confined to barracks.' Sandy smiled indulgently as a schoolmaster might at the prank of a favourite pupil.

'That was after a wee fight I had. A couple of weeks ago. Down at the disco . . . ' Danny started to explain, but again the defending officer took up the story. 'That was the fight when he got the blood on his cuff. It's in the evidence.'

'Tell me' – I spoke to our client who wouldn't have a favourite captain to help him give evidence in Court – 'just tell me in your own words.'

'It was a German boy what was taking the mickey out of my wife. Out of Hanni. I took him outside and gave him a couple of taps. He must have bled a bit.'

'A German boy with a class AB blood group just like the sergeant's?' I asked, feeling my side was getting over-confident. 'A blood group only enjoyed by 3 to 4 per cent of the population?' I stood up, put away my pen and started to tie up my brief. 'So it comes to this. You saw the sergeant alive at one in the morning. And he was found at 4 a.m. after the military police got an anonymous phone call.'

'From a German,' Sandy reminded me.

'In German, anyway. So. Giving the sergeant time to leave the bar, slip into his frock – wherever he did that – quarrel with whoever he quarrelled with . . . ' 'His friend, Helmut. Isn't that the most likely explanation?' Sandy interrupted, but I went on. 'When he was found he couldn't have been dead much more than two and a half hours.'

'The fellows prosecuting accept that.' Sandy was reassuring me.

'But do I accept it?' I asked, and Danny, who had been looking at me doubtfully, spoke, for the first time I thought, his mind. 'Don't you believe me, Mr Rumpole?'

'I'm not here to believe anything, I'm here to defend you,' I told my client. 'But some time or another it might be a bit of a help, old darling, if you started to tell me the truth.'

After we had left our client, I asked Sandy to drive me to the scene of the crime. The Rosenkavalier disco-bar looked small and somewhat dingy by daylight with its neon sign – an outline of a silver rose –

switched off. The place was locked up and we inspected the side alley which was, in fact, a narrow lane which joined the streets in front of and behind the disco, so a body might have been driven up from behind the building and delivered at the side entrance. On the other side of the lane was the high wall and regular windows of a tallish block of flats. Sandy's lurcher was sniffing at the side entrance, perhaps scenting old blood. I asked the captain, 'None of the neighbours saw or heard anything?'

'They wouldn't, would they?'

'Why do you say that?'

'They're all Germans.'

'The telephone call was made in German.'

'By his boyfriend perhaps.' The defending officer clearly had his own explanation of the crime.

'Boyfriend?'

'Helmut. He might not have been sure if he'd killed Jumbo Wilson. Perhaps he had a fit of remorse.'

'Why do you think "Jumbo" had a boyfriend? He was married.'

'What's that got to do with it?' Sandy smiled and then said seriously, 'You were right, of course, Danny wasn't telling you the whole truth. You know why Jumbo picked on him?'

'Tell me.'

'Because the sar'nt made a heavy pass and Danny Boy told him to satisfy his lust on the regimental goat, or words to that effect.'

I tried to think of the sequence of events. The sergeant had left the disco and gone somewhere, perhaps into the block of flats, changed into a bizarre costume, been knifed and dumped in the lane. 'So Helmut stabbed Jumbo in a lovers' quarrel after a bit of convivial dressing up?' I considered the captain's theory.

'Isn't that the obvious solution?' Sandy obviously regarded the problem as solved.

'I suppose it'd get you out of trouble,' I said, and when he laughed and asked, 'Me?', I explained, 'I mean, the regiment, of course.'

I was tired that night and I left the mess early. I got a torch from Borrow, the mess attendant, to light my way across the darkened square. As I left, Sandy had sat down to the piano, and I heard him singing: 'Kiss me goodnight, Sergeant Wilson, Tuck me in my little wooden bed . . . '

I came to the corner of the married quarters wing. I could hear the thin wail of the Boynes' baby, awake and crying, and I saw a curtain pulled back for a moment and a grey-haired, handsome woman, whom I took to be Mrs Wilson, looked out frowning with anger towards the source of the sound. Then she twitched the curtain across the window again, and I sank to my knees behind the dustbins at the foot of the iron staircase, and made a close examination, with the help of Borrow's torch, of the ground and the bottom stair.

I was in that position when Lieutenant Tony Ross, the duty officer in uniform that night, discovered me and looked down, as I thought, rather strangely. 'Hail to thee, Bright Seraph,' I greeted him. 'Thought I'd dropped a few marks down here. Must've had a hole in my pocket.'

'Can I help at all, sir?' the young officer asked.

'Not at all. No.' I struggled to my feet. 'Sleep well, Lieutenant. It's only money, isn't it?'

The court martial, which I don't think anyone suspected was my first, took place in an ornate nineteenth-century German civic building, and in a room with a great deal of carved stonework and a painted ceiling. Everyone was clearly identified, like the members of a television chat-show panel, by a little board with their title painted on it set on the table in front of them. The tribunal appointed to try Danny Boyne consisted of a president (a Brigadier Humphries of the Transport Corps, Sandy told me), a lieutenant-colonel, a major and two captains, one of whom was a uniformed, lady WRAC officer. And seated beside the president, I was surprised to see my old friend and one-time chamber mate, George Frobisher, who had deserted the dusty arena down the Bailey (well, George was never much of a cross-examiner) for the security of the Circuit Bench, and then, apparently in search of adventure, become a judge advocate, stationed in Germany advising court martials on the legal aspects of soldiers' trials. George sat beside the president now, wearing his wig and gown, and explained every point in the proceedings with tireless courtesy to the accused trooper, in a way which seemed to show the military as more civilised than some of the learned judges down the Bailey, notably his Honour Roger Bullingham known to me as the Mad Bull.

So, 04916323, Trooper Boyne of the 37th and 39th, the Duke of Clarence's Own Lancers, was charged with 'a civilian offence contrary to Section 70 of the Army Act 1955, that is to say, murder, in that on the 22nd and 23rd days of November last he murdered 75334188, Sergeant J. Wilson of the Duke of Clarence's Own'. A plea of not guilty was entered and after George had painstakingly explained the roles of everyone in Court, and advised Danny to relax and sit comfortably and make any comment that occurred to him to Mr Rumpole, his barrister, Lieutenant-Colonel Watford, was invited to rise from the prosecution table and outline the case against the trooper.

Sandy Ransom (at last parted from his lurcher, who was being cared for in the Special Investigations Branch Office) and I sat at the defence table next to our client, who had an NCO beside, and one behind him, holding his hat and belt, which he wouldn't wear, so Sandy explained, until he gave evidence. There was no dock, which again seemed a better arrangement than at the Bailey, where an accused person is penned into a sort of eminence which hints at their guilt. Taking George's advice, I sat comfortably and let the prosecuting officer begin.

And here was another plus. Lieutenant-Colonel Michael Watford, OBE, the Army Legal Services, was tall, youngish (almost everyone seems youngish to me), bespectacled and sensible. He had trained as a solicitor, and had, as it so happened, been well known to me as young Mike Watford, articled clerk with Butchers & Stringfellow, a firm who had often briefed me at the Bailey and who sent young Mike out to help with taking notes and witness statements, a task he performed a great deal better than the senior partners. So, from the whirligig of time, Mike Watford was known to me as a good egg; in fact, I would go so far as to say that he was a double yolker.

As Lieutenant-Colonel Mike outlined his case, my eyes strayed to our judges or, would they more correctly be called, the jury of army officers, because they would decide all the facts and leave the law to George. I had never had to face a jury in uniform before. I tried flashing a charming smile at the WRAC officer but it had no effect on her whatever. She was listening to Mike's opening with a frown of fierce concentration.

Mike's first witness was a young lady with a good deal of rather dried-up blonde hair, tricked out in tight, artificial leopard-skin trousers and a low-cut black silk vest. Chains and bracelets clinked as she moved, and she looked as though she had better things to do than take part in the army exercises of a foreign power. Her English was, however, so much better than my non-existent German that it was fully equal to all the demands made on it that day.

Mike Watford got her to admit that her name was Greta Schmerz, and she worked at hanging up the coats in the Rosenkavalier; when business was brisk, apparently, she also helped out at the bar. She identified the photograph of Sergeant Wilson as someone she had seen on occasions at the disco-bar. Mike then went so far as to tell her that we knew that, on the night in question, the sergeant was stabbed outside the disco-bar.

'We know nothing of the sort,' I rose to protest, and drove on through a mild 'Don't we, Mr Rumpole?' from George. 'We know he was found dead outside the disco. We haven't the foggiest idea where he was stabbed.'

'Very well' – Mike Watford conceded the point – 'he was found dead. Had you seen him in the disco that night?'

'I can't remember,' Greta told us after a pause.

'And *that* young man, Trooper Boyne, sitting there, was *he* in the disco that night?' the prosecutor asked.

'He was there, I remember him.' Miss Schmerz was sure. Having achieved this, Watford sat down and Rumpole arose.

'Fräulein Schmerz. So far as Sergeant Wilson, the man in the photograph, was concerned, he may have been there that night, or he may not. You simply don't know?'

'He was there. Danny and the other two saw him.' I got a loudly whispered reminder from the defending officer.

'Please, Captain. I do know your case!' I quietened Sandy and addressed the witness. 'Do you remember someone coming to the disco with spiky hair and black leather jacket?'

'I do remember.'

'Helmut!' Sandy whispered again triumphantly, and I muttered, 'I know it's much more exciting than manoeuvres, but do try and stay relatively calm.' I asked Miss Schmerz, 'What time did you see him?'

'How should I know that?'

'How indeed? Was it late?'

'I think . . . perhaps midnight . . . '

'Well, that's very helpful. Did he speak to you?'

'The punk man? He spoke to me.'

'In German?'

'Yes. He asked if I had seen the English sergeant.'

'Did he say the name Wilson?'

'He said that.'

'Tell me, Fräulein Schmerz.' I was curious to know. 'All the soldiers came to the disco in civilian clothes, didn't they? Jeans and anoraks and plimsolls – that sort of costume?'

'They weren't in soldier's dress,' she agreed.

'So you couldn't tell if that man in the photograph was a sergeant or not?'

'No.'

'Did you know his name was Wilson?'

'I didn't know his name.'

'So there seems very little point in the punk asking you the question? Yes, thank you, Fräulein Schmerz.'

I sat down, and Sandy looked at me with obvious displeasure. I was, it must have seemed to him, a very ordinary barrister indeed. 'What are you trying to do?' he asked me, and all I could whisper back was, 'Strangely enough, my dear old defending officer, I think I'm trying to find out the truth.'

The Court was still and respectful when the sergeant's widow was called to give her evidence. George asked her if she'd care to sit, and when she preferred to stand, tall, grey haired and dignified, by the witness chair, he assured her that she wouldn't be kept there long. In fact, Mike Watford only asked her a few questions. She identified the photograph of her dead husband, whom she had last seen alive when he left their flat in the married quarters not very long after nine o'clock on the night of 22 November. When I rose to cross-examine I told the witness that we all sympathised with her in the tragic situation in which she found herself, and went on to ask if Trooper Boyne and his German wife, Hanni, didn't live very near her little flat?

'Almost next door.' The voice was disapproving and the face stony.

'Did you see anything of them?'

'She was always at the dustbins. Putting things in them. Things the baby dirtied, most like.'

'Most likely.' I turned to another topic. 'You were at home all the evening and the night when your husband died?'

'Yes, I was. I never went out.'

'And Trooper Boyne was never in your flat at any time?'

'No.' The answer was decided.

'Did you ever ask either Mr or Mrs Boyne to your home?'

'Of course not.' The suggestion clearly struck her as ridiculous.

'Did you not invite them because your husband was a sergeant and my client was a humble trooper?'

'Not *just* because of that. She was one of them, wasn't she?'

'One of what?'

'One of them Germans.'

'You don't like Germans, Mrs Wilson?' The question seemed unnecessary; I asked it all the same.

'*They* did it.'

'They did what?'

'That's why he was out there in the street, out there dressed like that! They took him . . . He . . . he was gone . . . gone . . . '

'Don't distress yourself, madam.' George was using his best bed-side manner. 'Which Germans do you mean killed your husband?'

'I don't know. How could I know?' She was talking very quietly and calmly, like someone, I thought, on the verge of tears.

'You say some Germans killed him?'

'With respect' – I had to correct him – 'she didn't say that. She said Germans "took" him. Perhaps the shorthand writer . . . ' The lady with the shorthand book stood and found the phrase with unusual rapidity. 'She said "They took him . . . He was gone . . . " '

'I assume by "took" she meant kill.' George seemed to have little patience with my interruption.

'In my submission it would be extremely dangerous to assume anything of the sort,' I had to tell him. 'She said "took". The person who killed him may be someone entirely different.'

'What exactly are you suggesting, Mr Rumpole?' George frowned at me. It wasn't a fair question to an old Chambers mate who was, as yet, not entirely clear what he was suggesting. 'I hope that may become quite clear in my cross-examination of other witnesses,' I said to keep him quiet. 'I really don't want to prolong this witness's ordeal by keeping her in the witness-box a moment longer.' So I sat down and Sandy gave me another of his cross whispers, 'Why don't you ask her the vital question?'

'Which is?'

'Wasn't Jumbo Wilson a pooftah?'

'For a soldier, old darling,' I whispered back, 'you really know so little about murder. You don't endear yourself to the Court by asking the weeping widow if her husband wasn't a pooftah. It sort of adds insult to injury. No, I didn't ask the vital question. But I got the vital answer.'

'What was that?' Captain Sandy looked doubtful.

'They "took" him. That's what she said. Now wasn't that rather a curious way of putting it?' And as we sat in silence waiting for the next witness, some lines of old Robert Browning wandered idly into my mind: 'Some with lives that came to nothing, some with deeds as well undone,/Death stepped tacitly and *took* them where they never see the sun . . . ' So did Mrs Wilson mean that death had taken Jumbo, or did she mean something else entirely?

Now the door opened and an important-looking gentleman in the uniform of the Royal Army Medical Corps came to the witness table and was sworn by a member of the Court. I knew he would be the subject of my most important cross-examination, and I gazed at him with the close attention a matador gives to a bull as it enters the ring and does its preliminary business with the picadors. Lieutenant-Colonel Basil Borders, Doctor of Medicine and Fellow of The Royal College of Pathologists, was a tall, pale man with a thickening waist, ginger hair going thin, and rimless spectacles. He appeared, from the way he took the oath and answered Mike Watford's early questions, to have a considerable opinion of his own importance, and when he was asked to give his post-mortem findings he answered clearly enough.

'The deceased was a well-nourished man, forty-five years old, with no signs of disease,' Lieutenant-Colonel Borders told us. 'There were indications of a fairly recent high consumption of alcohol and a heavy meal. Death had been caused by a stab wound, with a flat, sharp object such as a knife which entered the abdomen and penetrated the abdominal aorta.'

I will not weary the reader with an account of the army patholo-gist's evidence-in-chief. It followed the lines of his statement and was thorough, painstaking and predictable. I opened my cross-examination with a dramatic performance which Captain Sandy had suggested and now staged with relish. He stood up with his back to me as I put an arm about his neck and appeared to stab him from behind with my pencil.

'One arm across the windpipe to stop the victim crying out and an upward stab from the back, penetrating the heart. Isn't that the accepted military manner of using a knife, Doctor?' I asked as I acted the commando role.

'That is the method taught in commando training.' Borders was clearly distressed by our courtroom histrionics.

'But the sergeant had a knife jabbed into the stomach?'

'Yes, indeed.'

'So inexpertly that it might not even have been fatal?'

'It might not have been.'

'If it hadn't happened to penetrate the aorta?'

'Indeed.'

'It looks far more like a civilian than a military job, doesn't it, Doctor?'

'Perhaps,' was as far as the witness would go, but Sandy whispered, 'Oh, I like it,' as he resumed his seat, his great moment over. I just hoped he would enjoy the rest of my cross-examination as much.

'And the knife – there's nothing to indicate that it was a bayonet?' I asked the pathologist.

'As I have said, I believe the blade was flat.'

'Not a bayonet or any sort of army knife?'

'There is no particular indication of that,' Borders agreed.

'It could've been the sort of sharp, pointed carving-knife available in any kitchen?'

'Yes, indeed.' He was finding the cross-examination easier than he had expected and was relaxed and smiling round the court. No one, I noticed, smiled back.

'Available to any civilian?'

'Available to Helmut!' the irrepressible Captain Sandy whispered as the witness answered, 'Yes.'

So far so good but I knew I was coming to an area of likely disagreement. I decided to lull the witness into a feeling of false security, hoping he would be taken by surprise when the attack was launched. I leant forward, spoke in a silken voice and poured out a double dose of flattery: 'Lieutenant-Colonel Borders, you are a very distinguished and experienced pathologist and no doubt you carried out a most thorough post-mortem examination.'

'Thank you.' The witness preened himself visibly. 'Indeed I did.'

'And we are all *most* grateful for the enormous trouble you have clearly taken in this matter.' George joined in the smiles now and the witness was even more grateful. 'Thank you very much.'

'Rarely have I heard such absolutely expert evidence!' Well, *I* wasn't on oath.

'You're very kind.'

'Just one small detail. What were your conclusions about the frock?'

'The frock?' He looked puzzled and I knew I was on to something.

'There is a cut in the scarlet frock the sergeant was wearing and a good deal of staining. Of course you fitted the hole in the dress to the hole in the body?' I assumed politely.

'I don't think I did.' The lieutenant-colonel looked at the Court as though it were a point of no importance, and I looked at him with rising and incredulous outrage. Finally, I managed a gasp of amazement on the word '*Indeed?*'

'The dress was a matter for the scientific officer. I don't believe I examined it at all.'

'Lieutenant-Colonel Borders!' I called the man to order. 'Are you representing yourself as an expert witness?'

'I am.' There was a flush now, rising to the roots of the ginger hair.

'A person capable of carrying out a post-mortem examination in a reasonably intelligent way?'

'Of course!'

'And you can't even tell this Court' – I spoke with rising fury – 'if the sergeant was wearing the frock when he was stabbed, or if it was cut and put on him *after his death?*'

'No, I can't tell you that, I'm afraid.' Again he did his best to make it sound as irrelevant as the weather in Manchester.

'You're afraid?' I gave my best performance of contemptuous anger. 'Then I'm afraid you're unlikely to have sufficient expertise to be of much assistance to the Court on another vital matter.'

'Mr Rumpole . . .' George was trying to call a halt to this mayhem, but I had done with the cape and was moving in with the sword and not to be interrupted. 'I refer to the time of death. Have you any useful contribution to make on that matter?'

'Mr Rumpole.' George could contain himself no longer. 'I know that you are in the habit of conducting murder cases at the Old Bailey with all the lack of inhibition of, shall we say, a commando raid.'

'Oh, sir.' I smiled at the old darling. 'You're too kind.'

'I think I should make it clear that the Army expects far more peaceful proceedings.' George spoke as severely as he knew how. 'The Military Court is accustomed to seeing all witnesses treated with quiet courtesy. I hope you'll find yourself able to fall into our way of doing things.'

'I'm extremely grateful, sir.' I thought it best to apologise. 'The Court will excuse me if I showed myself, for a moment, to be as clumsy and inexpert in my profession as this officer clearly is in his . . .'

'Mr Rumpole!' George was about to launch another missile in my direction, but I turned to the witness. 'Lieutenant-Colonel. Tell me, is that higher than a colonel?'

'No, lower.' Borders was not pleased.

'Oh, I'm sorry. I'm sure you'll soon earn promotion. You came from England to do this post-mortem?'

'Yes. I was flown out from the UK.'

'And were you told the brief facts of the case?'

'I was told that the suspect had been in a disco where the sergeant had been seen by witnesses around 01.00 hours.'

'And a telephone call about the stabbing had been received by the police at 03.45 hours. So when the army doctor arrived at 04.15 hours the Sergeant could only have been dead, say, about three hours?'

'That is so.'

'And yet there was a definite progress of rigor mortis?'

'Yes. That was found.' Borders was wary of another attack, and this was the vital part of my case. I pressed on quickly: 'Which you would not normally expect in the first three hours after death?'

'Rigor has been known to occur within thirty minutes,' he told *me*, who had won the Penge Bungalow case on rigor, among other factors.

'In *very* exceptional cases,' I told him.

'Well, yes . . . '

'And the temperature of the body had dropped by some six degrees.'

'Yes.'

'I have here Professor Ackerman's work *The Times of Death* in which he deals with falling temperatures.' In fact this volume, together with my old *Oxford Book of English Verse*, had been my constant bedtime reading in Germany. 'Let me put this to you. Normally wouldn't that indicate death at least six hours before?'

'It was a cold night in November, if you remember.'

'That is your answer?' I hope I sounded as though I couldn't believe it.

'Yes.' Borders looked at the faces of the Court members for comfort and received none. '*Hypostasis*,' I gave him the word as though I thought he might not have heard it before. 'The staining caused by blood settling down to the lower parts of the body after death. Were there not large areas of staining when the body was found? Just look at the photographs.' Borders opened the volume of post-mortem photographs on the witness table in front of him and I thought that he did so somewhat reluctantly. 'Isn't that degree of staining consistent with death, let's say, some six hours earlier?'

'It might be consistent with that, yes,' he admitted reluctantly. 'Hypostasis is subject to many variations.'

'In fact everything in those photographs is consistent with death having occurred around nine o'clock on the previous evening!'

'Mr Rumpole . . . ' George was now looking genuinely puzzled.

'Yes, sir?'

'Aren't you forgetting your own client's statement? And the statements of Troopers Finch and . . . '

'Goldsmith, sir,' I helped him.

'Goldsmith. Exactly so. They saw the sergeant in the disco at 1 a.m. He could hardly have died at nine the previous evening.'

'Oh, I don't know. Isn't there some sort of biblical parallel?' This was all the help I'd give old George. I said to the witness, 'One other little matter on the photographs. Are there not a number of pale patches on the stains?'

'Yes, there are.' He was looking at the pictures as though he hated them.

'Representing places where the body rested. Doesn't that indicate one thing clearly to you?'

'What do you mean exactly?'

'What do I mean? Exactly? I mean that the body had been moved after death. That's what I mean.'

There was a long pause, and then another reluctant admission from the witness who said, 'I think that may very well be so.'

It was over. A bit of a triumph, as I hope you will agree. I awarded myself two ears and a tail as I said, 'Thank you very much, Lieutenant Borders,' extremely politely and sat down.

Modestly satisfied as I had been with my cross-examination of the army pathologist, it had in no way delighted Captain Sandy Ransom, who sank lower in his seat during the course of it. As we came out of Court at the end of the day he was grumbling, 'Died by nine o'clock. He couldn't have! By nine o'clock he hadn't even met Helmut.'

'Helmut, of course.' I did my best to sound apologetic. 'Why do I always seem to forget about Helmut?'

'We thought we were getting an ordinary barrister. Do ordinary barristers try so damned hard to get their clients convicted?' Sandy was very angry. '*Someone*'s got to do something for that boy!' And he moved off to liberate his lurcher.

Then I heard the soft voice of a young woman who had clearly learnt to speak English with a Glasgow Irish accent.

'Mr Rumpole! About the blood on Danny's cuff . . . ' I turned to her and it was impossible, in spite of Mrs Wilson's evidence, to think of her as English or German – she was just an extremely beautiful girl in very great distress. 'Yes, I am Hanni Boyne. It was the old shirt,' she told me. 'He wore it when he had the fight. I hadn't washed it, you see. Then he wore it again that night. He didn't remember. I will say all that to them.'

I bet you will, I thought. What lies love makes people tell, for I couldn't imagine Hanni failing to wash Danny Boy's shirts. 'I really shouldn't be talking to you about your evidence,' I told her. Out of the corner of my eye I could see Lieutenant-Colonel Mike Watford coming out of Court.

'You will do your best for Danny, sir. We have been so happy, so awfully happy. The three of us.' I knew she was telling the truth then, but all I could do was mutter something about the case going reasonably well – nothing of any real use to her when she was sick for certainties – and take Mike Watford's arm and steer him to a quiet end of a marble-paved corridor and under the ponderous stone arches.

'Soft you, a word or two before you go, Mike,' I started, doing my best to cash in on the past. 'We used to get on moderately well, didn't we, when you were an articled clerk with Butchers & Stringfellow.'

'I always enjoyed our cases,' Mike admitted.

'Went after the evidence, didn't we, and got at the truth on more than one occasion?'

'You always had a nose for the evidence, Mr Rumpole.'

'So did you, as a young lad, Mike.'

'All this flattery means you're after something.' Lieutenant-Colonel Watford was not born yesterday.

'Oh, young Mike, as astute as ever. Be honest, you're not happy about the evidence on the time of death are you?'

There was a silence then. Mike Watford stopped walking and looked at me. I knew it would not be his style to tell me anything less than the truth. 'To be honest, not particularly.' And then he asked me. 'When do you think it was?'

'The time? Around 21.00 hours, as you would say,' I told him. 'The place, the bottom of the iron staircase outside the sergeant's married quarters. Looked for any blood traces round there, have you?'

'No. As a matter of fact.' He looked thoughtful. 'No.'

'Oh, young Mike Watford! What do you want to do? Win your case or discover the truth?'

'I think the Army would want us to discover the truth.' He had no doubt about it.

'Then, old darling, may I make a suggestion?' And I walked on with him, giving him a list of things to do as I had when we had worked together so happily down the Old Bailey.

When I got back to the barracks I sought an appointment with the colonel. After I had seen him, I went back to my quarters and soaked for a long time in the excellently hot water provided by the British Army. I wondered how many times I had washed away the exhaustion of a day in Court, and the invisible grime which comes from a long association with criminal behaviour, in an early evening bathtub. Then I put on a clean shirt and walked across the darkened barracks square to the mess.

My journey was interrupted by the roar and rattle of a jeep which drew up beside me. Captain Sandy Ransom and his lurcher jumped out, and I saw, with some sinking of the heart, that he was holding a rather muddy black leather jacket. 'Triumph!' he shouted at me. 'I've found it. I've found the evidence.'

It seemed that he had gone for a walk by the old Badweisheim canal after what he regarded as an extremely unsatisfactory day in Court. The lurcher had started to sniff around in a pile of loose earth, and there, by chance, someone had tried to bury the clear indication of their guilt. 'It's Helmut's jacket.' Sandy had no doubt about it.

'Of course it is,' I agreed, and went on to a more important matter. 'I've spoken to your colonel and he's dining in the mess tonight. I hope you can join us.'

'Aren't you going to ring Watford?' For a moment Sandy looked like a schoolboy deprived of a treat. 'Aren't you going to tell the prosecution about the new evidence?'

'I really think that can wait until after dinner.'

We were once again a small gathering in the mess: Colonel Undershaft, Major Sykes, Captain Ransom, Lieutenant Hammick and Ross, who was that night's duty officer. When the port was on the table I sat back and addressed them, having refused to answer any questions during the service of the usual excellent dinner. I felt that I was speaking to them as though I were in Court, and they formed the tribunal who would finally have to decide the strange case of the murder of Sergeant Jumbo Wilson. First I filled my glass and sent the decanter on round the table.

'I know you don't usually toast the regiment after dinner', I started, 'except on formal evenings in the mess. But it's such a power over you all, isn't it, the regiment? Blenheim, Malplaquet, Waterloo, Balaclava, El Alamein,' I intoned, looked round at them and raised my glass:

> 'This seraph-band . . .
> It was a heavenly sight!
> They stood as signals to the land,
> Each one a lovely light.

And the regiment always rallies round a Seraph in trouble. You told me that, didn't you, Sandy?'

'Of course we do.' Sandy was opposite me, nodding through the candlesticks. 'That's why we got you out here. Not that you've done much for the boy so far.'

'So when Sergeant Wilson was stabbed to death,' I went on with my final speech, 'you couldn't have it said that it was done by a Seraph, could you? Not by one of the heavenly band. Far better that the crime should have been committed by an unknown German called Helmut with a black leather jacket and a punk hairdo. Who better to take the blame, after all, than one of the old enemy? An enemy from the war you're all too young to remember.'

'Are you suggesting that the officers of this regiment . . . ?' The colonel had never looked more deeply disturbed.

'Not the officers, Colonel,' I hastened to answer him. 'One officer, the joker in the pack. Of course, pinning the crime on the mysterious Helmut took a lot of organisation and a good many risks. But perhaps that was part of the attraction. It took the place of war.'

The mess was very quiet; Borrow had left us. Old generals and defunct colonels on their rearing chargers looked down on us. Behind the flickering candles, Sandy was smiling. Hugh Undershaft asked me exactly what I knew.

'I'm not sure what I *know*, Colonel. Not for certain. But I'll tell you what I think. I think Danny Boy and his mates met by the dustbins at the foot of the sergeant's staircase and found him there. Dead. I think they told an officer. An officer who was there. With a jeep – his usual method of transport. Danny helped this officer move the body, hence the blood on his cuff. It was the sergeant's blood not the blood of another mysterious German. Then the lads, the young Seraphs, went into Der Rosenkavalier so they could lie and say they'd seen the sergeant there after midnight. Meanwhile, the captain of the Seraphs was unloading a body in a dark alley . . . '

'Dressed in a frock?' the colonel asked.

'That was your joker's contribution. Did he have a dress among the props for the pantomime, one large enough for the Dame? I think he dressed up a dead body.'

'Why on earth should anyone do that?' Sandy sounded incredulous.

'Why? To make some sort of homosexual crime of passion more credible, or as a sign of disapproval? The sergeant brought no credit on the regiment by having himself murdered, did he?'

There was a long silence then; the officers were looking at me, and I felt an intruder, never particularly welcome, in their private world. Then Sandy said, 'Aren't you forgetting Helmut?'

'Oh, I never believed in Helmut, the mysterious German who came so conveniently and asked for the sergeant by name. All the girl remembered was the spiky hair. What do you use in the pantomime, Sandy? Hair lacquer? Hair gel? Was that your own black leather jacket you found so conveniently?' The port had returned to me and I refilled my glass. I felt tired after a long case, and I wanted to leave them, to go home and forget their problem. 'I suppose, in a way, you were a first-rate defending officer. You wanted to get Danny Boy out of trouble and you thought he was guilty. I always believed he was innocent; he was a boy from Glasgow with the good sense to marry a German girl because they loved each other.'

There was another long, thoughtful silence, and then the colonel spoke to me, 'So, may we ask, who, in your opinion, killed Sar'nt Wilson?'

'Oh, don't worry,' I could reassure him, 'the joker never went so far as that. He could move his body, dress him in a frock, but not murder him.'

'Then who . . .'

'I always thought that it must've been bad enough to have been fancied by Sergeant Wilson. It must have been hell on earth to be married to him.' As I said it, in the warm mess, I shivered slightly. I was doing a job which wasn't mine, making accusations and bringing home guilt.

While I was talking to the officers of the Duke of Clarence's Own Lancers, a Captain Betteridge of the Special Investigations Branch called at the flat up the iron staircase in the married quarters. He found it spotlessly clean and shining. He saw the polished furniture and the framed photographs of Sergeant and Mrs Wilson on their wedding day, and of Mrs Wilson's father, a sergeant-major who had been killed at Arnhem. He opened a drawer in the sideboard and saw the gleaming, black-handled carving-knife, and he told Mrs Wilson that he wanted to question her further about the events around nine o'clock on the evening her husband died. It was not long before she told him everything, as she had been secretly longing to do since the day she killed Sergeant Wilson.

> *Farewell the plumed troop and the big wars,*
> *That make ambition virtue! O, farewell!*
> *Farewell the neighing steed and the shrill trump,*
> *The spirit-stirring drum, the ear-piercing fife,*
> *The royal banner, and all the quality,*
> * Pride, pomp and circumstance of glorious war!*

Farewell, anyway, to the barracks of the 37th and 39th Lancers at Badweisheim. Lieutenant Tony Ross drove me to the airport and Captain Ransom, for some reason, didn't turn out to say goodbye. Danny Boy thanked me a little brusquely, as though I had, after all, let down the regiment. Only his wife, Hanni, was genuinely and, I expect, everlastingly, grateful. I went back to Civvy Street and, in due course, I was ensconced with Hilda in the bar of the Old Gloucester.

'Where's ex-Major Johnnie?' I asked her.

'He got a job as secretary of a golf club in Devon. We had a farewell lunch. He bought me champagne.'

'Decent of him.'

'We had a really good chat. When you're with us, he told me, you do all the chatting.'

'Oh, do I?'

'He got me wondering.'

'Oh, really. What about?'

'I suppose what my life would have been like if I hadn't got you to marry me, Rumpole.'

'Did you do that?'

'Of course. You don't decide things like that on your own.'

She was right. I can make all sorts of decisions for my clients, but practically none for Rumpole.

'I might have kept up my singing', Hilda told me, 'if I hadn't married you, Rumpole. I can't help thinking about that.'

'No future in that, Hilda. No future at all in thinking about the past, or what we might have done. Let me give you a toast.' I raised my glass of indifferent claret. 'To the regiment! Coupled', I murmured under my breath, 'with the name of She Who Must Be Obeyed.'

Rumpole and the Tap End

There are many reasons why I could never become one of Her Majesty's judges. I am unable to look at my customer in the dock without feeling 'There but for the Grace of God goes Horace Rumpole.' I should find it almost impossible to order any fellow citizen to be locked up in a Victorian slum with a couple of psychopaths and three chamber-pots, and I cannot imagine a worse way of passing your life than having to actually listen to the speeches of the learned friends. It also has to be admitted that no sane Lord Chancellor would ever dream of the appointment of Mr Justice Rumpole. There is another danger inherent in the judicial office: a judge, any judge, is always liable to say, in a moment of boredom or impatience, something downright silly. He is then denounced in the public prints, his resignation is called for, he is stigmatised as malicious or at least mad and his Bench becomes a bed of nails and his ermine a hair shirt. There is, perhaps, no judge more likely to open his mouth and put his foot in it than that, on the whole well meaning, old darling, Mr Justice Featherstone, once Guthrie Featherstone, QC, MP, a Member of Parliament so uninterested in politics that he joined the Social Democrats and who, during many eventful years of my life, was Head of our Chambers in Equity Court. Now, as a judge, Guthrie Featherstone had swum somewhat out of our ken; but he hadn't lost his old talent for giving voice to the odd uncalled-for and disastrous phrase. He, I'm sure, will never forget the furore that arose when, in passing sentence in a case of attempted murder in which I was engaged for the defence, his Lordship made an unwise reference to the 'tap end' of a matrimonial bathtub. At least the account which follows may serve as a terrible warning to anyone contemplating a career as a judge.

★

I have spoken elsewhere, and on frequent occasions, of my patrons the Timsons, that extended family of South London villains for whom, over the years, I have acted as Attorney-General. Some of you may remember Tony Timson, a fairly mild-mannered receiver of stolen video-recorders, hi-fi sets and microwave ovens, married to that April Timson who once so offended her husband's male-chauvinist prejudices by driving a get-away car at a somewhat unsuccessful bank robbery. Tony and April lived in a semi on a large housing estate with their offspring, Vincent Timson, now aged eight, who I hoped would grow up in the family business and thus ensure a steady flow of briefs for Rumpole's future. Their house was brightly, not to say garishly, furnished with mock tiger-skin rugs, Italian-tile-style linoleum and wallpaper which simulated oak panelling. (I knew this from a large number of police photographs in various cases.) It was also equipped with almost every labour-saving device which ever dropped off the back of a lorry. On the day when my story starts this desirable home was rent with screams from the bathroom and a stream of soapy water flowing out from under the door. In the screaming, the word 'murderer' was often repeated at a volume which was not only audible to young Vincent, busy pushing a blue-flashing toy police car round the hallway, but to the occupants of the adjoining house and those of the neighbours who were hanging out their washing. Someone, it was not clear who it was at the time, telephoned the local cop shop for assistance.

In a surprisingly short while a real, flashing police car arrived and the front door was flung open by a wet and desperate April Timson, her leopard-skin-style towelling bath-robe clutched about her. As Detective Inspector Brush, an officer who had fought a running battle with the Timson family for years, came up the path to meet her she sobbed out, at the top of her voice, a considerable voice for so petite a redhead, 'Thank God, you've come! He was only trying to bloody murder me.' Tony Timson emerged from the bathroom a few seconds later, water dripping from his earlobe-length hair and his gaucho moustache. In spite of the word RAMBO emblazoned across his bath-robe, he was by no means a man of formidable physique. Looking down the stairs, he saw his wife in hysterics and his domestic hearth invaded by the Old Bill. No sooner had he reached the hallway than he was arrested and charged with attempted murder of his wife, the particulars being, that, while sharing a bath with her preparatory to going to a neighbour's party, he had tried to cause her death by drowning.

★

In course of time I was happy to accept a brief for the defence of Tony Timson and we had a conference in Brixton prison where the alleged wife-drowner was being held in custody. I was attended, on that occasion, by Mr Bernard, the Timsons' regular solicitor, and that up-and-coming young radical barrister, Mizz Liz Probert, who had been briefed to take a note and generally assist me in the *cause célèbre*.

'Attempted murderer, Tony Timson?' I opened the proceedings on a somewhat incredulous note. 'Isn't that rather out of your league?'

'April told me', he began his explanation, 'she was planning on wearing her skin-tight leatherette trousers with the revealing halter-neck satin top. That's what she was planning on wearing, Mr Rumpole!'

'A somewhat tasteless outfit, and not entirely *haute couture*,' I admitted. 'But it hardly entitles you to drown your wife, Tony.'

'We was both invited to a party round her friend Chrissie's. And that was the outfit she was keen on wearing . . .'

'She says you pulled her legs and so she became submerged.' Bernard, like a good solicitor, was reading the evidence.

' "The Brides in the Bath!" ' My mind went at once to one of the classic murders of all times. 'The very method! And you hit on it with no legal training. How did you come to be in the same bath, anyway?'

'We always shared, since we was courting.' Tony looked surprised that I had asked. 'Don't all married couples?'

'Speaking for myself and She Who Must Be Obeyed the answer is, thankfully, no. I can't speak for Mr Bernard.'

'Out of the question.' Bernard shook his head sadly. 'My wife has a hip.'

'Sorry, Mr Bernard. I'm really sorry.' Tony Timson was clearly an attempted murderer with a soft heart.

'Quite all right, Mr Timson,' Bernard assured him. 'We're down for a replacement.'

'April likes me to sit up by the taps.' Tony gave us further particulars of the Timson bathing habits. 'So I can rinse off her hair after a shampoo. Anyway, she finds her end that much more comfortable.'

'She makes you sit at the tap end, Tony?' I began to feel for the fellow.

'Oh, I never made no objection,' my client assured me. 'Although you can get your back a bit scalded. And those old taps does dig into you sometimes.'

'So were you on friendly terms when you both entered the water?' My instructing solicitor was quick on the deductions. 'She was all right then. We was both, well, affectionate. Looking forward to the party, like.'

'She didn't object to what you planned on wearing?' I wanted to cover all the possibilities.

'My non-structured silk-style suiting from Toy Boy Limited!' Tony protested. 'How could she object to that, Mr Rumpole? No. She washed her hair as per usual. And I rinsed it off for her. Then she told me who was going to be at the party, like.'

'Mr Peter Molloy,' Bernard reminded me. 'It's in the brief, Mr Rumpole.' Now I make it a rule to postpone reading my brief until the last possible moment so that it's fresh in my mind when I go into Court, so I said, somewhat testily, 'Of course I know that, but I thought I'd like to get the story from the client. Peanuts Molloy! Mizz Probert, we have a defence. Tony Timson's wife was taking him to a party attended by Peanuts Molloy.'

The full implications of this piece of evidence won't be apparent to those who haven't made a close study of my previous handling of the Timson affairs. Suffice it to say the Molloys are to the Timsons as the Montagues were to the Capulets or the Guelphs to the Ghibellines, and their feud goes back to the days when the whole of South London was laid down to pasture, and they were quarrelling about stolen sheep. The latest outbreak of hostilities occurred when certain Molloys, robbing a couple of elderly Timsons as *they* were robbing a bank, almost succeeded in getting Tony's relatives convicted for an offence they had not committed. Peter, better known as 'Peanuts', Molloy was the young hopeful of the clan Molloy and it was small wonder that Tony Timson took great exception to his wife putting on her leatherette trousers for the purpose of meeting the family enemy.

Liz Probert, however, a white-wig at the Bar who knew nothing of such old legal traditions as the Molloy–Timson hostility, said, 'Why should Mrs Timson's meeting Molloy make it all right to drown her?' I have to remind you that Mizz Liz was a pillar of the North Islington women's movement.

'It wasn't just that she was meeting him, Mr Rumpole,' Tony explained. 'It was the words she used.'

'What did she say?'

'I'd rather not tell you if you don't mind. It was humiliating to my pride.'

'Oh, for heaven's sake, Tony. Let's hear the worst.' I had never known a Timson behave so coyly.

'She made a comparison like, between me and Peanuts.'

'What comparison?'

Tony looked at Liz and his voice sank to a whisper. 'Ladies present,' he said.

'Tony,' I had to tell him, 'Mizz Liz Probert has not only practised in the criminal courts, but in the family division. She is active on behalf of gay and lesbian rights in her native Islington. She marches, quite often, in aid of abortion on demand. She is a regular reader of the woman's page of the *Guardian*. You and I, Tony, need have no secrets from Mizz Probert. Now, what was this comparison your wife made between you and Peanuts Molloy?'

'On the topic of virility. I'm sorry, miss.'

'That's quite all right.' Liz Probert was unshocked and unamused.

'What we need, I don't know if you would agree, Mr Rumpole,' Mr Bernard suggested, 'is a predominance of *men* on the jury.'

'Under-endowed males would condone the attempted murder of a woman, you mean?' The Probert hackles were up.

'Please. Mizz Probert.' I tried to call the meeting to order. 'Let us face this problem in a spirit of detachment. What we need is a sympathetic judge who doesn't want to waste his time on a long case. Have we got a fixed date for this, Mr Bernard?'

'We have, sir. Before the Red Judge.' Mr Bernard meant that Tony Timson was to be tried before the High Court judge visiting the Old Bailey.

'They're pulling out all the stops.' I was impressed.

'It *is* attempted murder, Mr Rumpole. So we're fixed before Mr Justice Featherstone.'

'Guthrie Featherstone.' I thought about it. 'Our one-time Head of Chambers. Now, I just wonder . . .'

We were in luck. Sir Guthrie Featherstone was in no mood to try a long case, so he summoned me and counsel for the prosecution to his room before the start of the proceedings. He sat robed but with his wig on the desk in front of him, a tall, elegant figure who almost always wore the slightly hunted expression of a man who's not entirely sure what he's up to – an unfortunate state of mind for a fellow who has to spend his waking hours coming to firm and just decisions. For all his indecision, however, he knew for certain that he didn't want to spend the whole day trying a ticklish attempted murder.

'Is this a long case?' the judge asked. 'I am bidden to take tea in the neighbourhood of Victoria. Can you fellows guess where?'

'Sorry, Judge. I give up.' Charles Hearthstoke, our serious-minded young prosecutor, seemed in no mood for party games.

'The station buffet?' I hazarded a guess.

'The station buffet!' Guthrie enjoyed the joke. 'Isn't that you all over, Horace? You will have your joke. Not far off, though.' The joke was over and he went on impressively. 'Buck House. Her Majesty has invited me – no, correction – "commanded" me to a Royal Garden Party.'

'God Save the Queen!' I murmured loyally.

'Not only Her Majesty,' Guthrie told us, 'more seriously one's lady wife, would be extremely put out if one didn't parade in grey top-hat order!'

'He's blaming it on his wife!' Liz Probert, who had followed me into the presence, said in a penetrating aside.

'So naturally one would have to be free by lunch-time. Hearthstoke, is this a long case from the prosecution point of view?' the judge asked.

'It is an extremely serious case, Judge.' Our prosecutor spoke like a man of twice his years. 'Attempted murder. We've put it down for a week.' I have always thought young Charlie Hearthstoke a megasized pill ever since he joined our Chambers for a blessedly brief period and tried to get everything run by a computer.

'I'm astonished', I gave Guthrie a little comfort, 'that my learned friend Mr Hearthrug should think it could possibly last so long.'

'Hearth*stoke*,' young Charlie corrected me.

'Have it your own way. With a bit of common sense we could finish this in half an hour.'

'Thereby saving public time and money.' Hope sprang eternal in the judge's breast.

'Exactly!' I cheered him up. 'As you know, it is an article of my religion never to plead guilty. But, bearing in mind all the facts in this case, I'm prepared to advise Timson to put his hands up to common assault. He'll agree to be bound over to keep the peace.'

'Common assault?' Hearthstoke was furious. 'Binding over? Hold on a minute. He tried to drown her!'

'Judge.' I put the record straight. 'He was seated at the tap end of the bath. His wife, lying back comfortably in the depths, passed an extremely wounding remark about my client's virility.'

It was then I saw Mr Justice Featherstone looking at me, apparently shaken to the core. 'The *tap end*,' he gasped. 'Did you say he was seated at the *tap end*, Horace?'

'I'm afraid so, Judge.' I confirmed the information sorrowfully.

'This troubles me.' Indeed the judge looked extremely troubled. 'How does it come about that he was seated at the tap end?'

'His wife insisted on it.' I had to tell him the full horror of the situation.

'This woman insisted that her husband sat with his back squashed up against the taps?' The judge's voice rose in incredulous outrage.

'She made him sit in that position so he could rinse off her hair.'

'At the *tap end*?' Guthrie still couldn't quite believe it.

'Exactly so.'

'You're sure?'

'There can be no doubt about it.'

'Hearthrug . . . I mean, *stoke*. Is this one of the facts agreed by the prosecution?'

'I can't see that it makes the slightest difference.' The prosecution was not pleased with the course its case was taking.

'You can't see! Horace, was this conduct in any way typical of this woman's attitude to her husband?'

'I regret to say, entirely typical.'

'Rumpole . . . ' Liz Probert, appalled by the chauvinist chatter around her, seemed about to burst, and I calmed her with a quiet 'Shut up, mizz.'

'So you are telling me that this husband deeply resented the position in which he found himself.' Guthrie was spelling out the implications exactly as I had hoped he would.

'What married man wouldn't, Judge?' I asked mournfully.

'And his natural resentment led to a purely domestic dispute?'

'Such as might occur, Judge, in the best bathrooms.'

'And you are content to be bound over to keep the peace?' His Lordship looked at me with awful solemnity.

'Reluctantly, Judge,' I said after a suitable pause for contemplation, 'I would agree to that restriction on my client's liberty.'

'Liberty to drown his wife!' Mizz Probert had to be 'shushed' again.

'Hearth*stoke*.' The judge spoke with great authority. 'My compliments to those instructing you and in my opinion it would be a gross waste of public funds to continue with this charge of attempted murder. We should be finished by half-past eleven.' He looked at his watch with the deep satisfaction of a man who was sure that he would be among those present at the Royal Garden Party, after the ritual visit to Moss Bros to hire the grey topper and all the trimmings. As we left the sanctum, I stood aside to let Mizz Probert out of the door. 'Oh, no, Rumpole, you're a man,' she whispered with her fury barely contained. 'Men always go first, don't they?'

So we all went into Court to polish off *R.* v. *Timson* and to make sure that Her Majesty had the pleasure of Guthrie's presence over the tea and strawberries. I made a token speech in mitigation, something of a formality as I knew that I was pushing at an open door. Whilst I was speaking, I was aware of the fact that the judge wasn't giving me his full attention. That was reserved for a new young shorthand writer, later to become known to me as a Miss (not, I'm sure in her case, a Mizz) Lorraine Frinton. Lorraine was what I believe used to be known as a 'bit of an eyeful', being young, doe-eyed and clearly surrounded by her own special fragrance. When I sat down, Guthrie thanked me absent-mindedly and reluctantly gave up the careful perusal of Miss Frinton's beauty. He then proceeded to pass sentence on Tony Timson in a number of peculiarly ill-chosen words.

'Timson,' his Lordship began harmlessly enough. 'I have heard about you and your wife's habit of taking a bath together. It is not for this Court to say that communal bathing, in time of peace when it is not in the national interest to save water, is appropriate conduct in married life. *Chacun à son goût*, as a wise Frenchman once said.' Miss Frinton, the shorthand writer, looked hopelessly confused by the words of the wise Frenchman. 'What throws a flood of light on this case', the judge went on, 'is that you, Timson, habitually sat at the tap end of the bath. It seems you had a great deal to put up with. And your wife, she, it appears from the evidence, washed her hair in the more placid waters of the other end. I accept that this was a purely domestic dispute. For the common assault to which you have pleaded guilty you will be bound over to keep the peace . . . ' And the judge added the terrible words, ' . . . in the sum of fifty pounds.'

So Tony Timson was at liberty, the case was over and a furious Mizz Liz Probert banged out of Court before Guthrie was half-way out of the door. Catching up with her, I rebuked my learned junior. 'It's not in the best traditions of the Bar to slam out before the judge in any circumstances. When we've just had a famous victory it's quite ridiculous.'

'A famous victory.' She laughed in a cynical fashion. 'For men!'

'Man, woman or child, it doesn't matter who the client is. We did our best and won.'

'Because he was a man! Why shouldn't he sit at the tap end? I've got to do something about it!' She moved away purposefully. I called after her. 'Mizz Probert! Where're you going?'

'To my branch of the women's movement. The protest's got to be organised on a national level. I'm sorry, Rumpole. The time for talking's over.'

And she was gone. I had no idea, then, of the full extent of the tide which was about to overwhelm poor old Guthrie Featherstone, but I had a shrewd suspicion that his Lordship was in serious trouble.

The Featherstones' two children were away at university, and Guthrie and Marigold occupied a flat which Lady Featherstone found handy for Harrods, her favourite shopping centre, and a country cottage near Newbury. Marigold Featherstone was a handsome woman who greatly enjoyed life as a judge's wife and was full of that strength of character and quickness of decision his Lordship so conspicuously lacked. They went to the Garden Party together with three or four hundred other pillars of the Establishment: admirals, captains of industry, hospital matrons and drivers of the royal train. Picture them, if you will, safely back home with Marigold kicking off her shoes on the sofa and Guthrie going out to the hall to fetch that afternoon's copy of the *Evening Sentinel*, which had just been delivered. You must, of course, understand that I was not present at the scene or other similar scenes which are necessary to this narrative. I can only do my best to reconstruct it from what I know of subsequent events and what the participants told me afterwards. Any gaps I have been able to fill in are thanks to the talent for fiction which I have acquired during a long career acting for the defence in criminal cases.

'There might just be a picture of us arriving at the Palace.' Guthrie brought back the *Sentinel* and then stood in horror, rooted to the spot by what he saw on the front page.

'Well, then. Bring it in here.' Marigold, no doubt, called from her reclining position.

'Oh, there's absolutely nothing to read in it. The usual nonsense. Nothing of the slightest interest. Well, I think I'll go and have a bath and get changed.' And he attempted to sidle out of the room, holding the newspaper close to his body in a manner which made the contents invisible to his wife.

'Why're you trying to hide that *Evening Sentinel*, Guthrie?'

'Hide it? Of course I'm not trying to hide it. I just thought I'd take it to read in the bath.'

'And make it all soggy? Let me have it, Guthrie.'

'I told you . . . '

'Guthrie. I want to see what's in the paper.' Marigold spoke in an authoritative manner and her husband had no alternative but to hand it over, murmuring the while, 'It's completely inaccurate, of course.'

And so Lady Featherstone came to read, under a large photograph of his Lordship in a full-bottomed wig, the story which was being enjoyed by every member of the legal profession in the Greater London area. CARRY ON DROWNING screamed the banner headline. ṪAP-END JUDGE'S AMAZING DECISION. And then came the full denunciation:

> Wives who share baths with their husbands will have to be care-
> ful where they sit in the future. Because 29-year-old April Tim-
> son of Bexleyheath made her husband Tony sit at the tap end
> the judge dismissed a charge of attempted murder against him.
> 'It seems you had a good deal to put up with,' 55-year-old
> Mr Justice Featherstone told Timson, a 36-year-old window
> cleaner. 'This is male chauvinism gone mad,' said a spokes-
> person of the Islington Women's Organisation. 'There will be
> protests up and down the country and questions asked in Parlia-
> ment. No woman can sit safely in her bath while this judge con-
> tinues on the bench.'

'It's a travesty of what I said, Marigold. You know exactly what these Court reporters are. Head over heels in Guinness after lunch,' Guthrie no doubt told his wife.

'This must have been in the morning. We went to the Palace after lunch.'

'Well, anyway. It's a travesty.'

'What do you mean, Guthrie? Didn't you say all that about the tap end?'

'Well, I may just have mentioned the tap end. Casually. In passing. Horace told me it was part of the evidence.'

'Horace?'

'Rumpole.'

'I suppose he was defending.'

'Well, yes . . .'

'You're clay in the hands of that little fellow, Guthrie. You're a Red Judge and he's only a junior, but he can twist you round his little finger,' I rather hope she told him.

'You think Horace Rumpole led me up the garden?'

'Of course he did! He got his chap off and he encouraged you to say something monumentally stupid about tap ends. Not, I suppose, that you needed much encouragement.'

'This gives an entirely false impression. I'll put it right, Marigold. I promise you. I'll see it's put right.'

'I think you'd better, Guthrie.' The judge's wife, I knew, was not a woman to mince her words. 'And for heaven's sake try not to put your foot in it again.'

So Guthrie went off to soothe his troubles up to the neck in bath water and Marigold lay brooding on the sofa until, so she told Hilda later, she was telephoned by the Tom Creevey Diary Column on the *Sentinel* with an enquiry as to which end of the bath she occupied when she and her husband were at their ablutions. Famous couples all over London, she was assured, were being asked the same question. Marigold put down the instrument without supplying any information, merely murmuring to herself, 'Guthrie! What have you done to us now?'

Marigold Featherstone wasn't the only wife appalled by the judge's indiscretions. As I let myself in to our mansion flat in the Gloucester Road, Hilda, as was her wont, called to me from the living-room, 'Who's that?'

'I am thy father's spirit,' I told her in sepulchral tones.

> *'Doomed for a certain term to walk the night,*
> *And for the day confined to fast in fires,*
> *Till the foul crimes done in my days of nature*
> *Are burnt and purged away.'*

'I suppose you think it's perfectly all right.' She was, I noticed, reading the *Evening Sentinel.*

'What's perfectly all right?'

'Drowning wives!' She said in the unfriendliest of tones. 'Like puppies. I suppose you think that's all perfectly understandable. Well, Rumpole, all I can say is, you'd better not try anything like that with me!'

'Hilda! It's never crossed my mind. Anyway, Tony Timson didn't drown her. He didn't come anywhere near drowning her. It was just a matrimonial tiff in the bathroom.'

'Why should *she* have to sit at the tap end?'

'Why indeed?' I made for the sideboard and a new bottle of Pommeroy's plonk. 'If she had, and if she'd tried to drown him because of it, I'd have defended her with equal skill and success. There you are, you see. Absolutely no prejudice when it comes to accepting a brief.'

'You think men and women are entirely equal?'

'Everyone is equal in the dock.'

'And in the home?'

'Well, yes, Hilda. Of course. Naturally. Although I suppose some are born to command.' I smiled at her in what I hoped was a soothing manner, well designed to unruffle her feathers, and took my glass of claret to my habitual seat by the gas-fire. 'Trust me, Hilda,' I told her. 'I shall always be a staunch defender of women's rights.'

'I'm glad to hear that.'

'I'm glad you're glad.'

'That means you can do the weekly shop for us at Safeway's.'

'Well, I'd really love that, Hilda,' I said eagerly. 'I should regard that as the most tremendous fun. Unfortunately I have to earn the boring stuff that pays for our weekly shop. I have to be at the service of my masters.'

'Husbands who try to drown their wives?' she asked unpleasantly.

'And vice versa.'

'They have late-night shopping on Thursdays, Rumpole. It won't cut into your work-time at all. Only into your drinking-time in Pommeroy's Wine Bar. Besides which I shall be far too busy for shopping from now on.'

'Why, Hilda? What on earth are you planning to do?' I asked innocently. And when the answer came I knew the sexual revolution had hit Froxbury Mansions at last.

'Someone has to stand up for women's rights', Hilda told me, 'against the likes of you and Guthrie Featherstone. I shall read for the Bar.'

Such was the impact of the decision in *R. v. Timson* on life in the

Rumpole home. When Tony Timson was sprung from custody he was not taken lovingly back into the bosom of his family. April took her baths alone and frequently left the house tricked out in her skin-tight, wet-look trousers and the exotic halter-neck. When Tony made so bold as to ask where she was going, she told him to mind his own business. Vincent, the young hopeful, also treated his father with scant respect and, when asked where he was off to on his frequent departures from the front door, also told his father to mind his own business.

When she was off on the spree, April Timson, it later transpired, called round to an off-licence in neighbouring Morrison Avenue. There she met the notorious Peanuts Molloy, also dressed in alluring leather, who was stocking up from Ruby, the large black lady who ran the 'offey', with raspberry crush, Champanella, crème de cacao and three-star cognac as his contribution to some party or other. He and April would embrace openly and then go off partying together. On occasion Peanuts would ask her how 'that wally of a husband' was getting on, and express his outrage at the lightness of the sentence inflicted on him. 'Someone ought to give that Tony of yours a bit of justice,' was what he was heard to say.

Peanuts Molloy wasn't alone in feeling that being bound over in the sum of fifty pounds wasn't an adequate punishment for the attempted drowning of a wife. This view was held by most of the newspapers, a large section of the public, and all the members of the North Islington Women's Movement (Chair, Mizz Liz Probert). When Guthrie arrived for business at the judge's entrance of the Old Bailey, he was met by a vociferous posse of women, bearing banners with the following legend:

> WOMEN OF ENGLAND,
> KEEP YOUR HEADS ABOVE WATER.
> GET JUSTICE FEATHERSTONE SACKED.

As the friendly police officers kept these angry ladies at bay, Guthrie took what comfort he might from the thought that a High Court judge can only be dismissed by a bill passed through both Houses of Parliament.

Something, he decided, would have to be done to answer his many critics. So Guthrie called Miss Lorraine Frinton, the doe-eyed short-hand writer, into his room and did his best to correct the record of his ill-considered judgment. Miss Frinton, breathtakingly decorative as ever, sat with her long legs neatly crossed in the judge's armchair and tried to grasp his intentions with regard to her short-hand note. I reconstruct this conversation thanks to Miss Frinton's later recollection. She was, she admits, very nervous at the time because she thought that the judge had sent for her because she had, in some way, failed in her duties. 'I've been living in dread of someone pulling me up about my short-hand,' she confessed. 'It's not my strongest suit, quite honestly.'

'Don't worry, Miss Frinton,' Guthrie did his best to reassure her. 'You're in no sort of trouble at all. But you are a shorthand writer, of course you are, and if we could just get to the point when I passed sentence. Could you read it out?'

The beautiful Lorraine looked despairingly at her notebook and spelled out with great difficultly, 'Mr Hearthstoke has quite wisely . . . '

'A bit further on.'

'Jackie a saw goo . . . a wise Frenchman . . . ' Miss Frinton was decoding.

'*Chacun à son goût!*'

'I'm sorry, my Lord. I didn't quite get the name.'

'*Ça ne fait rien.*'

'How are you spelling that?' She was now lost.

'Never mind.' The judge was at his most patient. 'A little further on, Miss Frinton. Lorraine. I'm sure you and I can come to an agreement. About a full stop.'

After much hard work, his Lordship had his way with Miss Frinton's shorthand note, and counsel and solicitors engaged in the case were assembled in Court to hear, in the presence of the gentlemen of the Press, his latest version of his unfortunate judgment.

'I have had my attention drawn to the report of the case in *The Times*', he started with some confidence, 'in which I am quoted as saying to Timson, "It seems you had a great deal to put up with. And your wife, she, it appears from the evidence, washed her hair in the more placid waters", etc. It's the full stop that has been misplaced. I have checked this carefully with the learned shorthand writer and she agrees with me. I see her nodding her head.' He looked down at Lorraine who nodded energetically, and the judge smiled at her. 'Very well, yes. The sentence in my judgment in fact read "It seems you had a great deal to put up with, and your wife." Full stop! What I intended to convey, and I should like the Press to take note of this, was that both Mr and Mrs Timson had a good deal to put up with. At different ends of the bath, of course. Six of one and half a dozen of the other. I hope that's clear?' It was, as I whispered to Mizz Probert sitting beside me, as clear as mud.

The judge continued. 'I certainly never said that I regarded being seated at the tap end as legal provocation to attempted murder. I would have said it was one of the facts that the jury might have taken into consideration. It might have thrown some light on this wife's attitude to her husband.'

'What's he trying to do?' *sotto voce* Hearthstoke asked me.

'Trying to get himself out of hot water,' I suggested.

'But the attempted murder charge was dropped,' Guthrie went on.

'He twisted my arm to drop it,' Hearthstoke was muttering.

'And the entire tap end question was really academic', Guthrie told us, 'as Timson pleaded guilty to common assault. Do you agree, Mr Rumpole?'

'Certainly, my Lord.' I rose in my most servile manner. 'You gave him a very stiff binding over.'

'Have you anything to add, Mr Hearthstoke?'

'No, my Lord.' Hearthstoke couldn't very well say anything else, but when the judge had left us he warned me that Tony Timson had better watch his step in future as Detective Inspector Brush was quite ready to throw the book at him.

Guthrie Featherstone left Court well pleased with himself and instructed his aged and extremely disloyal clerk, Wilfred, to send a bunch of flowers, or, even better, a handsome pot plant to Miss Lorraine Frinton in recognition of her loyal services. So Wilfred told me he went off to telephone Interflora and Guthrie passed his day happily trying a perfectly straightforward robbery. On rising he retired to his room for a cup of weak Lapsang and a glance at the *Evening Sentinel*. This glance was enough to show him that he had achieved very little more, by his statement in open Court, than inserting his foot into the mud to an even greater depth.

BATHTUB JUDGE SAYS IT AGAIN screamed the headline. *Putting her husband at the tap end may be a factor to excuse the attempted murder of a wife.* 'Did I say that?' the appalled Guthrie asked old Wilfred who was busy pouring out the tea.

'To the best of my recollection, my Lord, yes.'

There was no comfort for Guthrie when the telephone rang. It was old Keith from the Chancellor's office saying that the Lord Chancellor, as Head of the Judiciary, would like to see Mr Justice Featherstone at the earliest available opportunity.

'A bill through the Houses of Parliament.' A stricken Guthrie put down the telephone. 'Would they do it to me, Wilfred?' he asked, but answer came there none.

'You do look, my clerk, in a moved sort, as if you were dismayed.' In fact, Henry, when I encountered him in the clerk's room, seemed distinctly rattled. 'Too right, sir. I am dismayed. I've just had Mrs Rumpole on the telephone.'

'Ah. She Who Must wanted to speak to me?'

'No, Mr Rumpole. She wanted to speak to me. She said I'd be clerking for her in the fullness of time.'

'Henry,' I tried to reassure the man, 'there's no immediate cause for concern.'

'She said as she was reading for the Bar, Mr Rumpole, to make sure women get a bit of justice in the future.'

'Your missus coming into Chambers, Rumpole?' Uncle Tom, our oldest and quite briefless inhabitant, was pursuing his usual hobby of making approach shots to the waste-paper basket with an old putter.

'Don't worry, Uncle Tom.' I sounded as confident as I could. 'Not in the foreseeable future.'

'My motto as a barrister's clerk, sir, is anything for a quiet life,' Henry outlined his philosophy. 'I have to say that my definition of a quiet life does not include clerking for Mrs Hilda Rumpole.'

'Old Sneaky MacFarlane in Crown Office Row had a missus who came into his Chambers.' Uncle Tom was off down Memory Lane. 'She didn't come in to practice, you understand. She came in to watch Sneaky. She used to sit in the corner of his room and knit during all his conferences. It seems she was dead scared he was going to get off with one of his female divorce petitioners.'

'Mrs Rumpole, Henry, has only just written off for a legal course in the Open University. She can't yet tell provocation from self defence or define manslaughter.' I went off to collect things from my tray and Uncle Tom missed a putt and went on with his story. 'And you know what? In the end Mrs MacFarlane went off with a co-respondent she'd met at one of these conferences. Some awful fellow, apparently, in black and white shoes! Left poor old Sneaky high and dry. So, you see, it doesn't do to have wives in Chambers.'

'Oh, I meant to ask you, Henry. Have you seen my Ackerman on *The Causes of Death*?' One of my best-loved books had gone missing.

'I think Mr Ballard's borrowed it, sir.' And then Henry asked, still anxious, 'How long do they take then, those courses at the Open University?'

'Years, Henry,' I told him. 'It's unlikely to finish during our lifetime.'

When I went up to Ballard's room to look for my beloved Ackerman, the door had been left a little open. Standing in the corridor I could hear the voices of those arch-conspirators, Claude Erskine-Brown and Soapy Sam Ballard, QC. I have to confess that I lingered to catch a little of the dialogue.

'Keith from the Lord Chancellor's office sounded *you* out about Guthrie Featherstone?' Erskine-Brown was asking.

'As the fellow who took over his Chambers. He thought I might have a view.'

'And have you? A view, I mean.'

'I told Keith that Guthrie was a perfectly charming chap, of course.' Soapy Sam was about to damn Guthrie with the faintest of praise.

'Oh, perfectly charming. No doubt about that,' Claude agreed.

'But as a judge, perhaps, he lacks judgment.'

'Which is a pretty important quality in a judge,' Claude thought.

'Exactly. And perhaps there is some lack of . . . '

'*Gravitas?*'

'The very word I used, Claude.'

'There was a bit of lack of *gravitas* in Chambers, too,' Claude remembered, 'when Guthrie took a shine to a temporary typist . . . '

'So the upshot of my talk with Keith was . . . '

'What was the upshot?'

'I think we may be seeing a vacancy on the High Court Bench.' Ballard passed on the sad news with great satisfaction. 'And old Keith was kind enough to drop a rather interesting hint.'

'Tell me, Sam?'

'He said they might be looking for a replacement from the same stable.'

'Meaning these Chambers in Equity Court?'

'How could it mean anything else?'

'Sam, if you go on the Bench, we should need another silk in Chambers!' Claude was no doubt licking his lips as he considered the possibilities.

'I don't see how they could refuse you.' These two were clearly hand in glove.

'There's no doubt Guthrie'll have to go.' Claude pronounced the death sentence on our absent friend.

'He comes out with such injudicious remarks.' Soapy Sam put in another drop of poison. 'He was just like that at Marlborough.'

'Did you tell old Keith that?' Claude asked and then sat open-mouthed as I burst from my hiding-place with 'I bet you did!'

'Rumpole!' Ballard also looked put out. 'What on earth have you been doing?'

'I've been listening to the Grand Conspiracy.'

'You must admit, Featherstone J. has made the most tremendous boo-boo.' Claude smiled as though he had never made a boo-boo in his life.

'In the official view,' Soapy Sam told me, 'he's been remarkably stupid.'

'He wasn't stupid.' I briefed myself for Guthrie's defence. 'As a matter of fact he understood the case extremely well. He came to a wise decision. He might have phrased his judgment more elegantly, if he hadn't been to Marlborough. And let me tell you something, Ballard. My wife, Hilda, is about to start a law course at the Open University. She is a woman, as I know to my cost, of grit and deter-mination. I expect to see her Lord Chief Justice of England before you get your bottom within a mile of the High Court Bench!'

'Of course you're entitled to your opinion.' Ballard looked tolerant. 'And you got your fellow off. All I know for certain is that the Lord Chancellor has summoned Guthrie Featherstone to appear before him.'

The Lord Chancellor of England was a small, fat, untidy man with steel-rimmed spectacles which gave him the schoolboy look which led to his nickname 'The Owl of the Remove'. He was given to fits of teasing when he would laugh aloud at his own jokes and unpre-dictable bouts of biting sarcasm during which he would stare at his victims with cold hostility. He had been, for many years, the captain of the House of Lords croquet team, a game in which his ruthless cunning found full scope. He received Guthrie in his large, comfort-ably furnished room overlooking the Thames at Westminster, where his long wig was waiting on its stand and his gold-embroidered purse and gown were ready for his procession to the Woolsack. Two years after this confrontation, I found myself standing with Guthrie at a Christmas party given in our Chambers to members past and pres-ent, and he was so far gone in *Brut* (not to say Brutal) Pommeroy's

Méthode Champenoise as to give me the bare bones of this historic encounter. I have fleshed them out from my knowledge of both characters and their peculiar habits of speech.

'Judgeitis, Featherstone,' I hear the Lord Chancellor saying. 'It goes with piles as one of the occupational hazards of the judicial profession. Its symptoms are pomposity and self-regard. It shows itself by unnecessary interruptions during the proceedings or giving utterance to private thoughts far, far better left unspoken.'

'I did correct the press report, Lord Chancellor, with reference to the shorthand writer.' Guthrie tried to sound convincing.

'Oh, I read that.' The Chancellor was unimpressed. 'Far better to have left the thing alone. Never give the newspapers a second chance. That's my advice to you.'

'What's the cure for judgeitis?' Guthrie asked anxiously.

'Banishment to a golf club where the sufferer may bore the other members to death with recollections of his old triumphs on the Western Circuit.'

'You mean, a bill through two Houses of Parliament?' The judge stared into the future, dismayed.

'Oh, that's quite unnecessary!' The Chancellor laughed mirthlessly. 'I just get a judge in this room and say, "Look here, old fellow. You've got it badly. Judgeitis. The Press is after your blood and quite frankly you're a profound embarrassment to us all. Go out to Esher, old boy," I say, "and improve your handicap. I'll give it out that you're retiring early for reasons of health." And then I'll make a speech defending the independence of the judiciary against scurrilous and unjustified attacks by the Press.'

Guthrie thought about this for what seemed a silent eternity and then said, 'I'm not awfully keen on golf.'

'Why not take up croquet?' The Chancellor seemed anxious to be helpful. 'It's a top-hole retirement game. The women of England are against you. I hear they've been demonstrating outside the Old Bailey.'

'They were only a few extremists.'

'Featherstone, all women are extremists. You must know that, as a married man.'

'I suppose you're right, Lord Chancellor.' Guthrie now felt his position to be hopeless. 'Retirement! I don't know how Marigold's going to take it.'

The Lord Chancellor still looked like a hanging judge, but he stood up and said in businesslike tones, 'Perhaps it can be postponed in your case. I've talked it over with old Keith.'

'Your right-hand man?' Guthrie felt a faint hope rising.

'Exactly.' The Lord Chancellor seemed to be smiling at some private joke. 'You may have an opportunity some time in the future, in the not-too-distant future, let us hope, to make your peace with the women of England. You may be able to put right what they regard as an injustice to one of their number.'

'You mean, Lord Chancellor, my retirement is off ?' Guthrie could scarcely believe it.

'Perhaps adjourned. *Sine die.*'

'Indefinitely?'

'Oh, I'm so glad you keep up with your Latin.' The Chancellor patted Guthrie on the shoulder. It was an order to dismiss. 'So many fellows don't.'

So Guthrie had a reprieve and, in the life of Tony Timson also, dramatic events were taking place. April's friend Chrissie was once married to Shaun Molloy, a well-known safe breaker, but their divorce seemed to have severed her connections with the Molloy clan and Tony Timson had agreed to receive and visit her. It was Chrissie who lived on their estate and had given the party before which April and Tony had struggled in the bath together; but it was at Chrissie's house, it seemed, that Peanuts Molloy was to be a visitor. So Tony's friendly feelings had somewhat abated, and when Chrissie rang the chimes on his front door one afternoon when April was out, he received her with a brusque 'What you want?'

'I thought you ought to know, Tony. It's not right.'

'What's not right?'

'Your April and Peanuts. It's not right.'

'You're one to talk, aren't you, Chrissie? April was going round yours to meet Peanuts at a party.'

'He just keeps on coming to mine. I don't invite him. Got no time for Peanuts, quite honestly. But him and your April. They're going out on dates. It's not right. I thought you ought to know.'

'What you mean, dates?' As I have said, Tony's life had not been a bed of roses since his return home, but now he was more than usually troubled.

'He takes her out partying. They're meeting tonight round the offey in Morrison Avenue. Nine thirty time, she told me. Just thought you might like to know, that's all,' the kindly Chrissie added.

So it happened that at nine thirty that night, when Ruby was presiding over an empty off-licence in Morrison Avenue, Tony Timson entered it and stood apparently surveying the tempting bottles on

display but really waiting to confront the errant April and Peanuts
Molloy. He heard a door bang in some private area behind Ruby's
counter and then the strip lights stopped humming and the off-
licence was plunged into darkness. It was not a silent darkness, however; it was filled with the sound of footsteps, scuffling and heavy
blows.

Not long afterwards a police car with a wailing siren was screaming
towards Morrison Avenue; it was wonderful with what rapidity the
Old Bill was summoned whenever Tony Timson was in trouble.
When Detective Inspector Brush and his sergeant got into the off-
licence, their torches illuminated a scene of violence. Two bodies

were on the floor. Ruby was lying by the counter, unconscious, and
Tony was lying beside some shelves, nearer to the door, with a wound
in his forehead. The sergeant's torch beam showed a heavy cosh lying
by his right hand and pound notes scattered around him. 'Can't you
leave the women alone, boy?' the detective inspector said as Tony
Timson slowly opened his eyes.

So another Timson brief came to Rumpole, and Mr Justice Featherstone got a chance to redeem himself in the eyes of the Lord Chancellor and the women of Islington.

Like two knights of old approaching each other for combat, briefs at the ready, helmeted with wigs and armoured with gowns, the young black-haired Sir Hearthrug and the cunning old Sir Horace, with his faithful page Mizz Liz in attendance, met outside Number One Court at the Old Bailey and threw down their challenges.

'Nemesis,' said Hearthrug.

'What's that meant to mean?' I asked him.

'Timson's for it now.'

'Let's hope justice will be done,' I said piously.

'Guthrie's not going to make the same mistake twice.'

'Mr Justice Featherstone's a wise and upright judge,' I told him, 'even if his foot does get into his mouth occasionally.'

'He's a judge with the Lord Chancellor's beady eye upon him, Rumpole.'

'I wasn't aware that this case was going to be decided by the Lord Chancellor.'

'By him and the women of England.' Hearthstoke smiled at Mizz Probert in what I hoped she found a revolting manner. 'Ask your learned junior.'

'Save your breath for Court, Hearthrug. You may need it.' So we moved on, but as we went my learned junior disappointed me by saying, 'I don't think Tony Timson should get away with it again.'

'Happily, that's not for you to decide,' I told her. 'We can leave that to the good sense of the jury.'

However, the jury, when we saw them assembled, were not a particularly cheering lot. For a start, the women outnumbered the men by eight to four and the women in question looked large and severe. I was at once reminded of the mothers' meetings that once gathered round the guillotine and I seemed to hear, as Hearthstoke opened the prosecution case, the ghostly click of knitting needles.

His opening speech was delivered with a good deal of ferocity and he paused now and again to flash a white-toothed smile at Miss Lorraine Frinton, who sat once more, looking puzzled, in front of her shorthand notebook.

'Members of the jury,' Hearthrug intoned with great solemnity. 'Even in these days, when we are constantly sickened by crimes of violence, this is a particularly horrible and distressing event. An attack with this dangerous weapon' – here he picked up the cosh,

Exhibit One, and waved it at the jury – 'upon a weak and defenceless woman.'

'Did you say a *woman*, Mr Hearthstoke?' Up spoke the anxious figure of the Red Judge upon the Bench. I cannot believe that pure chance had selected Guthrie Featherstone to preside over Tony Timson's second trial.

Our judge clearly meant to redeem himself and appear, from the outset, as the dedicated protector of that sex which is sometimes called the weaker by those who have not the good fortune to be married to She Who Must Be Obeyed.

'I'm afraid so, my Lord,' Hearthstoke said, more in anger than in sorrow.

'This man Timson attacked a *woman!*' Guthrie gave the jury the benefit of his full outrage. I had to put some sort of a stop to this so I rose to say, 'That, my Lord, is something the jury has to decide.'

'Mr Rumpole,' Guthrie told me, 'I am fully aware of that. All I can say about this case is that should the jury convict, I take an extremely serious view of any sort of attack on a woman.'

'If they were bathing it wouldn't matter,' I muttered to Liz as I subsided.

'I didn't hear that, Mr Rumpole.'

'Not a laughing matter, my Lord,' I corrected myself rapidly.

'Certainly not. Please proceed, Mr Hearth*stoke*.' And here his Lordship whispered to his clerk, Wilfred, 'I'm not having old Rumpole twist me round his little finger in *this* case.'

'Very wise, if I may say so, my Lord,' Wilfred whispered back as he sat beside the judge, sharpening his pencils.

'Members of the jury,' an encouraged Hearthstoke proceeded. 'Mrs Ruby Churchill, the innocent victim, works in an off-licence near the man Timson's home. Later we shall look at a plan of the premises. The prosecution does not allege that Timson carried out this robbery alone. He no doubt had an accomplice who entered by an open window at the back of the shop and turned out the lights. Then, we say, under cover of darkness, Timson coshed the unfortunate Mrs Churchill, whose evidence you will hear. The accomplice escaped with most of the money from the till. Timson, happily for justice, slipped and struck his head on the corner of the shelves. He was found in a half-stunned condition, with the cosh and some of the money. When arrested by Detective Inspector Brush he said, "You got me this time, then." You may think that a clear admission of guilt.' And now Hearthstoke was into his peroration. 'Too long, Members of the jury,' he said, 'have women suffered in our Courts. Too long have men seemed licensed to attack them. Your verdict in this case will be awaited eagerly and hopefully by the women of England.'

I looked at Mizz Liz Probert and I was grieved to note that she was receiving this hypocritical balderdash with starry-eyed attention. During the mercifully short period when the egregious Hearthrug had been a member of our Chambers in Equity Court, I remembered, Mizz Liz had developed an inexplicably soft spot for the fellow. I was pained to see that the spot remained as soft as ever.

Even as we sat in Number One Court, the Islington women were on duty in the street outside bearing placards with the legend JUS-TICE FOR WOMEN. Erskine-Brown and Soapy Sam Ballard passed these demonstrators and smiled with some satisfaction. 'Guthrie's in the soup again, Ballard,' Claude told his new friend. 'They're taking to the streets!'

Ruby Churchill, large, motherly, and clearly anxious to tell the truth, was the sort of witness it's almost impossible to cross-examine effectively. When she had told her story to Hearthstoke, I rose and felt the silent hostility of both judge and jury.

'Before you saw him in your shop on the night of this attack,' I asked her, 'did you know my client, Mr Timson?'

'I knew him. He lives round the corner.'

'And you knew his wife, April Timson?'

'I know her. Yes.'

'She's been in your shop?'

'Oh, yes, sir.'

'With her husband?'

'Sometimes with him. Sometimes without.'

'Sometimes without? How interesting.'

'Mr Rumpole. Have you many more questions for this unfortunate lady?' Guthrie seemed to have been converted to the view that female witnesses shouldn't be subjected to cross-examination.

'Just a few, my Lord.'

'Please. Mrs Churchill,' his Lordship gushed at Ruby. 'Do take a seat. Make yourself comfortable. I'm sure we all admire the plucky way in which you are giving your evidence. *As a woman.*'

'And as a woman,' I made bold to ask, after Ruby had been offered all the comforts of the witness-box, 'did you know that Tony Timson had been accused of trying to drown his wife in the bath? And that he was tried and bound over?'

'My Lord. How can that possibly be relevant?' Hearthrug arose, considerably narked.

'I was about to ask the same question.' Guthrie sided with the prosecution. 'I have no idea what Mr Rumpole is driving at!'

'Oh, I thought your Lordship might remember the case,' I said casually. 'There was some newspaper comment about it at the time.'

'Was there really?' Guthrie affected ignorance. 'Of course, in a busy life one can't hope to read every little paragraph about one's cases that finds its way into the newspapers.'

'This found its way slap across the front page, my Lord.'

'Did it really? Do you remember that, Mr Hearthstoke?'

'I think I remember some rather ill-informed comment, my Lord.' Hearthstoke was not above buttering up the Bench.

'Ill-informed. Yes. No doubt it was. One has so many cases before one . . . ' As Guthrie tried to forget the past, I hastily drew the witness back into the proceedings. 'Perhaps your memory is better than his Lordship's?' I suggested to Ruby. 'You remember the case, don't you, Mrs Churchill?'

'Oh, yes. I remember it.' Ruby had no doubt.

'Mr Hearthstoke. Are you objecting to this?' Guthrie was looking puzzled.

'If Mr Rumpole wishes to place his client's previous convictions before the jury, my Lord, why should I object?' Hearthstoke looked at me complacently, as though I were playing into his hands, and Guthrie whispered to Wilfred, 'Bright chap, this prosecutor.'

'And can you remember what you thought about it at the time?' I went on plugging away at Ruby.

'I thought Mr Timson had got away with murder!'

The jury looked severely at Tony, and Guthrie appeared to think I had kicked a sensational own goal. 'I suppose that was hardly the answer you wanted, Mr Rumpole,' he said.

'On the contrary, my Lord. It was exactly the answer I wanted! And having got away with it then, did it occur to you that someone . . . some avenging angel, perhaps, might wish to frame Tony Timson on this occasion?'

'My Lord. That is pure speculation!' Hearthstoke arose, furious, and I agreed with him. 'Of course it is. But it's a speculation I wish to put in the mind of the jury at the earliest possible opportunity.' So I sat down, conscious that I had at least chipped away at the jury's certainty. They knew that I should return to the possibility of Tony having been framed and were prepared to look at the evidence with more caution.

That morning two events of great pith and moment occurred in the case of the Queen against Tony Timson. April went shopping in Morrison Avenue and saw something which considerably changed her attitude. Peanuts Molloy and her friend Chrissie were coming out of the off-licence with a plastic bag full of assorted bottles. As Peanuts held his car door open for Chrissie they engaged in a passionate and public embrace, unaware that they were doing so in the full view of Mrs April Timson, who uttered the single word 'Bastard!' in the hearing of the young hopeful Vincent who, being on his school holidays, was accompanying his mother. The other important matter was that Guthrie, apparently in a generous mood as he saw a chance of re-establishing his judicial reputation, sent a note to me and Hearthstoke asking if we would be so kind as to join him, and the other judges sitting at the Old Bailey, for luncheon.

Guthrie's invitation came as Hearthstoke was examining Miss Sweating, the schoolmistress-like scientific officer, who was giving evidence as to the bloodstains found about the off-licence on the night of the crime. As this evidence was of some importance I should record that blood of Tony Timson's group was traced on the floor and on the corner of the shelf by which he had fallen. Blood of the same group as that which flowed in Mrs Ruby Churchill's veins was to be found on the floor where she lay and on the cosh by Tony's hand. Talk of blood groups, as you will know, acts on me like the smell of greasepaint to an old actor, or the cry of hounds to John Peel. I was pawing the ground and snuffling a little at the nostrils as I rose to cross-examine.

'Miss Sweating,' I began. 'You say there was blood of Timson's group on the corner of the shelf?'

'There was. Yes.'

'And from that you assumed that he had hit his head against the shelf?'

'That seemed the natural assumption. He had been stunned by hitting his head.'

'Or by someone else hitting his head?'

'But the detective inspector told me . . . ' the witness began, but I interrupted her with 'Listen to me and don't bother about what the detective inspector told you!'

'Mr Rumpole!' That grave protector of the female sex on the Bench looked pained. 'Is that the tone to adopt? The witness is a woman!'

'The witness is a scientific officer, my Lord,' I pointed out, 'who pretends to know something about bloodstains. Looking at the photograph of the stains on the corner of the shelf, Miss Sweating, might not they be splashes of blood which fell when the accused was struck in that part of the room?'

Miss Sweating examined the photograph in question through her formidable horn-rims and we were granted two minutes' silence which I broke into at last with, 'Would you favour us with an answer, Miss Sweating? Or do you want to exercise a woman's privilege and not make up your mind?'

'Mr Rumpole!' The newly converted feminist judge was outraged. But the witness admitted, 'I suppose they might have got there like that. Yes.'

'They are consistent with his having been struck by an assailant. Perhaps with another weapon similar to this cosh?'

'Yes,' Miss Sweating agreed, reluctantly.

'Thank you. "Trip no further, pretty sweeting" . . . ' I whispered as I sat down, thereby shocking the shockable Mizz Probert.

'Miss Sweating' – Guthrie tried to undo my good work – 'you have also said that the bloodstains on the shelf are consistent with Timson having slipped when he was running out of the shop and striking his head against it?'

'Oh, yes,' Miss Sweating agreed eagerly. 'They are consistent with that, my Lord.'

'Very well.' His Lordship smiled ingratiatingly at the women of the jury. 'Perhaps the ladies of the jury would like to take a little light luncheon now?' And he added, more brusquely, 'The gentlemen too, of course. Back at five past two, Members of the jury.'

When we got out of Court, I saw my learned friend Charles Hearthstoke standing in the corridor in close conversation with the beautiful shorthand writer. He was, I noticed, holding her lightly and unobtrusively by the hand. Mizz Probert, who also noticed this, walked away in considerable disgust.

A large variety of judges sit at the Old Bailey. These include the Old Bailey regulars, permanent fixtures such as the Mad Bull Bullingham and the sepulchral Graves, judges of the lower echelon who wear black gowns. They also include a judge called the Common Sergeant, who is neither common nor a sergeant, and the recorder who wears red and is the senior Old Bailey judge – a man who has to face, apart from the usual diet of murder, robbery and rape, a daunting number of City dinners. These are joined by the two visiting High Court judges, the Red Judges of the Queen's Bench, of whom Guthrie was one, unless and until the Lord Chancellor decided to put him permanently out to grass. All these judicial figures trough together at a single long table in a back room of the Bailey. They do it, and the sight comes as something of a shock to the occasional visitor, wearing their wigs. The sight of Judge Bullingham's angry and purple face ingesting stew surmounted with horsehair is only for the strongest stomachs. They are joined by various City aldermen and officials wearing lace jabots and tailed coats and other guests from the Bar or from the world of business.

Before the serious business of luncheon begins, the company is served sherry, also taken whilst wearing wigs, and I was ensconced in a corner where I could overhear a somewhat strange preliminary conversation between our judge and counsel for the prosecution.

'Ah, Hearth*stoke*,' Guthrie greeted him. 'I thought I'd invite both counsel to break bread with me. Just want to make sure neither of you had anything to object to about the trial.'

'Of course not, Judge!' Hearthstoke was smiling. 'It's been a very pleasant morning. Made even more pleasant by the appearance of the shorthand writer.'

'The . . . ? Oh, yes! Pretty girl, is she? I hadn't noticed,' Guthrie fibbed.

'Hadn't you? Lorraine said you'd been extraordinarily kind to her. She so much appreciated the beautiful pot plant you sent her.'

'Pot plant?' Guthrie looked distinctly guilty, but Hearthstoke pressed on with 'Something rather gorgeous she told me. With pink blooms. Didn't she help you straighten out the shorthand note in the last Timson case?'

'She corrected her mistake,' Guthrie said carefully.

'*Her* mistake, was it?' Hearthstoke was looking at the judge. 'She said it'd been yours.'

'Perhaps we should all sit down now.' Guthrie was keen to end this embarrassing scene. 'Oh and, Hearthstoke, no need to mention that business of the pot plant around the Bailey. Otherwise they'll all be wanting one.' He gave a singularly unconvincing laugh. 'I can't give pink blooms to everyone, including Rumpole!'

'Of course, Judge.' Hearthstoke was understanding. 'No need to mention it at all *now*.'

'*Now?*'

'Now', the prosecutor said firmly, 'justice is going to be done to Timson. At last.'

Guthrie seemed thankful to move away and find his place at the table, until he discovered that I had been put next to him. He made the best of it, pushed one of the decanters in my direction and hoped I was quite satisfied with the fairness of the proceedings.

'Are *you* content with the fairness of the proceedings?' I asked him.

'Yes, of course. I'm the judge, aren't I?'

'Are you sure?'

'What on earth's that meant to mean?'

'Haven't you asked yourself why you, a High Court judge, a Red Judge, have been given a paltry little robbery with violence?' I refreshed myself with a generous gulp of the City of London's claret.

'I suppose it's the luck of the draw.'

'Luck of the draw, my eye! I detect the subtle hand of old Keith from the Lord Chancellor's office.'

'Keith?' His Lordship looked around him nervously.

'Oh, yes. "Give Guthrie *Timson*," he said. "Give him a chance to redeem himself by potting the fellow and sending him down for ten years. The women of England will give three hearty cheers and Featherstone will be the Lord Chancellor's blue-eyed boy again." Don't fall for it! You can be better than that, if you put your mind to it. Sum up according to the evidence and the hell with the Lord Chancellor's office!'

'Horace! I don't think I've heard anything you've been saying.'

'It's up to you, old darling. Are you a man or a rubber stamp for the Civil Service?'

Guthrie looked round desperately for a new subject of conversation and his eye fell on our prosecutor who was being conspicuously bored by an elderly alderman. 'That young Hearthstoke seems a pretty able sort of fellow,' he said.

'Totally ruthless,' I told him. 'He'd stop at nothing to win a case.'

'Nothing?'

'Absolutely nothing.'

Guthrie took the decanter and started to pour wine into his own glass. His hand was trembling slightly and he was staring at Hearthstoke in a haunted way.

'Horace,' he started confidentially, 'you've been practising at the Old Bailey for a considerable number of years.'

'Almost since the dawn of time.'

'And you can see nothing wrong with a judge, impressed by the hard work of a court official, say a shorthand writer, for instance, sending that official some little token of gratitude?'

'What sort of token are you speaking of, Judge?'

'Something like' – he gulped down wine – 'a pot plant.'

'A plant?'

'In a pot. With pink blossoms.'

'Pink blossoms, eh?' I thought it over. 'That sounds quite appropriate.'

'You can see nothing in any way improper in such a gift, Horace?' The judge was deeply grateful.

'Nothing improper at all. A "Busy Lizzie"?'

'I think her name's Lorraine.'

'Nothing wrong with that.'

'You reassure me, Horace. You comfort me very much.' He took another swig of the claret and looked fearfully at Hearthstoke. Poor old Guthrie Featherstone, he spent most of his judicial life painfully perched between the horns of various dilemmas.

'In the car after we arrested him, driving away from the off-licence, Tony Timson said, "You got me this time, then." ' This was the evidence of that hammer of the Timsons, Detective Inspector Brush. When he had given it, Hearthstoke looked hard at the jury to emphasise the point, thanked the officer profusely and I rose to cross-examine.

'Detective Inspector. Do you know a near neighbour of the Timsons named Peter, better known as "Peanuts", Molloy?'

'Mr Peter Molloy is known to the police, yes,' the inspector answered cautiously.

'He and his brother Greg are leading lights of the Molloy firm? Fairly violent criminals?'

'Yes, my Lord,' Brush told the judge.

'Have you known both Peanuts and his brother to use coshes like this one in the course of crime?'

'Well. Yes, possibly . . . '

'My Lord, I really must object!' Hearthstoke was on his feet and Guthrie said, 'Mr Rumpole. Your client's own character . . . '

'He is a petty thief, my Lord.' I was quick to put Tony's character before the jury. 'Tape-recorders and freezer-packs. No violence in his record, is there, Inspector?'

'Not up to now, my Lord,' Brush agreed reluctantly.

'Very well. Did you think he had been guilty of that attempted murder charge, after he and his wife quarrelled in the bathroom?'

'I thought so, yes.'

'You were called to the scene very quickly when the quarrel began.'

'A neighbour called us.'

'Was that neighbour a member of the Molloy family?'

'Mr Rumpole, I prefer not to answer that question.'

'I won't press it.' I left the jury to speculate. 'But you think he got off lightly at his first trial?' I was reading the note Tony Timson had scribbled in the dock while listening to the evidence as D. I. Brush answered, 'I thought so, yes.'

'What he actually said in the car was "I suppose you think you got me this time, then?" '

'No.' Brush looked at his notebook. 'He just said, "You got me this time, then." '

'You left out the words "I suppose you think" because you don't want him to get off lightly this time?'

'Now would I do a thing like that, sir?' Brush gave us his most honestly pained expression.

'That, Inspector Brush, is a matter for this jury to decide.' And the jury looked, by now, as though they were prepared to consider all the possibilities.

Lord Justice MacWhitty's wife, it seems, met Marigold Featherstone in Harrods, and told her she was sorry that Guthrie had such a terrible attitude to women. There was one old judge, apparently, who made his wife walk behind him when he went on Circuit, carrying the luggage, and Lady MacWhitty said she felt that poor Marigold was married to just such a tyrant. When we finally discussed the whole history of the Tony Timson case at the Chambers party, Guthrie told me that Marigold had said that she was sick and tired of women coming up to her and feeling sorry for her in Harrods.

'You see', Guthrie had said to his wife, 'if Timson gets off, the Lord Chancellor and all the women of England will be down on me like a ton of bricks. But the evidence isn't entirely satisfactory. It's just possible he's innocent. It's hard to tell where a fellow's duty lies.'

'Your duty, Guthrie, lies in keeping your nose clean!' Marigold had no doubt about it.

'My nose?'

'Clean. For the sake of your family. And if this Timson has to go inside for a few years, well, I've no doubt he richly deserves it.'

'Nothing but decisions!'

'I really don't know what else you expected when you became a judge.' Marigold poured herself a drink. Seeking some comfort after a hard day, the judge went off to soak in a hot bath. In doing so, I believe Lady Featherstone made it clear to him, he was entirely on his own.

Things were no easier in the Rumpole household. I was awakened at some unearthly hour by the wireless booming in the living-room

and I climbed out of bed to see Hilda, clad in a dressing-gown and hairnet, listening to the device with her pencil and notebook poised whilst it greeted her brightly with 'Good morning, students. This is first-year Criminal Law on the Open University. I am Richard Snellgrove, law teacher at Hollowfield Polytechnic, to help you on this issue ... Can a wife give evidence against her husband?'

'Good God!' I asked her, 'what time does the Open University open?'

'For many years a wife could not give evidence against her

husband,' Snellgrove told us. 'See *R.* v. *Boucher* 1952. Now, since the
Police and Criminal Evidence Act 1984, a wife can be called to give
such evidence.'

'You see, Rumpole.' Hilda took a note. 'You'd better watch out!' I
found and lit the first small cigar of the day and coughed gratefully.
Snellgrove continued to teach me law. 'But she can't be compelled to.
She has been a competent witness for the defence of her husband
since the Criminal Evidence Act 1898. But a judgment in the House
of Lords suggests she's not compellable . . . '

'What's that mean, Rumpole?' She asked me.

'Well, we could ask April Timson to give evidence for Tony. But
we couldn't make her,' I began to explain, and then, perhaps because
I was in a state of shock from being awoken so early, I had an idea of
more than usual brilliance. 'April Timson!' I told Hilda. 'She won't
know she's not compellable. I don't suppose she tunes into the
"Open at Dawn University". Now I wonder . . . '

'What, Rumpole. What do you wonder?'

'Quarter to six.' I looked at the clock on the mantelpiece. 'High
time to wake up Bernard.' I went to the phone and started to dial my
instructing solicitor's number.

'You see how useful I'll be to you' – Hilda looked extremely
pleased with herself – 'when I come to work in your Chambers.'

'Oh, Bernard,' I said to the telephone, 'wake you up, did I? Well,
it's time to get moving. The Open University's been open for hours.
Look, an idea has just crossed my mind . . . '

'It crossed *my* mind, Rumpole,' Hilda corrected me. 'And I was
kind enough to hand it on to you.'

When Mr Bernard called on April Timson an hour later, there was
no need for him to go into the nice legal question of whether she was a
compellable witness or not. Since she had seen Peanuts and her
friend Chrissie come out of the 'offey' she was, she made it clear,
ready and willing to come to Court and tell her whole story.

'Mrs April Timson,' I asked Tony's wife when, to the surprise of
most people in Court including my client, she entered the witness-
box, as a witness for the defence, 'some while ago you had a quarrel
with your husband in a bathtub. What was that quarrel about?'

'Peanuts Molloy.'

'About a man called Peter "Peanuts" Molloy. What did you tell
your husband about Peanuts?'

'About him as a man, like . . . ?'

'Did you compare the virility of these two gentlemen?'

'Yes, I did.' April was able to cope with this part of the evidence without embarrassment.

'And who got the better of the comparison?'

'Peanuts.' Tony, lowering his head, got his first look of sympathy from the jury.

'Was there a scuffle in your bath then?'

'Yes.'

'Mrs April Timson, did your husband ever try to drown you?'

'No. He never.' Her answer caused a buzz in Court. Guthrie stared at her, incredulous.

'Why did you suggest he did?' I asked. 'My Lord. I object. What possible relevance?' Hearthrug tried to interrupt but I and everyone else ignored him. 'Why did you suggest he tried to murder you?' I repeated.

'I was angry with him, I reckon,' April told us calmly, and the prosecutor lost heart and subsided. The judge, however, pursued the matter with a pained expression. 'Do I understand', he asked, 'you made an entirely false accusation against your husband?'

'Yes.' April didn't seem to think it an unusual thing to do.

'Don't you realise, madam,' the judge said, 'the suffering that accusation has brought to innocent people?' 'Such as you, old cock,' I muttered to Mizz Liz.

'What was that, Rumpole?' the judge asked me. 'Such as the man in the dock, my Lord,' I repeated.

'And other innocent, innocent people.' His Lordship shook his head sadly and made a note.

'After your husband's trial did you continue to see Mr Peanuts Molloy?' I went on with my questions to the uncompellable witness.

'We went out together. Yes.'

'Where did you meet?'

'We met round the offey in Morrison Avenue. Then we went out in his car.'

'Did you meet him at the off-licence on the night this robbery took place?'

'I never.' April was sure of it.

'Your husband says that your neighbour Chrissie came round and told him that you and Peanuts Molloy were going to meet at the off-licence at nine thirty that evening. So he went up there to put a stop to your affair.'

'Well, Chrissie was well in with Peanuts by then, wasn't she?' April smiled cynically. 'I reckon he sent her to tell Tony that.'

'Why do you reckon he sent her?'

Hearthstoke rose again, determined. 'My Lord, I must object,' he said. 'What this witness "reckons" is entirely inadmissible.' When he had finished, I asked the judge if I might have a word with my learned friend in order to save time. I then moved along our row and whispered to him vehemently, 'One more peep out of you, Hearthrug, and I lay a formal complaint on your conduct!'

'What conduct?' he whispered back.

'Trying to blackmail a learned judge on the matter of a pot plant sent to a shorthand writer.' I looked across at Lorraine. 'Not in the best traditions of the Bar, that!' I left him thinking hard and went back to my place. After due consideration he said, 'My Lord. On second thoughts, I withdraw my objection.'

Hearthstoke resumed his seat. I smiled at him cheerfully and continued with April's evidence. 'So why do you think Peanuts wanted to get your husband up to the off-licence that evening?'

'Pretty obvious, innit?'

'Explain it to us.'

'So he could put him in the frame. Make it look like Tony done Ruby up, like.'

'So he could put him in the frame. An innocent man!' I looked at the jury. 'Had Peanuts said anything to make you think he might do such a thing?'

'After the first trial.'

'After Mr Timson was bound over?'

'Yes. Peanuts said he reckoned Tony needed a bit of justice, like. He said he was going to see he got put inside. 'Course, Peanuts didn't mind making a bit hisself, out of robbing the offey.'

'One more thing, Mrs Timson. Have you ever seen a weapon like that before?'

I held up the cosh. The usher came and took it to the witness.

'I saw that one. I think I did.'

'Where?'

'In Peanuts' car. That's where he kept it.'

'Did your husband ever own anything like that?'

'What, Tony?' April weighed the cosh in her hand and clearly found the idea ridiculous. 'Not him. He wouldn't have known what to do with it.'

When the evidence was complete and we had made our speeches, Guthrie had to sum up the case of *R. v. Timson* to the jury. As he turned his chair towards them, and they prepared to give him their full attention, a distinguished visitor slipped unobtrusively into the back of the Court. He was none other than old Keith from the Lord Chancellor's office. The judge must have seen him, but he made no apology for his previous lenient treatment of Tony Timson.

'Members of the jury,' he began. 'You have heard of the false accusation of attempted murder that Mrs Timson made against an innocent man. Can you imagine, Members of the jury, what misery that poor man has been made to suffer? Devoted to ladies as he may be, he has been called a heartless "male chauvinist". Gentle and harmless by nature, he has been thought to connive at crimes of violence. Perhaps it was even suggested that he was the sort of fellow who would make his wife carry heavy luggage! He may well have been shunned in the streets, hooted at from the pavements, and the wife he truly loves has perhaps been unwilling to enter a warm, domestic bath with him. And then, consider', Guthrie went on, 'if the unhappy Timson may not have also been falsely accused in relation to the robbery with violence of his local "offey". Justice must be done, Members of the jury. We must do justice even if it means we do nothing else for the rest of our lives but compete in croquet competitions.' The judge was looking straight at Keith from the Lord Chancellor's office as he said this. I relaxed, lay back and closed my eyes. I knew, after all his troubles, how his Lordship would feel about a man falsely accused, and I had no further worries about the fate of Tony Timson.

When I got home, Hilda was reading the result of the trial in the *Evening Sentinel*. 'I suppose you're cock-a-hoop, Rumpole,' she said.

'Hearthrug routed!' I told her. 'The women of England back on our side and old Keith from the Lord Chancellor's office looking extremely foolish. And a miraculous change came over Guthrie.'

'What?'

'He suddenly found courage. It's something you can't do without, not if you concern yourself with justice.'

'That April Timson!' Hilda looked down at her evening paper. 'Making it all up about being drowned in the bath-water.'

'When lovely woman stoops to folly' – I went to the sideboard and poured a celebratory glass of Château Thames Embankment – 'And finds too late that men betray,/What charm can soothe her melancholy . . .'

'I'm not going to the Bar to protect people like her, Rumpole.' Hilda announced her decision. 'She's put me to a great deal of trouble. Getting up at a quarter to six every morning for the Open University.'

' "What art can wash her guilt away?" *What* did you say, Hilda?'

'I'm not going to all that trouble, learning Real Property and Company Law and eating dinners and buying a wig, not for the likes of April Timson.'

'Oh, Hilda! Everyone in Chambers will be extremely disappointed.'

'Well, I'm sorry.' She had clearly made up her mind. 'They'll just have to do without me. I've really got better things to do, Rumpole, than come home cock-a-hoop just because April Timson changes her mind and decides to tell the truth.'

'Of course you have, Hilda.' I drank gratefully. 'What sort of better things?'

'Keeping you in order for one, Rumpole. Seeing you wash up properly.' And then she spoke with considerable feeling. 'It's disgusting!'

'The washing up?'

'No. People having baths together.'

'Married people?' I reminded her.

'I don't see that makes it any better. Don't you ever ask me to do that, Rumpole.'

'Never, Hilda. I promise faithfully.' To hear, of course, was to obey.

That night's *Sentinel* contained a leading article which appeared under the encouraging headline BATHTUB JUDGE PROVED RIGHT. *Mrs April Timson,* it read, *has admitted that her husband never tried to drown her and the jury have acquitted Tony Timson on a second trumped-up charge. It took a judge of Mr Justice Featherstone's perception and experience to see through this woman's inventions and exaggerations and to uphold the law without fear or favour. Now and again the British legal system produces a judge of exceptional wisdom and integrity who refuses to yield to pressure groups and does justice though the heavens fall. Such a one is Sir Guthrie Featherstone.*

Sir Guthrie told me later that he read these comforting words whilst lying in a warm bath in his flat near Harrods. I have no doubt at all that Lady Featherstone was with him on that occasion, seated at the tap end.

Rumpole and the Bubble Reputation

It is now getting on for half a century since I took to crime, and I can honestly say I haven't regretted a single moment of it.

Crime is about life, death and the liberty of the subject; civil law is entirely concerned with that most tedious of all topics, money. Criminal law requires an expert knowledge of bloodstains, police-men's notebooks and the dark flow of human passion, as well as the argot currently in use round the Elephant and Castle. Civil law calls for a close study of such yawn-producing matters as bills of ex-change, negotiable instruments and charter parties. It is true, of course, that the most enthralling murder produces only a small and long-delayed Legal Aid cheque, sufficient to buy a couple of dinners at some Sunday supplement eatery for the learned friends who practise daily in the commercial courts. Give me, however, a sym-pathetic jury, a blurred thumbprint and a dodgy confession, and you can keep *Mega-Chemicals Ltd* v. *The Sunshine Bank of Florida* with all its fifty days of mammoth refreshers for the well-heeled bar-risters involved.

There is one drawback, however, to being a criminal hack; the judges and the learned friends are apt to regard you as though you were the proud possessor of a long line of convictions. How many times have I stood up to address the tribunal on such matters as the importance of intent or the presumption of innocence only to be stared at by the old darling on the Bench as though I were sporting a black mask or carrying a large sack labelled S W A G ? Often, as I walk through the Temple on my way down to the Bailey, my place of work, I have seen bowler-hatted commercial or revenue men pass by on the other side and heard them mutter, 'There goes old Rumpole. I wonder if he's doing a murder or a rape this morning?' The sad truth of the matter is that civil law is regarded as the Harrods and crime the Tesco's of the legal profession. And of all the varieties of civil action the most elegant, the smartest, the one which attracts the best barristers like bees to the honey-pot, is undoubtedly the libel action. Star in a libel case on the civilised stage of the High Court of Justice and fame and fortune will be yours, if you haven't got them already.

It's odd, isn't it? Kill a person or beat him over the head and remove his wallet, and all you'll get is an Old Bailey judge and an Old Bailey hack. Cast a well-deserved slur on his moral character, ridicule his nose or belittle his bank balance and you will get a High Court judge and some of the smoothest silks in the business. I can only remember doing one libel action, and after it I asked my clerk, Henry, to find me a nice clean assault or an honest break and entering. Exactly why I did so will become clear to you when I have revealed the full and hitherto unpublished details of *Amelia Nettleship* v. *The Daily Beacon and Maurice Machin*. If, after reading what went on in that particular defamation case, you don't agree that crime presents a fellow with a more honourable alternative, I shall have to think seriously about issuing a writ for libel.

You may be fortunate enough never to have read an allegedly 'historical' novel by that much-published authoress Miss Amelia Nettleship. Her books contain virginal heroines and gallant and gentlemanly heroes and thus present an extremely misleading account of our rough island story. She is frequently photographed wearing cotton print dresses, with large spectacles on her still pretty nose, dictating to a secretary and a couple of long-suffering cats in a wistaria-clad Tudor cottage somewhere outside Godalming. In the interviews she gives, Miss Nettleship invariably refers to the evils of the permissive society and the consequences of sex before marriage. I have never, speaking for myself, felt the slightest urge to join the permissive society; the only thing which would tempt me to such a course is hearing Amelia Nettleship denounce it.

Why, you may well ask, should I, whose bedtime reading is usually confined to *The Oxford Book of English Verse* (the Quiller-Couch edition), Archbold's *Criminal Law* and Professor Ackerman's *Causes of Death*, become so intimately acquainted with Amelia Nettleship? Alas, she shares my bed, not in person but in book form, propped up on the bosom of She Who Must Be Obeyed, alias my wife, Hilda, who insists on reading her far into the night. While engrossed in *Lord Stingo's Fancy*, I distinctly heard her sniff, and asked if she had a cold coming on. 'No, Rumpole,' she told me. 'Touching!'

'Oh, I'm sorry.' I moved further down the bed.

'Don't be silly. The book's touching. Very touching. We all thought Lord Stingo was a bit of a rake but he's turned out quite differently.'

'Sounds a sad disappointment.'

'Nonsense! It's ending happily. He swore he'd never marry, but Lady Sophia has made him swallow his words.'

'And if they were written by Amelia Nettleship I'm sure he found them extremely indigestible. Any chance of turning out the light?'

'Not yet. I've got another three chapters to go.'

'Oh, for God's sake! Can't Lord Stingo get on with it?' As I rolled over, I had no idea that I was soon to become legally involved with the authoress who was robbing me of my sleep.

My story starts in Pommeroy's Wine Bar to which I had hurried for medical treatment (my alcohol content had fallen to a dangerous low) at the end of a day's work. As I sipped my large dose of Château Thames Embankment, I saw my learned friend Erskine-Brown, member of our Chambers at Equity Court, alone and palely loitering. 'What can ail you, Claude?' I asked, and he told me it was his practice.

'Still practising?' I raised an eyebrow. 'I thought you might have got the hang of it by now.'

'I used to do a decent class of work,' he told me sadly. 'I once had a brief in a libel action. You were never in a libel, Rumpole?'

'Who cares about the bubble reputation? Give me a decent murder and a few well-placed bloodstains.'

'Now, guess what I've got coming up?' The man was wan with care.

'Another large claret for me, I sincerely hope.'

'Actual bodily harm and affray in the Kitten-A-Go-Go Club, Soho.' Claude is married to the Portia of our Chambers, the handsome Phillida Erskine-Brown, QC, and they are blessed with issue rejoicing in the names of Tristan and Isolde. He is, you understand, far more at home in the Royal Opera House than in any Soho Stripperama. 'Two unsavoury characters in leather jackets were duelling with broken Coca-Cola bottles.'

'Sounds like my line of country,' I told him.

'Exactly! I'm scraping the bottom of your barrel, Rumpole. I mean, you've got a reputation for sordid cases. I'll have to ask you for a few tips.'

'Visit the *locus in quo*,' was my expert advice. 'Go to the scene of the crime. Inspect the geography of the place.'

'The geography of the Kitten-A-Go-Go? Do I have to?'

'Of course. Then you can suggest it was too dark to identify anyone, or the witness couldn't see round a pillar, or . . . '

But at that point we were interrupted by an eager, bespectacled fellow of about Erskine-Brown's age who introduced himself as Ted Spratling from the *Daily Beacon*. 'I was just having an argument with my editor over there, Mr Rumpole,' he said. 'You do libel cases, don't you?'

'Good heavens, yes!' I lied with instant enthusiasm, sniffing a brief. 'The law of defamation is mother's milk to me. I cut my teeth on hatred, ridicule and contempt.' As I was speaking, I saw Claude Erskine-Brown eyeing the journalist like a long-lost brother. 'Slimey Spratling!' he hallooed at last.

'Collywobbles Erskine-Brown!' The hack seemed equally amazed. There was no need to tell me that they were at school together.

'Look, would you join my editor for a glass of Bolly?' Spratling invited me.

'What?'

'Bollinger.'

'I'd love to!' Erskine-Brown was visibly cheered.

'Oh, you too, Colly. Come on, then.'

'Golly, Colly!' I said as we crossed the bar towards a table in the corner. 'Bolly!'

So I was introduced to Mr Maurice – known as 'Morry' – Machin, a large silver-haired person with distant traces of a Scots accent, a blue silk suit and a thick gold ring in which a single diamond winked sullenly. He was surrounded with empty Bolly bottles and a master-ful-looking woman whom he introduced as Connie Coughlin, the features editor. Morry himself had, I knew, been for many years at the helm of the tabloid *Daily Beacon*, and had blasted many precious reputations with well-aimed scandal stories and reverberating 'revela-tions'. 'They say you're a fighter, Mr Rumpole, that you're a terrier, sir, after a legal rabbit,' he started, as Ted Spratling performed the deputy editor's duty of pouring the bubbly.

'I do my best. This is my learned friend, Claude Erskine-Brown, who specialises in affray.'

'I'll remember you, sir, if I get into a scrap.' But the editor's real business was with me. 'Mr Rumpole, we are thinking of briefing you. We're in a spot of bother over a libel.'

'Tell him', Claude muttered to me, 'you can't do libel.'

'I never turn down a brief in a libel action.' I spoke with confidence, although Claude continued to mutter, 'You've never been offered a brief in a libel action.'

'I don't care', I said, 'for little scraps in Soho. Sordid stuff. Give me a libel action, when a reputation is at stake.'

'You think that's important?' Morry looked at me seriously, so I treated him to a taste of *Othello*. ' "Good name in man or woman, dear my lord" ' (I was at my most impressive),

> *'Is the immediate jewel of their souls;*
> *Who steals my purse steals trash; 'tis something, nothing.*
> *'Twas mine, 'tis his, and has been slave to thousands;*
> *But he that filches from me my good name*
> *Robs me of that which not enriches him,*
> *And makes me poor indeed.'*

Everyone, except Erskine-Brown, was listening reverently. After I had finished there was a solemn pause. Then Morry clapped three times.

'Is that one of your speeches, Mr Rumpole?'

'Shakespeare's.'

'Ah, yes . . . '

'Your good name, Mr Machin, is something I shall be prepared to defend to the death,' I said.

'Our paper goes in for a certain amount of fearless exposure,' the *Beacon* editor explained.

'The "*Beacon* Beauties".' Erskine-Brown was smiling. 'I catch sight of it occasionally in the clerk's room.'

'Not that sort of exposure, Collywobbles!' Spratling rebuked his old school-friend. 'We tell the truth about people in the public eye.'

'Who's bonking who and who pays,' Connie from features explained. 'Our readers love it.'

'I take exception to that, Connie. I really do,' Morry said piously. 'I don't want Mr Rumpole to get the idea that we're running any sort of a cheap scandal-sheet.'

'Scandal-sheet? Perish the thought!' I was working hard for my brief.

'You wouldn't have any hesitation in acting for the *Beacon*, would you?' the editor asked me.

'A barrister is an old taxi plying for hire. That's the fine tradition of our trade,' I explained carefully. 'So it's my sacred duty, Mr Morry Machin, to take on anyone in trouble. However repellent I may happen to find them.'

'Thank you, Mr Rumpole.' Morry was genuinely grateful.

'Think nothing of it.'

'We are dedicated to exposing hypocrisy in our society. Wherever it exists. High or low.' The editor was looking noble. 'So when we find this female pretending to be such a force for purity and parading her morality before the Great British Public . . . '

'Being all for saving your cherry till the honeymoon,' Connie Coughlin translated gruffly.

'Thank you, Connie. Or, as I would put it, denouncing pre-marital sex,' Morry said.

'She's even against the *normal* stuff!' Spratling was bewildered.

'Whereas her own private life is extremely steamy. We feel it our duty to tell our public. Show Mr Rumpole the article in question, Ted.'

I don't know if they had expected to meet me in Pommeroy's but the top brass of the *Daily Beacon* had a cutting of the alleged libel at the ready. THE PRIVATE LIFE OF AMELIA NETTLESHIP BY BEACON GIRL ON THE SPOT, STELLA JANUARY I read, and then glanced at the story that followed. 'This wouldn't be *the* Amelia Nettleship?' I was beginning to warm to my first libel action. 'The expert bottler of pure historical bilge-water?'

'The lady novelist and hypocrite,' Morry told me. 'Of course I've never met the woman.'

'She robs me of my sleep. I know nothing of her morality, but her prose style depraves and corrupts the English language. We shall need a statement from this Stella January.' I got down to business.

'Oh, Stella left us a couple of months ago,' the editor told me.

'And went where?'

'God knows. Overseas, perhaps. You know what these girls are.'

'We've got to find her,' I insisted and then cheered him up with 'We shall fight, Mr Machin – Morry. And we shall conquer! Remember, I never plead guilty.'

'There speaks a man who knows damn all about libel.' Claude Erskine-Brown had a final mutter.

It might be as well if I quoted here the words in Miss Stella January's article which were the subject of legal proceedings. They ran as follows:

> Miss Amelia Nettleship is a bit of a puzzle. The girls in her historical novels always keep their legs crossed until they've got a ring on their fingers. But her private life is rather different. Whatever lucky young man leads the 43-year-old Amelia to the altar will inherit a torrid past which makes Mae West sound like Florence Nightingale. Her home, Hollyhock Cottage, near Godalming, has been the scene of one-night stands and longer liaisons so numerous that the neighbours have given up counting. There is considerably more in her jacuzzi than bath salts. Her latest Casanova, so far unnamed, is said to be a married man who's been seen leaving in the wee small hours.

From the style of this piece of prose you may come to the conclusion that Stella January and Amelia Nettleship deserved each other.

One thing you can say for my learned friend Claude Erskine-Brown is that he takes advice. Having been pointed in the direction of the Kitten-A-Go-Go, he set off obediently to find a cul-de-sac off Wardour Street with his instructing solicitor. He wasn't to know, and it was entirely his bad luck, that Connie Coughlin had dreamt up a feature on 'London's Square Mile of Sin' for the *Daily Beacon* and ordered an ace photographer to comb the sinful purlieus between Oxford Street and Shaftesbury Avenue in search of nefarious goings-on.

Erskine-Brown and a Mr Thrower, his sedate solicitor, found the Kitten-A-Go-Go, paid a sinister-looking myrmidon at the door ten quid each by way of membership and descended to a damp and darkened basement where two young ladies were chewing gum and removing their clothes with as much enthusiasm as they might bring to the task of licking envelopes. Claude took a seat in the front row and tried to commit the geography of the place to memory. It must be said, however, that his eyes were fixed on the plumpest of the

disrobing performers when a sudden and unexpected flash preserved his face and more of the stripper for the five million readers of the *Daily Beacon* to enjoy with their breakfast. Not being a particularly observant barrister, Claude left the strip joint with no idea of the ill luck that had befallen him.

Whilst Erskine-Brown was thus exploring the underworld, I was closeted in the Chambers of that elegant Old Etonian civil lawyer Robin Peppiatt, QC, who, assisted by his junior, Dick Garsington, represented the proprietor of the *Beacon*. I was entering the lists in the defence of Morry Machin, and our joint solicitor was an anxious little man called Cuxham, who seemed ready to pay almost any amount of someone else's money to be shot of the whole business. Quite early in our meeting, almost as soon, in fact, as Peppiatt had poured Earl Grey into thin china cups and handed round the *petit' beurres*, it became clear that everyone wanted to do a deal with the other side except my good self and my client, the editor.

'We should work as a team,' Peppiatt started. 'Of which, as leading counsel, I am, I suppose, the captain.'

'Are we playing cricket, old chap?' I ventured to ask him.

'If we were it would be an extremely expensive game for the *Beacon*.' The QC gave me a tolerant smile. 'The proprietors have contracted to indemnify the editor against any libel damages.'

'I insisted on that when I took the job,' Morry told us with considerable satisfaction.

'Very sensible of your client, no doubt, Rumpole. Now, you may not be used to this type of case as you're one of the criminal boys . . .'

'Oh, I know' – I admitted the charge – 'I'm just a juvenile delinquent.'

'But it's obvious to me that we mustn't attempt to justify these serious charges against Miss Nettleship's honour.' The captain of the team gave his orders and I made bold to ask, 'Wouldn't that be cricket?'

'If we try to prove she's a sort of amateur tart the jury might bump the damages up to two or three hundred grand,' Peppiatt explained as patiently as he could.

'Or four.' Dick Garsington shook his head sadly. 'Or perhaps half a million.' Mr Cuxham's mind boggled.

'But you've filed a defence alleging that the article's a true bill.' I failed to follow the drift of these faint-hearts.

'That's our bargaining counter.' Peppiatt spoke to me very slowly, as though to a child of limited intelligence.

'Our what?'

'Something to give away. As part of the deal.'

'When we agree terms with the other side we'll abandon all our allegations. Gracefully,' Garsington added.

'We put up our hands?' I contemptuously tipped ash from my small cigar on to Peppiatt's Axminster. Dick Garsington was sent off to get 'an ashtray for Rumpole'.

'Peregrine Landseer's agin us.' Peppiatt seemed to be bringing glad tidings of great joy to all of us. 'I'm lunching with Perry at the Sheridan Club to discuss another matter. I'll just whisper the thought of a quiet little settlement into his ear.'

'Whisper sweet nothings!' I told him. 'I'll not be party to any settlement. I'm determined to defend the good name of my client Mr Maurice Machin as a responsible editor.'

'At our expense?' Peppiatt looked displeased.

'If necessary. Yes! He wouldn't have published that story unless there was some truth in it. Would you?' I asked Morry, assailed by some doubt.

'Certainly not' – my client assured me – 'as a fair and responsible journalist.'

'The trouble is that there's no evidence that Miss Nettleship has done any of these things.' Clearly Mr Cuxham had long since thrown in the towel.

'Then we must find some! Isn't that what solicitors are for?' I asked, but didn't expect an answer. 'I'm quite unable to believe that anyone who writes so badly hasn't got *some* other vices.'

A few days later I entered the clerk's room of our Chambers in Equity Court to see our clerk, Henry, seated at his desk looking at the centre pages of the *Daily Beacon*, which Dianne, our fearless but somewhat hit-and-miss typist, was showing him. As I approached, Dianne folded the paper, retreated to her desk and began to type furiously. They both straightened their faces and the smiles of astonishment I had noticed when I came in were replaced by looks of legal seriousness. In fact Henry spoke with almost religious awe when he handed me my brief in *Nettleship* v. *The Daily Beacon and anor.* Not only was a highly satisfactory fee marked on the front but refreshers, that is the sum required to keep a barrister on his feet and talking, had been agreed at no less than five hundred pounds a day.

'You *can* make the case last, can't you, Mr Rumpole?' Henry asked with understandable concern.

'Make it last?' I reassured him. 'I can make it stretch on till the trump of doom! We have serious and lengthy allegations, Henry. Allegations that will take days and days, with any luck. For the first time in a long career at the Bar I begin to see . . . '

'See what, Mr Rumpole?'

'A way of providing for my old age.'

The door then opened to admit Claude Erskine-Brown. Dianne and Henry regarded him with a solemn pity, as though he'd had a death in his family.

'Here comes the poor old criminal lawyer,' I greeted him. 'Any more problems with your affray, Claude?'

'All under control, Rumpole. Thank you very much. Morning, Dianne. Morning, Henry.' Our clerk and secretary returned his greeting in mournful voices. At that point, Erskine-Brown noticed Dianne's copy of the *Beacon*, wondered who the 'Beauty' of that day might be, and picked it up before she could stop him.

'What've you got there? The *Beacon*! A fine crusading paper. Tells the truth without fear or favour.' My refreshers had put me in a remarkably good mood. 'Are you feeling quite well, Claude?'

Erskine-Brown was holding the paper in trembling hands and had gone extremely pale. He looked at me with accusing eyes and managed to say in strangled tones, '*You* told me to go there!'

'For God's sake, Claude! Told you to go where?'

'The *locus in quo*!'

I took the *Beacon* from him and saw the cause of his immediate concern. The *locus in quo* was the Kitten-A-Go-Go, and the blown-up snap on the centre page showed Claude closely inspecting a young lady who was waving her underclothes triumphantly over her head. At that moment, Henry's telephone rang and he announced that Soapy Sam Ballard, our puritanical Head of Chambers, founder member of the Lawyers As Christians Society (LAC) and the Savonarola of Equity Court, wished to see Mr Erskine-Brown in his room without delay. Claude left us with the air of a man climbing up into the dock to receive a stiff but inevitable sentence.

I wasn't, of course, present in the Head of Chambers' room where Claude was hauled up. It was not until months later, when he had recovered a certain calm, that he was able to tell me how the embarrassing meeting went and I reconstruct the occasion for the purpose of this narrative.

'You wanted to see me, Ballard?' Claude started to babble. 'You're looking well. In wonderful form. I don't remember when I've seen you looking so fit.' At that early stage he tried to make his escape from the room. 'Well, nice to chat. I've got a summons, across the road.'

'Just a minute!' Ballard called him back. 'I don't read the *Daily Beacon*.'

'Oh, don't you? Very wise,' Claude congratulated him. 'Neither do I. Terrible rag. Half-clad beauties on page four and no law reports. So they tell me. Absolutely no reason to bother with the thing!'

'But, coming out of the Temple tube station, Mr Justice Fishwick pushed this in my face.' Soapy Sam lifted the fatal newspaper from his desk. 'It seems he's just remarried and his new wife takes in the *Daily Beacon*.'

'How odd!'

'What's odd?'

'A judge's wife. Reading the *Beacon*.'

'Hugh Fishwick married his cook,' Ballard told him in solemn tones.

'Really? I didn't know. Well, that explains it. But I don't see why he should push it in your face, Ballard.'

'Because he thought I ought to see it.'

'Nothing in that rag could be of the slightest interest to you, surely?'

'Something is.'

'What?'

'You.'

Ballard held out the paper to Erskine-Brown, who approached it gingerly and took a quick look.

'Oh, really? Good heavens! Is that me?'

'Unless you have a twin brother masquerading as yourself. You feature in an article on "London's Square Mile of Sin".'

'It's all a complete misunderstanding!' Claude assured our leader.

'I'm glad to hear it.'

'I can explain everything.'

'I hope so.'

'You see, I got into this affray.'

'You got into what?' Ballard saw even more cause for concern.

'This fight' – Claude wasn't improving his case – 'in the Kitten-A-Go-Go.'

'Perhaps I ought to warn you, Erskine-Brown.' Ballard was being judicial. 'You needn't answer incriminating questions.'

'No, *I* didn't get into a fight.' Claude was clearly rattled. 'Good heavens, no. I'm doing a case, about a fight. An affray. With Coca-Cola bottles. And Rumpole advised me to go to this club.'

'Horace Rumpole is an *habitué* of this house of ill repute? At *his* age?' Ballard didn't seem to be in the least surprised to hear it.

'No, not at all. But he said I ought to take a view. Of the scene of the crime. This wretched scandal-sheet puts the whole matter in the wrong light. Entirely.'

There was a long and not entirely friendly pause before Ballard proceeded to judgment. 'If that is so, Erskine-Brown,' he said, 'and I make no further comment while the matter is *sub judice*, you will no doubt be suing the *Daily Beacon* for libel?'

'You think I should?' Claude began to count the cost of such an action.

'It is quite clearly your duty. To protect your own reputation and the reputation of this Chambers.'

'Wouldn't it be rather expensive?' I can imagine Claude gulping, but Ballard was merciless.

'What is money', he said, 'compared to the hitherto unsullied name of Number three, Equity Court?'

Claude's next move was to seek out the friend of his boyhood, 'Slimey' Spratling, whom he finally found jogging across Hyde Park. When he told the *Beacon* deputy editor that he had been advised to issue a writ, the man didn't even stop and Erskine-Brown had to trot along beside him. 'Good news!' Spratling said. 'My edition seems to enjoy libel actions. Glad you liked your pic.'

'Of course I didn't like it. It'll ruin my career.'

'Nonsense, Collywobbles.' Spratling was cheerful. 'You'll get briefed by all the clubs. You'll be the strippers' QC.'

'However did they get my name?' Claude wondered.

'Oh, I recognised you at once,' Slimey assured him. 'Bit of luck, wasn't it?' Then he ran on, leaving Claude outraged. They had, after all, been at Winchester together.

When I told the helpless Cuxham that the purpose of solicitors was to gather evidence, I did so without much hope of my words stinging him into any form of activity. If evidence against Miss Nettleship were needed, I would have to look elsewhere, so I rang up that great source of knowledge 'Fig' Newton and invited him for a drink at Pommeroy's.

Ferdinand Isaac Gerald, known to his many admirers as 'Fig' Newton, is undoubtedly the best in the somewhat unreliable band of professional private eyes. I know that Fig is now knocking seventy; that, with his filthy old mackintosh and collapsing hat, he looks like a scarecrow after a bad night; that his lantern jaw, watery eye and the frequently appearing drip on the end of the nose don't make him an immediately attractive figure. Fig may look like a scarecrow but he's a very bloodhound after a clue.

'I'm doing civil work now, Fig,' I told him when we met in Pommeroy's. 'Just got a big brief in a libel action which should provide a bit of comfort for my old age. But my instructing solicitor is someone we would describe, in legal terms, as a bit of a wally. I'd be obliged if you'd do his job for him and send him the bill when we win.'

'What is it that I am required to do, Mr Rumpole?' the great detective asked patiently.

'Keep your eye on a lady.'

'I usually am, Mr Rumpole. Keeping my eye on one lady or another.'

'This one's a novelist. A certain Miss Amelia Nettleship. Do you know her works?'

'Can't say I do, sir.' Fig had once confessed to a secret passion for Jane Austen. 'Are you on to a winner?'

'With a bit of help from you, Fig. Only one drawback here, as in most cases.'

'What's that, sir?'

'The client.' Looking across the bar I had seen the little group from the Beacon round the Bollinger. Having business with the editor, I left Fig Newton to his work and crossed the room. Sitting myself beside my client I refused champagne and told him that I wanted him to do something about my learned friend Claude Erskine-Brown.

'You mean the barrister who goes to funny places in the afternoon? What're you asking me to do, Mr Rumpole?'

'Apologise, of course. Print the facts. Claude Erskine-Brown was in the Kitten-A-Go-Go purely in pursuit of his legal business.'

'I love it!' Morry's smile was wider than ever. 'There speaks the great defender. You'd put up any story, wouldn't you, however improbable, to get your client off.'

'It happens to be true.'

'So far as we are concerned' – Morry smiled at me patiently – 'we printed a pic of a gentleman in a pin-striped suit examining the goods on display. No reason to apologise for that, is there, Connie? What's your view, Ted?'

'No reason at all, Morry.' Connie supported him and Spratling agreed.

'So you're going to do nothing about it?' I asked with some anger.

'Nothing we *can* do.'

'Mr Machin.' I examined the man with distaste. 'I told you it was a legal rule that a British barrister is duty-bound to take on any client however repellent.'

'I remember you saying something of the sort.'

'You are stretching my duty to the furthest limits of human endurance.'

'Never mind, Mr Rumpole. I'm sure you'll uphold the best traditions of the Bar!'

When Morry said that I left him. However, as I was wandering away from Pommeroy's towards the Temple station, Gloucester Road, home and beauty, a somewhat breathless Ted Spratling caught up with me and asked me to do my best for Morry. 'He's going through a tough time.' I didn't think the man was entirely displeased by the news he had to impart. 'The proprietor's going to sack him.'

'Because of this case?'

'Because the circulation's dropping. Tits and bums are going out of fashion. The wives don't like it.'

'Who'll be the next editor?'

'Well, I'm the deputy now . . . ' He did his best to sound modest.

'I see. Look' – I decided to enlist an ally – 'would you help me with the case? In strict confidence, I want some sort of a lead to this Stella January. Can you find how her article came in? Get hold of the original. It might have an address. Some sort of clue . . . '

'I'll have a try, Mr Rumpole. Anything I can do to help old Morry.' Never had I heard a man speak with such deep insincerity.

The weather turned nasty, but, in spite of heavy rain, Fig Newton kept close observation for several nights on Hollyhock Cottage, home of Amelia Nettleship, without any particular result. One morning I entered our Chambers early and on my way to my room I heard a curious buzzing sound, as though an angry bee were trapped in the lavatory. Pulling open the door, I detected Erskine-Brown plying a cordless electric razor.

'Claude,' I said, 'you're shaving!'

'Wonderful to see the workings of a keen legal mind.' The man sounded somewhat bitter.

'I'm sorry about all this. But I'm doing my best to help you.'

'Oh, please!' He held up a defensive hand. 'Don't try and do anything else to help me. "Visit the scene of the crime," you said. "Inspect the *locus in quo*!" So where has your kind assistance landed me? My name's mud. Ballard's as good as threatened to kick me out of Chambers. I've got to spend my life's savings on a speculative libel action. And my marriage is on the rocks. Wonderful what you can do, Rumpole, with a few words of advice. Your clients must be everlastingly grateful.'

'Your marriage, on the rocks, did you say?'

'Oh, yes. Philly was frightfully reasonable about it. As far as she was concerned, she said, she didn't care what I did in the afternoons. But we'd better live apart for a while, for the sake of the children. She didn't want Tristan and Isolde to associate with a father dedicated to the exploitation of women.'

'Oh, Portia!' I felt for the fellow. 'What's happened to the quality of mercy?'

'So, thank you very much, Rumpole. I'm enormously grateful. The next time you've got a few helpful tips to hand out, for God's sake keep them to yourself!'

He switched on the razor again. I looked at it and made an instant deduction. 'You've been sleeping in Chambers. You want to watch that, Claude. Bollard nearly got rid of me for a similar offence.'

'Where do you expect me to go? Phillida's having the locks changed in Islington.'

'Have you no friends?'

'Philly and I have reached the end of the line. I don't exactly want to advertise the fact among my immediate circle. I seem to remember, Rumpole, when you fell out with Hilda you planted yourself on us!' As he said this I scented danger and tried to avoid what I knew was coming.

'Oh. Now. Erskine-Brown. Claude. I was enormously grateful for your hospitality on that occasion.'

'Quite an easy run in on the Underground, is it, from Gloucester Road?' He spoke in a meaningful way.

'Of course. My door is always open. I'd be delighted to put you up, just until this mess is straightened out. But . . . '

'The least you could do, I should have thought, Rumpole.'

'It's not a sacrifice I could ask, old darling, even of my dearest friend. I couldn't ask you to shoulder the burden of daily life with She Who Must Be Obeyed. Now I'm sure you can find a very comfortable little hotel, somewhere cheap and cosy, around the British Museum. I promise you, life is by no means a picnic, in the Gloucester Road.'

Well, that was enough, I thought, to dissuade the most determined visitor from seeking hospitality under the Rumpole roof. I went about my daily business and, when my work was done, I thought I should share some of the good fortune brought with my brief in the libel action with She Who Must Be Obeyed. I lashed out on two bottles of Pommeroy's bubbly, some of the least exhausted flowers to be found outside the tube station and even, such was my reckless mood, lavender water for Hilda.

'All the fruits of the earth,' I told her. 'Or, let's say, the fruits of the first cheque in *Nettleship* v. *The Beacon*, paid in advance. The first of many, if we can spin out the proceedings.'

'You're doing that awful case!' She didn't sound approving.

'That awful case will bring us in five hundred smackers a day in refreshers.'

'Helping that squalid newspaper insult Amelia Nettleship.' She looked at me with contempt.

'A barrister's duty, Hilda, is to take on all comers. However squalid.'

'Nonsense!'

'What?'

'Nonsense. You're only using that as an excuse.'

'Am I?'

'Of course you are. You're doing it because you're jealous of Amelia Nettleship!'

'Oh, I don't think so,' I protested mildly. 'My life has been full of longings, but I've never had the slightest desire to become a lady novelist.'

'You're jealous of her because she's got high principles.' Hilda was sure of it. 'You haven't got high principles, have you, Rumpole?'

'I told you. I will accept any client, however repulsive.'

'That's not a principle, that's just a way of making money from the most terrible people. Like the editor of the *Daily Beacon*. My mind is quite made up, Rumpole. I shall not use a single drop of that corrupt lavender water.'

It was then that I heard a sound from the hallway which made my heart sink. An all-too-familiar voice was singing '*La donna e mobile*' in a light tenor. Then the door opened to admit Erskine-Brown wearing my dressing-gown and very little else. 'Claude telephoned and told me all his troubles.' Hilda looked at the man with sickening sympathy. 'Of course I invited him to stay.'

'You're wearing my dressing-gown!' I put the charge to him at once.

'I had to pack in a hurry.' He looked calmly at the sideboard. 'Thoughtful of you to get in champagne to welcome me, Rumpole.'

'Was the bath all right, Claude?' Hilda sounded deeply concerned.

'Absolutely delightful, thank you, Hilda.'

'What a relief! That geyser can be quite temperamental.'

'Which is your chair, Horace?' Claude had the courtesy to ask.

'I usually sit by the gas-fire. Why?'

'Oh, do sit there, Claude,' Hilda urged him and he gracefully agreed to pinch my seat. 'We mustn't let you get cold, must we. After your bath.'

So they sat together by the gas-fire and I was allowed to open champagne for both of them. As I listened to the rain outside the window my spirits, I had to admit, had sunk to the lowest of ebbs. And around five o'clock the following morning, Fig Newton, the rain falling from the brim of his hat and the drop falling off his nose, stood watching Hollyhock Cottage. He saw someone – he was too far away to make an identification – come out of the front door and get into a parked car. Then he saw the figure of a woman in a nightdress, no doubt Amelia Nettleship, standing in the lit doorway waving goodbye. The headlights of the car were switched on and it drove away.

When the visitor had gone, and the front door was shut, Fig moved nearer to the cottage. He looked down at the muddy track on which the car had been parked and saw something white. He stooped to pick it up, folded it carefully and put it in his pocket.

On the day that *Nettleship* v. *The Beacon* began its sensational course, I breakfasted with Claude in the kitchen of our so-called 'mansion' flat in the Gloucester Road. I say breakfasted, but Hilda told me that bacon and eggs were off as our self-invited guest preferred a substance, apparently made up of sawdust and bird

droppings, which he called muesli. I was a little exhausted, having
been kept awake by the amplified sound of grand opera from the
spare bedroom, but Claude explained that he always found that a little Wagner settled him down for the night. He then asked for some
of the goat's milk that Hilda had got in for him specially. As I coated
a bit of toast with Oxford marmalade, the man only had to ask for
organic honey to have it instantly supplied by She Who Seemed
Anxious to Oblige.

'And what the hell', I took the liberty of asking, 'is organic
honey?'

'The bees only sip from flowers grown without chemical fertilisers,' Claude explained patiently.

'How does the bee know?'

'What?'

'I suppose the other bees tell it. "Don't sip from that, old chap. It's
been grown with chemical fertilisers." '

So, ill-fed and feeling like a cuckoo in my own nest, I set off to the
Royal Courts of Justice, in the Strand, that imposing turreted château
which is the Ritz Hotel of the legal profession, the place where a gentleman is remunerated to the tune of five hundred smackers a day. It
is also the place where gentlemen prefer an amicable settlement to the
brutal business of fighting their cases.

I finally pitched up, wigged and robed, in front of the Court which
would provide the battleground for our libel action. I saw the combat-
ants, Morry Machin and the fair Nettleship, standing a considerable
distance apart. Peregrine Landseer, QC, counsel for the plaintiff, and
Robin Peppiatt, QC, for the proprietor of the *Beacon*, were meeting
on the central ground for a peace conference, attended by assorted
juniors and instructing solicitors.

'After all the publicity, my lady couldn't take less than fifty thousand.' Landseer, Chairman of the Bar Council and on the brink of
becoming a judge, was nevertheless driving as hard a bargain as any
second-hand car dealer.

'Forty and a full and grovelling apology.' And Peppiatt added
the bonus. 'We could wrap it up and lunch together at the
Sheridan.'

'It's steak and kidney pud day at the Sheridan,' Dick Garsington
remembered wistfully.

'Forty-five.' Landseer was not so easily tempted. 'And that's my
last word on the subject.'

'Oh, all right,' Peppiatt conceded. 'Forty-five and a full apology.
You happy with that, Mr Cuxham?'

'Well, sir. If you advise it.' Cuxham clearly had no stomach for the fight.

'We'll chat to the editor. I'm sure we're all going to agree' – Peppiatt gave me a meaningful look – 'in the end.'

While Landseer went off to sell the deal to his client, Peppiatt approached my man with 'You only have to join in the apology, Mr Machin, and the *Beacon* will pay the costs and the forty-five grand.'

' "Who steals my purse steals trash," ' I quoted thoughtfully. '"But he that filches from me my good name . . . " You're asking my client to sign a statement admitting he printed lies.'

'Oh, for heaven's sake, Rumpole!' Peppiatt was impatient. 'They gave up quoting that in libel actions fifty years ago.'

'Mr Rumpole's right.' Morry nodded wisely. 'My good name – I looked up the quotation – it's the immediate jewel of my soul.'

'Steady on, old darling,' I murmured. 'Let's not go *too* far.' At which moment Peregrine Landseer returned from a somewhat heated discussion with his client to say that there was no shifting her and she was determined to fight for every penny she could get.

'But Perry . . . ' Robin Peppiatt lamented, 'the case is going to take two weeks!' At five hundred smackers a day I could only thank God for the stubbornness of Amelia Nettleship.

So we went into Court to fight the case before a jury and Mr Justice Teasdale, a small, highly opinionated and bumptious little person who is unmarried, lives in Surbiton with a Persian cat, and was once an unsuccessful Tory candidate for Weston-super-Mare North. It takes a good deal of talent for a Tory to lose Weston-super-Mare North. Worst of all, he turned out to be a devoted fan of the works of Miss Amelia Nettleship.

'Members of the jury,' Landseer said in opening the plaintiff's case, 'Miss Nettleship is the authoress of a number of historical works.'

'Rattling good yarns, Members of the jury,' Mr Justice Teasdale chirped up.

'I beg your Lordship's pardon.' Landseer looked startled.

'I said "rattling good yarns", Mr Peregrine Landseer. The sort your wife might pick up without the slightest embarrassment. Unlike so much of the distasteful material one finds between hard covers today.'

'My Lord.' I rose to protest with what courtesy I could muster.

'Yes, Mr Rumbold?'

'Rum*pole*, my Lord.'

'I'm so sorry.' The judge didn't look in the least apologetic. 'I understand you are something of a stranger to these Courts.'

'Would it not be better to allow the jury to come to their own conclusions about Miss Amelia Nettleship?' I suggested, ignoring the Teasdale manners.

'Well. Yes. Of course. I quite agree.' The judge looked serious and then cheered up. 'And when they do they'll find she can put together a rattling good yarn.'

There was a sycophantic murmur of laughter from the jury, and all I could do was subside and look balefully at the judge. I felt a pang of nostalgia for the Old Bailey and the wild stampede of the mad Judge Bullingham.

As Peregrine Landseer bored on, telling the jury what terrible harm the *Beacon* had done to his client's hitherto unblemished reputation, Ted Spratling, the deputy editor, leant forward in the seat behind me and whispered in my ear. 'About that Stella January article,' he said. 'I bought a drink for the systems manager. The copy's still in the system. One rather odd thing.'

'Tell me . . . '

'The logon – that's the identification of the word processor. It came from the editor's office.'

'You mean it was written there?'

'No one writes things any more.'

'Of course not. How stupid of me.'

'It looks as if it had been put in from his word processor.'

'That is extremely interesting.'

'If Mr Rum*pole* has quite finished his conversation!' Peregrine Landseer was rebuking me for chattering during his opening speech.

I rose to apologise as humbly as I could. 'My Lord, I can assure my learned friend I was listening to every word of his speech. It's such a rattling good yarn.'

So the morning wore on, being mainly occupied by Landseer's opening. The luncheon adjournment saw me pacing the marble corridors of the Royal Courts of Justice with that great source of information, Fig Newton. He gave me a lengthy account of his observation on Hollyhock Cottage, and when he finally got to the departure of Miss Nettleship's nocturnal visitor, I asked impatiently, 'You got the car number?'

'Alas. No. Visibility was poor and weather conditions appalling.' The sleuth's evidence was here interrupted by a fit of sneezing.

'Oh, Fig!' I was, I confess, disappointed. 'And you didn't see the driver?'

'Alas. No, again.' Fig sneezed apologetically. 'However, when Miss Nettleship had closed the door and extinguished the lights, presumably in order to return to bed, I proceeded to the track in front of the house where the vehicle had been standing. There I retrieved an article which I thought might just possibly have been dropped by the driver in getting in or out of the vehicle.'

'For God's sake, show me!'

The detective gave me his treasure trove, which I stuffed into a pocket just as the usher came out of Court to tell me that the judge was back from lunch, Miss Nettleship was entering the witness-box, and the world of libel awaited my attention.

If ever I saw a composed and confident witness, that witness was Amelia Nettleship. Her hair was perfectly done, her black suit was perfectly discreet, her white blouse shone, as did her spectacles. Her features, delicately cut as an intaglio, were attractive, but her beauty was by no means louche or abundant. So spotless did she seem that she might well have preserved her virginity until what must have been, in spite of appearances to the contrary, middle age. When she had finished her evidence-in-chief the judge thanked her and urged her to go on writing her 'rattling good yarns'. Peppiatt then rose to his feet to ask her a few questions designed to show that her books were still selling in spite of the *Beacon* article. This she denied, saying that sales had dropped off. The thankless task of attacking the fair name of Amelia was left to Rumpole.

'Miss Nettleship,' I started off with my guns blazing, 'are you a truthful woman?'

'I try to be.' She smiled at his Lordship, who nodded encouragement.

'And you call yourself an historical novelist?'

'I try to write books which uphold certain standards of morality.'

'Forget the morality for a moment. Let's concentrate on the history.'

'Very well.'

One of the hardest tasks in preparing for my first libel action was reading through the works of Amelia Nettleship. Now I had to quote from Hilda's favourite. 'May I read you a short passage from an alleged historical novel of yours entitled *Lord Stingo's Fancy*?' I asked as I picked up the book.

'Ah, yes.' The judge looked as though he were about to enjoy a treat. 'Isn't that the one which ends happily?'

'Happily, all Miss Nettleship's books end, my Lord,' I told him. 'Eventually.' There was a little laughter in Court, and I heard Landseer whisper to his junior, 'This criminal chap's going to bump up the damages enormously.'

Meanwhile I started quoting from *Lord Stingo's Fancy*. ' "Sophia had first set eyes on Lord Stingo when she was a dewy eighteen-year-old and he had clattered up to her father's castle, exhausted from the Battle of Nazeby," ' I read. ' "Now at the ball to triumphantly celebrate the gorgeous, enthroning coronation of the Merry Monarch King Charles II they were to meet again. Sophia was now in her twenties but, in ways too numerous to completely describe, still an unspoilt girl at heart." You call that a *historical* novel?'

'Certainly,' the witness answered unashamed.

'Haven't you forgotten something?' I put it to her.

'I don't think so. What?'

'Oliver Cromwell.'

'I really don't know what you mean.'

'Clearly, if this Sophia . . . this girl . . . How do you describe her?'

' "Dewy", Mr Rumpole.' The judge repeated the word with relish.

'Ah, yes. "Dewy". I'm grateful to your Lordship. I had forgotten the full horror of the passage. If this dew-bespattered Sophia had been eighteen at the time of the Battle of Naseby in the reign of Charles I, she would have been thirty-three in the year of Charles II's coronation. Oliver Cromwell came in between.'

'I am an artist, Mr Rumpole.' Miss Nettleship smiled at my pettifogging objections.

'What kind of an artist?' I ventured to ask.

'I think Miss Nettleship means an artist in words,' was how the judge explained it.

'Are you, Miss Nettleship?' I asked. 'Then you must have noticed that the short passage I have read to the jury contains two split infinitives and a tautology.'

'A what, Mr Rumpole?' The judge looked displeased.

'Using two words that mean the same thing, as in "the enthroning coronation". My Lord, t a u . . . ' I tried to be helpful.

'I can *spell*, Mr Rumpole.' Teasdale was now testy.

'Then your Lordship has the advantage of the witness. I notice she spells Naseby with a "z".'

'My Lord. I hesitate to interrupt.' At least I was doing well enough to bring Landseer languidly to his feet. 'Perhaps this sort of cross-examination is common enough in the criminal courts, but I cannot see how it can possibly be relevant in an action for libel.'

'Neither can I, Mr Landseer, I must confess.' Of course the judge agreed.

I did my best to put him right. 'These questions, my Lord, go to the heart of this lady's credibility.' I turned to give the witness my full attention. 'I have to suggest, Miss Nettleship, that as an historical novelist you are a complete fake.'

'My Lord. I have made my point.' Landseer sat down then, looking well pleased, and immediately whispered to his junior, 'We'll let him go on with that line and they'll give us four hundred thousand.'

'You have no respect for history and very little for the English language.' I continued to chip away at the spotless novelist.

'I try to tell a story, Mr Rumpole.'

'And your evidence to this Court has been, to use my Lord's vivid expression, "a rattling good yarn"?' Teasdale looked displeased at my question.

'I have sworn to tell the truth.'

'Remember that. Now let us see how much of this article is correct.' I picked up Stella January's offending contribution. 'You do live at Hollyhock Cottage, near Godalming, in the county of Surrey?'

'That is so.'

'You have a jacuzzi?'

'She has *what*, Mr Rumpole?' I had entered a world unknown to a judge addicted to cold showers.

'A sort of bath, my Lord, with a whirlpool attached.'

'I installed one in my converted barn,' Miss Nettleship admitted. 'I find it relaxes me, after a long day's work.'

'You don't twiddle round in there with a close personal friend occasionally?'

'That's worth another ten thousand to us,' Landseer told his junior, growing happier by the minute. In fact the jury members were looking at me with some disapproval.

'Certainly not. I do not believe in sex before marriage.'

'And have no experience of it?'

'I was engaged once, Mr Rumpole.'

'Just once?'

'Oh, yes. My fiancé was killed in an air crash ten years ago. I think about him every day, and every day I'm thankful we didn't – ' she looked down modestly – 'do anything before we were married. We were tempted, I'm afraid, the night before he died. But we resisted the temptation.'

'Some people would say that's a very moving story,' Mr Justice Teasdale told the jury after a reverent hush.

'Others might say it's the story of *Sally on the Somme*, only there the fiancé was killed in the war.' I picked up another example of the Nettleship *oeuvre*.

'That, Mr Rumpole,' Amelia looked pained, 'is a book that's particularly close to my heart. At least I don't do anything my heroines wouldn't do.'

'He's getting worse all the time,' Robin Peppiatt, the *Beacon* barrister, whispered despairingly to his junior, Dick Garsington, who came back with 'The damages are going to hit the roof!'

'Miss Nettleship, may I come to the last matter raised in the article?'

'I'm sure the jury will be grateful that you're reaching the end, Mr Rumpole,' the judge couldn't resist saying, so I smiled charmingly and told him that I should finish a great deal sooner if I were allowed to proceed without further interruption. Then I began to read Stella January's words aloud to the witness. ' "Her latest Casanova, so far unnamed, is said to be a married man who's been seen leaving in the wee small hours." '

'I read that,' Miss Nettleship remembered.

'You had company last night, didn't you? Until what I suppose might be revoltingly referred to as "the wee small hours"?'

'What are you suggesting?'

'That someone was with you. And when he left at about five thirty in the morning you stood in your nightdress waving goodbye and blowing kisses. Who was it, Miss Nettleship?'

'That is an absolutely uncalled-for suggestion.'

'You called for it when you issued a writ for libel.'

'Do I have to answer?' She turned to the judge for help. He gave her his most encouraging smile and said that it might save time in the end if she were to answer Mr Rumpole's question.

'That is absolutely untrue!' For the first time Amelia's look of serenity vanished and I got, from the witness-box, a cold stare of hatred. 'Absolutely untrue.' The judge made a grateful note of her answer. 'Thank you, Miss Nettleship. I think we might continue with this tomorrow morning, if you have any further questions, Mr Rumpole?'

'I have indeed, my Lord.' Of course I had more questions and by the morning I hoped also to have some evidence to back them up.

★

I was in no hurry to return to the alleged 'mansion' flat that night. I rightly suspected that our self-invited guest, Claude Erskine-Brown, would be playing his way through *Die Meistersinger* and giving Hilda a synopsis of the plot as it unfolded. As I reach the last of a man's Seven Ages I am more than ever persuaded that life is too short for Wagner, a man who was never in a hurry when it came to composing an opera. I paid a solitary visit to Pommeroy's well-known watering-hole after Court in the hope of finding the representatives of the *Beacon*; but the only one I found was Connie Coughlin, the features editor, moodily surveying a large gin and tonic. 'No champagne tonight?' I asked as I wandered over to her table, glass in hand.

'I don't think we've got much to celebrate.'

'I wanted to ask you' – I took a seat beside the redoubtable Connie – 'about Miss Stella January. Our girl on the spot. Bright, attractive kind of reporter, was she?'

'I don't know,' Connie confessed.

'But surely you're the features editor?'

'I never met her.' She said it with the resentment of a woman whose editor had been interfering with her page.

'Any idea how old she was, for instance?'

'Oh, young, I should think.' It was the voice of middle age speaking. 'Morry said she was young. Just starting in the business.'

'And I was going to ask you . . .'

'You're very inquisitive.'

'It's my trade.' I downed what was left of my claret. ' . . . About the love life of Mr Morry Machin.'

'Good God. Whose side are you on, Mr Rumpole?'

'At the moment, on the side of the truth. Did Morry have some sort of a romantic interest in Miss Stella January?'

'Short-lived, I'd say.' Connie clearly had no pity for the girl if she'd been enjoyed and then sacked.

'He's married?'

'Oh, two or three times.' It occurred to me that at some time, during one or other of these marriages, Morry and La Coughlin might have been more than fellow hacks on the *Beacon*. 'Now he seems to have got some sort of steady girlfriend.' She said it with some resentment.

'You know her?'

'Not at all. He keeps her under wraps.'

I looked at her for a moment. A woman, I thought, with a lonely evening in an empty flat before her. Then I thanked her for her help and stood up.

'Who are you going to grill next?' she asked me over the rim of her gin and tonic.

'As a matter of fact,' I told her, 'I've got a date with Miss Stella January.'

Quarter of an hour later I was walking across the huge floor, filled with desks, telephones and word processors, where the *Beacon* was produced, towards the glass-walled office in the corner, where Morry sat with his deputy Ted Spratling, seeing that all the scandal that was fit to print, and a good deal of it that wasn't, got safely between the covers of the *Beacon*. I arrived at his office, pulled open the door and was greeted by Morry, in his shirtsleeves, his feet up on the desk. 'Working late, Mr Rumpole? I hope you can do better for us tomorrow,' he greeted me with amused disapproval.

'I hope so too. I'm looking for Miss Stella January.'

'I told you, she's not here any more. I think she went overseas.'

'I think she's here,' I assured him. He was silent for a moment and then he looked at his deputy. 'Ted, perhaps you'd better leave me to have a word with my learned counsel.'

'I'll be on the back bench.' Spratling left for the desk on the floor which the editors occupied.

When he had gone, Morry looked up at me and said quietly, 'Now then, Mr Rumpole, sir. How can I help you?'

'Stella certainly wasn't a young woman, was she?' I was sure about that.

'She was only with us a short time. But she was young, yes,' he said vaguely.

'A quotation from her article that Amelia Nettleship "makes Mae West sound like Florence Nightingale". No young woman today's going to have heard of Mae West. Mae West's as remote in history as Messalina and Helen of Troy. That article, I would hazard a guess, was written by a man well into his middle age.'

'Who?'

'You.'

There was another long silence and the editor did his best to smile. 'Have you been drinking at all this evening?'

'I took a seat then on the edge of his desk and lit a small cigar. 'Of course I've been drinking *at all*. You don't imagine I have these brilliant flashes of deduction when I'm perfectly sober, do you?'

'Then hadn't you better go home to bed?'

'So you wrote the article. No argument about that. It's been found in the system with your word processor number on it. Careless, Mr Machin. You clearly have very little talent for crime. The puzzling thing is, why you should attack Miss Nettleship when she's such a good friend of yours.'

'Good friend?' He did his best to laugh. 'I told you. I've never even met the woman.'

'It was a lie, like the rest of this pantomime lawsuit. Last night you were with her until past five in the morning. And she said goodbye to you with every sign of affection.'

'What makes you say that?'

'Were you in a hurry? Anyway, this was dropped by the side of your car.' Then I pulled out the present Fig Newton had given me outside Court that day and put it on the desk.

'Anyone can buy the *Beacon*.' Morry glanced at the mud-stained exhibit.

'Not everyone gets the first edition, the one that fell on the editor's desk at ten o'clock that evening. I would say that's a bit of a rarity around Godalming.'

'Is that all?'

'No. You were watched.'

'Who by?'

'Someone I asked to find out the truth about Miss Nettleship.

Now he's turned up the truth about both of you.'

Morry got up then and walked to the door which Ted Spratling had left half open. He shut it carefully and then turned to me. 'I went down to ask her to drop the case.'

'To use a legal expression, pull the other one, it's got bells on it.'

'I don't know what you're suggesting.'

And then, as he stood looking at me, I moved round and sat in the editor's chair. 'Let me enlighten you.' I was as patient as I could manage. 'I'm suggesting a conspiracy to pervert the course of justice.'

'What's that mean?'

'I told you I'm an old taxi, waiting on the rank, but I'm not prepared to be the get-away driver for a criminal conspiracy.'

'You haven't said anything? To anyone?' He looked older and very frightened.

'Not yet.'

'And you won't.' He tried to sound confident. 'You're my lawyer.'

'Not any longer, Mr Machin. I don't belong to you any more. I'm an ordinary citizen, about to report an attempted crime.' It was then I reached for the telephone. 'I don't think there's any limit on the sentence for conspiracy.'

'What do you mean, "conspiracy"?'

'You're getting sacked by the *Beacon*; perhaps your handshake is a bit less than golden. Sales are down on historical virgins. So your steady girlfriend and you get together to make half a tax-free million.'

'I wish I knew how.' He was doing his best to smile.

'Perfectly simple. You turn yourself into Stella January, the unknown girl reporter, for half an hour and libelled Amelia. She sues the paper and collects. Then you both sail into the sunset and share the proceeds. There's one thing I shan't forgive you for.'

'What's that?'

'The plan called for an Old Bailey hack, a stranger to the civilised world of libel who wouldn't settle, an old war-horse who'd attack La Nettleship and inflame the damages. So you used me, Mr Morry Machin!'

'I thought you'd be accustomed to that.' He stood over me, suddenly looking older. 'Anyway, they told me in Pommeroy's that you never prosecute.'

'No, I don't, do I? But on this occasion, I must say, I'm sorely tempted.' I thought about it and finally pushed away the telephone. 'Since it's a libel action I'll offer you terms of settlement.'

'What sort of terms?'

'The fair Amelia to drop her case. You pay the costs, including the fees of Fig Newton, who's caught a bad cold in the course of these proceedings. Oh, and in the matter of my learned friend Claude Erskine-Brown . . . '

'What's he got to do with it?'

' . . . Print a full and grovelling apology on the front page of the *Beacon*. And get them to pay him a substantial sum by way of damages. And that's my last word on the subject.' I stood up then and moved to the door.

'What's it going to cost me?' was all he could think of saying.

'I have no idea, but I know what it's going to cost me. Two weeks at five hundred a day. A provision for my old age.' I opened the glass door and let in the hum and clatter which were the birth-pangs of the *Daily Beacon*. 'Good-night, Stella,' I said to Mr Morry Machin. And then I left him.

So it came about that next morning's *Beacon* printed a grovelling apology to 'the distinguished barrister Mr Claude Erskine-Brown' which accepted that he went to the Kitten-A-Go-Go Club purely in the interests of legal research and announced that my learned friend's hurt feelings would be soothed by the application of substantial, and tax-free, damages. As a consequence of this, Mrs Phillida Erskine-Brown rang Chambers, spoke words of forgiveness and love to her husband, and he arranged, in his new-found wealth, to take her to dinner at Le Gavroche. The cuckoo flew from our nest, Hilda and I were left alone in the Gloucester Road, and we never found out how *Die Meistersinger* ended.

In Court my one and only libel action ended in a sudden outburst of peace and goodwill, much to the frustration of Mr Justice Teasdale, who had clearly been preparing a summing-up which would encourage the jury to make Miss Nettleship rich beyond the dreams of avarice. All the allegations against her were dropped; she had no doubt been persuaded by her lover to ask for no damages at all and the *Beacon*'s editor accepted the bill for costs with extremely bad grace. This old legal taxi moved off to ply for hire elsewhere, glad to be shot of Mr Morry Machin. 'Is there a little bit of burglary around, Henry?' I asked our clerk, as I have recorded. 'Couldn't you get me a nice little gentle robbery? Something which shows human nature in a better light than civil law?'

'Good heavens!' Hilda exclaimed as we lay reading in the matrimonial bed in Froxbury Mansions. I noticed that there had been a change in her reading matter and she was already well into *On the*

Make by Suzy Hutchins. 'This girl's about to go to Paris with a man old enough to be her father.'

'That must happen quite often.'

'But it seems he *is* her father.'

'Well, at least you've gone off the works of Amelia Nettleship.'

'The way she dropped that libel action. The woman's no better than she should be.'

'Which of us is? Any chance of turning out the light?' I asked She Who Must Be Obeyed, but she was too engrossed in the doings of her delinquent heroine to reply.

Rumpole à la Carte

I suppose, when I have time to think about it, which is not often during the long day's trudge round the Bailey and more down-market venues such as the Uxbridge Magistrates Court, the law represents some attempt, however fumbling, to impose order on a chaotic universe. Chaos, in the form of human waywardness and uncontrollable passion, is ever bubbling away just beneath the surface and its sporadic outbreaks are what provide me with my daily crust, and even a glass or two of Pommeroy's plonk to go with it. I have often noticed, in the accounts of the many crimes with which I have been concerned, that some small sign of disorder – an unusual number of milk bottles on a doorstep, a car parked on a double yellow line by a normally law-abiding citizen, even, in the Penge Bungalow Murders, someone else's mackintosh taken from an office peg – has been the first indication of anarchy taking over. The clue that such dark forces were at work in La Maison Jean-Pierre, one of the few London eateries to have achieved three Michelin stars and to charge more for a bite of dinner for two than I get for a legal aid theft, was very small indeed.

Now my wife, Hilda, is a good, plain cook. In saying that, I'm not referring to She Who Must Be Obeyed's moral values or passing any judgment on her personal appearance. What I can tell you is that she cooks without flights of fancy. She is not, in any way, a woman who lacks imagination. Indeed some of the things she imagines Rumpole gets up to when out of her sight are colourful in the extreme, but she doesn't apply such gifts to a chop or a potato, being quite content to grill the one and boil the other. She can also boil a cabbage into submission and fry fish. The nearest her cooking comes to the poetic is, perhaps, in her baked jam roll, which I have always found to be an emotion best recollected in tranquillity. From all this, you will gather that Hilda's honest cooking is sufficient but not exotic, and that happily the terrible curse of *nouvelle cuisine* has not infected Froxbury Mansions in the Gloucester Road.

So it is not often that I am confronted with the sort of fare photographed in the Sunday supplements. I scarcely ever sit down to an octagonal plate on which a sliver of monkfish is arranged in a composition of pastel shades, which also features a brush stroke of pink sauce, a single peeled prawn and a sprig of dill. Such gluttony is, happily, beyond my means. It wasn't, however, beyond the means of Hilda's cousin Everard, who was visiting us from Canada, where he carried on a thriving trade as a company lawyer. He told us that he felt we stood in dire need of what he called 'a taste of gracious living' and booked a table for three at La Maison Jean-Pierre.

So we found ourselves in an elegantly appointed room with subdued lighting and even more subdued conversation, where the waiters padded around like priests and the customers behaved as though they were in church. The climax of the ritual came when the dishes were set on the table under silvery domes, which were lifted to the whispered command of '*Un, deux, trois!*' to reveal the somewhat mingy portions on offer. Cousin Everard was a grey-haired man in a pale grey suiting who talked about his legal experiences in greyish tones. He entertained us with a long account of a take-over bid for the Winnipeg Soap Company which had cleared four million dollars for his clients, the Great Elk Bank of Canada. Hearing this, Hilda said accusingly, 'You've never cleared four million dollars for a client, have you, Rumpole? You should be a company lawyer like Everard.'

'Oh, I think I'll stick to crime,' I told them. 'At least it's a more honest type of robbery.'

'Nonsense. Robbery has never got us a dinner at La Maison Jean-Pierre. We'd never be here if Cousin Everard hadn't come all the way from Saskatchewan to visit us.'

'Yes, indeed. From the town of Saskatoon, Hilda.' Everard gave her a greyish smile.

'You see, Hilda. Saskatoon as in *spittoon*.'

'Crime doesn't pay, Horace,' the man from the land of the igloos told me. 'You should know that by now. Of course, we have several fine-dining restaurants in Saskatoon these days, but nothing to touch this.' He continued his inspection of the menu. 'Hilda, may I make so bold as to ask, what is your pleasure?'

During the ensuing discussion my attention strayed. Staring idly round the consecrated area I was startled to see, in the gloaming, a distinct sign of human passion in revolt against the forces of law and order. At a table for two I recognised Claude Erskine-Brown, opera buff, hopeless cross-examiner and long-time member of our Chambers in Equity Court. But was he dining tête-à-tête with his wife, the handsome and successful QC, Mrs Phillida Erskine-Brown, the Portia of our group, as law and order demanded? The answer to that was no. He was entertaining a young and decorative lady solicitor named Patricia (known to herself as Tricia) Benbow. Her long golden hair (which often provoked whistles from the cruder junior clerks round the Old Bailey) hung over her slim and suntanned shoulders and one generously ringed hand rested on Claude's as she gazed, in her usual appealing way, up into his eyes. She couldn't gaze into them for long as Claude, no doubt becoming uneasily aware of the unexpected presence of a couple of Rumpoles in the room, hid his face behind a hefty wine list.

At that moment an extremely superior brand of French head waiter manifested himself beside our table, announced his presence with a discreet cough, and led off with, '*Madame, messieurs.* Tonight Jean-Pierre recommends, for the main course, *la poésie de la poitrine du canard aux céleris et épinards crus.*'

'*Poésie* . . . ' Hilda sounded delighted and kindly explained, 'That's poetry, Rumpole. Tastes a good deal better than that old Wordsworth of yours, I shouldn't be surprised.'

'Tell us about it, Georges.' Everard smiled at the waiter. 'Whet our appetites.'

'This is just a few wafer-thin slices of breast of duck, marinated in a drop or two of Armagnac, delicately grilled and served with a celery *rémoulade* and some leaves of spinach lightly steamed . . . '

'And mash . . . ?' I interrupted the man to ask.

'*Excusez-moi?*' The fellow seemed unable to believe his ears.

'Mashed spuds come with it, do they?'

'Ssh, Rumpole!' Hilda was displeased with me, but turned all her charms on Georges. 'I will have the *poésie*. It sounds delicious.'

'A culinary experience, Hilda. Yes. *Poésie* for me too, please.' Everard fell into line.

'I would like a *poésie* of steak and kidney *pudding*, not pie, with mashed potatoes and a big scoop of boiled cabbage. *English* mustard, if you have it.' It seemed a reasonable enough request.

'Rumpole!' Hilda's whisper was menacing. 'Behave yourself!'

'This . . . "pudding" ' – Georges was puzzled – 'is not on our menu.'

' "Your pleasure is our delight". It says that on your menu. Couldn't you ask Cookie if she could delight me? Along those lines.'

' "Cookie"? I do not know who M'sieur means by "Cookie". Our *maître de cuisine* is Jean-Pierre O'Higgins himself. He is in the kitchen now.'

'How very convenient. Have a word in his shell-like, why don't you?'

For a tense moment it seemed as though the looming, priestly figure of Georges was about to excommunicate me, drive me out of the temple, or at least curse me by bell, book and candle. However, after muttering, '*Si vous le voulez. Excusez-moi,*' he went off in search of higher authority. Hilda apologised for my behaviour and told Cousin Everard that she supposed I thought I was being funny. I assured her that there was nothing particularly funny about a steak and kidney pudding.

Then I was aware of a huge presence at my elbow. A tall, fat, red-faced man in a chef's costume was standing with his hands

on his hips and asking, 'Is there someone here wants to lodge a complaint?'

Jean-Pierre O'Higgins, I was later to discover, was the product of an Irish father and a French mother. He spoke in the tones of those Irishmen who come up in a menacing manner and stand far too close to you in pubs. He was well known, I had already heard it rumoured, for dominating both his kitchen and his customers; his phenomenal rudeness to his guests seemed to be regarded as one of the attractions of his establishment. The gourmets of London didn't feel that their dinners had been entirely satisfactory unless they were served up, by way of a savoury, with a couple of insults from Jean-Pierre O'Higgins.

'Well, yes,' I said. 'There is someone.'

'Oh, yes?' O'Higgins had clearly never heard of the old adage about the customer always being right. 'And are you the joker that requested mash?'

'Am I to understand you to be saying', I enquired as politely as I knew how, 'that there are to be no mashed spuds for my delight?'

'Look here, my friend. I don't know who you are . . .' Jean-Pierre went on in an unfriendly fashion and Everard did his best to introduce me. 'Oh, this is Horace Rumpole, Jean-Pierre. The *criminal* lawyer.'

'*Criminal* lawyer, eh?' Jean-Pierre was unappeased. 'Well, don't commit your crimes in my restaurant. If you want "mashed spuds", I suggest you move down to the working-men's caff at the end of the street.'

'That's a very helpful suggestion.' I was, as you see, trying to be as pleasant as possible.

'You might get a few bangers while you're about it. And a bottle of OK sauce. That suit your delicate palate, would it?'

'Very well indeed! I'm not a great one for wafer-thin slices of anything.'

'You don't look it. Now, let's get this straight. People who come into my restaurant damn well eat as I tell them to!'

'And I'm sure you win them all over with your irresistible charm.' I gave him the retort courteous. As the chef seemed about to explode, Hilda weighed in with a well-meaning 'I'm sure my husband doesn't mean to be rude. It's just, well, we don't dine out very often. And this is such a delightful room, isn't it?'

'Your husband?' Jean-Pierre looked at She Who Must Be Obeyed with deep pity. 'You have all my sympathy, you unfortunate woman. Let me tell you, Mr Rumpole, this is La Maison Jean-Pierre. I have three stars in the Michelin. I have thrown out an Arabian king because he ordered *filet mignon* well cooked. I have sent film stars away in tears because they dared to mention Thousand Island dressing. I am Jean-Pierre O'Higgins, the greatest culinary genius now working in England!'

I must confess that during this speech from the patron I found my attention straying. The other diners, as is the way with the English at the trough, were clearly straining their ears to catch every detail of the row whilst ostentatiously concentrating on their plates. The pale, bespectacled girl making up the bills behind the desk in the corner seemed to have no such inhibitions. She was staring across the room and looking at me, I thought, as though I had thoroughly deserved the O'Higgins rebuke. And then I saw two waiters approach Erskine-Brown's table with domed dishes, which they laid on the table with due solemnity.

'And let me tell you,' Jean-Pierre's oration continued, 'I started my career with salads at La Grande Bouffe in Lyons under the great Ducasse. I was *rôtisseur* in Le Crillon, Boston. I have run this restaurant for twenty years and I have never, let me tell you, in my whole career, served up a mashed spud!'

The climax of his speech was dramatic but not nearly as startling as the events which took place at Erskine-Brown's table. To the count of '*Un, deux, trois!*' the waiters removed the silver covers and from under the one in front of Tricia Benbow sprang a small, alarmed brown mouse, perfectly visible by the light of a table candle, which had presumably been nibbling at the *poésie*. At this, the elegant lady solicitor uttered a piercing scream and leapt on to her chair. There she stood, with her skirt held down to as near her knees as possible, screaming in an ever-rising scale towards some ultimate crescendo. Meanwhile the stricken Claude looked just as a man who'd planned to have a quiet dinner with a lady and wanted to attract no one's attention would look under such circumstances. 'Please, Tricia,' I could hear his plaintive whisper, 'don't scream! People are noticing us.'

'I say, old darling,' I couldn't help saying to that three-star man O'Higgins, 'they had a mouse on that table. Is it the *spécialité de la maison?*'

A few days later, at breakfast in the mansion flat, glancing through the post (mainly bills and begging letters from Her Majesty, who seemed to be pushed for a couple of quid and would be greatly obliged if I'd let her have a little tax money on account), I saw a glossy brochure for a hotel in the Lake District. Although in the homeland of my favourite poet, Le Château Duddon, 'Lakeland's Paradise of Gracious Living', didn't sound like old Wordsworth's cup of tea, despite the 'king-sized four-poster in the Samuel Taylor Coleridge suite'.

'Cousin Everard wants to take me up there for a break.' Hilda, who was clearing away, removed a half-drunk cup of tea from my hand.

'A break from what?' I was mystified.

'From you, Rumpole. Don't you think I need it? After that disastrous evening at La Maison?'

'Was it a disaster? I quite enjoyed it. England's greatest chef laboured and gave birth to a ridiculous mouse. People'd pay good money to see a trick like that.'

'*You* were the disaster, Rumpole,' she said, as she consigned my last piece of toast to the tidy-bin. 'You were unforgivable. Mashed spuds! Why ever did you use such a vulgar expression?'

'Hilda,' I protested, I thought, reasonably, 'I have heard some fairly fruity language round the Courts in the course of a long life of crime. But I've never heard it suggested that the words "mashed spuds" would bring a blush to the cheek of the tenderest virgin.'

'Don't try to be funny, Rumpole. You upset that brilliant chef, Mr O'Higgins. You deeply upset Cousin Everard!'

'Well' – I had to put the case for the defence – 'Everard kept on suggesting I didn't make enough to feed you properly. Typical commercial lawyer. Criminal law is about life, liberty and the pursuit of happiness. Commercial law is about money. That's what I think, anyway.'

Hilda looked at me, weighed up the evidence and summed up, not entirely in my favour. 'I don't think you made that terrible fuss because of what you thought about the commercial law,' she said. 'You did it because you have to be a "character", don't you? Wherever you go. Well, I don't know if I'm going to be able to put up with your "character" much longer.'

I don't know why but what she said made me feel, quite suddenly and in a most unusual way, uncertain of myself. What was Hilda talking about exactly? I asked for further and better particulars.

'You have to be one all the time, don't you?' She was clearly getting into her stride. 'With your cigar ash and steak and kidney and Pommeroy's Ordinary Red and your arguments. Always arguments! Why do you have to go on arguing, Rumpole?'

'Arguing? It's been my life, Hilda,' I tried to explain.

'Well, it's not mine! Not any more. Cousin Everard doesn't argue in public. He is quiet and polite.'

'If you like that sort of thing.' The subject of Cousin Everard was starting to pall on me.

'Yes, Rumpole. Yes, I do. That's why I agreed to go on this trip.'

'Trip?'

'Everard and I are going to tour all the restaurants in England with stars. We're going to Bath and York and Devizes. And you can stay here and eat all the mashed spuds you want.'

'What?' I hadn't up till then taken Le Château Duddon entirely seriously. 'You really mean it?'

'Oh, yes. I think so. The living is hardly gracious here, is it?'

On the way to my place of work I spent an uncomfortable quarter of an hour thinking over what She Who Must Be Obeyed had said about me having to be a 'character'. It seemed an unfair charge. I drink Château Thames Embankment because it's all I can afford. It keeps me regular and blots out certain painful memories, such as a bad day in Court in front of Judge Graves, an old darling who undoubtedly passes iced water every time he goes to the gents'. I enjoy the fragrance of a small cigar. I relish an argument. This is the way of life I have chosen. I don't have to do any of these things in order to be a character. Do I?

I was jerked out of this unaccustomed introspection on my arrival in the clerk's room at Chambers. Henry, our clerk, was striking bargains with solicitors over the telephone whilst Dianne sat in front of her typewriter, her head bowed over a lengthy and elaborate manicure. Uncle Tom, our oldest inhabitant, who hasn't had a brief in Court since anyone can remember, was working hard at improving his putting skills with an old mashie niblick and a clutch of golf balls, the hole being represented by the waste-paper basket laid on its side. Almost as soon as I got into this familiar environment I was comforted by the sight of a man who seemed to be in far deeper trouble than I was. Claude Erskine-Brown came up to me in a manner that I can only describe as furtive.

'Rumpole,' he said, 'as you may know, Philly is away in Cardiff doing a long fraud.'

'Your wife', I congratulated the man, 'goes from strength to strength.'

'What I mean is, Rumpole' – Claude's voice sank below the level of Henry's telephone calls – 'you may have noticed me the other night. In La Maison Jean-Pierre.'

'Noticed you, Claude? Of course not! You were only in the company of a lady who stood on a chair and screamed like a banshee with toothache. No one could have possibly noticed you.' I did my best to comfort the man.

'It was purely a business arrangement,' he reassured me.

'Pretty rum way of conducting business.'

'The lady was Miss Tricia Benbow. My instructing solicitor in the VAT case,' he told me, as though that explained everything.

'Claude, I have had some experience of the law and it's a good plan, when entertaining solicitors in order to tout for briefs, *not* to introduce mice into their *plats du jour*.'

The telephone by Dianne's typewriter rang. She blew on her nail lacquer and answered it, as Claude's voice rose in anguished protest. 'Good heavens. You don't think I did *that*, do you, Rumpole? The whole thing was a disaster! An absolute tragedy! Which may have appalling consequences . . . ' 'Your wife on the phone, Mr Erskine-Brown,' Dianne interrupted him and Claude went to answer the call with all the eager cheerfulness of a French aristocrat who is told the tumbrel is at the door. As he was telling his wife he hoped things were going splendidly in Cardiff, and that he rarely went out in the evenings, in fact usually settled down to a scrambled egg in front of

the telly, there was a sound of rushing water without and our Head of
Chambers joined us.

'Something extremely serious has happened.' Sam Ballard, QC,
made the announcement as though war had broken out. He is a pallid
sort of person who usually looks as though he has just bitten into a
sour apple. His hair, I have to tell you, seems to be slicked down with
some kind of pomade.

'Someone nicked the nail-brush in the Chambers loo?' I suggested
helpfully.

'How did you guess?' He turned on me, amazed, as though I had
the gift of second sight.

'It corresponds to your idea of something serious. Also I notice
such things.'

'Odd that you should know immediately what I was talking about,
Rumpole.' By now Ballard's amazement had turned to deep suspicion.

'Not guilty, my Lord,' I assured him. 'Didn't you have a meeting
of your God-bothering society here last week?'

'The Lawyers As Christians committee. We met here. What of it?'

' "Cleanliness is next to godliness." Isn't that their motto? The
devout are notable nail-brush nickers.' As I said this, I watched
Erskine-Brown lay the telephone to rest and leave the room with the
air of a man who has merely postponed the evil hour. Ballard was still
on the subject of serious crime in the facilities. 'It's of vital importance in any place of work, Henry,' he batted on, 'that the highest
standards of hygiene are maintained! Now I've been instructed by the
City Health Authority in an important case, it would be extremely
embarrassing to me personally if my Chambers were found wanting
in the matter of a nail-brush.'

'Well, don't look at me, Mr Ballard.' Henry was not taking this lec-
ture well.

'I am accusing nobody.' Ballard sounded unconvincing. 'But look
to it, Henry. Please, look to it.'

Then our Head of Chambers left us. Feeling my usual reluctance
to start work, I asked Uncle Tom, as something of an expert in these
matters, if it would be fair to call me a 'character'.

'A what, Rumpole?'

'A "character", Uncle Tom.'

'Oh, they had one of those in old Sniffy Greengrass's Chambers in
Lamb Court,' Uncle Tom remembered. 'Fellow called Dalrymple.
Lived in an absolutely filthy flat over a chemist's shop in Chancery
Lane and used to lead a cat round the Temple on a long piece of pink

tape. "Old Dalrymple's a character," they used to say, and the other fellows in Chambers were rather proud of him.'

'I don't do anything like that, do I?' I asked for reassurance.

'I hope not,' Uncle Tom was kind enough to say. 'This Dalrymple finally went across the road to do an undefended divorce. In his pyjamas! I believe they had to lock him up. I wouldn't say you were a "character", Rumpole. Not yet, anyway.'

'Thank you, Uncle Tom. Perhaps you could mention that to She Who Must?'

And then the day took a distinct turn for the better. Henry put down his phone after yet another call and my heart leapt up when I heard that Mr Bernard, my favourite instructing solicitor (because he keeps quiet, does what he's told and hardly ever tells me about his bad back), was coming over and was anxious to instruct me in a new case which was 'not on the legal aid'. As I left the room to go about this business, I had one final question for Uncle Tom. 'That fellow Dalrymple. He didn't play golf in the clerk's room did he?'

'Good heavens, no.' Uncle Tom seemed amused at my ignorance of the world. 'He was a character, do you see? He'd hardly do anything normal.'

Mr Bernard, balding, pin-striped, with a greying moustache and a kindly eye, through all our triumphs and disasters remained imperturbable. No confession made by any client, however bizarre, seemed to surprise him, nor had any revelation of evil shocked him. He lived through our days of murder, mayhem and fraud as though he were listening to *Gardeners' Question Time*. He was interested in growing roses and in his daughter's nursing career. He spent his holidays in remote spots like Bangkok and the Seychelles. He always went away, he told me, 'on a package' and returned with considerable relief. I was always pleased to see Mr Bernard, but that day he seemed to have brought me something far from my usual line of country.

'My client, Mr Rumpole, first consulted me because his marriage was on the rocks, not to put too fine a point of it.'

'It happens, Mr Bernard. Many marriages are seldom off them.'

'Particularly so if, as in this case, the wife's of foreign extraction. It's long been my experience, Mr Rumpole, that you can't beat foreign wives for being vengeful. In this case, extremely vengeful.'

'Hell hath no fury, Mr Bernard?' I suggested.

'Exactly, Mr Rumpole. You've put your finger on the nub of the case. As you would say yourself.'

'I haven't done a matrimonial for years. My divorce may be a little rusty,' I told him modestly.

'Oh, we're not asking you to do the divorce. We're sending that to Mr Tite-Smith in Crown Office Row.'

Oh, well, I thought, with only a slight pang of disappointment, good luck to little Tite-Smith.

'The matrimonial is not my client's only problem,' Mr Bernard told me.

' "When sorrows come," Mr Bernard, "they come not single spies, But in battalions!" Your chap got something else on his plate, has he?'

'On his plate!' The phrase seemed to cause my solicitor some amusement. 'That's very apt, that is. And apter than you know, Mr Rumpole.'

'Don't keep me in suspense! Who is this mysterious client?'

'I wasn't to divulge the name, Mr Rumpole, in case you should refuse to act for him. He thought you might've taken against him, so he's coming to appeal to you in person. I asked Henry if he'd show him up as soon as he arrived.'

And, dead on cue, Dianne knocked on my door, threw it open and announced, 'Mr O'Higgins.' The large man, dressed now in a deafening checked tweed jacket and a green turtle-necked sweater, looking less like a chef than an Irish horse coper, advanced on me with a broad grin and his hand extended in a greeting, which was in strong contrast to our last encounter.

'I rely on you to save me, Mr Rumpole,' he boomed. 'You're the man to do it, sir. The great criminal defender!'

'Oh? I thought *I* was the criminal in your restaurant,' I reminded him.

'I have to tell you, Mr Rumpole, your courage took my breath away! Do you know what he did, Mr Bernard? Do you know what this little fellow here had the pluck to do?' He seemed determined to impress my solicitor with an account of my daring in the face of adversity. 'He only ordered mashed spuds in La Maison Jean-Pierre. A risk no one else has taken in all the time I've been *maître de cuisine*.'

'It didn't seem to be particularly heroic,' I told Bernard, but O'Higgins would have none of that. 'I tell you, Mr Bernard' – he moved very close to my solicitor and towered over him – 'a man who could do that to Jean-Pierre couldn't be intimidated by all the judges of the Queen's Bench. What do you say then, Mr Horace Rumpole? Will you take me on?'

I didn't answer him immediately but sat at my desk, lit a small cigar and looked at him critically. 'I don't know yet.'

'Is it my personality that puts you off?' My prospective client folded himself into my armchair, with one leg draped over an arm. He grinned even more broadly, displaying a judiciously placed gold tooth. 'Do you find me objectionable?'

'Mr O'Higgins.' I decided to give judgment at length. 'I think your restaurant pretentious and your portions skimpy. Your customers eat in a dim, religious atmosphere which seems to be more like evensong than a good night out. You appear to be a self-opinionated and self-satisfied bully. I have known many murderers who could teach you a lesson in courtesy. However, Mr Bernard tells me that you are prepared to pay my fee and, in accordance with the great traditions of the Bar, I am on hire to even the most unattractive customer.'

There was a silence and I wondered if the inflammable restaurateur were about to rise and hit me. But he turned to Bernard with even greater enthusiasm. 'Just listen to that! How's that for eloquence? We picked the right one here, Mr Bernard!'

'Well, now. I gather you're in some sort of trouble. Apart from your marriage, that is.' I unscrewed my pen and prepared to take a note.

'This has nothing to do with my marriage.' But then he frowned unhappily. 'Anyway, I don't think it has.'

'You haven't done away with this vengeful wife of yours?' Was I to be presented with a murder?

'I should have, long ago,' Jean-Pierre admitted. 'But no. Simone is still alive and suing. Isn't that right, Mr Bernard?'

'It is, Mr O'Higgins,' Bernard assured him gloomily. 'It is indeed. But this is something quite different. My client, Mr Rumpole, is being charged under the Food and Hygiene Regulations 1970 for offences relating to dirty and dangerous practices at La Maison. I have received a telephone call from the Environmental Health Officer.'

It was then, I'm afraid, that I started to laugh. I named the guilty party. 'The mouse!'

'Got it in one.' Jean-Pierre didn't seem inclined to join in the joke.

'The "wee, sleekit, cow'rin, tim'rous beastie",' I quoted at him. 'How delightful! We'll elect for trial before a jury. If we can't get you off, Mr O'Higgins, at least we'll give them a little harmless entertainment.'

Of course it wasn't really funny. A mouse in the wrong place, like too many milk bottles on a doorstep, might be a sign of passions stretched beyond control.

I have always found it useful, before forming a view about a case, to inspect the scene of the crime. Accordingly I visited La Maison Jean-Pierre one evening to study the ritual serving of dinner.

Mr Bernard and I stood in a corner of the kitchen at La Maison Jean-Pierre with our client. We were interested in the two waiters who had attended table eight, the site of the Erskine-Brown assignation. The senior of the two was Gaston, the station waiter, who had four tables under his command. 'Gaston Leblanc,' Jean-Pierre told us, as he identified the small, fat, cheerful, middle-aged man who trotted between the tables. 'Been with me for ever. Works all the hours God gave to keep a sick wife and their kid at university. Does all sorts of

other jobs in the daytime. I don't enquire too closely. Georges Pitou, the head waiter, takes the orders, of course, and leaves a copy of the note on the table.'

We saw Georges move, in a stately fashion, into the kitchen and hand the order for table eight to a young cook in a white hat, who stuck it up on the kitchen wall with a magnet. This was Ian, the *sous-chef*. Jean-Pierre had 'discovered' him in a Scottish hotel and wanted to encourage his talent. That night the bustle in the kitchen was muted, and as I looked through the circular window into the dining-room I saw that most of the white-clothed tables were standing empty, like small icebergs in a desolate polar region. When the prosecution had been announced there had been a headline in the *Evening Standard* which read GUESS WHO'S COMING TO DINNER? MOUSE SERVED IN TOP LONDON RESTAURANT and since then attendances at La Maison had dropped off sharply.

The runner between Gaston's station and the kitchen was the *commis* waiter, Alphonse Pascal, a painfully thin, dark-eyed young man with a falling lock of hair who looked like the hero of some nineteenth-century French novel, interesting and doomed. 'As a matter of fact,' Jean-Pierre told us, 'Alphonse is full of ambition. He's starting at the bottom and wants to work his way up to running a hotel. Been with me for about a year.'

We watched as Ian put the two orders for table eight on the serving-table. In due course Alphonse came into the kitchen and called out, 'Number Eight!' 'Ready, frog face,' Ian told him politely, and Alphonse came back with, '*Merci*, idiot.'

'Are they friends?' I asked my client.

'Not really. They're both much too fond of Mary.'

'Mary?'

'Mary Skelton. The English girl who makes up the bills in the restaurant.'

I looked again through the circular window and saw the unmemorable girl, her head bent over her calculator. She seemed an unlikely subject for such rivalry. I saw Alphonse pass her with a tray, carrying two domed dishes and, although he looked in her direction, she didn't glance up from her work. Alphonse then took the dishes to the serving-table at Gaston's station. Gaston looked under one dome to check its contents and then the plates were put on the table. Gaston mouthed an inaudible '*Un, deux, trois!*', the domes were lifted before the diners and not a mouse stirred.

'On the night in question,' Bernard reminded me, 'Gaston says in his statement that he looked under the dome on the gentleman's plate.'

'And saw no side order of mouse,' I remembered.

'Exactly! So he gave the other to Alphonse, who took it to the lady.'

'And then . . . Hysterics!'

'And then the reputation of England's greatest *maître de cuisine* crumbled to dust!' Jean-Pierre spoke as though announcing a national disaster.

'Nonsense!' I did my best to cheer him up. 'You're forgetting the reputation of Horace Rumpole.'

'You think we've got a defence?' my client asked eagerly. 'I mean, now that you've looked at the kitchen?'

'Can't think of one for the moment,' I admitted, 'but I expect we'll cook up something in the end.'

Unencouraged, Jean-Pierre looked out into the dining-room, muttered, 'I'd better go and keep those lonely people company,' and left us. I watched him pass the desk, where Mary looked up and smiled and I thought, however brutal he was with his customers, at least Jean-Pierre's staff seemed to find him a tolerable employer. And then, to my surprise, I saw him approach the couple at table eight, grinning in a most ingratiating manner, and stand chatting and bowing as though they could have ordered doner kebab and chips and that would have been perfectly all right by him.

'You know,' I said to Mr Bernard, 'it's quite extraordinary, the power that can be wielded by one of the smaller rodents.'

'You mean it's wrecked his business?'

'No. More amazing than that. It's forced Jean-Pierre O'Higgins to be polite to his clientele.'

After my second visit to La Maison events began to unfold at breakneck speed. First our Head of Chambers, Soapy Sam Ballard, made it known to me that the brief he had accepted on behalf of the Health Authority, and of which he had boasted so flagrantly during the nailbrush incident, was in fact the prosecution of J.-P. O'Higgins for the serious crime of being in charge of a rodent-infested restaurant. Then She Who Must Be Obeyed, true to her word, packed her grip and went off on a gastronomic tour with the man from Saskatoon. I was left to enjoy a lonely high-calorie breakfast, with no fear of criticism over the matter of a fourth sausage, in the Taste-Ee-Bite café, Fleet Street. Seated there one morning, enjoying the company of *The Times* crossword, I happened to overhear Mizz Liz Probert, the dedicated young radical barrister in our Chambers, talking to her close friend, David Inchcape, whom she had persuaded us to take on in a somewhat devious manner – a barrister as young but, I think, at heart, a touch less radical than Mizz Liz herself.

'You don't really *care*, do you, Dave?' she was saying.

'Of course I care. I care about you, Liz. Deeply.' He reached out over their plates of muesli and cups of decaff to grasp her fingers.

'That's just physical.'

'Well. Not just physical. I don't suppose it's *just*. Mainly physical, perhaps.'

'No one cares about old people.'

'But you're not old people, Liz. Thank God!'

'You see. You don't care about them. My dad was saying there's old people dying in tower blocks every day. Nobody knows about it for weeks, until they decompose!' And I saw Dave release her hand and say, 'Please, Liz. I *am* having my breakfast.'

'You see! You don't want to know. It's just something you don't want to hear about. It's the same with battery hens.'

'What's the same about battery hens?'

'No one wants to know. That's all.'

'But surely, Liz. Battery hens don't get lonely.'

'Perhaps they do. There's an awful lot of loneliness about.' She looked in my direction. 'Get off to Court then, if you have to. But do *think* about it, Dave.' Then she got up, crossed to my table, and asked what I was doing. I was having my breakfast, I assured her, and not doing my yoga meditation.

'Do you always have breakfast alone, Rumpole?' She spoke, in the tones of a deeply supportive social worker, as she sat down opposite me.

'It's not always possible. Much easier now, of course.'

'Now. Why *now*, exactly?' She looked seriously concerned.

'Well. Now my wife's left me,' I told her cheerfully.

'Hilda!' Mizz Probert was shocked, being a conventional girl at heart.

'As you would say, Mizz Liz, she is no longer sharing a one-on-one relationship with me. In any meaningful way.'

'Where does that leave you, Rumpole?'

'Alone. To enjoy my breakfast and contemplate the crossword puzzle.'

'Where's Hilda gone?'

'Oh, in search of gracious living with her Cousin Everard from Saskatoon. A fellow with about as many jokes in him as the Dow Jones Average.'

'You mean, she's gone off with another man?' Liz seemed unable to believe that infidelity was not confined to the young.

'That's about the size of it.'

'But, Rumpole. *Why?*'

'Because he's rich enough to afford very small portions of food.'

'So you're living by yourself? You must be terribly lonely.'

' "Society is all but rude," ' I assured her, ' "To this delicious solitude." '

There was a pause and then Liz took a deep breath and offered her assistance. 'You know, Rumpole. Dave and I have founded the YRL. Young Radical Lawyers. We don't only mean to reform the legal system, although that's part of it, of course. We're going to take on social work as well. We could always get someone to call and take a look at your flat every morning.'

'To make sure it's still there?'

'Well, no, Rumpole. As a matter of fact, to make sure you are.'

Those who are alone have great opportunities for eavesdropping, and Liz and Dave weren't the only members of our Chambers I heard engaged in a heart-to-heart that day. Before I took the journey back to the She-less flat, I dropped into Pommeroy's and was enjoying the ham roll and bottle of Château Thames Embankment which would constitute my dinner, seated in one of the high-backed, pew-like stalls Jack Pommeroy has installed, presumably to give the joint a vaguely medieval appearance and attract the tourists. From behind my back I heard the voices of our Head of Chambers and Claude Erskine-Brown, who was saying, in his most ingratiating tones, 'Ballard. I want to have a word with you about the case you've got against La Maison Jean-Pierre.'

To this, Ballard, in thoughtful tones, replied unexpectedly, 'A strong chain! It's the only answer.' Which didn't seem to follow.

'It was just my terrible luck, of course,' Erskine-Brown complained, 'that it should happen at my table. I mean, I'm a pretty well-known member of the Bar. Naturally I don't want my name connected with, well, a rather ridiculous incident.'

'Fellows in Chambers aren't going to like it.' Ballard was not yet with him. 'They'll say it's a restriction on their liberty. Rumpole, no doubt, will have a great deal to say about Magna Carta. But the only answer is to get a new nail-brush and chain it up. Can I have your support in taking strong measures?'

'Of course, you can, Ballard. I'll be right behind you on this one.' The creeping Claude seemed only too anxious to please. 'And in this case you're doing, I don't suppose you'll have to call the couple who actually *got* the mouse?'

'The couple?' There was a pause while Ballard searched his memory. 'The mouse was served – appalling lack of hygiene in the workplace – to a table booked by a Mr Claude Erskine-Brown and guest. Of course he'll be a vital witness.' And then the penny dropped. He stared at Claude and said firmly, '*You'll* be a vital witness.'

'But if I'm a witness of any sort, my name'll get into the papers and Philly will know I was having dinner.'

'Why on earth *shouldn't* she know you were having dinner?' Ballard was reasoning with the man. 'Most people have dinner. Nothing to be ashamed of. Get a grip on yourself, Erskine-Brown.'

'Ballard. Sam.' Claude was trying the appeal to friendship. 'You're a married man. You should understand.'

'Of course I'm married. And Marguerite and I have dinner. On a regular basis.'

'But I wasn't having dinner with Philly.' Claude explained the matter carefully. 'I was having dinner with an instructing solicitor.'

'That was your guest?'

'Yes.'

'A solicitor?'

'Of course.'

Ballard seemed to have thought the matter over carefully, but he was still puzzled when he replied, remembering his instructions. 'He apparently leapt on to a chair, held down his skirt and screamed three times!'

'Ballard! The solicitor was Tricia Benbow. You don't imagine I'd spend a hundred and something quid on feeding the face of Mr Bernard, do you?'

There was another longish pause, during which I imagined Claude in considerable suspense, and then our Head of Chambers spoke again. 'Tricia Benbow?' he asked.

'Yes.'

'Is that the one with the long blonde hair and rings?'

'That's the one.'

'And your wife knew nothing of this?'

'And must never know!' For some reason not clear to me, Claude seemed to think he'd won his case, for he now sounded grateful.

'Thank you, Ballard. Thanks awfully, Sam. I can count on you to keep my name out of this. I'll do the same for you, old boy. Any day of the week.'

'That won't be necessary.' Ballard's tone was not encouraging, although Claude said, 'No? Well, thanks, anyway.'

'It *will* be necessary, however, for you to give evidence for the pro-secution.' Soapy Sam Ballard pronounced sentence and Claude yelped, 'Have a heart, Sam!'

'Don't you "Sam" me.' Ballard was clearly in a mood to notice the decline of civilisation as we know it. 'It's all part of the same thing, isn't it? Sharp practice over the nail-brush. Failure to assist the authorities in an important prosecution. You'd better prepare yourself for Court, Erskine-Brown. And to be cross-examined by Rumpole for the defence. Do your duty! And take the consequences.'

A moment later I saw Ballard leaving for home and his wife, Mar-guerite, who, you will remember, once held the position of matron at the Old Bailey. No doubt he would chatter to her of nail-brushes and barristers unwilling to tell the whole truth. I carried my bottle of plonk round to Claude's stall in order to console the fellow.

'So,' I said, 'you lost your case.'

'What a bastard!' I have never seen Claude so pale.

'You made a big mistake, old darling. It's no good appealing to the warm humanity of a fellow who believes in chaining up nail-brushes.'

So the intrusive mouse continued to play havoc with the passions of a number of people, and I prepared myself for its day in Court. I told Mr Bernard to instruct Ferdinand Isaac Gerald Newton, known in the trade as Fig Newton, a lugubrious scarecrow of a man who is, without doubt, our most effective private investigator, to keep a watchful eye on the staff of La Maison. And then I decided to call in at the establishment on my way home one evening, not only to get a few more facts from my client but because I was becoming bored with Pommeroy's ham sandwiches.

Before I left Chambers an event occurred which caused me deep satisfaction. I made for the downstairs lavatory, and although the door was open, I found it occupied by Uncle Tom who was busily engaged at the basin washing his collection of golf balls and scrub-bing each one to a gleaming whiteness with a nail-brush. He had been putting each one, when cleaned, into a biscuit tin and as I entered he dropped the nail-brush in also.

'Uncle Tom!' – I recognised the article at once – 'that's the Cham-bers nail-brush! Soapy Sam's having kittens about it.'

'Oh, dear. Is it, really? I must have taken it without remembering. I'll leave it on the basin.'

But I persuaded him to let me have it for safe-keeping, saying I longed to see Ballard's little face light up with joy when it was restored to him.

When I arrived at La Maison the disputes seemed to have become a great deal more dramatic than even in Equity Court. The place was not yet open for dinner, but I was let in as the restaurant's legal adviser and I heard raised voices and sounds of a struggle from the kitchen. Pushing the door open, I found Jean-Pierre in the act of forcibly removing a

knife from the hands of Ian, the *sous-chef*, at whom an excited Alphonse Pascal, his lock of black hair falling into his eyes, was shouting abuse in French. My arrival created a diversion in which both men calmed down and Jean-Pierre passed judgment on them. 'Bloody lunatics!' he said. 'Haven't they done this place enough harm already? They have to start slaughtering each other. Behave yourselves. *Soyez sages!* And what can I do for *you*, Mr Rumpole?'

'Perhaps we could have a little chat,' I suggested as the tumult died down. 'I thought I'd call in. My wife's away, you see, and I haven't done much about dinner.'

'Then what would you like?'

'Oh, anything. Just a snack.'

'Some pâté, perhaps? And a bottle of champagne?' I thought he'd never ask.

When we were seated at a table in a corner of the empty restaurant, the patron told me more about the quarrel. 'They were fighting again over Mary Skelton.'

I looked across at the desk, where the unmemorable girl was getting out her calculator and preparing for her evening's work. 'She doesn't look the type, exactly,' I suggested.

'Perhaps', Jean-Pierre speculated, 'she has a warm heart? My wife Simone looks the type, but she's got a heart like an ice-cube.'

'Your wife. The vengeful woman?' I remembered what Mr Bernard had told me.

'Why should she be vengeful to me, Mr Rumpole? When I'm a particularly tolerant and easy-going type of individual?'

At which point a couple of middle-aged Americans, who had strayed in off the street, appeared at the door of the restaurant and asked Jean-Pierre if he were serving dinner. 'At six thirty? No! And we don't do teas, either.' He shouted across at them, in a momentary return to his old ways, 'Cretins!'

'Of course', I told him, 'you're a very parfait, gentle cook.'

'A great artist needs admiration. He needs almost incessant praise.'

'And with Simone', I suggested, 'the admiration flowed like cement?'

'You've got it. Had some experience of wives, have you?'

'You might say, a lifetime's experience. Do you mind?' I poured myself another glass of unwonted champagne.

'No, no, of course. And your wife doesn't understand you?'

'Oh, I'm afraid she does. That's the worrying thing about it. She blames me for being a "character".'

'They'd blame you for anything. Come to divorce, has it?'

'Not quite reached your stage, Mr O'Higgins.' I looked round the restaurant. 'So I suppose you have to keep these tables full to pay Simone her alimony.'

'Not exactly. You see she'll own half La Maison.' That hadn't been entirely clear to me and I asked him to explain.

'When we started off, I was a young man. All I wanted to do was to get up early, go to Smithfield and Billingsgate, feel the lobsters and smell the fresh scallops, create new dishes, and dream of sauces. Simone was the one with the business sense. Well, she's French, so she insisted on us getting married in France.'

'Was that wrong?'

'Oh, no. It was absolutely right, for Simone. Because they have a damned thing there called "community of property". I had to agree to give her half of everything if we ever broke up. You know about the law, of course.'

'Well, not everything about it.' Community of property, I must confess, came as news to me. 'I always found knowing the law a bit of a handicap for a barrister.'

'Simone knew all about it. She had her beady eye on the future.' He emptied his glass and then looked at me pleadingly. 'You're going to get us out of this little trouble, aren't you, Mr Rumpole? This affair of the mouse?'

'Oh, the mouse!' I did my best to reassure him. 'The mouse seems to be the least of your worries.'

Soon Jean-Pierre had to go back to his kitchen. On his way, he stopped at the cash desk and said something to the girl, Mary. She looked up at him with, I thought, unqualified adoration. He patted her arm and went back to his sauces, having reassured her, I suppose, about the quarrel that had been going on in her honour.

I did justice to the rest of the champagne and pâté de foie and started off for home. In the restaurant entrance hall I saw the lady who minded the cloaks take a suitcase from Gaston Leblanc, who had just arrived out of breath and wearing a mackintosh. Although large, the suitcase seemed very light and he asked her to look after it.

Several evenings later I was lying on my couch in the living-room of the mansion flat, a small cigar between my fingers and a glass of Château Fleet Street on the floor beside me. I was in vacant or in pensive mood as I heard a ring at the front-door bell. I started up, afraid that the delights of *haute cuisine* had palled for Hilda, and then I remembered that She would undoubtedly have come armed with a latchkey. I approached the front door, puzzled at the sound of young and excited voices without, combined with loud music. I got the door open and found myself face to face with Liz Probert, Dave Inchcape and five or six other junior hacks, all wearing sweatshirts with a picture of a wig and YOUNG RADICAL LAWYERS written on them. Dianne was also there in trousers and a glittery top, escorted by my clerk, Henry, wearing jeans and doing his best to appear young and swinging. The party was carrying various bottles and an article we know well down the Bailey (because it so often appears in lists of stolen property) as a ghetto blaster. It was from this contraption that the loud music emerged.

'It's a surprise party!' Mizz Liz Probert announced with considerable pride. 'We've come to cheer you up in your great loneliness.'

Nothing I could say would stem the well-meaning invasion. Within minutes the staid precincts of Froxbury Mansions were transformed into the sort of disco which is patronised by under-thirties on a package to the Costa del Sol. Bizarre drinks, such as rum and blackcurrant juice or advocaat and lemonade, were being mixed in what remained of our tumblers, supplemented by toothmugs from the bathroom. Scarves dimmed the lights, the ghetto blaster blasted ceaselessly and dancers gyrated in a self-absorbed manner, apparently oblivious of each other.

Only Henry and Dianne, practising a more old-fashioned ritual, clung together, almost motionless, and carried on a lively conversation with me as I stood on the outskirts of the revelry, drinking the best of the wine they had brought and trying to look tolerantly convivial.

'We heard as how Mrs Rumpole has done a bunk, sir.' Dianne looked sympathetic, to which Henry added sourly, 'Some people have all the luck!'

'Why? Where's your wife tonight, Henry?' I asked my clerk. The cross he has to bear is that his spouse has pursued an ambitious career in local government so that, whereas she is now the Mayor of Bexley-heath, he is officially her Mayoress.

'My wife's at a dinner of South London mayors in the Mansion House, Mr Rumpole. No consorts allowed, thank God!' Henry told me.

'Which is why we're both on the loose tonight. Makes you feel young again, doesn't it, Mr Rumpole?' Dianne asked me as she danced minimally.

'Well, not particularly young, as a matter of fact.' The music yawned between me and my guests as an unbridgeable generation gap. And then one of the more intense of the young lady radicals approached me, as a senior member of the Bar, to ask what the hell the Lord Chief Justice knew about being pregnant and on probation at the moment your boyfriend's arrested for dope. 'Very little, I should imagine,' I had to tell her, and then, as the telephone was bleating pathetically beneath the din, I excused myself and moved to answer it. As I went, a Y R L sweatshirt whirled past me; Liz, dancing energetically, had pulled it off and was gyrating in what appeared to be an ancient string-vest and a pair of jeans.

'Rumpole!' the voice of She Who Must Be Obeyed called to me, no doubt from the banks of Duddon. 'What on earth's going on there?'

'Oh, Hilda. Is it you?'

'Of course it's me.'

'Having a good time, are you? And did Cousin Everard enjoy his sliver of whatever it was?'

'Rumpole. What's that incredible noise?'

'Noise? Is there a noise? Oh, yes. I think I do hear music. Well . . .' Here I improvised, as I thought brilliantly. 'It's a play, that's what it is, a play on television. It's all about young people, hopping about in a curious fashion.'

'Don't talk rubbish!' Hilda, as you may guess, sounded far from convinced. 'You know you never watch plays on television.'

'Not usually, I grant you,' I admitted. 'But what else have I got to do when my wife has left me?'

Much later, it seemed a lifetime later, when the party was over, I settled down to read the latest addition to my brief in the O'Higgins case. It was a report from Fig Newton, who had been keeping observation on the workers at La Maison. One afternoon he followed Gaston Leblanc, who left his home in Ruislip with a large suitcase, with which he travelled to a smart address at Egerton Crescent in Knightsbridge. This house, which had a bunch of brightly coloured balloons tied to its front door, Fig kept under surveillance for some time. A number of small children arrived, escorted by nannies, and were let in by a manservant. Later, when all the children had been received, Fig, wrapped in his Burberry with his collar turned up against the rain, was able to move so he got a clear view into the sitting-room.

What he saw interested me greatly. The children were seated on the floor watching breathlessly as Gaston Leblanc, station waiter and part-time conjuror, dressed in a black robe ornamented with stars, entertained them by slowly extricating a live and kicking rabbit from a top hat.

★

For the trial of Jean-Pierre O'Higgins we drew the short straw in the shape of an Old Bailey judge aptly named Gerald Graves. Judge Graves and I have never exactly hit it off. He is a pale, long-faced, unsmiling fellow who probably lives on a diet of organic bran and carrot juice. He heard Ballard open the proceedings against La Maison with a pained expression, and looked at me over his half-glasses as though I were a saucepan that hadn't been washed up properly. He was the last person in the world to laugh a case out of Court and I would have to manage that trick without him.

Soapy Sam Ballard began by describing the minor blemishes in the restaurant's kitchen. 'In this highly expensive, allegedly three-star establishment, the Environmental Health Officer discovered cracked tiles, open waste-bins and gravy stains on the ceiling.'

'The ceiling, Mr Ballard?' the judge repeated in sepulchral tones.

'Alas, yes, my Lord. The ceiling.'

'Probably rather a tall cook,' I suggested, and was rewarded with a freezing look from the Bench.

'And there was a complete absence of nail-brushes in the kitchen handbasins.' Ballard touched on a subject dear to his heart. 'But wait, Members of the jury, until you get to the —' 'Main course?' I suggested in another ill-received whisper and Ballard surged on '— the very heart of this most serious case. On the night of May the 18th, a common house mouse was served up at a customer's dinner table.'

'We are no doubt dealing here, Mr Ballard,' the judge intoned solemnly, 'with a defunct mouse?'

'Again, alas, no, my Lord. The mouse in question was alive.'

'And kicking,' I muttered. Staring vaguely round the Court, my eye lit on the public gallery where I saw Mary Skelton, the quiet restaurant clerk, watching the proceedings attentively.

'Members of the jury' – Ballard had reached his peroration – 'need one ask if a kitchen is in breach of the Food and Hygiene Regulations if it serves up a living mouse? As proprietor of the restaurant, Mr O'Higgins is, say the prosecution, absolutely responsible. Whomsoever in his employ he seeks to blame, Members of the jury, he must take the consequences. I will now call my first witness.'

'Who's that pompous imbecile?' Jean-Pierre O'Higgins was adding his two pennyworth, but I told him he wasn't in his restaurant now and to leave the insults to me. I was watching a fearful and embarrassed Claude Erskine-Brown climb into the witness-box and take the oath as though it were the last rites. When asked to give his full names he appealed to the judge.

'My Lord. May I write them down? There may be some publicity about this case.' He looked nervously at the assembled reporters.

'Aren't you a member of the Bar?' Judge Graves squinted at the witness over his half-glasses.

'Well, yes, my Lord,' Claude admitted reluctantly.

'That's nothing to be ashamed of – in most cases.' At which the judge aimed a look of distaste in my direction and then turned back to the witness. 'I think you'd better tell the jury who you are, in the usual way.'

'Claude . . . ' The unfortunate fellow tried a husky whisper, only to get a testy 'Oh, do speak up!' from his Lordship. Whereupon, turning up the volume a couple of notches, the witness answered, 'Claude Leonard Erskine-Brown.' I hadn't known about the Leonard.

'On May the 18th were you dining at La Maison Jean-Pierre?' Ballard began his examination.

'Well, yes. Yes. I did just drop in.'

'For dinner?'

'Yes,' Claude had to admit.

'In the company of a young lady named Patricia Benbow?'

'Well. That is . . . Er . . . er.'

'Mr Erskine-Brown' – Judge Graves had no sympathy with this sudden speech impediment – 'it seems a fairly simple question to answer, even for a member of the Bar.'

'I was in Miss Benbow's company, my Lord,' Claude answered in despair.

'And when the main course was served were the plates covered?'

'Yes. They were.'

'And when the covers were lifted what happened?'

Into the expectant silence, Erskine-Brown said in a still, small voice, 'A mouse ran out.'

'Oh, do speak up!' Graves was running out of patience with the witness, who almost shouted back, 'A mouse ran out, my Lord!'

At this point Ballard said, 'Thank you, Mr Erskine-Brown,' and sat down, no doubt confident that the case was in the bag – or perhaps the trap. Then I rose to cross-examine.

'Mr Claude Leonard Erskine-Brown,' I weighed in, 'is Miss Benbow a solicitor?'

'Well. Yes . . . ' Claude looked at me sadly, as though wanting to say, *Et tu*, Rumpole?

'And is your wife a well-known and highly regarded Queen's Counsel?'

Graves's face lit up at the mention of our delightful Portia. 'Mrs

Erskine-Brown has sat here as a recorder, Members of the jury.' He smiled sickeningly at the twelve honest citizens.

'I'm obliged to your Lordship.' I bowed slightly and turned back to the witness. 'And is Miss Benbow instructed in an important forthcoming case, that is the Balham Mini-Cab Murder, in which she is intending to brief Mrs Erskine-Brown, QC?'

'Is – is she?' Never quick off the mark, Claude didn't yet realise that help was at hand.

'And were you taking her out to dinner so you might discuss the defence in that case, your wife being unfortunately detained in Cardiff?' I hoped that made my good intentions clear, even to a barrister.

'Was I?' Erskine-Brown was still not with me.

'Well, weren't you?' I was losing patience with the fellow.

'Oh, yes.' At last the penny dropped. 'Of course I was! I do remember now. Naturally. And I did it all to help Philly. To help my wife. Is that what you mean?' He ended up looking at me anxiously.

'Exactly.'

'Thank you, Mr Rumpole. Thank you very much.' Erskine-Brown's gratitude was pathetic. But the judge couldn't wait to get on to the exciting bits. 'Mr Rumpole,' he boomed mournfully, 'when are we coming to the mouse?'

'Oh, yes. I'm grateful to your Lordship for reminding me. Well. What sort of animal was it?'

'Oh, a very small mouse indeed.' Claude was now desperately anxious to help me. 'Hardly noticeable.'

'A very small mouse and hardly noticeable,' Graves repeated as he wrote it down and then raised his eyebrows, as though, when it came to mice, smallness was no excuse.

'And the first you saw of it was when it emerged from under a silver dish-cover? You couldn't swear it got there in the kitchen?'

'No, I couldn't.' Erskine-Brown was still eager to cooperate.

'Or if it was inserted in the dining-room by someone with access to the serving-table?'

'Oh, no, Mr Rumpole. You're perfectly right. Of course it might have been!' The witness's cooperation was almost embarrassing, so the judge chipped in with 'I take it you're not suggesting that this creature appeared from a dish of duck breasts by some sort of miracle, are you, Mr Rumpole?'

'Not a miracle, my Lord. Perhaps a trick.'

'Isn't Mr Ballard perfectly right?' Graves, as was his wont, had joined the prosecution team. 'For the purposes of this offence it doesn't matter *how* it got there. A properly run restaurant should not serve up a mouse for dinner! The thing speaks for itself.'

'A talking mouse, my Lord? What an interesting conception!' I got a loud laugh from my client and even the jury joined in with a few friendly titters. I also got, of course, a stern rebuke from the Bench. 'Mr Rumpole!' – his Lordship's seriousness was particularly deadly – 'this is not a place of entertainment! You would do well to remember that this is a most serious case from your client's point of view. And I'm sure the jury will wish to give it the most weighty consideration. We will continue with it after luncheon. Shall we say, five past two, Members of the jury?'

Mr Bernard and I went down to the pub, and after a light snack of shepherd's pie, washed down with a pint or two of Guinness, we hurried back into the Palais de Justice and there I found what I hoped for. Mary Skelton was sitting quietly outside the Court, waiting for the proceedings to resume. I lit a small cigar and took a seat with my instructing solicitor not far away from the girl. I raised my voice a little and said, 'You know what's always struck me about this case, Mr Bernard? There's no evidence of droppings or signs of mice in the kitchen. So someone put the mouse under the cover deliberately. Someone who wanted to ruin La Maison's business.'

'Mrs O'Higgins?' Bernard suggested.

'Certainly not! She'd want the place to be as prosperous as possible because she owned half of it. The guilty party is someone who wanted Simone to get nothing but half a failed eatery with a ruined reputation. So what did this someone do?'

'You tell me, Mr Rumpole.' Mr Bernard was an excellent straight man.

'Oh, broke a lot of little rules. Took away the nail-brushes and the lids of the tidy-bins. But a sensation was needed, something that'd hit the headlines. Luckily this someone knew a waiter who had a talent for sleight of hand and a spare-time job producing livestock out of hats.'

'Gaston Leblanc?' Bernard was with me.

'Exactly! He got the animal under the lid and gave it to Alphonse to present to the unfortunate Miss Tricia Benbow. Consequence: ruin for the restaurant and a rotten investment for the vengeful Simone. No doubt someone paid Gaston well to do it.'

I was silent then. I didn't look at the waiting girl, but I was sure she was looking at me. And then Bernard asked, 'Just who are we talking about, Mr Rumpole?'

'Well, now. Who had the best possible reason for hating Simone, and wanting her to get away with as little as possible?'

'Who?'

'Who but our client?' I told him. 'The great *maître de cuisine*, Jean-Pierre O'Higgins himself.'

'No!' I had never heard Mary Skelton speaking before. Her voice was clear and determined, with a slight North Country accent. 'Excuse me.' I turned to look at her as she stood up and came over to us. 'No, it's not true. Jean-Pierre knew nothing about it. It was my idea entirely. Why did *she* deserve to get anything out of us?'

I stood up, looked at my watch, and put on the wig that had been resting on the seat beside me. 'Well, back to Court. Mr Bernard, take a statement from the lady, why don't you? We'll call her as a witness.'

Whilst these events were going on down the Bailey, another kind of drama was being enacted in Froxbury Mansions. She Who Must Be Obeyed had returned from her trip with Cousin Everard, put on the kettle and surveyed the general disorder left by my surprise party with deep disapproval. In the sitting-room she fanned away the bar-room smell, drew the curtains, opened the windows and clicked her tongue at the sight of half-empty glasses and lipstick-stained fag ends. Then she noticed something white nestling under the sofa, pulled it out and saw that it was a Young Radical Lawyers sweat-shirt, redolent of Mizz Liz Probert's understated yet feminine perfume.

Later in the day, when I was still on my hind legs performing before Mr Justice Graves and the jury, Liz Probert called at the mansion flat to collect the missing garment. Hilda had met Liz at occasional Chambers parties but when she opened the door she was, I'm sure, stony-faced, and remained so as she led Mizz Probert into the sitting-room and restored to her the sweatshirt which the Young Radical Lawyer admitted she had taken off and left behind the night before. I have done my best to reconstruct the following dialogue, from the accounts given to me by the principal performers. I can't vouch for its total accuracy, but this is the gist, the meat you understand. It began when Liz explained she had taken the sweatshirt off because she was dancing and it was quite hot.

'You were *dancing* with Rumpole?' Hilda was outraged. 'I knew he was up to something. As soon as my back was turned. I heard all that going on when I telephoned. Rocking and rolling all over the place. At his age!'

'Mrs Rumpole. Hilda . . . ' Liz began to protest but only provoked a brisk 'Oh, please. Don't you Hilda me! Young Radical Lawyers, I suppose that means you're free and easy with other people's husbands!' At which point I regret to report that Liz Probert could scarcely contain her laughter and asked, 'You don't think I fancy Rumpole, do you?'

'I don't know why not.' Hilda has her moments of loyalty. 'Rumpole's a "character". Some people like that sort of thing.'

'Hilda. Look, please listen,' and Liz began to explain. 'Dave Inchcape and I and a whole lot of us came to give Rumpole a party. To cheer him up. Because he was lonely. He was missing you so terribly.'

'He was *what*?' She Who Must could scarcely believe her ears, Liz told me. 'Missing you,' the Young Radical repeated. 'I saw him at breakfast. He looked so sad. "She's left me", he said, "and gone off with her Cousin Everard." '

'Rumpole said that?' Hilda no longer sounded displeased.

'And he seemed absolutely broken-hearted. He saw nothing ahead, I'm sure, but a lonely old age stretching out in front of him. Anyone could tell how much he cared about you. Dave noticed it as well. Please can I have my shirt back now?'

'Of course.' Hilda was now treating the girl as though she were the prodigal grandchild or some such thing. 'But, Liz . . . '

'What, Hilda?'

'Wouldn't you like me to put it through the wash for you before you take it home?'

Back in the Ludgate Circus verdict factory, Mary Skelton gave evidence along the lines I have already indicated and the time came for me to make my final speech. As I reached the last stretch I felt I was making some progress. No one in the jury-box was asleep, or suffering from terminal bronchitis, and a few of them looked distinctly sympathetic. The same couldn't be said, however, of the scorpion on the Bench.

'Ladies and gentlemen of the jury.' I gave it to them straight. 'Miss Mary Skelton, the cashier, was in love. She was in love with her boss, that larger-than-life cook and "character", Jean-Pierre O'Higgins. People do many strange things for love. They commit suicide or leave home or pine away sometimes. It was for love that Miss Mary Skelton caused a mouse to be served up in La Maison Jean-Pierre, after she had paid the station waiter liberally for performing the trick. She it was who wanted to ruin the business, so that my client's vengeful wife should get absolutely nothing out of it.'

'Mr Rumpole!' His Lordship was unable to contain his fury.

'And my client knew nothing whatever of this dire plot. He was entirely innocent.' I didn't want to let Graves interrupt my flow, but he came in at increased volume, 'Mr Rumpole! If a restaurant serves unhygienic food, the proprietor is guilty. In law it doesn't matter in the least how it got there. Ignorance by your client is no excuse. I presume you have some rudimentary knowledge of the law, Mr Rumpole?'

I wasn't going to tangle with Graves on legal matters. Instead I confined my remarks to the more reasonable jury, ignoring the judge. 'You're not concerned with the law, Members of the jury,' I told them, 'you are concerned with justice!'

'That is a quite outrageous thing to say! On the admitted facts of this case, Mr O'Higgins is clearly guilty!' His Honour Judge Graves had decided but the honest twelve would have to return the verdict and I spoke to them. 'A British judge has no power to direct a British jury to find a defendant guilty! I know that much at least.'

'I shall tell the jury that he is guilty in law, I warn you.' Graves's warning was in vain. I carried on regardless.

'His Lordship may tell you that to his heart's content. As a great Lord Chief Justice of England, a judge superior in rank to any in this Court, once said, "It is the duty of the judge to tell you as a jury what to do, but you have the power to do exactly as you like." And what you do, Members of the jury, is a matter entirely between God and your own consciences. Can you really find it in your consciences to condemn a man to ruin for a crime he didn't commit?' I looked straight at them. 'Can any of you? Can you?' I gripped the desk in front of me, apparently exhausted. 'You are the only judges of the facts in this case, Members of the jury. My task is done. The future career of Jean-Pierre O'Higgins is in your hands, and in your hands alone.' And then I sat down, clearly deeply moved.

At last it was over. As we came out of the doors of the Court, Jean-Pierre O'Higgins embraced me in a bear hug and was, I greatly feared, about to kiss me on both cheeks. Ballard gave me a look of pale disapproval. Clearly he thought I had broken all the rules by asking the jury to ignore the judge. Then a cheerful and rejuvenated Claude came bouncing up bleating, 'Rumpole, you were brilliant!'

'Oh yes,' I told him. 'I've still got a win or two in me yet.'

'Brilliant to get me off. All that nonsense about a brief for Philly.'

'Not nonsense, Leonard. I mean, Claude. I telephoned the fair Tricia and she's sending your wife the Balham Mini-Cab Murder.

Are you suggesting that Rumpole would deceive the Court?'

'Oh' – he was interested to know – 'am I getting a brief too?'

'She said nothing of that.'

'All the same, Rumpole' – he concealed his disappointment – 'thank you very much for getting me out of a scrape.'

'Say no more. My life is devoted to helping the criminal classes.'

As I left him and went upstairs to slip out of the fancy dress, I had one more task to perform. I walked past my locker and went on into the silks' dressing-room, where a very old QC was seated in the shadows snoozing over the *Daily Telegraph*. I had seen Ballard downstairs, discussing the hopelessness of an appeal with his solicitor, and it was the work of a minute to find his locker, feel in his jacket pocket and haul a large purse out of it. Making sure that the sleeping silk hadn't spotted me, I opened the purse, slipped in the nail-brush I had rescued from Uncle Tom's tin of golf balls, restored it to the pocket and made my escape undetected.

I was ambling back up Fleet Street when I heard the brisk step of Ballard behind me. He drew up alongside and returned to his favourite topic. 'There's nothing for it, Rumpole,' he said, 'I shall chain the next one up.'

'The next what?'

'The next nail-brush.'

'Isn't that a bit extreme?'

'If fellows, and ladies, in Chambers can't be trusted,' Ballard said severely, 'I am left with absolutely no alternative. I hate to have to do it, but Henry is being sent out for a chain tomorrow.'

We had reached the newspaper stand at the entrance to the Temple and I loitered there. 'Lend us 20p for the *Evening Standard*, Bollard. There might be another restaurant in trouble.'

'Why are you never provided with money?' Ballard thought it typical of my fecklessness. 'Oh, all right.' And then he put his hand in his pocket and pulled out the purse. Opening it, he was amazed to find his ten pees nestling under an ancient nail-brush. 'Our old nail-brush!' The reunion was quaintly moving. 'I'd recognise it anywhere. How on earth did it get in there?'

'Evidence gets in everywhere, old darling,' I told him. 'Just like mice.'

When I got home and unlocked the front door, I was greeted with the familiar cry of 'Is that you, Rumpole?'

'No,' I shouted back, 'it's not me. I'll be along later.'

'Come into the sitting-room and stop talking rubbish.'

I did as I was told and found the room swept and polished and that She, who was looking unnaturally cheerful, had bought flowers.

'Cousin Everard around, is he?' I felt, apprehensively, that the floral tributes were probably for him.

'He had to go back to Saskatoon. One of his clients got charged with fraud, apparently.' And then Hilda asked, unexpectedly, 'You knew I'd be back, didn't you, Rumpole?'

'Well, I *had* hoped . . . ' I assured her.

'It seems you almost gave up hoping. You couldn't get along without me, could you?'

'Well, I had a bit of a stab at it,' I said in all honesty.

'No need for you to be brave any more. I'm back now. That nice Miss Liz Probert was saying you missed me terribly.'

'Oh, of course. Yes. Yes, I missed you.' And I added as quietly as possible, 'Life without a boss . . . '

'What did you say?'

'You were a great loss.'

'And Liz says you were dreadfully lonely. I was glad to hear that, Rumpole. You don't usually say much about your feelings.'

'Words don't come easily to me, Hilda,' I told her with transparent dishonesty.

'Now you're so happy to see me back, Rumpole, why don't you

take me out for a little celebration? I seem to have got used to dining *à la carte.*'

Of course I agreed. I knew somewhere where we could get it on the house. So we ended up at a table for two in La Maison and discussed Hilda's absent relative as Alphonse made his way towards us with two covered dishes.

'The trouble with Cousin Everard', Hilda confided in me, 'is he's not a "character".'

'Bit on the bland side?' I enquired politely.

'It seems that unless you're with a "character", life can get a little tedious at times,' Hilda admitted.

The silver domes were put in front of us, Alphonse called out, '*Un, deux, trois!*' and they were lifted to reveal what I had no difficulty in ordering that night: steak and kidney pud. Mashed spuds were brought to us on the side.

'Perhaps that's why I need you, Rumpole.' She Who Must Be Obeyed was in a philosophic mood that night. 'Because you're a "character". And you need me to tell you off for being one.'

Distinctly odd, I thought, are the reasons why people need each other. I looked towards the cashier's desk, where Jean-Pierre had his arm round the girl I had found so unmemorable. I raised a glass of the champagne he had brought us and drank to their very good health.

Rumpole and the Children of the Devil

Sometimes, when I have nothing better to occupy my mind, when I am sitting in the bath, for instance, or in the doctor's surgery having exhausted the entertainment value of last year's *Country Life*, or when I am in the corner of Pommeroy's Wine Bar waiting for some generous spirit in Chambers, and there aren't many of them left, to come in and say, 'Care for a glass of Château Fleet Street, Rumpole?', I wonder what I would have done if I had been God. I mean, if I had been responsible for creating the world in the first place, would I have cobbled up a globe totally without the minus quantities we have grown used to, a place with no fatal diseases or traffic jams or Mr Justice Graves – and one or two others I could mention? Above all, would I have created a world entirely without evil? And, when I come to think rather further along these lines, it seems to me that a world without evil might possibly be a damned dull world – or an undamned dull world, perhaps I should say – and it would certainly be a world which would leave Rumpole without an occupation. It would also put the Old Bill and most of Her Majesty's judges, prosecutors, prison officers and screws on the breadline. So perhaps a world where everyone rushes about doing good to each other and everyone, including the aforesaid Graves, is filled with brotherly love, is not such a marvellous idea after all.

Brooding a little further on this business of evil, it occurs to me that the world is fairly equally divided between those who see it everywhere because they are always looking for it and those who hardly notice it at all. Of course, the mere fact that some people recognise devilment in the most everyday matters doesn't mean that it isn't there. I have known the first indication that evil was present, in various cases that I have been concerned with, to be a missing library ticket, a car tyre punctured or the wrong overcoat taken from the cloakroom of an expensive restaurant. At other times, the signs of evil are so blatant that they are impossible to ignore, as in the dramatic start to the case which I have come to think of as concerning the children of the Devil. They led to a serious and, at times, painful inquiry into the machinations of Satan in the borough of Crockthorpe.

Crockthorpe is a large, sprawling, in many parts dejected, in others rather too cosy for comfort, area south of the Thames. Its inhabitants include people speaking many languages, many without jobs, many gainfully employed in legal and not so legal businesses – and the huge Timson clan, which must by now account for a sizeable chunk of the population. The Timsons, as those of you who have followed my legal career in detail will know, provide not only the bread and marge, the Vim and Brasso, but quite often the beef and butter of our life in Froxbury Mansions, Gloucester Road. A proportion of my intake of Château Thames Embankment, and my wife Hilda's gin and tonic, comes thanks to the tireless activities of the Timson family. They are such a large group, their crime rate is so high, and their success rate so comparatively low, that they are perfect clients for an Old Bailey hack. They go in for theft, shop breaking and receiving stolen property but they have never produced a master crook. If you are looking for sensational crimes, the Timsons won't provide them or, it would be more accurate to say, they didn't until the day that Tracy Timson apparently made a pact with the Devil.

The story began in the playground of Crockthorpe's Stafford Cripps Junior School. The building had not been much repaired since it was built in the heady days of the first post-war Labour Government, and the playground had been kicked to pieces by generations of scuffling under-twelves. It was during the mid-morning break when the children were out fighting, ganging up on each other, or unhappy because they had no one to play with – among the most active, and about to pick a fight with a far larger black boy, was Dominic Molloy, angel-faced and Irish, who will figure in this narrative – when evil appeared.

Well, as I say, it was half-way through break and the headmistress, a certain Miss Appleyard, a woman in her early forties who would have been beautiful had not the stress of life in the Stafford Cripps Junior aged her prematurely, was walking across the playground, trying to work out how to make fifty copies of *The Little Green Reading Book* go round two hundred pupils, when she heard the sound of concerted, eerie and high-pitched screaming coming from one of the doors that led on to the playground.

Turning towards the sound of the outcry, Miss Appleyard saw a strange sight. A small posse of children, about nine of them, all girls and all screaming, came rushing out like a charge of miniature cavalry. Who they were was, at this moment, a mystery to the headmistress for each child wore a similar mask. Above the dresses and the jeans and pullovers hung the scarlet and black, grimacing and evil faces of nine devils.

At this sight even the bravest and most unruly children in the playground were taken aback, many retreated, some of the younger ones adding to the chorus of screams. Only young Dominic Molloy, it has to be said, stood his ground and viewed the scene that followed with amusement and contempt. He saw Miss Appleyard step forward fearlessly and, when the charge halted, she plucked off the devil's mask and revealed the small, heart-shaped face of the eight-year-old Tracy, almost the youngest, and now apparently the most devilish, of the Timson family.

Events thereafter took an even more sinister turn. At first the headmistress looked grim, confiscated the masks and ordered the children back to the classroom, but didn't speak to them again about the extraordinary demonstration. Unfortunately she laid the matter before the proper authority, which in this case was the Social Services and Welfare Department of the Crockthorpe Council. So the wheels were set in motion that would end up with young Tracy Timson being taken into what is laughingly known as care, this being the punishment meted out to children who fail to conform to a conventional and rational society.

Childhood has, I regret to say, like much else, got worse since I was a boy. We had school bullies, we had headmasters who were apparently direct descendants of Captain Bligh of the *Bounty*, we had cold baths, inedible food and long hours in chapel on Sundays, but there was one compensation. No one had invented social workers. Now British children, it seems, can expect the treatment we once thought was only meted out to the political opponents of the late unlamented Joseph Stalin. They must learn to dread the knock at the door, the tramp of the Old Bill up the stairs, and being snatched from their nearest and dearest by a member of the alleged caring professions.

The dreaded knock was to be heard at six thirty one morning on the door of the semi in Morrison Close, where that young couple Cary and Rosemary (known as Roz) Timson lived with Tracy, their only child. There was a police car flashing its blue light outside the house and a woman police constable in uniform on the step. The knock was administered by a social worker named Mirabelle Jones, of whom we'll hear considerably more later. She was a perfectly pleasant-looking girl with well-tended hair who wore, whenever I saw her, a linen jacket and a calf-length skirt of some ethnic material. When she spoke she modulated her naturally posh tones into some semblance of a working-class accent, and she always referred to the parents of the children who came into her possession as Mum and Dad and spoke with friendliness and deep concern.

When the knock sounded, Tracy was asleep in the company of someone known as Barbie doll, which I have since discovered to be a miniature American person with a beehive hairdo and a large wardrobe. Cary Timson was pounding down the stairs in his pyjamas, unhappily convinced that the knock was in some way connected with the break-in at a shop in Gunston Avenue about which he had been repeatedly called in for questioning, although he had made it clear, on each occasion, that he knew absolutely bugger all about it.

By the time he had pulled open the door his wife, Roz, had appeared on the stairs behind him, so she was able to hear Mirabelle telling her husband, after the parties had identified each other, that she had 'come about young Tracy'. From the statements which I was able to read later it appears that the dialogue then went something like this. It began with a panic-stricken cry from Roz of 'Tracy? What about our Tracy? She's asleep upstairs. Isn't she asleep upstairs?'

'Are you Mum?' Mirabelle then asked.

'What do you mean, am I Mum? Course I'm Tracy's mum. What do you want?' Roz clearly spoke with rising hysteria and Mirabelle's reply sounded, as always, reasonable.

'We want to look after your Tracy, Mum. We feel she needs rather special care. I'm sure you're both going to help us. We do rely on Mum and Dad to be *very* sensible.'

Roz was not deceived by the soothing tones and concerned smile. She got the awful message and the shock of it brought her coldly to her senses. 'You come to take Tracy away, haven't you?' And before the question was answered she shouted, 'You're not bloody taking her away!'

'We just want to do the very best for your little girl. That's all, Mum.' At which Mirabelle detached a dreaded and official-looking document from the clipboard she was carrying. 'We do have a court order. Now shall we go and wake Tracy up? Ever so gently.'

It would be unnecessarily painful to dwell on the scene that followed. Roz fought like a tigress for her young and had to be restrained, at first by her husband, who had learned, as a juvenile, the penalty for assaulting the powers of justice, and then by the

uniformed officer who was called in from the car. The Timsons were
told that they would be able to argue the case in court eventually, the
woman police officer helped pack a few clothes for Tracy in a small
case and, as the child was removed from the house, Mirabelle took
the Barbie doll from her, explaining that it was bad for children in
such circumstances to have too many things that reminded them of
home. So young Tracy Timson was taken into custody and her parents came nearer to heartbreak than they ever had in their lives, even
when Cary got a totally unexpected two years' for the theft of a
clapped-out Volvo Estate from Safeway's car-park. Throughout it all
it's fair to say that Miss Mirabelle Jones behaved with the tact and
consideration which made her such a star of the Social Services and
such a dangerous witness in the Juvenile Court.

Tracy Timson was removed to a gloomy Victorian villa now
known as The Lilacs, Crockthorpe Council Children's Home, where
she will stay for the remainder of this story, and Mirabelle set out to
interview what she called Tracy's peers, by which she meant the other
kids Tracy was at school with, and, in the course of her activities, she
called at another house in Morrison Close, this one being occupied
by the father and mother of young Dominic Molloy. Now anyone
who knows anything about the world we live in, anyone who keeps his
or her ear to the ground and picks up as much information as possible
about family rivalry in the Crockthorpe area, will know that the Molloys and the Timsons are chalk and cheese and as deadly rivals as the

Montagues and the Capulets, the Guelphs and the Ghibellines, or York and Lancaster. The Molloys are an extended family; they are also villains, but of a more purposeful and efficient variety. To the Timsons' record of small-time thieving the Molloys added wounding, grievous bodily harm and an occasional murder. Now Mirabelle called on the eight-year-old Dominic Molloy and, after a preliminary consultation with him and his parents, he agreed to help her with her inquiries. This, in turn, led to a further interview in an office at the school with young Dominic which was immortalised on videotape.

I remember my first conference with Tracy's parents, because on that morning Hilda and I had a slight difference of opinion on the subject of the Scales of Justice Ball. This somewhat grisly occasion is announced annually on a heavily embossed card which arrived, with the gas bill and various invitations to insure my life and go on Mediterranean cruises, on the Rumpole breakfast table.

I had launched this invitation towards the tidy-bin to join the tea-leaves and the eggshells when Hilda, whose eagle eye misses nothing, immediately retrieved it, shook various particles of food off it and challenged me with, 'And why are you throwing this away, Rumpole?'

'You don't want to go, Hilda.' I did my best to persuade her. 'Disgusting sight, Her Majesty's judges, creaking round in the foxtrot at the Savoy Hotel. You wouldn't enjoy it.'

'I suppose not, Rumpole. Not in the circumstances.'

'Not in what circumstances?'

'It's too humiliating.'

'I quite agree.' I saw her point at once. 'When Mr Justice Graves breaks into the veleta I hang my head in shame.'

'It's humiliating for me, Rumpole, when other chaps in Chambers lead their wives out on to the floor.'

'Not a pretty sight, I have to agree, the waltzing Bollards, the pirouetting Erskine-Browns.'

'Why do you never lead me out on to the dance floor nowadays, Rumpole?' She asked me the question direct. 'I sometimes dream about it. We're at the Scales of Justice Ball. At the Savoy Hotel. And you lead me out on to the floor, as the first lady in Chambers.'

'You are, Hilda,' I hastened to agree with her, 'you're quite definitely the senior . . .'

'But you never lead me out, Rumpole! We have to sit there, staring at each other across the table, while all around us couples are dancing the night away.'

'Hilda' – I decided to disclose my defence – 'I have, as you know, many talents, but I'm not Nijinsky. Anyway, we don't get much practice at dancing down the Old Bailey.'

'Oh, it doesn't matter. When is the ball? Marigold Featherstone told me but I can't quite remember.' I saw, with a sort of dread, that she was checking the food-stained invitation to answer her question. 'November the 18th! It just happens to be my birthday. Well, we'll stay at home, as usual. At least I won't have to sit and watch other happy people dancing together.' And now she applied the corner of a handkerchief to her eye.

'Please, Hilda,' I begged, 'not the waterworks!' At which she sniffed bravely and dismissed me from her presence.

'No, of course not. Go along now. You've got to get to work. Work's the only thing that matters to you. You'd rather defend a murderer than dance with your wife.'

'Well, yes. Perhaps,' I had to admit. 'Look, do cheer up, old thing. Please.' She gave me her last lament as I moved towards the door.

'Old, yes, I suppose. We're both too old for a party. And I'll just have to get used to the fact that I didn't marry a dancer.'

'Sorry, Hilda.'

So I left She Who Must Be Obeyed, sitting alone in the kitchen and looking, as I thought, genuinely unhappy. I had seen her miffed before. I had seen her outraged. I had seen her, all too frequently, intensely displeased at some item of Rumpole's behaviour which fell short of perfection. But I was unprepared for the sadness which seemed to have engulfed her. Had she spent her life imagining she was Ginger Rogers, and was she at last reconciled to the fact that I had neither the figure nor the top hat to play whatever his name was – Astaire? For a moment a sensation to which I am quite unused came over me. I felt inadequate. However, I pulled myself together and pointed myself in the direction of my Chambers in the Temple, where I knew I had a conference with a couple of Timsons in what I imagined would be no more than a routine case of petty thievery.

I had acted for Cary before in a little matter of lead removed from the roof of Crockthorpe Methodist Church. He was tall and thin, and usually spoke in a slow, mocking way as though he found the whole of life slightly amusing. He didn't look amused now. His wife, Roz, was a solid girl in her late twenties with broad cheek-bones and capable hands. In attendance was the faithful Mr Bernard, who, from time immemorial, has acted as the solicitor-general to the Timson family.

'They wouldn't let Tracy take even a doll. Not one of her Barbies. How do you think people could do that to a child?' Roz asked me when Mr Bernard had outlined the facts of the case. Her eyes were red and swollen and, as she sat in my client's chair, nervously twisting her wedding ring, she looked not much older than a child herself.

'Nicking your kid. That's what it's come to. Well, I'll allow us Timsons may have done a fair bit of mischief in our time. But no one in the family's ever stooped to that, Mr Rumpole.' And Cary Timson added for greater emphasis, 'People what nick kids get boiling cocoa poured on their heads, when they're inside like.'

'Cary worships that girl, Mr Rumpole,' Roz told me. 'No matter what they say.'

'Take a look at these' – her husband was already pulling out his wallet – 'and you'll see the reason why.' So the brightly coloured snaps were laid proudly on my desk and I saw the three of them on a Spanish beach, at a theme park or on days out in the country. The mother and father held their child aloft, in the manner of successful athletes with a golden prize, triumphantly and with unmistakable delight.

'Bloody marvellous, isn't it?' Cary's gentle mocking had turned to genuine anger. 'Eight years old and our Trace needs a brief.'

'You'll get Tracy back for us, won't you, Mr Rumpole?' I thought Roz must have given birth to this much-loved daughter when she was about seventeen. 'She'll be that unhappy.'

'You seen the photos, Mr Rumpole.' And Cary asked, 'Does she have the look of a villain?'

'I'd say not a hardened criminal,' I had to admit.

'What's her crime, Mr Rumpole? That's what Roz and I wants to know. It's not as though she nicked things ever.'

'Well, not really -' And Roz admitted, 'She'll take a Jaffa cake when I'm not looking, or a few sweets occasionally.'

'Our Tracy's too young for any serious nicking.' Her father was sure of it. 'What you reckon she done, Mr Rumpole? What they got on her charge-sheet?'

'Childhood itself seems a crime to some people.' It's a point that has often struck me.

'We can't seem to get any sense out of that Miss Jones.' Roz looked helpless.

'Jones?'

'Officer in charge of case. Tracy's social worker.'

'One of the "caring" community.' I was sure of it.

'All she'll say is that she's making further inquiries,' Mr Bernard told me.

'I never discovered what I'd done when they banged me up in a draughty great boarding-school at the age of eight.' I looked back down the long corridor of years and began to reminisce.

'Hear that, Roz?' Cary turned to his wife. 'They banged up Mr Rumpole when he was a kid.'

'Did they, Mr Rumpole? Did they really?'

But before I could give them further and better particulars of the bird I had done at Linklaters, that down-market public school I attended on the Norfolk coast, Mr Bernard brought us back to the fantastic facts of the case and the nature of the charges against Tracy. 'I've been talking to the solicitor for the local authority', he reported, 'and their case is that the juvenile Timson has been indulging in devil-worship, hellish rituals and satanic rights.'

It might be convenient if I were to give you an account of that filmed interview with Dominic Molloy which, as I have told you, we finally saw at the trial. Before that, Mr Bernard had acquired a transcript of this dramatic scene, so we were, by bits and pieces, made aware of the bizarre charges against young Tracy, a case which began to look as though it should be transferred from Crockthorpe Juvenile Court to Seville to be decided by hooded inquisitors in the darkest days of the Spanish Inquisition.

The scene was set in the headmistress's office in Stafford Cripps Junior. Mirabelle Jones, at her most reassuring, sat smiling on one side of the desk, while young Dominic Molloy, beaming with self-importance, played the starring role on the other.

'You remember the children wearing those horrid masks at school, do you, Dominic?' Mirabelle kicked off the proceedings.

'They scared me!' Dominic gave a realistic shudder.

'I'm sure they did.' The social worker made a note, gave the camera – no doubt installed in the corner of the room – the benefit of her smile and then returned to the work in hand.

'Did you see who was leading those children?'

'In the end I did.'

'Who was it?'

'Trace.'

'Tracy Timson?'

'Yes.'

'Your mum said you went round to Tracy Timson's a few times. After school, was that?'

'Yes. After school like.'

'And then you said you went somewhere else. Where else, exactly?'

'Where they put people.'

'A churchyard. Was it a churchyard?' Mirabelle gave us a classic example of a leading question. Dominic nodded approval and she made a note. 'The one in Crockthorpe Road, the church past the roundabout? St Elphick's?' Mirabelle suggested and Dominic nodded again. 'It was the churchyard. Was it dark?' Dominic nodded so eagerly that his whole body seemed to rock backwards and forwards and he was in danger of falling off his chair.

'After school and late. A month ago? So it was dark. Did a grown-up come with you? A man, perhaps. Did a man come with you?'

'He said we was to play a game.' Now Dominic had resorted to a kind of throaty whisper, guaranteed to make the flesh creep.

'What sort of game?'

'He put something on his face.'

'A mask?'

'Red and horns on it.'

'A devil's mask.' Mirabelle was scribbling enthusiastically. 'Is that right, Dominic? He wanted you to play at devils? This man did?'

'He said he was the Devil. Yes.'

'He was to be the Devil. And what were you supposed to be?'

Dominic didn't answer that, but sat as if afraid to move.

'Perhaps you were the Devil's children?'

At this point Dominic's silence was more effective than any answer.

'What was the game you had to play?' Mirabelle tried another approach.

'Dance around.' The answer came in a whisper.

'Dance around. Now I want you to tell me, Dominic, when did you meet this man? At Tracy Timson's house? Is that where you met him?' More silence from Dominic, so Mirabelle tried again. 'Do you know who he was, Dominic?' At which Dominic nodded and looked round fearfully.

'Who was he, Dominic? You've been such a help to me so far. Can't you tell me who he was?'

'Tracy's dad.'

Everything changes and with ever-increasing rapidity. Human beings no longer sell tickets at the Temple tube station. Machines and not disillusioned waitresses dispense the so-called coffee in the Old Bailey canteen and, when I became aware that Dianne, our long-time typist and close personal friend to Henry, our clerk, had left the service, I feared and expected that she might be replaced by a robot. However, what I found behind the typewriter, when I blew into the clerk's room after a hard day's work on an Actual Bodily Harm in Acton a few weeks after my conference with Tracy's parents, was nothing more mechanical than an unusually pretty and very young woman, wearing a skirt as short as a suspended sentence and a smile so ready that it seemed never to leave her features entirely but to be waiting around for the next opportunity to beam. Henry introduced her as Miss Clapton. 'Taken over from Dianne, Mr Rumpole, who has just got herself married. I don't know if you've heard the news.'

'Married? Henry, I'm sorry.'

'To a junior clerk in a bankruptcy set.' He spoke with considerable disgust. 'I told her she'd live to regret it.'

'Welcome to Equity Court, Miss Clapton,' I said. 'If you behave really well, you might get parole in about ten years.' She gave me the smile at full strength, but my attention was diverted by the sight of Mizz Liz Probert who had just picked up a brief from the mantelpiece and was looking at it with every sign of rapture. Liz, the daughter of Red Ron Probert, Labour leader on the Crockthorpe Council, is the most radical member of our Chambers. I greeted her with, 'Soft you now! The fair Mizz Probert! What are you fondling there, old thing?' Or words to that effect.

'What does it look like, Rumpole?'

'It looks suspiciously like a brief.'

'Got it in one!' Mizz Liz was in a perky mood that evening.

'Time marches on! My ex-pupil has begun to acquire briefs. What is it? Bad case of Non-Renewed Dog Licence?'

'A bit more serious than that. I'm for the Crockthorpe local authority, Rumpole.'

'I am suitably overawed.' I didn't ask whether the presence of Red Ron on the council had anything to do with this manna from heaven, and Mizz Liz went on to tell a familiar story.

'A little girl had to be taken into care. She's in terrible danger in the home. You know what it is – the father's got a criminal record. As a matter of fact, it's a name that might be familiar to you. Timson.'

'So they took away a Timson child because the father's got form?' I asked innocently, hoping for further information.

'Not just that. Something rather awful was going on. Devil-worship! The family were deeply into it. Quite seriously. It's a shocking case.'

'Is it really? Tell me, do you believe in the Devil?'

'Of course I don't, Rumpole. Don't be so ridiculous! Anyway, that's hardly the point.'

'Isn't it? It interests me, though. You see, I'm likely to be against you in the Juvenile Court.'

'You, Rumpole! On the side of the Devil?' Mizz Probert seemed genuinely shocked.

'Why not? They tell me he has the best lines.'

'Defending devil-worshippers, in a *children's* case! That's really not on, is it, Rumpole?'

'I really can't think of anyone I wouldn't defend. That's what I believe in. I was just on my way to Pommeroy's. Mizz Liz, old thing, will you join me in a stiffener?'

'I don't really think we should be seen drinking together, not now I'm appearing for the local authority.'

'For the local authority, of course!' I gave her a respectful bow on leaving. 'A great power in the land! Even if they do rather interfere with the joy of living.'

No sooner had I got to Pommeroy's Wine Bar and chalked up the first glass of Jack Pommeroy's Very Ordinary when Claude Erskine-Brown of our Chambers came into view in a state of considerable excitement about the new typist. 'An enormous asset, don't you think? Dot will bring a flood of spring sunshine into our clerk's room.'

'Dot?' I was puzzled. 'What are you babbling about?'

'Her name's Dot, Rumpole. She told me that. I said it was a beautiful name.'

I didn't need to tell the fellow he was making a complete ass of himself; this was a fact too obvious to mention.

'I've told her she must come to me if she has any problems work-wise.' Claude is, of course, married to Phillida Erskine-Brown, QC, the attractive and highly competent Portia of our Chambers. Perhaps it's because he has to play second fiddle to this powerful advocate that Claude is forever on the look-out for alternative company, a pursuit which brings little but embarrassment to himself and those around him. I saw nothing but trouble arising from the appearance of this Dot upon the Erskine-Brown horizon, but now the fellow completely changed the subject and said, 'You know Charlie Wisbeach?'

'I've never heard of him.'

'Wisbeach, Bottomley, Perkins & Harris.' Erskine-Brown spoke in an awe-struck whisper as though repeating a magic formula.

'Good God! Are they *all* here?'

'I rather think Claude's talking about my dad's firm.' This came from a plumpish but fairly personable young man who was in the offing, holding a bottle of champagne and a glass, which he now refilled and also gave a shower of bubbles to Erskine-Brown.

'Just the best firm in the City, Rumpole. Quality work. And Charlie here's come to the Bar. He wants a seat in Chambers.' Erskine-Brown sounded remarkably keen on the idea, no doubt hoping for work from the firm of Wisbeach, Bottomley, Perkins & Harris.

'Oh, yes?' I sniffed danger. 'And where would he like it? There might be an inch or two available in the downstairs loo. Didn't we decide we were full up at the last Chambers meeting?'

'I say, you must be old Rumpole!' Young Wisbeach was looking at me as though I were some extinct species still on show in the Natural History Museum.

'I'm afraid I've got very little choice in the matter,' I had to admit.

'You're not still practising, are you?' Charlie Wisbeach had the gall to ask.

'Not really. I suppose I've learned how to do it by now.'

'Oh, but Claude Erskine-Brown told me you'd soon be retiring.'

'Did you, Claude? Did you tell young Charlie that?' I turned upon the treacherous Erskine-Brown the searchlight eyes and spoke in the pained tones of the born cross-examiner.

'Well, no. Not exactly, Rumpole.' The man fumbled for words. 'Well, of course, I just assumed you'd be retiring sometime.'

'Don't count on it, Erskine-Brown. Don't you ever count on it!'

'And Claude told me that when you retired, old chap, there might be a bit of space in your Chambers.' The usurper Wisbeach apparently found the situation amusing. 'A pretty enormous space is what I think he said. Didn't you, Claude?'

'Well no, Charlie. No . . . Not *quite*.' Erskine-Brown's embarrassment proved his guilt.

'It sounds like an extremely humorous conversation.' I gave them both the look contemptuous.

'Charlie has a pretty impressive c.v., Rumpole.' Erskine-Brown tried to change the subject as his new-found friend gave him another slurp.

'See what?'

'Curriculum vitae. Eton . . . '

'Oh. Good at that as well, is he? I thought it was mainly drinkin'.'

'Claude's probably referring to the old school.' Wisbeach could not, of course, grasp the Rumpole joke.

'Oh, Eton! Well, I've no doubt you'll rise above the handicaps of a deprived childhood. In somebody else's Chambers.'

'As a matter of fact Claude showed me *your* room.' Wisbeach gave the damning evidence. 'Very attractive accommodation.'

'You did *what*, Claude?'

'Charlie and I . . . Well, we . . . called in to see you. But you were doing that long arson in Snaresbrook.'

'Historic spot, your room!' Wisbeach told me as though I'd never seen the place before. 'Fine views over the churchyard. Don't you look straight down at Dr Johnson's tomb?'

'It's Oliver Goldsmith's, as it so happens.' Eton seemed to have done little for the man's store of essential knowledge.

'No, Johnson's!' You can't tell an old Etonian anything.

'Goldsmith,' I repeated, with the last of my patience.

'Want to bet?'

'Not particularly.'

'Your old room needs a good deal of decorating, of course. And some decent furniture. But the idea is, we might share. While you're still practising, Rumpole.'

'That's not an idea. It's a bad dream.' I directed my rejection of the offer at Erskine-Brown, who started up a babble of 'Rumpole! Think of the work that Wisbeach could send us!'

'And I would like to let it be known that *I* still have work of my own to do, and I do it best alone. As a free spirit! Wrongs are still righted.' Here I drained my plonk to the dregs and stood up, umbrella in hand. 'Mr Justice Graves is still putting the boot in. Chief Inspector Brush is still referring to his unreliable notebook. And an eight-year-old Timson has been banged up against her will, not in Eton College like you, Master Charlie, but in the tender care of the Crockthorpe local authority. The child is suspected of devil-worship. Can you believe it? An offence which I thought went out with the burning of witches.'

'Is that your case, Rumpole?' Erskine-Brown looked deeply interested.

'Indeed, yes. And I have a formidable opponent. None other than Mizz Liz Probert, with the full might of the local authority behind her. So, while there are such challenges to be overcome, let me tell you, Claude, and you, Charlie Whatsit, Rumpole shall never sheath the sword. Never!'

So I left the bar with my umbrella held aloft like the weapon of a crusader, and the effect of this exit was only slightly marred by my colliding with a couple of trainee solicitors who were blocking the fairway. As I apologised and lowered the umbrella I could distinctly hear the appalling Wisbeach say, 'Funny old buffer!'

In all my long experience down the Bailey and in lesser courts I have not known a villain as slithery and treacherous as Claude Erskine-

Brown proved on that occasion. As soon as he could liberate himself from the cuckoo he intended to place in my nest, he dashed up to Equity Court in search of our Head of Chambers, Samuel Ballard, QC. Henry, who was working late on long-delayed fee notes, told him that Soapy Sam was at a service with his peer group, the Lawyers As Christians Society, in the Temple church. Undeterred, Claude set off to disturb the holy and devoutly religious Soapy at prayer. It was, he told a mystified Henry as he departed, just the place to communicate the news he had in mind.

I am accustomed to mix with all sorts of dubious characters in pursuit of evidence and, when I bought a glass of Pommeroy's for an LAC (member of the Lawyers As Christians Society), I received an astonishing account of Claude's entry into evensong. Pushing his way down the pew he arrived beside our Head of Chambers, who had risen to his feet to an organ accompaniment and was about to give vent to a hymn. Attending worshippers were able to hear dialogue along the following lines.

'Erskine-Brown. Have you joined us?' Ballard was surprised.

'Of course I've joined LACS. Subscription's in the post. But I had to tell you about Rumpole, as a matter of urgency.'

'Please, Erskine-Brown. This is no place to be talking about such matters as Rumpole.'

'*Devil-worshippers*. Rumpole's in with devil-worshippers,' Claude said in a voice calculated to make our leader's flesh creep.

However, at this moment, the hymn-singing began and Ballard burst out with:

> '*God moves in a mysterious way*
> *His wonders to perform;*
> *He plants his footsteps in the sea,*
> *And rides upon the storm.*'

Betraying a certain talent for improvisation, my informant told me that he distinctly heard Claude Erskine-Brown join in with:

> '*Rumpole in his mischievous way*
> *Has taken on a case*
> *About some devil-worshippers.*
> *He's had them in your place!*
> *Your Chambers, I mean.*'

At which point Ballard turned and looked at the conniving Claude with deep and horrified concern.

★

It was a time when everyone seemed intent on investigating the alleged satanic cult. Mirabelle Jones continued to make films for showing before the Juvenile Court and this time she interviewed Tracy Timson in a room, also equipped with a camera and recording apparatus, in the children's home.

Mirabelle arrived, equipped with dolls, not glamorous pin-up girls, but a somewhat drab and unsexy family consisting of a Mum and Dad, Grandpa and Grandma, who looked like solemn New England farm-workers. Tracy was ordered to play with this group, and when, without any real interest in the matter, she managed to get Grandpa lying on top of Mum, Miss Jones sucked in her breath and made a note which she underlined heavily.

Later, Tracy was shown a book in which there was a picture of a devil with a forked tail, who looked like an opera singer about to undertake Mephisto-pheles in Faust. The question-ing, as recorded in the trans-cript, then went along these lines.

'You know who he is, don't you, Tracy?' Mirabelle was being particularly compassion-ate as she asked this.

'No.'

'He's the Devil. You know about devils, don't you?' And she added, still smiling, 'You put on a devil's mask at school, didn't you, Tracy?'

'I might have done.' Tracy made an admission.

'So what do you think of the Devil, then?'

'He looks funny.' Tracy was smiling, which I thought, in all the circumstances, was remarkably brave of her.

'Funny?'

'He's got a tail. The tail's funny.'

'Who first told you about the Devil, Tracy?'

'I don't know,' the child answered, but the persistent inquisitor was not to be put off so easily.

'Oh, you must know. Did you hear about the Devil at home? Was that it? Did Dad tell you about the Devil?'

Tracy shook her head. Mirabelle Jones sighed and tried again. 'Does that picture of the Devil remind you of anyone, Tracy?' Still getting no answer, Mirabelle resorted to a leading question, as was her way in these interviews. 'Do you think it looks like your dad at all?'

In search of an answer to Miss Jones's unanswered question, I summoned Cary and Roz to my presence once again. When they arrived, escorted by the faithful Bernard, I put the matter as bluntly as I knew how. At the mention of evil, Tracy's mother merely looked puzzled. 'The Devil? Tracy don't know nothing about the Devil.'

'Of course not!' Cary's denial was immediate. 'It's not as if we went to church, Mr Rumpole.'

'You've never heard of such a suggestion before?' I looked hard at Tracy's father. 'The Devil. Satan. Beelzebub. Are you saying the Timson family knows nothing of such matters?'

'Nothing at all, Mr Rumpole.'

'When they came that morning . . .'

'When they came to get our Tracy?' Roz's eyes filled with tears as she relived the moment.

'Yes. When they came for that. What did you *think* was going on exactly?' I asked Cary the question.

'I thought they come about that shop that got done over, Wedges, down Gunston Avenue. They've had me down the nick time and time again about it.'

'And it wasn't you?'

'Straight up, Mr Rumpole. Would I deceive you?'

'It has been known, but I'll believe you. Do you know who did it?' I asked Cary.

'No, Mr Rumpole. No, I won't grass. That I won't do. I've had enough trouble being accused of grassing on Gareth Molloy when he was sent down for the Tobler Road supermarket job.'

'The Timsons and the Molloys are deadly enemies. How could you know what they were up to?'

'My mate Barry Peacock was driving for them on that occasion. They thought I knew something and grassed to Chief Inspector Brush. Would I do a thing like that?'

'No, I don't suppose you would. So you thought the Old Bill were just there about ordinary, legitimate crime. You had no worries about Tracy?'

'She's a good girl, Mr Rumpole. Always has been,' Roz was quick to remind me.

'Always cheerful, isn't she, Roz?' Her husband added to the evidence of character. 'I enjoys her company.'

'So where the devil do these ideas come from? Sorry, perhaps I shouldn't've said that . . . You know Dominic Molloy told the social worker you taught a lot of children satanic rituals.'

'You ever believed a Molloy, have you, Mr Rumpole, in Court or out of it?' Cary Timson had a good point there, but I rather doubted if I could convince the Juvenile Court of the wisdom learned at the Old Bailey.

When our conference was over I showed my visitors out and I thought I saw, peering from a slightly open doorway at the end of the corridor, the face of Erskine-Brown, as horrified and intent as a passer-by who suddenly notices that, on the other side of the street, a witches' coven is holding its annual beano. The door shut as soon as I clocked him and Claude vanished within. Twenty minutes later I received a visit from Soapy Sam Ballard, QC, our so-called Head of Chambers. I don't believe that these events were unconnected. As soon as he got in, Ballard sniffed the air as though detecting the scent of brimstone and said, 'You've had them in here, Rumpole?'

'Had who in here, Bollard?'

'Those who owe allegiance to the Evil One.'

'You mean the Mr Justice Graves fan club? No. They haven't been near the place.'

'Rumpole! You know perfectly well who I mean.'

'Oh, yes. Of course.' I decided to humour the fellow. 'They were all here. Lucifer, Beelzebub, Belial. All present and correct.

> 'High on a throne of royal state, which far
> Outshone the wealth of Ormus and of Ind,
> Or where the gorgeous East with richest hand
> Showers on her kings barbaric pearl and gold,
> Satan exalted sat, by merit raised
> To that bad eminence; and from despair
> Thus high uplifted beyond hope.

'Grow up, Bollard! I am representing an eight-year-old child who's been torn from the bosom of her family and banged up without trial. You see here Rumpole, the protector of the innocent.'

'The protector of devil-worshippers!' Ballard said.

'Those too. If necessary.' I sat down at the desk and picked up the papers in a somewhat tedious affray.

'Rumpole. Every decent Chambers has to draw the line some-where.'

'Does it?'

'There are certain cases, certain clients even, which are simply, well, not acceptable.'

'Oh, I do agree.'

'Do you?'

'Oh, yes. I agree entirely.'

'Well, then. I'm glad to hear it.' Soapy Sam looked as gratified as a cleric hearing a deathbed confession from a lifelong heathen.

'Didn't I catch sight of you prosecuting an accountant for unpaid VAT?' I asked the puzzled QC. 'Some cases are simply unaccept-able. Far too dull to be touched by a decent barrister with a bargepole. Don't you agree, old darling?'

'Rumpole, there's something I meant to raise with you.' The saintly Sam was growing distinctly ratty.

'Then buck up and raise it, I'm busy.' I returned to the affray.

'Young Charlie Wisbeach wants to come into these Chambers. He'd bring us a great deal of high-class, *commercial* work from his father's firm. Unfortunately we have no room for him at the moment.'

'Has he thought of a cardboard box in Middle Temple Lane?' I thought this a helpful suggestion; Bollard didn't agree.

'This is neither the time nor the place for one of your jokes, Rumpole. You have a tenancy here and tenancies can be brought to an end. Especially if the tenant in question is carrying on a practice not in the best traditions of 3 Equity Court. There is something in this room which makes me feel uneasy.'

'Oh, I do so agree. Perhaps you'll be leaving shortly.'

'I'm giving you fair warning, Rumpole. I expect you to think it over.' At which our leader made for the door and I called after him, 'Oh, before you go, Bollard, why don't you look up "exorcism" in the *Yellow Pages*? I believe there's an unfrocked bishop in Stepney who'll quote you a very reasonable price. And if you call again, don't forget the holy water!'

But the man had gone and I was left alone to wonder exactly what devilment Cary Timson had been up to.

I have, or at a proper moment I will have, a confession to make. At this time I was presenting She Who Must Be Obeyed with a mystery which she no doubt found baffling, although I'm afraid a probable solution presented itself to her mind far too soon. I had reason to telephone a Miss Tatiana Fern and, not wishing to do so with Hilda's knowledge, and as the lady in question left her house early, I called when I thought She was still asleep. I now suspect Hilda was listening in on the bedroom extension, although she lay motionless and with her eyes closed when I came back to bed. Later I discovered that when Hilda went off to shop in Harrods she spotted me coming out of Knightsbridge tube station, a place far removed from the Temple and the Old Bailey, and sleuthed me to a house in Mowbray Crescent which she saw me enter when the front door was opened by the aforesaid Tatiana Fern. So it came about that She met Marigold, Mr Justice Featherstone's outspoken wife, and together they formed the opinion that Rumpole was up to no good whatsoever.

Of course, She didn't tackle me openly about this, but I could sense what was in the wind when she started up a conversation about the male libido at breakfast one morning. It followed from something she had read in her *Daily Telegraph*.

'They're doing it again, Rumpole.'

'Who are?'

'Men.'

'Ah.'

'Causing trouble in the workplace.'

'Yes. I suppose so.'

'Brushing up against their secretaries. Unnecessarily. I suppose that's something you approve of, Rumpole?'

'I haven't got a secretary, Hilda. I've got a clerk called Henry. I've never felt the slightest temptation to brush up against Henry.' And that answer you might have thought would finish the matter, but Hilda had more information from the *Telegraph* to impart.

'They put it all down to glands. Men've got too much something in their glands. That's a fine excuse, isn't it?'

'Never tried it.' But I thought it over. 'I suppose I might: "My client intends to rely on the glandular defence, my Lord." '

'It wouldn't wash.' Hilda was positive. 'When I was a child we were taught to believe in the Devil.'

'I'm sure you were.'

'He tempts people. Particularly men.'

'I thought it was Eve.'

'What?'

'I thought it was Eve he tempted first.'

'That's you all over, Rumpole.'

'Is it?'

'Blame it all on a woman! That's men all over.'

'Hilda, there's nothing I'd like more than to sit here with you all day, discussing theology. But I've got to get to work.' I was making my preparations for departure when She said darkly, 'Enjoy your lunch-hour!'

'What did you say?'

'I said, "I hope you enjoy your lunch-hour", Rumpole.'

'Well, I probably shall. It's Thursday. Steak pie day at the pub in Ludgate Circus. I shall look forward to that.'

'And a few other little treats besides, I should imagine.'

Hilda was immersed in her newspaper again when I left her. I knew then that, no matter what explanation I had given, She Who Must Be Obeyed had come to the firm conclusion that I was up to something devilish.

It's a strange fact that it was not until nearly the end of the threescore years and ten allotted to me by the psalmist that I was first called upon to perform in a Juvenile Court. It was, as I was soon to discover, a place in which the law as we know and occasionally love it had very little place. It was also a soulless chamber in Crockthorpe's already chipped and crumbling glass and concrete courthouse complex. Tracy's three judges – a large motherly-looking magistrate as chairwoman, flanked by a small, bright-eyed Sikh justice in a sari, and a lean and anxious headmaster – sat with their clerk, young, officious and bespectacled, to keep them in order. The defence team, Rumpole and the indispensable Bernard, together with the prosecutor, Mizz Liz Probert, and a person from the council solicitor's office, sat at another long table opposite the justices. Miss Mirabelle Jones, armed with a ponderous file, was comfortably ensconced in the witness chair and a large television set was playing that hit video, the interview with Dominic Molloy.

We had got to the familiar dialogue which started with Mirabelle's question: 'He wanted you to play at devils? This man did?'

'He said he was the Devil. Yes,' the picture of the boy Dominic alleged.

'He was to be the Devil. And what were you supposed to be? Perhaps you were the Devil's children?'

At which point Rumpole ruined the entertainment by rearing to his hind legs and making an objection, a process which in this court seemed as unusual and unwelcome as a guest lifting his soup plate to his mouth and slurping the contents at a state banquet at Buckingham Palace. When I said I was objecting, the clerk switched off the telly with obvious reluctance.

'That was a leading question by the social worker,' I said, although the fact would have been obvious to the most superficial reader of *Potted Rules of Evidence*. 'It and the answer are entirely inadmissible, as your clerk will no doubt tell you.' And I added, in an extremely audible whisper to Bernard, 'If he knows his business.'

'Mr Rumpole' – the chairwoman gave me her most motherly smile – 'Miss Mirabelle Jones is an extremely experienced social worker. We think we can rely on her to put her questions in the proper manner.'

'I was just venturing to point out that on this occasion she put her question in an entirely improper manner,' I told her, 'madam.'

'My Bench will see the film to the end, Mr Rumpole. You'll have a chance to make any points later.' The clerk gave his decision in a manner which caused me to whisper to Mr Bernard, 'Her Master's Voice.' I hope they all heard, but to make myself clear I said to Madam Chair, 'My point is that you shouldn't be seeing this film at all.'

'We are going to continue with it now, Mr Rumpole.' The learned clerk switched on the video again. Miss Jones appeared to ask, 'What was the game you had to play?' And Dominic answered, 'Dance around.'

'Dance around.' Mirabelle Jones's shadow repeated in case we had missed the point. 'Now I want you to tell me, Dominic, when did you meet this man? At Tracy Timson's house? Is that where you met him?'

'It's a leading question!' I said aloud, but the performance continued and Mirabelle asked, 'Do you know who he was?' And on the screen Dominic nodded politely.

'Who was he?' Mirabelle asked and Dominic replied, 'Tracy's dad.'

As the video was switched off, I was on my feet again. 'You're not going to allow that evidence?' I couldn't believe it. 'Pure hearsay! What a child who isn't called as a witness said to Miss Jones here, a child we've had no opportunity of cross-examining said, is nothing but hearsay. Absolutely worthless.'

'Madam Chairwoman.' Mizz Probert rose politely beside me.

'Yes, Miss Probert.' Liz got an even more motherly smile; she was the favourite child and Rumpole the black sheep of the family.

'Mr Rumpole is used to practising at the Old Bailey —'

'And has managed to acquire a nodding acquaintance of the law of evidence,' I added.

'And of course *this* Court is not bound by strict rules of evidence. Where the welfare of a child is concerned, you're not tied down by a lot of legal quibbles about hearsay.'

'Quibbles, Mizz Probert? Did I hear you say quibbles?' My righteous indignation was only half simulated.

'You are free,' Liz told the tribunal, 'with the able assistance of Miss Mirabelle Jones, to get at the truth of this matter.'

'My learned friend was my pupil.' I was, I must confess, more than a little hurt. 'I spent months, a year of my life, in bringing her up with some rudimentary knowledge of the law. And when she says that the rule against hearsay is a legal quibble . . . '

'Mr Rumpole, I don't think my Bench wants to waste time on a legal argument.' The clerk of the Court breathed heavily on his glasses and polished them briskly.

'Do they not? Indeed!' I was launched on an impassioned protest and no one was going to stop me. 'So does it come to this? Down at the Old Bailey, that backward and primitive place, no villain can be sent down to chokey as a result of a leading question, or a bit of gossip in the saloon bar, or what a child said to a social worker and wasn't even cross-examined. But little Tracy Timson, eight years old, can be banged up for an indefinite period, snatched from the family that loves her, without the protection the law affords to the most violent bank robber! Is that the proposition that Mizz Liz Probert is putting before the court? And which apparently finds favour in the so-called legal mind of the court official who keeps jumping up like a jack-in-the-box to tell you what to do?'

Even as I spoke the clerk, having shined up his spectacles to his total satisfaction, was whispering to his well-upholstered chair.

'Mr Rumpole, my Bench would like to get on with the evidence. Speeches will come later,' the chairwoman handed down her clerk's decision.

'They will, madam. They most certainly will,' I promised. And then, as I sat down, profoundly discontented, Liz presumed to teach me my business.

'Let me give you a tip, Rumpole,' she whispered. 'I should keep off the law if I were you. They don't like it around here.'

While I was recovering from this lesson given to me by my ex-pupil, our chairwoman was addressing Mirabelle as though she were a mixture of Mother Teresa and Princess Anne. 'Miss Jones,' she purred, 'we're grateful for the thoroughness with which you've gone into this difficult case on behalf of the local authority.'

'Oh, thank you so much, Madam Chair.'

'And we've seen the interview you carried out with Tracy on the video film. Was there anything about that interview which you thought especially significant?'

'It was when I showed her the picture of the Devil,' Mirabelle answered. 'She wasn't frightened at all. In fact she laughed. I thought . . . '

'Is there any point in my telling you that what this witness thought isn't evidence?' I sent up a cry of protest.

'Carry on, Miss Jones. If you'd be so kind.' Madam Chair decided to ignore the Rumpole interruption.

'I thought it was because it reminded her of someone she knew pretty well. Someone like Dad.' Mirabelle put in the boot with considerable delicacy.

'Someone like Dad. Yes.' Our chair was now making a careful note, likely to be fatal to Tracy's hopes of liberty. 'Have you any questions, Mr Rumpole?'

So I rose to cross-examine. It's no easy task to attack a personable young woman from one of the caring professions, but this Mirabelle Jones was, so far as my case was concerned, a killer. I decided that there was only one way to approach her and that was to go in with all guns firing. 'Miss Jones' – I loosed the first salvo – 'you are, I take it, against cruelty to children?'

'Of course. That goes without saying.'

'Does it? Can you think of a more cruel act, to a little child, than coming at dawn with the Old Bill and snatching it away from its mother and father, without even a Barbara doll for consolation?'

'Barbie doll, Mr Rumpole,' Roz whispered urgently.

'What?'

'It's a Barbie doll, Mrs Timson says,' Mr Bernard instructed me on what didn't seem to be the most vital point in the case.

'Very well, Barbie doll.' And I returned to the attack on Mirabelle. 'Without that, or a single toy?'

'We don't want the children to be distracted.'

'By thoughts of home?'

'Well, yes.'

'You wanted Tracy to concentrate on your dotty idea of devil-worship!' I put it bluntly.

'It wasn't a dotty idea, Mr Rumpole, and I had to act quickly. Tracy had to be removed from the presence of evil.'

'Evil? What do you mean by that exactly?' The witness hesitated, momentarily at a loss for a suitable definition in a rational age, and Mizz Liz Probert rose to the rescue.

'You ought to know, Mr Rumpole. Haven't you had plenty of experience of that down at the Old Bailey?'

'Oh, well played, Mizz Probert!' I congratulated her loudly. 'Your pupilling days are over. Now, Miss Mirabelle Jones' – I returned to my real opponent – 'let's come down, if we may, from the world of legend and hearsay and gossip and fantasy, to what we call, down at the Old Bailey, hard facts. You know that my client, Mr Cary Timson, is a small-time thief and a minor villain?'

'I have given the Bench the list of Dad's criminal convictions, yes.' Mirabelle looked obligingly into her file.

'It's not the sort of record, is it, Mr Rumpole, that you might expect a good father to have?' The chair smiled as she invited me to agree but I declined to do so.

'Oh, I don't know,' I said. 'Are only the most law-abiding citizens meant to have children? Are we about to remove their offspring from share-pushers, insider dealers and politicians who don't tell the truth? If we did, even this tireless local authority would run out of children's homes to bang them up in.'

'Speeches come later, Mr Rumpole.' The loquacious clerk could keep silent no longer.

'They will,' I promised him. 'Cary Timson is a humble member of the Clan Timson, that vast family of South London villains. Now, remind us of the name of that imaginative little boy you interviewed on prime-time television.'

'Dominic Molloy.' Mirabelle knew it by heart.

'Molloy, yes. And, as we've been told so often, you are an extremely experienced social worker.'

'I think so.'

'With a vast knowledge of the social life in this part of South London?'

'I get to know a good deal. Yes, of course I do.'

'Of course. So it will come as no surprise to you if I suggest that the Molloys are a large family of villains of a slightly more dangerous nature than the Timsons.'

'I didn't know that. But if you say so . . . '

'Oh, I do say so. Did you meet Dominic's mother, Mrs Peggy Molloy?'

'Oh, yes. I had a good old chat with Mum. Over a cuppa.' The Bench and Mirabelle exchanged smiles.

'And over a cuppa did she tell you that her husband, Gareth, Dominic's dad, was in Wandsworth as a result of the Tobler Road supermarket affair?'

'Mr Rumpole. My Bench is wondering if this is entirely relevant.' The clerk had been whispering to the chair and handed the words down from on high.

'Then let your Bench keep quiet and listen,' I told him. 'It'll soon find out. So what's the answer, Miss Jones? Did you know that?'

'I didn't know that Dominic's dad was in prison.' Miss Jones adopted something of a light, insouciant tone.

'And that he suspected Tracy's dad, as you would call him, Cary Timson, of having been the police informer who put him there?'

'Did he?' The witness seemed to find all this talk of adult crime somewhat tedious.

'Oh, yes. And I shall be calling hearsay evidence to prove it. Miss Jones, are you telling this Bench that you, an experienced social worker, didn't bother to find out about the deep hatred that exists between the Molloys and the Timsons, stretching back over generations of villainy to the dark days when Crockthorpe was a village and the local villains swung at the crossroads?'

'I have nothing about that in my file,' Mirabelle told us, as though that made all such evidence completely unimportant.

'Nothing in your file. And your file hasn't considered the possibility that young Dominic Molloy might have been encouraged to put an innocent little girl of a rival family ''in the frame'', as we're in-clined to call it down the Old Bailey?'

'It seems rather far-fetched to me.' Mirabelle gave me her most superior smile.

'Far-fetched, Miss Jones, to you who believe in devil-worship?'

'I believe in evil influences on children.' Mirabelle chose her words carefully. 'Yes.'

'Then let us just examine that. Your superstitions were first excited by the fact that a number of children appeared in the playground of Crockthorpe Junior wearing masks?'

'Devil's masks. Yes.'

'Yet the only one you took into so-called care was Tracy Timson?'

'She was the ring-leader. I discovered that Tracy had brought the masks to school in the kit-bag with her lunch and her reading books.'

'Did you ask her where she got them from?'

'I did. Of course, she wouldn't tell me.' Mirabelle smiled and I knew a possible reason for Tracy's silence. Even if Cary had been indulging in satanic rituals his daughter would never have grassed on him.

'I assumed it was from her father.' Mirabelle inserted her elegant boot once more.

'Miss Mirabelle Jones. Let's hope that at some point we'll get to a little reliable evidence, and that this case doesn't rely entirely on your assumptions.'

The lunch-break came none too soon and Mr Bernard and I went in search of a convenient watering-hole. The Jolly Grocer was to Pom-meroy's Wine Bar what the Crockthorpe Court was to the Old Bailey. It was a large, bleak pub and the lounge bar was resonant with the bleeping of computer games and the sound of muzak. Pommeroy's claret may be at the bottom end of the market, but I suspected that The Jolly Grocer's red would be pure paint stripper. I refreshed myself on a couple of bottles of Guinness and a pork pie, which was only a little better than minced rubber encased in cardboard, and then we started the short walk back to the Crockthorpe *Palais de Justice*.

On the way I let Bernard know my view of the proceedings so far. 'It's all very well to accuse the deeply caring Miss Mirabelle Jones of guessing,' I told him, 'but we've got to tell the old darlings on the Bench, bonny Bernard, where the hell the masks came from.'

'Our client, Mr Cary Timson . . . '

'You mean "Dad"?'

'Yes. He denies all knowledge.'

'Does he?' And then, quite suddenly, I came to a halt. I found myself outside a shop called Wedges Carnival and Novelty Stores. The window was full of games, fancy-dress, hats, crackers, Hallowe'en costumes, Father Christmas costumes, masks and other equipment for parties and general merry-making. It was while I was gazing with a wild surmise at these goods on display that I said to Mr Bernard, in the somewhat awe-struck tone of a watcher of the skies when a new planet swims into his ken, 'Well, he would, wouldn't he? The honour of the Timsons.'

'What do you mean, Mr Rumpole?'

'What's the name of this street? Is it by any chance . . . ?'

It was. My instructing solicitor, looking up at a street sign, said, 'Gunston Avenue.'

'Who robbed Wedges?' We had arrived back at the courthouse with ten minutes in hand and I found Cary Timson smoking a last fag on the gravel outside the main entrance. His wife was with him and I lost no time in asking the vital question.

'Mr Rumpole' – Tracy's dad looked round and lowered his voice – 'you know I can't—'

'Grass? It's the code of the Timsons, isn't it? Well, let me tell you, Cary. There's something even more important than your precious code.'

'I don't know it, then.'

'Oh, yes, you do. You know it perfectly well. Get that wallet out, why don't you? Look at the photographs you were so pleased to show me. Look at them, Cary!'

Cary took out his wallet and looked obediently at the pictures of the much-loved Tracy.

'Is she less important than honour among thieves?' I asked them both. Roz looked at her husband, her jaw set and her eyes full of determination. I knew then what the answer to my question would have to be.

The afternoon's proceedings dragged on without any new drama, and although Cary had told me what I needed to know I hadn't yet got his leave to use the information. The extended Timson family would have to be consulted. When the day's work was done I took the tube back to the Temple and, with my alcohol content having sunk to a dangerous low, I went at once to Pommeroy's for first aid.

Then I was unfortunate enough to meet my proposed cuckoo, the old Etonian Charlie Wisbeach, who, being not entirely responsible for his actions, was administering champagne to a toothy and Sloaney girl solicitor called, if I can bring myself to remember the occasion when she instructed me in a robbery and forgot to summon the vital witness, Miss Arabella Munday. Wisbeach greeted me with a raucous cry of 'Rumpole, old man! Glass of Bolly?'

'Why? What are you celebrating?' I did my best to sound icy; all the same I possessed myself of a glass, which he filled unsteadily.

'Ballard asked me in for a chat. It seems there may be a vacancy in your Chambers, Rumpole.'

'Wherever Ballard is there's always a vacancy. What do you mean exactly?'

'Pity you blotted your copy-book.'

'My what?'

'Not very clever of you, was it? Defending devil-worshippers with such a remarkably devout Head of Chambers. It seems I may soon be occupying your room, old man, looking down on the Temple church and Oliver Goldsmith's tomb.'

I looked at the slightly swaying Wisbeach for a long time and then, as I sized up the enemy, a kind of plot began to form itself in my mind. 'Dr Johnson's,' I corrected the man again.

'You told me it was Oliver Goldsmith's.'

'No, I told you it was Dr Johnson's.'

'Goldsmith's.'

'Johnson's.'

'You want to bet?' Charlie Wisbeach's face moved uncomfortably close to mine. 'Does the old roly-poly Rumpole want to put his money where his mouth is, does he?'

'Ten quid says it's Johnson.'

'I'm going to give you odds.' Charlie was clearly an experienced gambler. 'Three to one against Johnson. Olly Goldsmith evens. Twenty to one the field. Since I'm taking over the room we'll check on it tomorrow.'

'Why not now?' I challenged him.

'What?'

'Why not check on it now?' I repeated. 'Thirty quid in my pocket and I can take a taxi home.'

'Ten quid down and you'll walk. All right, then. Come on, Arabella. Bring the bottle, old girl.'

As they left Pommeroy's, I hung behind and then went to the telephone on the wall by the gents'. I had seen the light in Ballard's window when I came up from Temple station. He usually worked late,

partly because he was a slow study so far as even the simplest brief
was concerned and partly, I believe, because of a natural reluctance
to go home to his wife, Marguerite, a trained nurse, who had once
been the Old Bailey's merciless matron. I put in a quick telephone call
to Soapy Sam and advised him to look out of his window in about five
minutes' time and pay particular attention to any goings-on in the
Temple churchyard. Then I went to view the proceedings from a safe
distance.

What I saw, and what Sam Ballard saw from his grandstand
view, was Charlie Wisbeach holding a bottle and a blonde. He

gave a triumphant cry of
'Oliver Goldsmith!' and
then mounted the tomb as
though it were a hunter
and, alternately swigging
from the bottle and kissing
Miss Arabella Munday,
he laughed loudly at his triumph over Rumpole. It
was a satanic sound so
far as our Head of Cham-
bers was concerned, and
this appalling graveyard
ritual convinced him that
Charlie Wisbeach, who no
doubt spent his spare mo-
ments reciting the Lord's
Prayer backwards, was a
quite unsuitable candidate
for a place in a Christian Chambers such as 3 Equity Court.

That night important events were also taking place in my client's
home in Morrison Close, Crockthorpe. Numerous Timsons were
assembled in the front room, assisted by minor villains and their
wives. Cary's Uncle Fred, the undisputed head of the family, was
there, as was Uncle Dennis, who should long ago have retired from a
life of crime to his holiday home on the Costa del Sol. I have done my
best to reconstruct the debate from the account given to me by Roz.
After a general family discussion and exchange of news, Uncle Fred
gave his opinion of the Wedges job. 'Bloody joke shop. I always said it
was a bad idea, robbing a joke shop.'

'There was always money left in the till overnight. Our info told us that. And the security was hopeless. Through the back door, like.' Uncle Dennis explained the thinking behind the enterprise.

'What you want to leave the stuff round my place for?' Cary was naturally aggrieved because the booty had, it transpired, included a box of satanic masks to which, as they were left in her father's garage, young Tracy had easy access. 'You should have known how dangerous them things were, what with young kids and social workers about.'

'Well, Fred's was under constant surveillance,' Uncle Dennis explained. 'As was mine. And seeing as you and Roz was away on Monday . . . '

'Oh, thank you very much!' Cary was sarcastic.

'And Den knowing where you kept your garage key . . . ' Uncle Fred was doing his best to protect Uncle Dennis from charges of carelessness.

'Lucky the Bill never thought of looking there,' Cary pointed out.

'I meant to come back for the stuff sometime. It was a bit of a trivial matter. It slipped my memory, quite honestly.' Uncle Dennis was notoriously forgetful, once having left his Fisherman's Diary containing his name and address at the scene of a crime.

'Well, it wasn't no trivial matter for our Tracy.'

'No, I knows, Roz. Sorry about that.'

'Look, Den,' Cary started, 'we're not asking you to put your hands up to Chief Brush . . . '

'Yes, we are, Cary.' Roz was in deadly earnest. 'That's just what we're asking. You got to do it for our Tracy.'

'Hang about a bit.' Uncle Dennis looked alarmed. 'Who says we got to?'

And then Roz told him, 'Mr Rumpole.'

So the next morning Dennis Timson gave evidence in the Juvenile Court. Although I had been careful to explain his criminal record he looked, in his comfortable tweed jacket and cavalry twill trousers, the sort of chap that might star on *Gardeners' Question Time* and I could see that Madam Chair took quite a shine to him. After some preliminaries we got to the heart of the matter.

'I was after the money, really,' Dennis told the Bench. 'But I suppose I got a bit greedy, like. I just shoved a few of those boxes in the back of the vehicle. Then I didn't want to take them round to my place, so I left them in Cary's garage.'

'Why did you do that?' I asked.

'Well, young Cary didn't have anything to do with the Wedges job, so I thought they'd be safe enough there. Of course, I was under considerable pressure of work at that time, and it slipped my mind to tell Cary and Roz about it.'

'Did you see what was in any of those cases?'

'I had a little look-in. Seemed like a lot of carnival masks. That sort of rubbish.'

'So young Tracy getting hold of the devil's masks was just the usual Timson cock-up, was it?'

'What did you say, Mr Rumpole?' The chairwoman wasn't quite sure she could believe her ears.

'It was a stock-up, for Christmas, Madam Chair,' I explained. 'Oh, one more thing, Mr Dennis Timson. Do you know why young Dominic Molloy has accused Tracy and her father of fiendish rituals in a churchyard?'

'Course I do.' Uncle Den had no doubt. 'Peggy Molloy told Barry Peacock's wife and Barry's wife told my Doris down the Needle Arms last Thursday.'

'We can't possibly have this evidence!' Liz Probert rose to object. Perhaps she'd caught the habit from me.

'Oh, really, Miss Probert?' I looked at her in amazement. 'And why ever not?'

'What Barry's wife told Mrs Timson is pure hearsay.' Mizz Probert was certain of it.

'Of course it is.' And I gave her back her own argument. 'And pure hearsay is totally acceptable in the Juvenile Court. Where the interest of the child is at stake we are not bound by legal quibbles. I agree, Madam Chair, with every word which has fallen from your respected and highly learned clerk. Now then, Mr Timson, what did you hear exactly?'

'Gareth thought Cary had grassed on him over the Tobler Road supermarket job. So they got young Dominic to put the frame round Tracy and her dad.'

'So what you are telling us, Mr Timson, is that this little boy's evidence was a pure invention.' At last Madam Chair seemed to have got the message.

Uncle Dennis gave her the most charming and friendliest of smiles as he said, 'Well, you can't trust the Molloys, can you, my Lady? Everyone knows they're a right family of villains.'

There comes a time in many cases when the wind changes, the tide turns and you're either blown on to the rocks or make safe harbour. Uncle Dennis's evidence changed the weather, and after it I noticed that Madam Chair no longer returned Miss Mirabelle Jones's increasingly anxious smile, Mizz Probert's final address was listened to in stony silence, and I was startled to hear a distinct 'thank you' from the Bench as I sat down. After a short period of retirement the powers that were to shape young Tracy Timson's future announced that they were dissatisfied by the evidence of any satanic rituals and she was, accordingly, to be released from custody forthwith. Before this judgment was over, the tears which Roz had fought to control since the dawn raid were released and, at her moment of joy, she cried helplessly.

I couldn't resist it. I got into Mr Bernard's car and followed the Timson Cortina to the Children's Home. We waited until we saw the mother and father emerge from that gaunt building, each holding one of their daughter's hands. As they came down the steps to the street they swung her in the air between them, and when they got into the car they were laughing. Miss Mirabelle Jones, who had brought the order for release, stood in the doorway of The Lilacs and watched without expression, and then Tracy's legal team drove away to do other cases with less gratifying results.

When I got home, after a conference in an obtaining credit by fraud and a modest celebration at Pommeroy's Wine Bar, Hilda was not in the best of moods. When I told her that I brought glad tidings all She said was, 'You seem full of yourself, Rumpole. Been having a good time, have you?'

'A great time! Managed to extricate young Tracy Timson from the clutches of the caring society and she's back in the bosom of her family. And I'll be getting another brief defending Dennis Timson on a charge of stealing from Wedges Carnival Novelties. Well, I expect I'll think of something.'

I poured myself a glass of wine to lighten the atmosphere and Hilda said, somewhat darkly, 'You never wanted to be a judge, did you, Rumpole?'

'Judging people? Condemning them? No, that's not my line, exactly. Anyway, judges are meant to keep quiet in Court.'

'And they're much more restricted, aren't they?' It may have sounded an innocent question on a matter of general interest, but her voice was full of menace.

'Restricted?' I repeated, playing for time.

'Stuck in Court all day, in the public eye and on their best behaviour. They have far less scope than you to indulge in other activities . . .'

'Activities, Hilda?'

'Oh, yes. Perhaps it's about time we really talked for once,

Rumpole. Is there something that you feel you ought to tell me?'

'Well. Yes, Hilda. Yes. As a matter of fact there is.' I had in fact done something which I found it strangely embarrassing to mention.

'I suppose you've had time to think up some ridiculous defence.'

'Oh, no. I plead guilty. There are no mitigating circumstances.'

'Rumpole! How could you?' The Court was clearly not going to be moved by any plea for clemency.

'Temporary insanity. But I did it at enormous expense.'

'You had to pay!' It would scarcely be an exaggeration to say that Hilda snorted.

'Well. They don't give these things away for nothing.'

'I imagine not!'

'One hundred smackers. But it *is* your birthday next week.'

'Rumpole! I can't think what my birthday's got to do with it.' At least I had managed to puzzle her a little.

'Everything, Hilda. I've just bought us two tickets for the Scales of Justice Ball. Now, what was it *you* wanted us to talk about?'

All I can say is that Hilda looked extremely confused. It was as though Mr Injustice Graves was just about to pass a stiff sentence of chokey and had received a message that, as it was the Queen's birthday, there would be a general amnesty for all prisoners.

'Well,' she said, 'not at the moment. Perhaps some other time.' And she rescued the lamb chops from the oven with the air of a woman suddenly and unexpectedly deprived of a well-justified and satisfactory outburst of rage.

Matters were not altogether resolved when we found ourselves at a table by the dance floor in the Savoy Hotel in the company of Sam Ballard and his wife, Marguerite, who always, even in a ball gown, seemed to carry with her a slight odour of antiseptic and sensible soap. Also present were Marigold Featherstone, wife of a judge whose foot was never far from his mouth, Claude Erskine-Brown and Liz Probert with her partner, co-mortgagee and fellow member of 3 Equity Court, young Dave Inchcape.

'Too bad Guthrie's sitting at Newcastle!' Claude commiserated with Marigold Featherstone on the absence of her husband and told her, 'Philly's in Swansea. Prosecuting the Leisure Centre Murder.'

'Never mind, Claude.'

And Marguerite Ballard added menacingly, 'I'll dance with you.'

'Oh, yes, Erskine-Brown' – her husband was smiling – 'you have my full permission to shake a foot with my wife.'

'Oh, well. Yes. Thank you very much. I say, I thought Charlie

Wisbeach and his girlfriend were going to join us?' Claude seemed unreasonably disappointed.

'No, Erskine-Brown.' The Ballard lips were even more pursed than usual. 'Young Wisbeach won't be joining us. Not at the ball. And certainly not in Chambers.'

'Oh, really? I thought it was more or less fixed.'

'I think, Claude, it's become more or less unstuck,' I disillusioned him. In the ensuing chatter I could hear Marigold Featherstone indulging in some whispered dialogue with my wife which went something like this.

'Have you faced him with it yet, Hilda?'

'I was just going to do it when he told me we were coming here. He behaved well for once.'

'They do that, occasionally. Don't let it put you off.'

Further whispers were drowned as Erskine-Brown said to Ballard in a loud and challenging tone, 'May I ask you why Charlie Wisbeach isn't joining us, after all?'

'Not on this otherwise happy occasion, Erskine-Brown. I can only say . . . practices.'

'Well, of course he practises. In the Commercial Court.' And Claude turned to me, full of suspicion. 'Do you know anything about this, Rumpole?'

'Me? Know anything? Nothing whatever.' I certainly wasn't prepared to incriminate myself.

'I have told Wisbeach we simply have no accommodation. I do not regard him as a suitable candidate to share Rumpole's room. It will be far better for everyone if we never refer to the matter again.' So our Head of Chambers disposed of the case of *Rumpole* v. *Wisbeach* and the band played an old number from the days of my youth called 'Smoke Gets in Your Eyes'.

'Now, as Head of Chambers' – Ballard claimed his alleged rights – 'I think I should lead my wife out on to the floor.'

'No. No, Ballard. With all due respect' – I rose to my feet – 'as the longest-serving Chambers wife, She, that is Mrs Rumpole, should be led out first. Care for a dance, Hilda?'

'Rumpole! Are you sure you can manage it?' Hilda was astonished.

'Perfectly confident, thank you.' And, without a moment's hesitation, I applied one hand to her waist, seized her hand with the other, and steered her fearlessly out on to the parquet, where, though I say it myself, I propelled my partner for life in strict time to the music. I even indulged in a little fancy footwork as we cornered in front of a table full of solicitors.

'You're *chasséing*, Rumpole!' She was astounded.

'Oh, yes. I do that quite a lot nowadays.'

'Wherever did you learn?'

'To be quite honest with you . . .'

'If you're capable of such a thing.' She had not been altogether won over.

'From a Miss Tatiana Fern. I looked her up in the *Yellow Pages*. One-time Southern Counties Ballroom Champion. I took a few lessons.'

'*Where* did you take lessons?'

'Place called Mowbray Crescent.'

'Somewhere off Sloane Street?'

'Hilda! You knew?'

'Oh, don't ever think you can do anything I don't know about.' At which point the Ballards passed us, not dancing in perfect harmony. 'You're really quite nippy on your feet, Rumpole. Marguerite Ballard's looking absolutely green with envy.' And then, after a long period of severity, she actually smiled at me. 'You are an old devil, Rumpole!' she said.

Rumpole and the Family Pride

My daily round doesn't often bring me into contact with the upper crust, those who figure in Debrett and fill the gossip columns. I don't imagine they are any more law-abiding than the rest of society, but their crimes – drug abuse for the young hopefuls and city frauds for the dads – seldom come Rumpole's way as they tend to hire the most expensive, and not necessarily the best, legal hacks available. In Froxbury Mansions the blue-blooded didn't appear, nor were they much discussed until She Who Must Be Obeyed began to take in *Coronet* magazine, a glossy publication given to chronicling the goings-on in stately homes.

We were seated at breakfast one morning and I was reading the papers in a committal I was doing in Thames Magistrates Court when Hilda suddenly said, 'How extraordinary! The ffrench-Uffingtons are together again. His romance with Lady Fiona Armstead is apparently over.'

As I could make nothing of this, I gave her even more startling news from my brief. 'Walter "The Wally" Wilkinson walked into Beddoes Road nick uninvited and confessed to the Southwark triple murder. Isn't that even more extraordinary?'

Totally uninterested in this curious event, Hilda continued to read the news from her copy of *Coronet*. 'And here's Harry ffrench-Uffington enjoying a joke with his lovely wife Myrtle during the Save the Starving Ball at the Dorchester Hotel.'

'A sixty-year-old man of no fixed address. The Old Bill washed him down, thanked him very much and locked him up!' I interrupted her and then let her into the past life of The Wally. 'Form: drunk in charge, numerous; theft, numerous also, fraud on the social services. Pretty down-market stuff for a triple murderer.'

'Lord Luxter's put on weight', was Hilda's news. 'Don't you
remember him when he was so slim and handsome on the polo
field?'

'Please, Hilda. Do you *know* any of these people?'

'You can read all about them in Debby's Diary in *Coronet*
magazine.'

'*You* can read all about them. I've never heard of them.'

'Well, you should, Rumpole. Then you might learn about gracious
living. You might get out of the habit of blowing on your tea to cool it
down.'

'I'm in a hurry!' I explained. 'What do you expect me to do, fan it
with my hat?'

'Ah. There it is!' Hilda turned a page and cried triumphantly,
'That's what I was looking for! Sackbut Castle.'

'What're you going to do with it, Hilda, now you've found it?'

'Seat of the Sackbut family since the fourteenth century,' She read
out. 'Romantic setting near Welldyke on the Yorkshire Moors. The
17th Baron Sackbut occupies the private wing with his young second
wife, Rosemary, née Wystan. You see, Rumpole, it's *not* all about
people you've never heard of.'

'You mean this Rosemary Sackbut, whatever?'

'Née W*ystan*, Rumpole!'

'It doesn't ring a bell,' I had to confess.

'Oh, really. What's my name, Rumpole?'

'She Who Must – I mean Hilda,' I corrected myself hastily.

'Hilda *what*?'

'Hilda Rumpole, of course.' During the above exchange I was
darting into the hall and back to the kitchen and collecting the hat and
mac while polishing off the remnants of my breakfast.

'Oh, well done!' She congratulated me ironically. 'Now, then.
Hilda Rumpole, née *what*?'

'Oh, I see! Née Wystan!'

'Uncle Freddie's son was Hungerford Wystan who went into
Assorted Chemicals and Rosemary's his youngest. She's my first
cousin once removed,' Hilda explained.

'Once removed to a castle?'

'So that's why I take in *Coronet*. I knew Rosemary'd turn up in it
sooner or later.'

'Section 62 committal,' I muttered as I packed the brief away in my
bag. 'We'll try and get The Wally's conviction chucked out in the
Magistrates Court.'

'Oh, Rumpole!' Hilda was looking at me with disapproval. 'I bet you that no one at Sackbut Castle eats breakfast with his hat on. No wonder they didn't ask us to the wedding.'

I duly arrived at Thames Magistrates Court where I found that my opponent was Mizz Liz Probert, radical member of our Chambers, who was looking far from happy. 'You're not going to object to being sent for trial, are you?' she more or less snapped at me.

'Ask not what I am going to do, Mizz Liz. Watch me in Court. If I'm on my feet I'm probably being objectionable.'

'I shall be led by Sam Ballard at the trial,' she warned me.

'If he's prosecuting, there must be some hope for the defence.'

'Oh, please, don't try to be funny, Rumpole. Quite honestly, I just don't feel like it today.'

So I left her and went to ask a police officer if my client had arrived. I was surprised to find that he was delighted to have The Wally Wilkinson on the premises. 'You mean our triple, Mr Rumpole? We're all feeling just that little bit chuffed about having his case. It's not every day you get a triple murderer walk in with his hands up. Your solicitor's there already. Know your way down, sir, do you?'

I knew my way down and found my client and Mr Bernard in a police cell. The Wally Wilkinson was a small, chirpy man with wispy hair and an unreliable look in his eyes. Despite his age, he seemed wiry and energetic. The prison officer ushered me in, saying, 'Your brief's arrived, Walter. Got all you want, have you?' There was an unexpected note of obsequious respect in the official voice which The Wally, who was smoking a fag and holding a mug, seemed to think was no more than his due. '*This* tea?' he said. 'I wouldn't call it tea. Pour it back in the horse.'

'We're just putting on another brew. Want a couple of biscuits with that, do you, Walter?'

'I wouldn't say no.'

'I see you're all right for smokes.' The prison officer seemed relieved.

'Mr Bernard obliged,' The Wally told him. 'Oh, by the way, Perce, anything in the paper about my case, is there?'

'Just general background. The house. Victims. All that. Today's court'll be in the *Standard.*'

'Save us one, would you?'

'No probs.'

'You seem to be getting the four-star treatment,' I said when the turnkey had left us.

'Well, I'm on a triple, aren't I, Mr Rumpole?' The Wally looked modestly pleased. 'Something out of the ordinary, a very serious crime indeed. Naturally they respects you for it.'

The very serious crime occurred on the night of 12 February in a done-up Victorian house near Southwark Cathedral. It was shared by a merchant banker and his friend who was also something in the City. The third, and younger, victim was a social worker named Gerald Vulmay, who was apparently a guest staying the night.

'That Gerald,' The Wally told us, 'he was the one who let me into the house.'

'You were on your way home' – I consulted The Wally's proof of evidence – 'and you asked him for money and told him you couldn't find a place to sleep, all the hostel beds were taken because of the cold weather.'

'Even the warm spots over the hotel kitchens. Round the Savoy and the Regent Palace. They were all booked up. So he just looked at me and said, "All right. There's a spare bed in here. I'm sure they'll let you stay." '

'Did you meet all three of them?' I asked.

'Oh yes. They give me a meal, after they'd run a hot bath for me. Kitted me out in a pair of pyjamas. Some sort of Greek stuff, they was eating. I had to pretend I liked it.'

'Then what happened? Can you remember?'

'That's the terrible thing, Mr Rumpole. It's like my mind went a total blank on the subject. They put words into my mouth, like, when I made the confession.'

'All right. Do you remember walking into the Beddoes Road nick?'

'Sort of.'

'What made you do that?'

'I dunno, Mr Rumpole.' The Wally looked vague.

'Did they say you could see a lawyer?'

'No, they never. And them two officers what interviewed me, they were very aggressive.'

The prison officer returned with refreshments and said, 'There you are, Walter. Bit of a better brew. And a few ginger nuts. We'll save you that *Evening Standard*.'

'Thanks, Perce. I call that very kind.' And as he drank his tea, The Wally smiled at me. 'I tell you, Mr Rumpole. This beats sleeping in a cardboard box any day of the week.'

I fought that committal for three days in the Magistrates Court and did my best to exclude the confession. I knew it was a hopeless case, and after The Wally, who didn't seem particularly disappointed, was sent for trial, I came out of Court to find Liz Probert sitting on a bench in the entrance hall looking more disconsolate than ever. I tried to cheer her up by saying, 'You won the day. Next step the Old Bailey. I wonder if we can find twelve sleepers in cardboard boxes to sit on the jury. By the way, have you seen young David Inchcape lately? We're co-defending in an affray.'

'No, I *haven't* seen "young Inchcape", as you call him. You'd better find him for yourself.'

'Mizz Probert. Liz. What on earth's the matter?'

'Absolutely nothing's the matter!'

'You don't usually burst into tears when you win cases.' I could see, with embarrassment, distinct signs of the waterworks.

'I'm not bursting into tears at all. Why should you assume that I've burst into tears, just because I'm a woman?' she sniffed unhappily. 'It must be my contact lenses.'

'Someone in Chambers upset your contact lenses?' And then I hazarded a guess. 'Anything wrong between you and young Inchcape?'

'Isn't that you all over, Rumpole? It's just stereotypical male vanity! I'm a woman, so if I'm upset it must be about a man? Men are the only things women have got to be upset about, aren't they?' She searched in vain for a tissue in her handbag and I offered her a stereotypical male handkerchief.

'No, thanks. Oh, all right, it *is* about bloody Dave Inchcape.'

'I'm sorry. What's he done?'

'It's not what he's done. It's what he *is*! What he's been in secret all these years. And he's never had the guts to tell me about it.'

'Secretly married?' I wondered.

'I could cope with that. No. It's something . . . Well, it's really unmentionable. Ugh!' she shuddered. 'Awful. He's not worth worrying about.'

Naturally I was eager to hear more, but an officer came up to tell me that my wife was on the phone and I could take it in the police room. When I heard her news, told in a voice of almost uncontainable excitement, I didn't know if I could take it. The distant cousin, Rosemary, it seemed had come through at last. We were invited for a weekend at the castle by Lord and Lady Sackbut. When I came out of the police room I saw my red and white spotted handkerchief on the bench and Liz gone. I left Thames Court and, out into the street, a press photographer snapped me just as I was blowing my nose.

Sackbut Castle, near the small town of Welldyke, was built to defend a large area of North Yorkshire. It had been besieged three times during the Wars of the Roses. Other great historical events had taken place there, but when Richard, the 17th baron, brought home his young second wife, it was a peaceful enough place. And so it remained until shortly before the Rumpole visit when Jonathan Sackbut, thirteen years old and on holiday from Eton, was taking Monty the family labrador for an early run by the lake. On approaching the water the dog barked and then stood on the edge, whining. When the Hon. Jonathan joined the labrador he saw, indeed they must have both seen, the body of an elderly woman face-down in the water. She was wearing a drenched, rabbity fur coat and the big, plastic shopping-bag she still clutched was floating like water-wings. It became clear, when she was fished out, that she was some kind of a bag lady, a female tramp. Photographs taken later showed a large, broad-cheeked face which might once have been pretty.

The boy ran home to tell his father and stepmother, for Jonathan was the son of Lord Sackbut by his first and divorced wife. In due course, the police, the ambulance, the pathologist Dr Matthew Malkin, and Lord Sackbut himself, gathered by the lake. They were joined by Dr Hugo Swabey, the local coroner, and Mr Pringle, the coroner's officer. Swabey, as I got to know him, was a self-important and officious man in his sixties, dressed as though anxious to give the impression that he was a local squire or country landowner, although his clothes were far too new for the role. Pringle, the officer who accompanied him, was a stout and elderly ex-policeman with a Yorkshire accent and a perpetual, inappropriate smile. The coroner welcomed the pathologist, told the police he wanted the deceased's personal effects sent over to his office as soon as possible, and spoke with careful politeness to the castle owner. 'Good-morning, my Lord. I thought it right to get my inquiries going as soon as possible. I must ask you, have you seen the body?'

'Yes, of course,' Richard Sackbut told him. 'My boy found it.'

'Can you help us, then. Anyone you can recognise?'

'No. No, of course not,' Lord Sackbut told him. 'No one I've ever set eyes on.' And with this he got into his Range Rover and drove back to the castle.

For our weekend visit, Hilda seemed to have packed a wardrobe that would have seen us through a long summer holiday. Our taxi from the station dropped us outside the main entrance at the West Gate. As I staggered in with our suitcases, the attendant told us to leave our luggage with him and said, 'The rest of you've gone up. Hurry along.' So we climbed the wide stone staircase and found ourselves in a great hall with narrow windows, bare of furniture except for suits of armour and brutal-looking weapons arranged in great circles on the walls. In the distance we saw a group of people and a man in a dark suit who was signalling to us and calling out, 'Over here, my party!'

'Why does he call it "his" party, Rumpole?' Hilda was puzzled, and I let her wonder on as the man showed us the view from a window. 'From here you get a good view of the East Tower. See that narrow window up at the top there? That's what they called My Lady's Boudoir. Little room where they say the 7th Baron Sackbut locked up his lady wife on account as she'd got overly familiar with the steward. Not a very comfortable boudoir, by all accounts.'

'Is the family about?' Hilda cut him short by asking.

'Lord and Lady Sackbut are in residence,' he told her. 'Yes. They occupy the East Wing, which was built as a family mansion in the year 1792. We will now go down to the moat and the formal gardens. Come along, my party.' But Hilda had seen a door beside where a notice read PRIVATE APARTMENTS. NO ADMISSION. 'In here, Rumpole!' She gave the order as she led the way through it.

'Madam!' the tour guide said, 'that's not open to the public.'

'We are *not* the public,' Hilda said as she swept out of view. I followed murmuring an apologetic 'She Who Must . . . ' to the out-raged guide.

Through the magic doorway we found ourselves in a long passage which led to the open door of a drawing-room. When we reached it, we found it comfortably furnished, with chairs and sofas, a big fireplace and family pictures on the walls, a line of Sackbuts' faces, predominantly male. High windows opened on to the terrace of the castle. Sitting in a window-seat a pale boy was alone, reading a book. He looked up and peered through his glasses as Hilda approached.

'We are the Rumpoles. We have been invited for the weekend,' said Hilda.

The boy stared at Hilda silently.

'Is your mother . . . I mean, is Rosemary?'

'They're not back yet, I'm afraid. There's only me.'

'Oh, well. I'm Hilda Rumpole. This is my husband,' said Hilda. Jonathan put down his book carefully, having turned down the page, and advanced on Rumpole with his hand stretched out. 'Good after-noon, sir. I'm Jonathan Sackbut.'

'Horace Rumpole.' We shook hands.

'I'm Rosemary's cousin, you know.' Hilda made her position clear.

'Once removed,' I added.

'Really, Rumpole, don't let's go into all that.' At this moment, a young woman came in and called from the doorway, 'Aunty Hilda!' She had a rather solemn, sad face and floating brown hair. Her youth made her attractive; in middle age her looks might harden. She talked in a brisk manner with the brightness of youth.

'Oh, Rosemary, there you are at last!' Hilda was relieved.

'I'm sorry. Richard's driving the lorry back from Welldyke Show. I took the car. I was terrified of keeping you waiting.' And Rosemary told me, 'You must be Uncle Horace.'

'I've got no alternative.'

'Jonathan,' Rosemary spoke to the boy for the first time, 'I hope you've been entertaining the Rumpoles.'

'Not really.' He picked up his book and went out on to the terrace. Rosemary looked after him. Theirs, I thought was not an easy rela-tionship; stepmothers have a difficult time.

'Let's see if we can rustle up some tea.' Rosemary pushed a bell near the fireplace. 'Richard was so disappointed you couldn't come to the wedding.'

'Were we asked?' I wondered.

'Of course! Well, I'm sure you were. We sent out so many invita-tions . . . Perhaps you were away?'

'We're hardly ever away. Are we, Rumpole?'

'Oh, hardly ever,' I confirmed Hilda's evidence.

'You know, Rosemary dear, it was so funny when we arrived. They treated us like members of the public! Wasn't it funny, Rumpole?'

'Oh, hilarious,' I agreed.

'You *would* like a cup of tea, wouldn't you, Uncle Horace?' Rosemary was clearly trying to make up for the absence of a wedding invitation.

'Well, if you have got anything in the nature of a bottle of red. Nothing of any particular distinction. Peasants' claret would be perfectly acceptable.'

'Rumpole!' She Who Must Be Obeyed was not pleased.

'No, Aunty Hilda. Let Uncle Horace have what he wants. We're going to spoil him. Do sit down, Uncle Horace. You must be exhausted after all those absolutely splendid court cases you do.' Rosemary put her hand on my arm and guided me to a chair.

'Splendid cases?' And Hilda said, with some contempt, 'Like Walter The Wally Wilkinson!' But Rosemary continued to look at me with admiration. 'My dad', she said, 'saw you in action in some case at the Old Bailey. He said you were absolutely super! Had the jury eating out of your hand. I remember what he told us: "In the court room nobody dares say Boo to Rumpole." '

'Well,' I told her modestly, 'I can be rather magnificent at times.'

'And didn't you do one hugely famous case? Oh, yonks and yonks ago. Something about a bungalow?'

'You might possibly be thinking of the Penge Bungalow Murders.'

'That's right! I say, you *must* tell us all about it. It sounds riveting. I know Richard can't wait to meet you.'

A melancholy-looking manservant did bring us tea, and I had a bottle of Château Château, but Rosemary's husband had not returned by the time we went upstairs to change. 'Of course,' Hilda had told me, 'they'll dress for dinner at the castle.' So she had brought a long ball gown, and encased in a heavy silver breastplate she looked armoured and ready to take on allcomers. I managed to button up a dinner-jacket which seemed to have shrunk over the years as Hilda told me that Rosemary had said that old Lord 'Plunger' Plumstead was expected for dinner.

'Why Plunger. Does he dive?'

'He used to gamble terribly. Really, Rumpole, you ought to keep up with Debby's Diary.'

So we went down to our first castle dinner and found that all our guests and the Sackbuts had this in common – none of them were in

evening-dress. The men were without ties, in sweaters, or tweed
jackets worn with cord trousers. Plunger Plumstead, whose head was
sunk, like that of an aged tortoise, into a collar several sizes too large
for him, sported an ancient black velvet jacket and a silk scarf. The
women were dressed casually, but no one commented on what now
seemed our eccentric attire. Richard Sackbut had finally appeared
and turned out to be a man, perhaps in his late forties, whose long
chin, gingery hair and blue eyes were echoed in all the family portraits
we had seen. For some reason, which I could not fathom, he seemed
extremely glad to see me and kept saying it was 'jolly sporting of you
to come all the way to North Yorkshire for a weekend'. This was an
opinion with which I had to agree as I looked round the dinner-table
that night.

There was Plunger's wife, Mercia, a stately woman who looked
embalmed and, so far as I can remember, never spoke. There was a
young couple called the Yarroways, Tarquin and Helen, who talked
in very loud voices about people I didn't know, and sports and pas-

times of which I had no experience. Pippa and Gavin Bastion were older, I suppose in their early fifties, and more sophisticated. Gavin made cynical remarks in quiet, amused tones and Pippa, a collapsing beauty, drank a good deal and smoked between courses.

Towards the end of dinner they began to discuss Dr Hugh Swabey, the local coroner. He clearly wasn't a favourite with the upper crust. 'Of course, he's enjoying every minute of your business, Richard,' Gavin Bastion said. 'Best thing that's happened to him since he had coach lamps put round his pool-side area.'

'Where's all the money come from?' Helen Yarrowby asked.

'Expensive nose jobs in Leeds, and other sorts of jobs, no doubt,' Pippa Bastion suggested.

'You've seen him out hunting, haven't you, Plunger?' Helen asked the lord who turned to me and said, 'Absolutely everything wrong about the chap, Rumbold. He comes out like a dog's dinner.'

'That should give him a deep understanding of foxes,' I said, but nobody laughed.

'Don't expect Swabey's ever got near enough to see a fox. He comes out with a string on his top hat!' Pippa said it as though the unfortunate coroner had committed rape on the hunting field.

'And a red coat when no one's asked him to wear such a thing,' Gavin added to the indictment.

'No, darling. That's not the point. The point is, a red coat with *flat buttons.*' And Pippa turned to Hilda for support. 'Imagine that, Mrs Rumpole!'

'Oh, dear. Of course. Flat buttons! How very extraordinary.' My wife did her best to sound appalled, while I asked in all innocence, 'You mean you'd prefer them *round?*'

'Flat, shiny buttons without a hunt crest on them,' Gavin explained. 'Means he just got the thing off the peg at Moss Bros.'

'Is that a serious offence?'

'I suppose it depends on what you think is serious in this world.' Plunger looked as though I were prepared to excuse any crime, however heinous.

'Oh, I'm only used to murder and robbery,' I told him. 'Suchlike trivialities. I'd never heard of the crime of *flat buttons* before.'

There was a silence then, broken by Richard Sackbut. 'We had rather a nasty accident here, Rumpole. Some old tramp woman managed to drown herself in the castle lake.'

'Is Swabey going to be a pain in the neck about it, Richard?' Gavin Bastion asked.

'Oh, you know what he is. He wants to get his name in the papers, make a sensational trial of it. He thinks he's going to discover all sorts of things that aren't there to be discovered. It's just a bore, quite honestly.'

'Well, I don't see that you're responsible for anything,' Plunger assured our host. 'Most people have got a *lake* of some sort, haven't they, Rumbold?'

'Well, we have to make do with rather a small one, in the Gloucester Road.' This was another joke which went down like a lead balloon, but Rosemary came to my rescue. 'Talking of sensational trials, darling, Uncle Horace was telling me about that one he did yonks ago. In a bungalow, wasn't it, Uncle Horace?'

Then I lent back and prepared to enjoy myself for the first time since we arrived in the castle. 'It was an extraordinary case. I was a young man then, a white wig really, and I won it alone and without a leader. It raised some most interesting questions about bruising and the time of death. I mean, it should be relatively simple to discover if a bruise were pre- or post-mortem, of course. A careless pathologist could cause bruising when removing the tongue during an autopsy. That's what happened in the Penge Bungalow Murders.' There was a somewhat embarrassed pause, and I felt that neither my jokes nor my tales from the morgue were greatly appreciated. Pippa said, 'Where is Penge, actually?'

'Isn't it somewhere near Bognor?' Tarquin Yarroway guessed. But Richard gave a signal to his wife at the other end of the table, at which she rose, saying, 'Oh, yes. Well. Shall we leave the men to their . . .'

'Post-mortems, apparently,' Gavin finished her sentence for her gloomily.

After the ladies had left us, the masculine conversation flowed like cement. Nobody told improper jokes, and, after a while, Plunger Plumstead, who had been staring at me balefully, growled, 'I say, Rumbold. Can you get your gamekeepers to eat rook?'

'Well, now you mention it. I've never really tried.'

'When I was a boy, gamekeepers pretty well lived on rook. Their wives used to make them up into pies. You won't find a woman who'll do that now.'

'Tell the truth, I don't have any gamekeepers – or rooks either, come to that.'

'Odd! I thought you said you had a place in Gloucester.'

I was saved further embarrassment as Richard moved from his place at the head of the table to sit next to me. Then, as Gavin Bastion started a long story about some local adultery, our host said, confidentially, 'Mr Rumpole, Rosemary was telling me you've had a great deal of success in your cases.'

'I suppose I have acquired a certain reputation round the Brixton cells,' I told him. 'I never knew I was famous in castles.'

'And a good many of your cases', he went on, 'have concerned, well, dead people.'

'Dead people? Yes. I've always found, contrary to popular belief, that they can tell you a lot.'

'I wonder if you'd have time for a bit of a chat tomorrow?' he asked tentatively.

'I'm yours for the weekend.'

'You're still available for business?'

'Always. Always available.'

'Good! That's very good.' He seemed relieved and, for the first time, I saw him smile. 'Well, now. Shall we join the ladies?'

'Why not? Let's join them' – I tried a final joke – 'and make one huge, enormous lady!' Lord Sackbut was still smiling politely, but he didn't laugh. He was a man, I was later to discover, who sometimes missed the point.

As I was tearing off the stiff collar in a large and draughty bedroom, I told Hilda that I need never have gone through that blunt execution. 'I thought they were slackly dressed for a castle,' she said. 'Never mind. *We* looked smart, Rumpole.'

'We wore the wrong things, but they never referred to it. You noticed that? They never said a word.'

'It was sweet of them to ask us, wasn't it?'

'Why do you suppose they did?'

'Well, we're family, aren't we?'

'Not because we're family and not even because they never asked us to the wedding. My Lord Richard Sackbut's in trouble, Hilda. At least he's got that in common with Walter The Wally Wilkinson. He needs a good brief.'

The next morning there didn't seem to be very much to do but look around the house. At the end of the row of family portraits I saw a man who looked so like our host that he could only have been Richard's father, a long-chinned, blue-eyed, gingery-haired man in army uniform. Under the picture the legend was CAPTAIN THE LORD SACKBUT MP, DSO. BORN 1912, DIED 1972. By the drawing-room fireplace Rosemary was taking Hilda through a number of volumes of family photographs leading up to an extensive record of the wedding which we had unfortunately missed. As I couldn't gasp at the length of the bride's train, or the good looks of the bridegroom, I returned down the passage to the part of the castle thrown open to the public, with whom I had decided to mingle.

I had hardly entered the Great Hall, or heard much of the guide's monologue, when a man in assertive tweeds emerged from the *hoi polloi*, and introduced himself as Dr Hugo Swabey. 'We met briefly, Mr Rumpole,' he said, 'when you came up to Leeds on that stabbing in the old people's home.'

'Of course. And you gave some rather novel evidence on the direction of knife wounds.'

'Well, thank you, thank you very much.' I hadn't meant it as a compliment, and, in fact, Swabey's evidence was generally ignored. 'One is sometimes able to throw a new light in dark corners, you know, given a sound medical knowledge and the sort of mind that asks the occasional awkward question. I suppose that's why they landed me with the coroner's job.'

'I hear you're enjoying it.'

'Yes, well . . . Seeing the sights of North Yorkshire, are you?'

'No, as a matter of fact. We're guests of the Sackbuts.'

'You're privileged! I've never been invited on to the other side of that door, into the Holy of Holies, strange as it may seem. Though I go out with the hunt and I'm pretty well known in the neighbourhood. His Lordship invited you, did he?'

'Oh, I think it was his wife.'

'It must have been his Lordship. Women don't make many decisions in the Sackbut clan. Come to think of it, it may have been rather an intelligent move with the inquest coming up.'

'I heard about that. Some poor old lady tumbled into the lake, one of the homeless.'

'Homeless? Is that what she was? Or was she looking for a home?

My officer's downstairs now, taking statements. Who was she, when was she killed, how did she die? These are the questions my Court will have to answer. Meanwhile, I thought I'd just wander around and soak up the castle atmosphere. All these suits of armour, for instance, maximum protection and nothing much inside them. Typical Sackbut.'

'Have you come to see my client?' I asked him.

'Oh, is his Lordship that already?' Dr Swabey seemed delighted. 'That *will* be fun. I think we'll be able to offer you a few surprises.'

'Good! I shall look forward to it,' I promised.

'I hope his Lordship will too. Just one thing you might be asking your client to explain, among others.'

'What's that?'

'I had the dead woman's possessions sent over to my office. The police like to hang on to their things, but I insisted. Well, she had a big plastic bag, full of old clothes and rotting food and a gin bottle almost empty. But there was a sort of plastic purse, pretty well waterproof. You might be interested in its contents.'

'Might I?'

'There was a return coach ticket to Victoria, so she wasn't a local tramp, nothing like that. But more interestingly, a photograph, taken on the terrace of this castle. An old photograph. Shows a woman holding a baby and a man in uniform. No doubt who the man was. Absolutely no mistaking the family features. It was Lord Sackbut's father. Now how do you imagine a homeless old bag lady got hold of that, Mr Rumpole?' There was, I thought, a certain amount of triumph in his voice as he asked me the question.

'I really have no idea.'

'I wonder if your client has. I'm telling you all this for your assistance, of course.' As he said it, I thought that the Welldyke coroner had absolutely no intention of helping Lord Sackbut who had never invited him beyond the door marked PRIVATE.

'I'm very grateful.'

Dr Swabey was looking down to the far end of the Great Hall to where the conducted tour was filing out under the command of their guide. 'I mustn't miss my chance of another look around the grounds – and the lake, of course.'

That morning I also inspected the lake. I took a turn round the gardens and then found my host in the stables, talking to a girl in jodhpurs about the lameness of one of the horses whose solemn faces, peering over their stable doors, put me in mind of the portraits of the

Sackbut family. At my request he drove me down to the lake in his Range Rover, and took me to the spot where the drowned bag lady had been pulled out of the water. It had been a wet summer in North Yorkshire, and there were plenty of tyre marks on the grass path. Richard told me he drove past there often, on his way to a field where he had horses out.

So I looked down to the weedy, muddy water from the top of a steep, slippery bank, and at the odd branches and tree stumps on the way down. I stooped to look at a branch, freshly broken, and then I told my client that I'd met the local coroner, who didn't seem to like his Lordship very much.

'The feeling's mutual.'

It was a heavy day, with a low sky which seemed darker than the bright fields and green trees. There were insects buzzing and a party of ducks on the lake floated lethargically as though half asleep. I looked at my client and wondered what secrets he was keeping from me. 'What on earth are you worrying about?' I asked him.

'What do you mean?'

'Why call on the expert services of Rumpole of the Bailey, who has studied causes of death by cross-examining the great Professor Andrew Ackerman, King of the Morgues. An old bag lady slipped and drowned herself in your grounds. Sad but hardly a threat to your peace of mind, I might have thought.'

'We're open to the public,' he tried to explain, 'I mean, they might say we're not safe . . . '

'Nonsense! You're not responsible for tramps in the night-time. What's the real problem? And what's making the Grand Inquisitor of Welldyke so excited?'

'Perhaps . . . ' But if he were about to tell me something, he changed his mind. 'It's entirely a family matter. We'd better be getting back.'

'Tell me,' I asked him again, 'I'm used to hearing about family matters. Murder's a family matter, nine times out of ten.'

'Murder?' He seemed surprised. 'Who said anything about murder?'

'Nothing yet. But dear old Dr Swabey looks as though he's longing to come out with it.'

I didn't get any more from my client, and he drove me back to the castle, promising a treat for the afternoon: a dog show, bowling for a pig, a tombola and other delights in the castle grounds. It sounded like a fête worse than death, a comment I kept to myself.

When I entered the drawing-room, in search of She Who Must Be Obeyed, I thought, at first, that the room was empty. Then I heard a boy's voice, only just audible, repeating words which were well known to me. Jonathan was alone, sitting on his window-seat with a book, but he wasn't reading, he was reciting, only occasionally reminding himself of the lines:

> '*So through the darkness and the cold we flew,*
> *And not a voice was idle; with the din,*
> *Meanwhile, the precipices rang aloud;*
> *The leafless trees and every icy crag*
> *Tinkled like iron; while the distant hills*
> *Into the tumult sent an alien sound . . . '*

Jonathan continued to recite quietly, and I joined in with:

> '*Of melancholy not unnoticed, while the stars*
> *Eastward were sparkling clear, and in the West*
> *The orange sky of evening died away . . . '*

The boy closed the book as soon as he heard my voice, and now he looked embarrassed.

'You like that?' I asked him.

'Well, yes. The sound of it,' he admitted reluctantly.

'So do I. I like the sound of it very much.' I went to sit at the fireside, in front of a big coffee table piled with the family photograph albums Hilda and Rosemary had been looking at. I began to turn the pages idly. 'You live here with your father in the holidays?' I asked.

'With Father, yes.'

'See much of your mother, do you?'

'Not really.'

'Why's that?'

Perhaps he wouldn't have answered my question if we hadn't recited Wordsworth together, but he said, 'I went once or twice. Now it seems easier if I don't go. I didn't enjoy it much, really.'

Then there was a silence

while I turned more pages of the albums. 'Fascinating', I said at last, 'these old family photographs.' I found a page with Jonathan, aged about five, sitting on a Shetland pony. 'Is that you when you were really small and insignificant?'

He got up and stood beside me. 'That's me on Mouse.'

'Any pictures of your mother?'

'No, I don't think so.'

But perhaps there had been; there were blank spaces and small traces of paper having been torn out. 'Shall we take a dive back into history?' I found a volume dated 1940–50 and, after turning a number of pages, I found snaps of the man who looked so like Richard. 'That's your grandfather. I recognise him from his portrait.'

'Everyone says he looks just like my father,' Jonathan said. 'I don't seem to look like them at all.'

'Don't apologise. Here's Grandad on a horse, and playing tennis, and opening something and, oh, in uniform. That must have been in the last war. Is there anything like a wedding photograph?' There wasn't. What I found were the same blank spaces, the same traces of pictures torn out, the signs of a memory someone wanted to obliterate. 'Isn't that rather odd?' I asked Jonathan. 'Your grandmother doesn't seem to be here either.'

The sky remained dark, but the rain held off that afternoon. The castle walls were illuminated by a low shaft of sunlight directed from under gunmetal clouds. The stalls and tents were set out on a patch of grass under the East Tower. Hilda had gone off to buy what seemed, when I had to carry them back to London, a huge selection of jams, and I was chatting to Rosemary who was in charge of an old clothes stall which was being eagerly searched by the mothers and wives of the village. 'Got anything suitable for wearing in a cardboard box?' I asked her.

'You going to take up residence, Uncle Horace?' Rosemary asked.

'I've got a client who may have to go back to one. That is, if I manage to spring him from the nick. I had an interesting talk to Jonathan. He doesn't see much of his mother, does he?'

'Quite honestly, Richard thinks it best not. She made this ghastly second marriage.'

'To somebody ghastly?'

'To a chap who sold her a car. They live in Pinner or somewhere quite impossible. Can you imagine that after Richard and the castle?'

And then the loudspeakers announced that the contest for the dog who looked most like its owner was about to start. Hilda came hurrying up saying we mustn't miss this extraordinary entertainment and as we hurried towards the judging ring, she said, 'Just look at the castle, towering over us. Doesn't it make you feel we've been in the Middle Ages?'

'Lucky for you, we're not.'

'It must have been so romantic.'

'Not that I'd ever have locked you up in the East Tower, Hilda. I'd never have dreamt of doing anything like that, not being a lord.'

'Oh, really, Rumpole! I hope you weren't talking that sort of nonsense to Rosemary!'

'Not quite. We were talking about Richard's first wife. Not that it could have been her, of course – she's much too young. Besides which, she's alive and wed and living in Pinner . . . ' I was following a private train of thought and Hilda had stopped listening for we had arrived at the dog ring where owners were assembling with their four-footed look-alikes. There was a fat woman with a Pekinese, a hatchet-faced man with a lurcher, and a man who had taken off his shirt and was holding his grey, long-haired Yorkshire terrier against the grey hairs on his chest. Richard stood proudly beside Monty, the labrador, and old Plunger Plumstead was there with an ancient, watery-eyed and evil-looking bull-terrier to whom he might have been closely related. Hilda had wandered off to talk to the Yarroways, whom she had greeted as life-long friends, and I stood alone, watching, as Pippa Bastion, the judge, announced that the first prize went to Plunger's dog.

The prize was presented by the coroner who stood, in another suit of brilliant checks, at the judge's table. When he had been rewarded I went up to congratulate Plunger.

'Oh, Bo'sun and I win it every year. God knows what I'm going to do when the filthy dog snuffs it. Bottle of Cherry Bounce, presented by Dr Swabey. Revolting! Can't drink the stuff.'

I told him I had spotted a beer tent where we might find something more acceptable. 'Oh, very good,' he said. 'Good idea of yours, Rumbold. You have these sort of dos in your part of Gloucester?'

When we were in the tent, coping with large plastic tumblers full of North Yorkshire bitter, I said, 'Perhaps dogs grow to look like their masters in the way that men grow up to be reproductions of their dads.'

'Reproductions? Oh, Richard certainly is. Spitting image of old

Robert. Fine man, Robert. Had a bloody good war. Peace didn't treat him quite so kindly. Came back home. Found all sorts of things wrong. Lot of pheasant covers cut. Rooks out of control. Labour Government. Something seriously dicky about the roof. Things not so marvellous on the domestic front either, not too long afterwards his wife bolted off.'

'Did you know Richard's mother?'

'Depends what you mean by *know*. Not in the biblical sense, old chap!' He laughed, gulped his beer and went on. 'So I was probably in a minority. But she always seemed a perfectly nice woman to me. A bit affected. I remember she always called Richard, Riccardo, with a sort of funny Italian accent. Or was it Riccardino? Of course he hated it.'

'What was her name?'

'Margaret. Maggie was what we called her.'

'And what happened to her in the end?'

'In the end? Oh, in the end she died.'

That evening we were only four at dinner but, with due formality, Hilda and Rosemary left us men to our port and I began to ask Richard about his childhood. It was then he told me something that had occurred at his prep school, a story I shall never forget. 'I suppose I was about nine,' he said. 'Just nine. And the message came: "The Headmaster wants to see you in his study after prayers." Well, you know what that meant. You got that awful sort of feeling in the pit of your stomach and sweaty hands. All the usual symptoms of terror, I suppose. Anyway, I knocked on the study door and there he was. Snowy Slocombe. A hard man. But just. Perfectly just. I've got no complaints about that. Big tall fellow with snow-white hair. And he told me to close the door and come up to the desk and then he said, "Sackbut, I know you're going to take this like a man." And then, of course, I thought I knew exactly what I was in for. But he said, "I've just had your father on the telephone, Sackbut. And he's asked me to let you know. I'm afraid your mother's dead." And do you know what I felt, Rumpole? I felt a kind of enormous relief, because he wasn't going to beat me.'

We were silent for a little, then I asked, 'Did your father tell you how she died?'

'Not really. When I came home for the holidays he said, "I suppose Slocombe gave you the message." And I told him, "Yes." I don't think we discussed it much after that.'

'Do you know how? Or where?'

'I heard vaguely. I think she left home after I'd gone back to school.

She must have died soon after that, I suppose. Abroad somewhere. I've an idea it might have been Italy. France or Italy . . . '

'But didn't you make . . . any sort of inquiries?' I found it hard to believe.

'No.' He sounded quite matter of fact.

'Why not?'

'I don't think my father would have wanted me to.'

'You believed your father?'

'Of course.'

'On so little evidence?'

'I wouldn't have doubted him.'

'Do you have any idea', I asked, 'how old she'd be now? If she'd lived, I mean.'

'I suppose late sixties.'

'It never occurred to you that she might try to get in touch with you?'

'You mean, come back from the dead?' He was smiling.

'Yes. Something like that, I suppose.'

Our new friends, the Sackbuts, invited us to the opera where the Bastions had taken a box. Not to be caught out a second time I arrived in a blazer and grey flannels to find the rest of the party in evening-dress. 'They're so secretive,' She complained to me in the interval. 'They never let you know what they're going to wear.' But Richard did give me some interesting information over the champagne and sandwiches. After telling me that the fellow on the stage looked a great deal too fat to be accepted into the Egyptian Army he said, 'I say, Rumpole. I think I've got a young relative in your Chambers. David Luxter. His grandfather was Lord Chancellor and his father's my cousin.'

'You mean the present Lord Luxter?' Hilda has Debrett ever at her fingertips.

'No' – I had to disappoint Hilda – 'I'm afraid we've got no Luxter in our stable.'

'Oh, he did an odd thing,' Richard told us. 'Didn't want to rely on his family name, can't think why. So the Luxter boy went into the law under an alias. He found a name in some poem or other, Harry Luxter told me, something about a bell and a rock.'

' " . . . The vessel strikes with a shivering shock – 'O Christ! it is the Inchcape Rock!' " Not a great poet, Southey, but I suppose young David found him useful.'

'That's the name! Inchcape!'

'Born the son of a lord?' And I thought I knew the reason for Mizz Probert's sorrow. I wondered if she would ever forgive him.

When the opera was over, Hilda woke me with a sharp nudge and we set off to walk down to the Savoy where the Sackbuts were standing us dinner. We took a short cut down the narrow street behind the Strand Palace Hotel and there, men and women, young and old, were settling down for the night as near as possible to the grille where a certain amount of hot air came streaming up from the hotel's kitchen. As our rather grand procession swept by a voice called my name from a doorway and I turned to see a small dosser, with a bobble hat pulled down over his eyes, holding out a tattered copy of the *Evening Standard* which had formed part of his bedding. 'Mr Rumpole! I recognise you, sir.' He handed me the snap of me blowing my nose. 'I see your picture in this old paper. As you was defending Walter The Wally in the big murder case. I have got some info for you on that one, sir.' As I loitered to speak further to the man, I heard Richard say, 'What's happened to your husband?'

'I'm afraid he's met a friend,' Hilda told him, so they walked on, sure I suppose, that I'd catch them up. I didn't do so immediately as I wanted to hear the story old Arnie, as he'd introduced himself, had to tell. He would not speak of it however, until I'd bought him a cup of tea and a couple of ham rolls in a rather affected caff, dressed up as a Parisian bar in the 1890s, in the Covent Garden Piazza. Those patrons sitting down wind of Arnie moved to other tables as he munched contentedly.

'I was with The Wally that night, Mr Rumpole,' he told me. 'We was all down under Hungerford Bridge. And he got into a bit of an argument, like, with Bronco Billington. Always a bit of a pain up the bum, Bronco, in a manner of speaking. Nick! Never seen anything like it. Well. He had Wally's drop of gin and his pie off him and a punch-up started. And a bit of manual strangulation. Wally's strong, like, when he's roused up and he left Bronco flattened. So we went off sharpish round Centrepoint where there was still spaces. And next day we read in the papers about the triple murder. But The Wally was with me, all that night. Straight up, he was. Only thing, he reckoned he'd done in poor old Bronco, who was never in good health at the best of times. Cough his bloody guts out soon as you touch him.'

'And had he done in Bronco?'

'Bless you, no. Bronco was in the Cut, Waterloo, Thursday midnight. Singing his head off on a bottle of meths. I'd've told The Wally, only I didn't know where they got him banged up. You'll be seeing him, will you?'

'Not just yet,' I told him. 'I'm defending a lord.'

'Oh, wonderful, Mr Rumpole. Going up in the world, are we? You couldn't spare . . .'

Of course I could. I handed him a couple of crisp tenners and told him not to waste it all on tea. Then I wondered if I could recover my outlay from the legal aid fund.

As the inquest drew near, I began to make my preparations. Cursitor & Carlill of Welldyke were the family solicitors, and I saw the prim and elderly Mr Cursitor at my Chambers on one of his visits to London. I suggested that he must have been sure that Richard's mother had died, because if she were alive she might have had some claim against the estate on his father's death.

'Not really, Mr Rumpole.' Mr Cursitor actually put the tips of his fingers together when he spoke, something he must have seen family solicitors doing in old movies. 'Richard's father had started divorce proceedings before his wife left England. She never appeared again and the case went through undefended. She was no longer married to the late Lord Sackbut, so she would have had no claim.'

'Did Richard know that?'

'I don't think we ever discussed it with him. I'm sure his father didn't.'

'And who was the man she ran off with?'

'An Italian prisoner-of-war. I believe she'd met him when he was working on one of the farms. I suppose she misconducted herself and joined him somewhere in Italy. She left no address.'

Before I parted from Mr Cursitor, I gave him a number of jobs to do and asked him to put an advertisement in the *Daily Telegraph* personal column. It was a long shot, a very long shot indeed, but then I had very little ammunition.

*

For someone who has had, in the course of a long life, a great deal to do with sudden and violent death, I have only rarely appeared in Coroner's Courts. The proceedings are directed by the coroner, who calls for witnesses and asks the questions. The legal hack is usually limited to putting a few supplementaries. The Welldyke Court was a dark and stately Victorian affair, set in a crumbling municipal building. For the inquest on the unknown bag lady, the place was packed with friends of the Sackbuts and, I suppose, some enemies, interested members of the Press and some who found an inquest a welcome addition to the pleasures of a holiday in North Yorkshire. There was a jury of local men and women, a shorthand writer and Mr Pringle, the coroner's officer, acting as the court usher. Dr Swabey sat, his face and glasses shining, thoroughly enjoying putting the grey-haired pathologist through his paces.

'Dr Malkin,' he said in his most patronising manner, 'please use layman's language. Not all of us understand the complexities of forensic medicine.'

'Including you, old darling,' I whispered to no one in particular, but the coroner apparently heard me. 'May I remind everyone in Court', he pontificated, 'this is a solemn proceeding. Mine is the ancient office of *custos placitorum*, the keeper of the decisions. We have the solemn duty, you and I, Members of the jury, to inquire into the mysteries of death. I hope we may do so, without interruption.'

'Just as soon as *you* stop interrupting.' I tried another whisper which the coroner wisely ignored and asked Malkin to continue his evidence. 'She was a woman in her late sixties or early seventies, in poor general health. I came to the conclusion that death was probably caused by a blow to the head with some blunt instrument before the body entered the water. I didn't think it was a case of death by drowning because there was no water in the lungs.'

'Might death have been caused by a deliberate attack?' Swabey asked eagerly. 'A blow to the head by some assailant?'

'I thought it might.' As the pathologist said this, there was a buzz of interest in court, but I sat, expressionless.

'Struck *before* the body was put into the lake?' Swabey asked.

'Yes.'

'Which would make this an unlawful killing. Or, to use a word with which the jury might be more familiar, murder.' The coroner was delighted to say this for the first time in the proceedings.

'I couldn't rule out that possibility. No.'

'Mr Rumpole. Do you wish to apply to ask the pathologist a question?' Swabey asked with a cheerless smile in my direction.

'Yes.' I rose purposefully to my hind legs. 'A good many questions.'

'Then I shall grant your application.'

'Very generous, sir. Dr Malkin. In a case of drowning it's possible for death to occur immediately, due to a sudden cardiac arrest. Is that not so? It's happened in the case of sailors falling off ships, for instance.'

'It *has* happened.'

'And in such a case, there might be no water in the lungs.'

'There *might* not be.'

'Such deaths have often occurred with drunken sailors. They fall off the deck and alcohol produces a state of hypersensitivity to sudden and unexpected contact with water.'

'It may do so.' The pathologist was reluctant to admit it.

'Dr Malkin. You have read the great Professor Ackerman's work, *The Causes of Death*, I'm sure?'

'Of course I've read it!' Dr Malkin was running out of patience before I ran out of questions.

'Professor who, Mr Rumpole?' The coroner was foolish enough to ask.

'Ackerman, sir. Required reading, I should have thought, for any keeper of the decisions.' After that enjoyable interruption, I returned to Dr Malkin and the business in hand. 'The professor quotes many such cases.'

'I believe he does.'

'And we know that this old lady had an almost empty gin bottle in her possession. You found a high level of alcohol in her blood, didn't you?'

'Fairly high.'

'Fairly high. So it remains a possibility, does it not, that this unfortunate lady met her death by drowning?'

There was a long pause before Dr Malkin, with the utmost reluctance said, 'It's a possibility. Yes.'

'Dealing with the blow to the head. This was a particularly steep bit of bank, was it not?'

'It was fairly steep.'

'With a number of branches and tree stumps. On some of which traces of blood were found.'

'Yes.'

'Can you rule out the possibility that this old lady, having drunk rather more gin than was good for her, slipped and fell into the lake, striking her head on one of those tree stumps as she fell?'

'I can't rule that out, altogether.' Clearly Dr Malkin hated to have to say it; murder was a far more exciting alternative.

'Thank you, Doctor. It seems we may have reached a sensible interpretation of the facts and one that should be obvious even to those who haven't read Professor Ackerman's great work.' As I sat down I looked meaningfully at Swabey, but he was busy trying to repair the damage I had done to his witness.

'Dr Malkin,' he said, 'we gather from your evidence that this blow to the head might have been accidental, or it might have been deliberate. Is that right?'

'Quite right, sir.'

'You, of course, didn't go into the circumstances in which someone might have had a motive for causing the death of this old lady.'

'No,' Malkin started but it was time for Rumpole to rise in, at least well-simulated, fury. 'I object to that question. How can Dr Malkin possibly answer it?'

'He can't, Mr Rumpole.' Swabey again smiled unconvincingly. 'That will be the subject of the next part of my investigation. I know you will wish to help me with it. Thank you, Dr Malkin. We would now like to ask Mr Saggers a few questions.'

Mr Saggers turned out to be the attendant at the West Gate who took charge of our luggage when we first visited the castle. He was a solid Yorkshireman, clearly reliable, and turned out to be a devastating witness. As soon as he was in the box and sworn in, Pringle, the coroner's officer, showed him the mortuary photograph of the dead bag lady, and, in particular, a close-up of her large, but possibly once pretty, face.

'Mr Saggers,' the coroner said, 'can you recognise the lady in that photograph?'

'The Lady in the Lake,' I whispered, and Swabey again made a public pronouncement. 'For those of us unused to court-room practice, I should say that silence is kept whilst a witness is giving evidence.'

'Wonder who his grandmother is?' I asked Cursitor. 'And can she suck eggs?' But now Saggers was telling a story I had to listen to. 'It was the day before they found her,' he said. 'She came up to the castle entrance and wanted to go in. She wasn't with any of the groups that'd paid already, so I asked her for two pounds. She said she hadn't got it, but she wanted to see his Lordship. I told her that wouldn't be possible. I didn't think she was anyone he'd want to see. So. Well, she sort of wandered off.'

'What time was that?' Swabey asked.

'Just before four, because I was going off for my tea-break. Then, as I was passing the formal gardens, you know, where the long border, the white border they call it, runs down to the statue? Well, I saw them there.'

'You saw who, Mr Saggers?'

'The old lady. And his Lordship.'

I whispered to his Lordship urgently taking instructions, but Richard shook his head and firmly denied the suggestion. This added considerably to my worries.

'What were they doing?' Swabey asked.

'Just talking together. I saw them and then I went on for my tea.'

'Have you any questions, Mr Rumpole?' The coroner was looking more cheerful than I felt as I rose to do my best with Saggers.

'Before you went on for your tea, how long did you see these two together?'

'Perhaps half a minute. I didn't stop to look at them.'

'And how far away were they down at the end of the border? Fifty yards?'

'About that.'

'It was afternoon. Was the sun behind them?'

'I think it was. Mind you, I'd seen the woman close to, at the gate.'

'So you said. But you couldn't see Lord Sackbut's face clearly in the garden?'

'I made sure it was his Lordship.'

'How was he dressed?'

'A tweed cap, and his jersey and cord trousers. Like he does. He'd been doing something with the horses.'

'He was dressed like many other men who might have been about the garden and the statues that day, Mr Saggers. When you say you *think* it was his Lordship, will you accept the possibility that you might have been mistaken?' I did my best, as you can see, but it didn't get very far. Saggers, the reliable witness, answered, 'I know what I saw, Mr Rumpole. To be quite honest with you I got no doubt about it.'

When we were getting ready for bed in the castle, I told Hilda my worries. 'Richard's going to tell a lie! He spoke to the old lady and now he's going to deny it.'

'Oh, Richard wouldn't do a thing like that.' She was sure of it.

'Why not? Because he's a lord? Because he lives in a castle? I tell you, Hilda. People have been lying here since the Wars of the Roses. Lying and locking up their wives or tearing their wives' photographs out of family albums. Behaving like that' – and, as I said it, I felt I had reached close to the heart of the case – 'because their fathers did it.'

The next day Lord Sackbut went into the witness-box at the coroner's request and Dr Swabey examined him in the manner of one who'd never been invited into the private apartments and wasn't going to let his Lordship forget it. To the thousand-dollar question Richard answered, 'The first time I saw the old lady was when her body was found in our lake. I had never set eyes on her before that.'

'My Lord. I remember you told me that at the time, and no doubt others heard you. But you have heard Mr Saggers's evidence. Is he lying?'

'I'm not saying that. I'm saying Mr Saggers is mistaken. I didn't speak to the old lady that afternoon.'

'Very well, Jury will have to make up their minds who's telling the truth.' Swabey gave the jury a trusting look and then turned to another subject. 'Lord Sackbut, when you were a boy, your mother left your father.'

'I fail to see what that's got to do with this case.'

'Bear with me, my Lord, I think it may have a great deal to do with it. At that time, did your father tell you that your mother was dead?'

'She was dead, yes.'

'But how did you know that?'

'Because my father said so.' Richard was clearly keeping his temper with difficulty. 'He told my school.'

'And you believed him?'

'Of course.'

'Did it ever occur to you that your father was so angry with your mother that he pretended she had died. He didn't want you to try to see her again?'

'It never occurred to me that my father would tell a lie, Dr Swabey. To me or anyone.'

'Do you not know that there have been many rumours, in your family and in the town, that your mother didn't die as your father said, but was alive many years later and living in Italy?'

'I never heard such rumours. Anyway, they would have been untrue.'

'This is becoming intolerable.' I gave another exhibition of the Rumpole wrath. 'Lord Sackbut's here to give evidence, not to deal with tittle-tattle.'

'Please, Mr Rumpole, don't excite yourself. You have reached an age when that might be injurious to your health. Mr Pringle, the photograph, please. Now. I pass to another matter.' Pringle was handing the photograph of Richard's father in uniform, sitting on the castle terrace with a woman and a baby. As Richard looked at it, Swabey went purring on, 'We have heard evidence that that photograph was found in the old lady's possession. Let's look at it, shall we? Is that the terrace of Sackbut Castle?'

'Yes.'

'And is the man in it your father, as he was at the end of the last war?'

'It is my father, yes.'

'Oh, I am so very much obliged. Now there is also a woman with a baby. Is that woman your mother?'

'I . . . really can't say,' Richard hesitated.

'You mean you can't remember what your own mother looked like?' Swabey spoke more in sorrow than in anger, but the jury looked at Richard with distinct disapproval.

'Not altogether clearly.'

'I suggest to you that it is a family group. Your father, your mother and yourself as a very young child.'

'I suppose that's a possibility,' the witness had to admit.

'Or a probability? Now. Can you tell the jury why this old lady had that photograph in her possession when she came visiting Sackbut Castle?'

'How on earth can my client know that?' I was up and fuming again.

'Then let me suggest an answer to assist Lord Sackbut.' And Swabey made a suggestion which was no help at all to Richard. 'Could it be because she *was* the lady your father, in a fit of wounded pride, had given out as dead?'

'I object to that!' I fumed on. 'Is this an inquest or a lesson in writing pulp fiction? There is not a scrap of evidence . . . '

'Oh, yes, there is, Mr Rumpole. There is a photograph. Now, you shall have your opportunity to ask questions later. Let me just put this final point to you, my Lord.' So I sat down reluctantly and the coroner concluded. 'If this old lady was the Dowager Lady Sackbut, fallen on evil days, she'd hardly be a welcome visitor at the castle, would she? After all that time. Come, no doubt, with a claim for money. Didn't it occur to you, my Lord, that she might be better dead, as your father had wished, so many, many years ago?'

His Lordship rejected the suggestion entirely and I took him through it all again and he denied it again. But during the rest of the day I had the strong feeling that the jury didn't like Lord Sackbut, the man who couldn't remember what his mother looked like. In the middle of the afternoon, however, Mr Cursitor, who had been out of Court, came back and whispered in my ear. He had a piece of news that gave us a hope of restoring the Sackbut name, and putting Dr Swabey in his place for ever. As soon as I heard it, I asked Swabey to adjourn the case until the next morning. He was about to make some trouble about this, until I reminded him that there was a writ of *mandamus* almost as old as Coroner's Courts, by which I could haul him up to the Lord Chief Justice. I might even have been right about the law. Anyway we took an early bath and returned the next morning to further good news from Mr Cursitor. I thought it right to keep the latest developments from the Sackbut family and, when we were back in Court, I passed a note of my further application up to the coroner.

'Mr Rumpole,' he said in his most official voice, 'you've asked me to take the evidence of this witness. Mrs . . . '

'Petronelli, sir.'

'Mrs Petronelli. And I have no idea what light she can throw on this dark subject.'

'Then let me help you out. She's here now, sir. Let her come in and be sworn.'

The door of the court room opened and Mr Cursitor appeared. Standing aside, he let in a woman, dressed in black. She must

have been almost seventy but she was still elegant, smiling, with fair hair touched with grey. Mr Pringle led her to the witness-box where she took the oath quietly. I started my questions before the coroner quite understood what was happening.

'What was your name, madam,' I asked, 'before you married Signor Petronelli?'

'It was Lady Sackbut.'

'And your son is?'

She looked at my client for the first time and said, 'Richard.' He had lowered his eyes and sat with his arms folded.

'Mr Rumpole, do I understand that this lady is your client's . . . ?'

'His mother, sir.'

'I still don't know what evidence she can give.'

'Then perhaps it would be better if I carried on. I think the story will become quite clear to everyone.'

'Very well, Mr Rumpole. Carry on for the moment. If you please.' The coroner was suffering from a sudden lack of energy as he saw his carefully built-up case of doubt and suspicion collapsing.

'It's many years since you saw your son?' I asked the witness.

'I'm afraid it's a great many years.'

'When Signor Petronelli was alive, I think you lived in Como?'

'Yes. My husband had a hotel there. When he died I decided to sell it and come back to England.'

'To where in England?'

'To London. I live in Southwark.' Then I summoned Pringle, who took the witness the photograph of the dead bag lady.

'Look at that photograph, will you? Since you have lived there, have you become interested in a charity dealing with homeless people?'

'There seem to be so many sleeping in the street in London. We give them meals. Try to find them beds. Even invite them home sometimes.' She looked at the photograph of the dead woman. 'That's Bertha.'

'Bertha?'

'When I first met her she was sleeping at the back of Waterloo station. I let her stay with me one night, when we couldn't find her a bed anywhere else. We began to talk. She told me about her husband, who'd been a builder and gone bankrupt and been sent to prison for some reason. And, I don't know why, I told her about Sackbut Castle and my son. I never talked much about it to anyone else. But with Bertha it seemed it wouldn't matter.'

'So she stayed the night in your house. Did she leave the next morning?'

'Yes. I never saw her again.'

'Was anything missing when she left?'

'Well, yes. A photograph I'd shown her when we were talking. I kept it in a desk. Not on display or anything. And when Bertha went, that went with her. I was very angry with her for stealing it.'

Pringle handed the witness another photograph, the group on the castle terrace.

'Is that the photograph you lost?'

'Yes, it is.'

'Who are the people in that group?'

'My first husband, myself and Richard when he was a baby.'

'One final question. Did your son Richard ever hit you over the head with a blunt instrument and push you into a lake?'

'No. No, he never did that to me. Even if he thought I deserved it.' And now the witness was looking at her son, half-smiling. He looked up at her.

After that, even Dr Swabey, for all his ingenuity, couldn't think of much to ask Signora Petronelli. The inquest was virtually over and the verdict inevitable. As soon as it was given, the Court rose, the room emptied and Lord Sackbut was left alone in it with the woman who had been dead to him so long. I knew we should get away early and we had packed our bags and taken them to the Court. Mr Cursitor's clerk found us a taxi and we drove straight to the station.

' "The jury in the Sackbut Castle inquest returned a verdict of accidental death", blah, blah.' We were at breakfast again in the kitchen at home and I was reading *The Times* and Hilda had her *Daily Telegraph*.

'Rumpole,' she sounded worried, 'you said Richard was lying in Court.'

'Oh, yes. Bertha waylaid him in the garden. Told him she had some news for him. Probably asked for money. He sent her away and wouldn't listen. She hung around Welldyke until the evening and then went back to the castle, full of gin and unsteady on her pins. It really was an accident. I don't know, Hilda. Perhaps he had a secret fear that Bertha *was* his mother. He hadn't seen the real one for thirty years. But recognising his mother would mean his father was a liar, the father who could do no wrong. So he pretended that he didn't have the faintest idea who she was.'

'That wasn't very nice of him.'

'People aren't always nice, especially if they're lords. Luckily his real mother reads the *Daily Telegraph*.'

'Why luckily?'

'Oh, didn't I tell you? I got old Mr Dry-as-Dust Cursitor to put an advertisement in the personal column: RICCARDINO WANTS TO SEE HIS MOTHER. VERY URGENT. PHONE THE SOLICITORS. And the Sackbuts read *The Times*.'

The phone on the wall was ringing. I went to answer it as Hilda was saying, 'Poor woman. Poor, poor woman.'

The call was from Mizz Liz Probert. She was off to Court early and wanted to let me know that the prosecution was offering no evidence against Walter The Wally Wilkinson. The man who really did it, apparently, was the social worker's lover and he had made a confession and there was enough forensic evidence to make it stick. Apparently they were all in a rather complicated emotional situation. That seemed a considerable understatement to me. Before she rang off I offered to buy Mizz Liz a drink in Pommeroy's that evening.

When I returned to my cooling tea and toast, I told Hilda another tale of social distinctions. 'You know why The Wally confessed to that triple murder?' I said. 'Snobbery, Hilda. Pure snobbery. He thought he'd done in an old dosser called Bronco Billington but he didn't want to be potted for anything so down-market. So he put his hands up to a smart triple murder. That way he'd join the upper crust in chokey and be treated like a lord by all the screws.'

'Rumpole,' She said thoughtfully, 'I don't think we'll go to Sackbut Castle again.'

'I don't think we'll be asked,' I told her.

That evening, at a corner table in Pommeroy's, and over a couple of glasses of Château Fleet Street, I broached a delicate subject with Mizz Probert. 'Liz, I wanted to tell you that I know all about the Honourable David Luxter, otherwise known as Inchcape.'

'The Hon. David!' Liz spat out the title. 'It's disgusting.'

'Instead of a decent upbringing in a one-parent family in Camden, he was cursed with ex-Lord Chancellor Luxter as a grandad. He was a deprived child.'

'A *what*?' Liz sounded puzzled.

'They all are, Mizz Liz. The lot of them. The lords and ladies and marquises of whatnot that figure in Debby's Diary in *Coronet* magazine. They turn their sons out of the home at a tender age. They put them into the care of some sort of young offenders' secure home like Eton. They lie to them and tell them that their mothers are dead. The dice are loaded, against the young of the upper crust.'

Then we drank in silence. When she had thought it over, Liz said, 'I suppose they are.'

'What Dave needs is counselling. He needs a supportive figure in a secure one-on-one situation. He needs the confidence-building skills that you alone can bring him.'

'Does he? I suppose he has been discriminated against, really . . . '

'One of society's outcasts, I'd say.'

'I shouldn't have withdrawn my support.'

'Replace it, Liz! Prop the poor fellow up.'

She took another gulp of the Ordinary red and came to a sensible conclusion. 'It's a bloody unjust world, Rumpole,' she said.

'You've been all these years in the law, Liz. And you've only just found that out?'

Rumpole on Trial

I have often wondered how my career as an Old Bailey hack would terminate. Would I drop dead at the triumphant end of my most moving final speech? 'Ladies and Gentlemen of the jury, my task is done. I have said my say. This trial has been but a few days out of your life, but for me it is the *whole* of my life. And that life I leave, with the utmost confidence, in your hands,' and then keel over and out. 'Rumpole snuffs it in Court'; the news would run like wild fire round the Inns of Court and I would challenge any jury to dare to convict after that forensic trick had been played upon them. Or will I die in an apoplexy after a particularly heated disagreement with Mr Injustice Graves, or Sir Oliver Oliphant? One thing I'm sure of, I shall not drift into retirement and spend my days hanging around Froxbury Mansions in a dressing-gown, nor shall I ever repair to the Golden Gate Retirement Home, Weston-super-Mare, and sit in the sun-lounge retelling the extraordinary case of the Judge's Elbow, or the Miracle in the Ecclesiastical Court which saved a vicar from an unfrocking. No, my conclusion had better come swiftly, and Rumpole's career should end with a bang rather than a whimper. When thinking of the alternatives available, I never expected I would finish by being kicked out of the Bar, dismissed for unprofessional conduct and drummed out of the monstrous regiment of learned friends. And yet this conclusion became a distinct possibility on that dreadful day when, apparently, even I went too far and brought that weighty edifice, the legal Establishment, crashing down upon my head.

The day dawned grey and wet after I had been kept awake most of the night by a raging toothache. I rang my dentist, Mr Lionel Leering, a practitioner whose company I manage to shun until the pain becomes unbearable, and he agreed to meet me at his Harley Street rooms at nine o'clock, so giving me time to get to the Old Bailey, where I was engaged in a particularly tricky case. So picture me at the start of what was undoubtedly the worst in a long career of difficult days, stretched out on the chair of pain and terror beside the bubbling spittoon. Mr Leering, the smooth, grey-haired master of the drill, who seemed perpetually tanned from a trip to his holiday home in Ibiza, was fiddling about inside my mouth while subliminal baroque music tinkled on the cassette player and the blonde nurse looked on with well-simulated concern.

'Busy day ahead of you, Mr Rumpole?' Mr Leering was keeping up the bright chatter. 'Open just a little wider for me, will you? What sort of terrible crime are you on today then?'

'Ans . . . lorter,' I did my best to tell him.

'My daughter?' Leering purred with satisfaction. 'How kind of you to remember. Well, Jessica's just done her A-levels and she's off to Florence doing the History of Art. You should hear her on the quattrocento. Knows a great deal more than I ever did. And of course, being blonde, the Italians are mad about her.'

'I said . . . Ans . . . lorter. Down the Ole . . . Ailey,' I tried to explain before he started the drill.

'My old lady? Oh, you mean Yolande. I'm not sure she'd be too keen on being called that. She's better now. Gone in for acupuncture. What were you saying?'

'An . . . cord . . . Tong . . . '

'Your tongue? Not hurting you, am I?'

'An . . . supposed . . . Illed is ife.'

'Something she did to her back,' Leering explained patiently. 'Playing golf. Golf covers a multitude of sins. Particularly for the women of Hampstead Garden Suburb.'

'Ell on the ender . . . '

The drill had stopped now, and he pulled the cotton wool rolls away from my gums. My effort to tell him about my life and work had obviously gone for nothing because he asked politely, 'Send her what? Your love? Yolande'll be tickled to death. Of course, she's never met you. But she'll still be tickled to death. Rinse now, will you? Now what were we talking about?'

'Manslaughter,' I told him once again as I spat out pink and chemicated fluid.

'Oh, no. Not really? Yolande can be extremely irritating at times. What woman can't? But I'm not actually tempted to bash her across the head.'

'No' – I was showing remarkable patience with this slow-witted dentist – 'I said I'm doing a case at the Old Bailey. My client's a man called Tong. Accused of manslaughter. Killed his wife, Mrs Tong. She fell down and her head hit the fender.'

'Oh, really? How fascinating.' Now he knew what I was talking about, Mr Leering had lost all interest in my case. 'I've just done a temporary stopping. That should see you through the day. But ring me up if you're in any trouble.'

'I think it's going to take a great deal more than a temporary stopping to see me through today,' I said as I got out of the chair and struggled into the well-worn black jacket. 'I'm before Mr Justice "Ollie" Oliphant.'

As I was walking towards the Old Bailey I felt a familiar stab of pain, warning me that the stopping might be extremely temporary. As I was going through the revolving doors, Mizz Liz Probert came flying in behind me, sent the door spinning, collided into my back, then went dashing up the stairs, calling, 'Sorry, Rumpole!' and vanished.

'Sorry, Rumpole!' I grumbled to myself. Mizz Probert cannons into you, nearly sends your brief flying and all she does is call out 'Sorry, Rumpole!' on the trot. Everyone, it seemed to me, said 'Sorry, Rumpole!' and didn't mean a word of it. They were sorry for sending my clients to chokey, sorry for not showing me all the prosecution statements, sorry for standing on my foot in the Underground, and now, no doubt, sorry for stealing my bands. For I had reached the robing-room and, while climbing into the fancy dress, searched for the little white hanging tabs that ornament a legal hack's neck and, lo and behold, these precious bands had been nicked. I looked down the robing-room in desperation and saw young Dave Inchcape, Mizz Liz Probert's lover and co-mortgagee, carefully tie a snow-white pair of crisp linen bands around his winged collar. I approached him in a hostile manner.

'Inchcape' – I lost no time in coming to the point – 'have you pinched my bands?'

'Sorry, Rumpole?' He pretended to know nothing of the matter.

'You have!' I regarded the case as proved. 'Honestly, Inchcape. Nowadays the barristers' robing-room is little better than a den of thieves!'

'These are my bands, Rumpole. There are some bands over there on the table. Slightly soiled. They're probably yours.'

'Slightly soiled? Sorry, Rumpole! Sorry, whoever they belonged to,' and I put them on. 'The bloody man's presumably got mine, anyway.'

When I got down, correctly if sordidly decorated about the throat, to Ollie Oliphant's Court One I found Claude Erskine-Brown all tricked out as an artificial silk and his junior, Mizz She Who Cannons Into You Probert.

'I want to ask you, Rumpole,' Claude said in his newly acquired QC's voice, 'about calling your client.'

'Mr Tong.'

'Yes. Are you calling him?'

'I call him Mr Tong because that's his name.'

'I mean,' he said with exaggerated patience, as though explaining the law to a white wig, 'are you going to put him in the witness-box? You don't have to, you know. You see, I've been asked to do a murder in Lewes. One does have so many demands on one's time in silk.

So if you're not going to call Mr Tong, I thought, well, perhaps we might finish today.'

While he was drooling on, I was looking closely at the man's neck. Then I came out with the accusation direct. 'Are those my bands you're wearing?' I took hold of the suspect tabs, lifted them and examined them closely. 'They look like my bands. They *are* my bands! What's that written on them?'

'C.E.B. stands for Claude Erskine-Brown.' This was apparently his defence.

'When did you write that?'

'Oh really, Rumpole! We don't even share the same robing-room now I'm in silk. How could I have got at your bands? Just tell me, are you calling your client?'

I wasn't satisfied with his explanation, but the usher was hurrying us in as the judge was straining at the leash. I pushed my way into Court, telling Erskine-Brown nothing of my plans.

I knew what I'd like to call my client. I'd like to call him a grade A, hundred-per-cent pain in the neck. In any team chosen to bore for England he would have been first in to bat. He was a retired civil servant and his hair, face, business suit and spectacles were of a uniform grey. When he spoke, he did so in a dreary monotone and never used one word when twenty would suffice. The only unexpected thing about him was that he ever got involved in the colourful crime of manslaughter. I had considered a long time before deciding to call Mr Tong as a witness in his own defence. I knew he would bore the jury to distraction and no doubt drive that North Country comedian Mr Justice Oliphant into an apoplexy. However, Mrs Tong had been found dead from a head wound in the sitting-room of their semi-detached house in Rickmansworth, and I felt her husband was called upon to provide some sort of an explanation.

You will have gathered that things hadn't gone well from the start of that day for Rumpole, and matters didn't improve when my client Tong stepped into the witness-box, raised the Testament on high and gave us what appeared to be a shortened version of the oath. 'I swear by', he said, carefully omitting any reference to the Deity, 'that the evidence I shall give shall be the truth, the whole truth and nothing but the truth.'

'Mr Rumpole. Your client has left something out of the oath.' Mr Justice Oliphant might not have been a great lawyer but at least he knew the oath by heart.

'So I noticed, my Lord.'

'Well, see to it, Mr Rumpole. Use your common sense.'

'Mr Tong,' I asked the witness, 'who is it you swear by?'

'One I wouldn't drag down to the level of this place, my Lord.'

'What's he mean, Mr Rumpole? Drag down to the level of this Court? What's he mean by that?' The judge's common sense was giving way to uncommon anger.

'I suppose he means that the Almighty might not wish to be seen in Court Number One at the Old Bailey,' I suggested.

'Not wish to be seen? I never heard of such a thing!'

'Mr Tong has some rather original ideas about theology, my Lord.' I did my best to deter further conversation on the subject. 'I'm sure he would go into the matter at considerable length if your Lordship was interested.'

'I'm not, Mr Rumpole, not interested in the least.' And here his Lordship turned on the witness with 'Are you saying, Mr . . . What's your name again?'

'Tong, my Lord. Henry Sebastian Tong.'

'Are you saying my Court isn't good enough for God? Is that what you're saying?'

'I am saying that this Court, my Lord, is a place of sin and worldliness and we should not involve a Certain Being in these proceedings. May I remind you of the Book of Ezekiel: "And it shall be unto them a false divination in their sight, to them that have sworn oaths." '

'Don't let's worry about the Book of Ezekiel.' This work clearly wasn't Ollie Oliphant's bedtime reading. 'Mr Rumpole, can't you control your client?'

'Unfortunately not, my Lord.'

'When I was a young lad, the first thing we learned at the Bar was to control our clients.' The judge was back on more familiar territory. 'It's a great pity you weren't brought up in a good old commonsensical Chambers in Leeds, Mr Rumpole.'

'I suppose I might have acquired some of your Lordship's charm and polish,' I said respectfully.

'Let's use our common sense about this, shall we? Mr Tong, do you understand what it is to tell the truth?'

'I have always told the truth. During my thirty years in the Ministry.'

'Ministry?' The judge turned to me in some alarm. 'Is your client a man of the cloth, Mr Rumpole?'

'I think he's referring to the Ministry of Agriculture and Fisheries, where he was a clerk for many years.'

'Are you going to tell the truth?' The judge addressed my client in a common-sense shout.

'Yes.' Mr Tong even managed to make a monosyllable sound boring.

'There you are, Mr Rumpole!' The judge was triumphant. 'That's the way to do it. Now, let's get on with it, shall we?'

'I assure your Lordship, I can't wait. Ouch!' The tooth Mr Leering had said would see me through the day disagreed with a sharp stab of pain. I put a hand to my cheek and muttered to my instructing solicitor, the faithful Mr Bernard, 'It's the temporary stopping.'

'Stopping? Why are you stopping, Mr Rumpole?' The judge was deeply suspicious.

Now I knew what hell was, examining a prize bore before Ollie Oliphant with a raging toothache. All the same, I soldiered on and asked Tong, 'Were you married to the late Sarah Tong?'

'We had met in the Min of Ag and Fish, where Sarah Pennington, as she then was, held a post in the typing pool. We were adjacent, as I well remember, on one occasion for the hot meal in the canteen.'

'I don't want to hurry you.'

'You hurry him, Mr Rumpole.'

'Let's come to your marriage,' I begged the witness.

'The 13th of March 1950, at the Church of St Joseph and All Angels, in what was then the village of Pinner.' Mr Tong supplied all the details. 'The weather, as I remember it, was particularly inclement. Dark skies and a late snow flurry.'

'Don't let's worry about the weather.' Ollie was using his common sense and longing to get on with it.

'I took it as a portent, my Lord, of storms to come.'

'Could you just describe your married life to the jury?' I tried a short cut.

'I can only, with the greatest respect and due deference, adopt the words of the psalmist. No doubt they are well known to his Lordship?'

'I shouldn't bet on it, Mr Tong,' I warned him, and, ignoring Ollie's apparent displeasure, added, 'Perhaps you could just remind us what the Good Book says?'

' "It is better to dwell in a corner of the housetop, than with a brawling woman in a wide house," ' Mr Tong recited. ' "It is better to dwell in the wilderness than with a contentious and angry woman." '

So my client's evidence wound on, accompanied by toothache and an angry judge, and I felt that I had finally fallen out of love with the art of advocacy. I didn't want to have to worry about Mr Tong or the precise circumstances in which Mrs Tong had been released from this world. I wanted to sit down, to shut up and to close my eyes in peace. She Who Must Be Obeyed had something of the same idea. She wanted me to become a judge. Without taking me into her confidence, she met Marigold Featherstone, the judge's wife, for coffee in Harrods for the purpose of furthering her plan. 'Rumpole gets so terribly tired at night,' Hilda said in the Silver Grill, and Marigold, with a heavy sigh, agreed.

'So does Guthrie. At night he's as flat as a pancake. Is Rumpole flat as a pancake too?'

'Well, not exactly.' Hilda told me she wasn't sure of the exact meaning of this phrase. 'But he's so irritable these days. So edgy, and then he's had this trouble with his teeth. If only he could have a job *sitting down*.'

'You mean, like a clerk or something?'

'Something like a judge.'

'Really?' Marigold was astonished at the idea.

'Oh, I don't mean a Red Judge,' Hilda explained. 'Not a really posh judge like Guthrie. But an ordinary sort of circus judge. And Guthrie does know such important people. You said he's always calling in at the Lord Chancellor's office.'

'Only when he's in trouble,' Marigold said grimly. 'But I suppose I might ask if he could put in a word about your Horace.'

'Oh, Marigold! Would you?'

'Why not? I'll wake the old fellow up and tell him.'

As it happened, my possible escape from the agonies of the Bar was not by such an honourable way out as that sought by Hilda in the Silver Grill. The route began to appear as Mr Tong staggered slowly towards the high point of his evidence. We had enjoyed numerous quotations from the Old Testament. We had been treated to a blow-by-blow account of a quarrel between him and his wife during a holiday in Clacton-on-Sea and many other such incidents. We had learned a great deal more about the Ministry of Agriculture and Fisheries than we ever needed to know. And then Ollie, driven beyond endurance, said, 'For God's sake—'

'My Lord?' Mr Tong looked deeply pained.

'All right, for all our sakes. When are we going to come to the facts of this manslaughter?'

So I asked the witness, 'Now, Mr Tong, on the night this *accident* took place.'

'Accident! That's a matter for the jury to decide!' Ollie exploded. 'Why do you call it an accident?'

'Why did your Lordship call it manslaughter? Isn't that a matter for the jury to decide?'

'Did I say that?' the judge asked. 'Did I say that, Mr Erskine-Brown?'

'Yes, you did,' I told him before Claude could stagger to his feet. 'I wondered if your Lordship had joined the prosecution team, or was it a single-handed effort to prejudice the jury?'

There was a terrible silence and I suppose I should never have said it. Mr Bernard hid his head in shame, Erskine-Brown looked disapproving and Liz appeared deeply worried. The judge controlled himself with difficulty and then spoke in quiet but dangerous tones. 'Mr Rumpole, that was a quite intolerable thing to say.'

'My Lord. That was a quite intolerable thing to do.' I was determined to fight on.

'I may have had a momentary slip of the tongue.' It seemed that the judge was about to retreat, but I had no intention of allowing him to do so gracefully. 'Or', I said, 'your Lordship's well-known common sense may have deserted you.'

There was another sharp intake of breath from the attendant legal hacks and then the judge kindly let me know what was in his mind. 'Mr Rumpole. I think you should be warned. One of these days you may go too far and behaviour such as yours can have certain consequences. Now, can we get on?'

'Certainly. I didn't wish to interrupt the flow of your Lordship's rebuke.' So I started my uphill task with the witness again. 'Mr Tong, on the night in question, did you and Mrs Tong quarrel?'

'As per usual, my Lord.'

'What was the subject of the quarrel?'

'She accused me of being overly familiar with a near neighbour. This was a certain Mrs Grabowitz, my Lord, a lady of Polish extraction, whose deceased husband had, by a curious coincidence, been a colleague of mine – it's a small world, isn't it? – in the Min of Ag and Fish.'

'Mr Tong, ignore the neighbour's deceased husband, if you'd be so kind. What did your wife do?'

'She ran at me, my Lord, with her nails poised, as though to scratch me across the face, as it was often her habit so to do. However, as ill-luck would have it, the runner in front of the gas-fire slipped beneath her feet on the highly polished flooring and she fell. As she did so, the back of her head made contact with the raised tiling in front of our hearth, my Lord, and she received the injuries which ultimately caused her to pass over.'

'Mr Rumpole, is that the explanation of this lady's death you wish to leave to the jury?' the judge asked with some contempt.

'Certainly, my Lord. Does your Lordship wish to prejudge the issue and are we about to hear a little premature adjudication?'

'Mr Rumpole! I have warned you twice, I shall not warn you again. I'm looking at the clock.'

'So I'd noticed.'

'We'll break off now. Back at ten past two, Members of the jury.' And then Ollie turned to my client and gave him the solemn warning which might help me into retirement. 'I understand you're on bail, Mr Tong, and you're in the middle of giving your evidence. It's vitally important that you speak to no one about your case during the lunchtime adjournment. And no one must speak to you, particularly your legal advisers. Is that thoroughly understood, Mr Rumpole?'

'Naturally, my Lord,' I assured him. 'I do know the rules.'

'I hope you do, Mr Rumpole. I sincerely hope you do.'

The events of that lunch-hour achieved a historic importance. After a modest meal of bean-shoot sandwiches in the Nut-house Vegetarian Restaurant down by the bank (Claude was on a regime calculated to make him more sylph-like and sexually desirable), he returned to the Old Bailey and was walking up to the silks' robing-room when he saw, through an archway, the defendant Tong seated and silent. Approaching nearer, he heard the following words (Claude was good enough to make a careful note of them at the time) shouted by Rumpole in a voice of extreme irritation.

'Listen to me,' my speech, which Claude knew to be legal advice to the client, began. 'Is this damn thing going to last for ever? Well, for God's sake, get on with it! You're driving me mad. Talk. That's all you do, you boring old fart. Just get on with it. I've got enough trouble with the judge without you causing me all this agony. Get it out. That's all. Short and snappy. Put us out of our misery. Get it out and then shut up!'

As I say, Claude took a careful note of these words but said nothing to me about them when I emerged from behind the archway. When we got back to court I asked my client a few more questions, which he answered with astounding brevity.

'Mr Tong. Did you ever intend to do your wife the slightest harm?'

'No.'

'Did you strike her?'

'No.'

'Or assault her in any way?'

'No.'

'Just wait there, will you?' – I sat down with considerable relief – 'in case Mr Erskine-Brown can think of anything to ask you.' Claude did have something to ask, and his first question came as something of a surprise to me.

'You've become very monosyllabic since lunch, haven't you, Mr Tong?'

'Perhaps it's something he ate,' I murmured to my confidant, Bernard.

'No' – Erskine-Brown wouldn't have this – 'it's nothing you ate, is it, as your learned counsel suggests? It's something Mr Rumpole said to you.'

'*Said* to him?' Ollie Oliphant registered profound shock. 'When are you suggesting Mr Rumpole spoke to him?'

'Oh, during the luncheon adjournment, my Lord.' Claude dropped the bombshell casually.

'Mr Rumpole!' Ollie gasped with horror. 'Mr Erskine-Brown, did I not give a solemn warning that no one was to speak to Mr Tong and he was to speak to no one during the adjournment?'

'You did, my Lord,' Claude confirmed it. 'That was why I was so surprised when I heard Mr Rumpole doing it.'

'You heard Mr Rumpole speaking to the defendant Tong?'

'I'm afraid so, my Lord.'

Again Bernard winced in agony, and there were varying reactions of shock and disgust all round. I didn't improve the situation by muttering loudly, 'Oh, come off it, Claude.'

'And what did Mr Rumpole say?' The judge wanted all the gory details.

'He told Mr Tong he did nothing but talk. And he was to get on with it and he was to get it out and make it snappy. Oh, yes, he said he was a boring old fart.'

'A boring old what, Mr Erskine-Brown?'

'Fart, my Lord.'

'And he's not the only one around here either,' I informed Mr Bernard.

If the judge heard this he ignored it. He went on in tones of the deepest disapproval to ask Claude, 'And, since that conversation, you say that the defendant Tong has been monosyllabic. In other words, he is obeying Mr Rumpole's quite improperly given instructions?'

'Precisely what I am suggesting, my Lord.' Claude was delighted to agree.

'Well, now, Mr Rumpole.' The judge stared balefully at me. 'What've you got to say to Mr Erskine-Brown's accusation?'

Suddenly a great weariness came over me. For once in my long life I couldn't be bothered to argue and this legal storm in a lunch-hour bored me as much as my client's evidence. I was tired of Tong, tired of judges, tired of learned friends, tired of toothache, tired of life. I rose wearily to my feet and said, 'Nothing, my Lord.'

'Nothing?' Mr Justice Oliphant couldn't believe it.

'Absolutely nothing.'

'So you don't deny that all Mr Erskine-Brown has told the Court is true?'

'I neither accept it nor deny it. It's a contemptible suggestion, made by an advocate incapable of conducting a proper cross-examination. Further than that I don't feel called upon to comment. So far as I know I am not on trial.'

'Not at the moment,' said the judge. 'I cannot answer for the Bar Council.'

'Then I suggest we concentrate on the trial of Mr Tong and forget mine, my Lord.' That was my final word on the matter.

When we did concentrate on the trial it went extremely speedily. Mr Tong remained monosyllabic, our speeches were brief, the judge, all passion spent by the drama of the lunch-hour, summed up briefly and by half-past five the jury were back with an acquittal. Shortly after that many of the characters important to this story had assembled in Pommeroy's Wine Bar.

Although he was buying her a drink, Liz Probert made no attempt to disguise her disapproval of the conduct of her learned leader, as she told me after these events had taken place. 'Why did you have to do that, Claude?' she asked in a severe manner. 'Why did you have to put that lunchtime conversation to Tong?'

'Rather brilliant, I thought,' he answered with some self-satisfaction and offered to split a half-bottle of his favourite Pouilly-Fumé with her. 'It got the judge on my side immediately.'

'And got the jury on Rumpole's side. His client was acquitted, I don't know if you remember.'

'Well, win a few, lose a few,' Claude said airily. 'That's par for the course, if you're a busy silk.'

'I mean, why did you do that to Rumpole?'

'Well, that was fair, wasn't it? He shouldn't have talked to his client when he was still in the box. It's just not on!'

'Are you sure he did?' Liz asked.

'I heard him with my own ears. You don't think I'd lie, do you?'

'Well, it has been known. Didn't you lie to your wife, about taking me to the opera?' Liz had no compunction about opening old wounds.

'That was love. Everyone lies when they're in love.'

'Don't ever tell me you're in love with me again. I shan't believe a single word of it. Did you really mean to get Rumpole disbarred?'

'Rumpole disbarred?' Even Claude sounded shaken by the idea. 'It's not possible.'

'Of course it's possible. Didn't you hear Ollie Oliphant?'

'That was just North Country bluff. I mean, they couldn't do a thing like that, could they? Not to Rumpole.'

'If you ask me, that's what they've been longing to do to Rumpole for years,' Liz told him. 'Now you've given them just the excuse they need.'

'Who needs?'

'The Establishment, Claude! They'll use you, you know, then they'll throw you out on the scrap-heap. That's what they do to spies.'

'My God!' Erskine-Brown was looking at her with considerable admiration. 'You're beautiful when you're angry!'

At which point Mizz Probert left him, having seen me alone, staring gloomily into a large brandy. Claude was surrounded by thirsty barristers, eager for news of the great Rumpole–Oliphant battle.

Before I got into conversation with Liz, who sat herself down at my table with a look of maddening pity on her face, I have to confess that I had been watching our clerk Henry at a distant table. He had bought a strange-looking white concoction for Dot Clapton, and was now sitting gazing at her in a way which made me feel that this was no

longer a rehearsal for the Bexleyheath Thespians but a real-life drama which might lead to embarrassing and even disastrous results. I didn't manage to earwig all the dialogue, but I learned enough to enable me to fill in the gaps later.

'You can't imagine what it was like, Dot, when my wife was mayor.' Henry was complaining, as he so often did, about his spouse's civic duties.

'Bet you were proud of her.' Dot seemed to be missing the point.

'Proud of her! What happened to my self-respect in those days when I was constantly referred to as the "Lady Mayoress"?'

'Poor old Henry!' Dot couldn't help laughing.

'Poor old Henry, yes. At council meetings I had to sit in the gallery known as the hen pen. I was sat there with the wives.'

'Things a bit better now, are they?' Dot was still hugely entertained.

'Now Eileen's reverted to Alderperson? Very minimally, Dot. She's on this slimming regime now. What shall I go back to? Lettuce salad and cottage cheese – you know, that white stuff. Tastes of soap. No drink, of course. Nothing alcoholic. You reckon you could go another Snowball?'

'I'm all right, thanks.' I saw Dot cover her glass with her hand.

'I know you are, Dot,' Henry agreed enthusiastically. 'You most certainly are all right. The trouble is, Eileen and I haven't exactly got a relationship. Not like *we've* got a relationship.'

'Well, she doesn't work with you, does she? Not on the fee notes,' Dot asked, reasonably enough.

'She doesn't work with me at all and, well, I don't feel close to her. Not as I feel close to you, Dot.'

'Well, don't get that close,' Dot warned him. 'I saw Mr Erskine-Brown give a glance in this direction.'

'Mr Erskine-Brown? He's always chasing after young girls. Makes himself ridiculous.' Henry's voice was full of contempt.

'I *had* noticed.'

'I'm not like that, Dot. I like to talk, you know, one on one. Have a relationship. May I ask you a very personal question?'

'No harm in asking.' She sounded less than fascinated.

'Do you like me, Dot? I mean, do you like me for myself?'

'Well, I don't like you for anyone else.' Dot laughed again. 'You're a very nice sort of person. Speak as you find.'

And then Henry asked anxiously, 'Am I a big part of your life?'

'Course you are!' She was still amused.

'Thank you, Dot! Thank you very much. That's all I need to

know.' Henry stood up, grateful and excited. 'That deserves another Snowball!'

I saw him set out for the bar in a determined fashion, so now Dot was speaking to his back, trying to explain herself. 'I mean, you're my boss, aren't you? That's a big part of my life.'

Things had reached this somewhat tricky stage in the Dot–Henry relationship by the time Liz came and sat with me and demanded my full attention with a call to arms. 'Rumpole,' she said, 'you've got to fight it. Every inch of the way!'

'Fight what?'

'Your case. It's the Establishment against Rumpole.'

'My dear Mizz Liz, there isn't any case.'

'It's a question of free speech.'

'Is it?'

'Your freedom to speak to your client during the lunch-hour. You're an issue of civil rights now, Rumpole.'

'Oh, am I? I don't think I want to be that.'

And then she looked at my glass and said, as though it were a sad sign of decline, 'You're drinking brandy!'

'Dutch courage,' I explained.

'Oh, Rumpole, that's not like you. You've never been afraid of judges.'

'Judges? Oh, no, as I always taught you, Mizz Liz, fearlessness is the first essential in an advocate. I can cope with judges. It's the other chaps that give me the jim-jams.'

'Which other chaps, Rumpole?'

'Dentists!' I took a large swig of brandy and shivered.

Time cures many things and in quite a short time old smoothy-chops Leering had the nagging tooth out of my head and I felt slightly better tempered. Time, however, merely encouraged the growth of the great dispute and brought me nearer to an event that I'd never imagined possible, the trial of Rumpole.

You must understand that we legal hacks are divided into Inns, known as Inns of Court. These Inns are ruled by the benchers, judges and senior barristers, who elect each other to the office rather in the manner of the council which ruled Venice during the Middle Ages. The benchers of my Inn, known as the Outer Temple, do themselves extremely proud and, once elected, pay very little for lunch in the Outer Temple Hall, and enjoy a good many ceremonial dinners, Grand Nights, Guest Nights and other such occasions, when they climb into a white tie and tails, enter the dining-hall with

bishops and generals on their arms, and then retire to the Parliament
Room for fruit, nuts, port, brandy, Muscat de Beaumes de Venise
and Romeo y Julieta cigars. There they discuss the hardships of judicial life and the sad decline in public morality and, occasionally,
swap such jokes as might deprave and corrupt those likely to hear
them.

On this particular Guest Night Mr Justice Graves, as treasurer of
the Inn, was presiding over the festivities. Ollie Oliphant was also
present, as was a tall, handsome, only slightly overweight QC called
Montague Varian, who was later to act as my prosecutor. Sam Ballard, the alleged Head of our Chambers and recently elected bencher,
was there, delighted and somewhat overawed by his new honour. It
was Ballard who told me the drift of the after-dinner conversation in
the Parliament Room, an account which I have filled up with invention founded on a hard-won knowledge of the characters concerned.
Among the guests present were a Lady Mendip, a sensible grey-
haired headmistress, and the Bishop of Bayswater. It was to this cleric
that Graves explained one of the quainter customs of the Outer
Temple dining process.

'My dear Bishop, you may have heard a porter ringing a handbell
before dinner. That's a custom we've kept up since the Middle Ages.
The purpose is to summon in such of our students as may be fishing
in the Fleet River.'

'Oh, I like that. I like that *very* much.' The bishop was full of enthusiasm for the Middle Ages. 'We regard it as rather a charming eccentricity.' Graves was smiling but his words immediately brought out the
worst in Oliphant.

'I've had enough of eccentricity lately,' he said. 'And I don't regard
it as a bit charming.'

'Ah, Oliver, I heard you'd been having a bit of trouble with Rumpole.' Graves turned the conversation to the scandal of the moment.

'You've got to admit, Rumpole's a genuine eccentric!' Montague
Varian seemed to find me amusing.

'Genuine?' Oliphant cracked a nut mercilessly. 'Where I come
from we know what genuine is. There's nothing more genuine than a
good old Yorkshire pudding that's risen in the oven, all fluffy and
crisp outside.'

At which a voice piped up from the end of the table singing a
Northern folk song with incomprehensible words, 'On Ilkley Moor
baht 'at!' This was Arthur Nottley, the junior bencher, a thin, rather
elegant fellow whose weary manner marked a deep and genuine cyn-
icism. He often said he only stayed on at the Bar to keep his basset

hound in the way to which it had become accustomed. Now he had not only insulted the Great Yorkshire Bore, but had broken one of the rules of the Inn, so Graves rebuked him.

'Master Junior, we don't sing on Guest Nights in this Inn. Only on the Night of Grand Revelry.'

'I'm sorry, Master Treasurer.' Nottley did his best to sound apologetic.

'Please remember that. Yes, Oliver? You were saying?'

'It's all theatrical,' Oliphant grumbled. 'Those old clothes to make himself look poor and down-at-heel, put on to get a sympathy vote from the jury. That terrible old bit of waistcoat with cigar ash and gravy stains.'

'It's no more than a façade of a waistcoat,' Varian agreed. 'A sort of dickie!'

'The old Lord Chief would never hear argument from a man he suspected of wearing a backless waistcoat.' Oliphant quoted a precedent. 'Do you remember him telling Freddy Ringwood, "It gives me little pleasure to listen to an argument from a gentleman in light trousers"? You could say the same for Rumpole's waistcoat. When he waves his arms about you can see his shirt.'

'You're telling me, Oliver!' Graves added to the horror, 'Unfortunately I've seen more than that.'

'Of course, we do have Rumpole in Chambers.' Ballard, I'm sure, felt he had to apologise for me. 'Unfortunately. I inherited him.'

'Come with the furniture, did he?' Varian laughed.

'Oh, *I'd* never have let him in,' the loyal Ballard assured them. 'And I must tell you, I've tried to raise the matter of his waistcoat on many occasions, but I can't get him to listen.'

'Well, there you go, you see.' And Graves apologised to the cleric, 'But we're boring the bishop.'

'Not at all. It's fascinating.' The Bishop of Bayswater was enjoying the fun. 'This Rumpole you've been talking about. I gather he's a bit of a character.'

'You could say he's definitely got form.' Varian made a legal joke.

'Previous convictions that means, Bishop,' Graves explained for the benefit of the cloth.

'We get them in our business,' the bishop told them. 'Priests who try to be characters. They've usually come to it later in life. Preach eccentric sermons, mention Saddam Hussein in their prayers, pay undue attention to the poor of north Bayswater and never bother to drop in for a cup of tea with the perfectly decent old ladies in the south. Blame the Government for all the sins of mankind in the faint hope of getting their mugs on television. "Oh, please God", that's my nightly prayer, "save me from characters".'

Varian passed him the Madeira and when he had refilled his glass the bishop continued: 'Give me a plain, undistinguished parish priest, a chap who can marry them, bury them and still do a decent Armistice Day service for the Veterans Association.'

'Or a chap who'll put his case, keep a civil tongue in his head and not complain when you pot his client,' Oliphant agreed.

'By the way,' Graves asked, 'what did Freddy Ringwood *do* in the end? Was it that business with his girl pupil? The one who tried to slit her wrists in the women's robing-room at the Old Bailey?'

'No, I don't think that was it. Didn't he cash a rubber cheque in the Circuit mess?' Arthur Nottley remembered.

'That was cleared. No' – Varian put them right – 'old Freddy's trouble was that he spoke to his client while he was in the middle of giving evidence.'

'It sounds familiar!' Ollie Oliphant said with relish. 'And in Rumpole's case there was also the matter of the abusive language he used to me on the Bench. Not that I mind for myself. I can use my common sense about that, I hope. But when you're sitting representing Her Majesty the Queen it amounts to *lèse majesté*.'

'High treason, Oliver?' suggested Graves languidly. 'There's a strong rumour going round the Sheridan Club that Rumpole called you a boring old fart.'

At which Arthur Nottley whispered to our leader, 'Probably the only true words spoken in the case!' and Ballard did his best to look disapproving at such impertinence.

'I know what he said.' Oliphant was overcome with terrible common sense. 'It was the clearest Contempt of Court. That's why I felt it was my public duty to report the matter to the Bar Council.'

'And they're also saying' – Varian was always marvellously well informed – 'that Rumpole's case has been put over to a disciplinary tribunal.'

'And may the Lord have mercy on his soul,' Graves intoned. 'Rumpole on trial! You must admit, it's rather an amusing idea.'

The news was bad and it had better be broken to She Who Must Be Obeyed as soon as possible. I had every reason to believe that when she heard it, the consequent eruption of just wrath against the tactless bloody-mindedness of Rumpole would register on the Richter scale as far away as Aldgate East and West Hampstead. So it was in the tentative and somewhat nervous way that a parent on Guy Fawkes night lights the blue touch-paper and stands well back that I said to Hilda one evening when we were seated in front of the gas-fire, 'Old thing, I've got something to tell you.'

'And I've got something to tell *you*, Rumpole.' She was drinking coffee and toying with the *Telegraph* crossword and seemed in an unexpectedly good mood.

All the same, I had to confess, 'I think I've about finished with this game.'

'What game is that, Rumpole?'

'Standing up and bowing, saying, "If your Lordship pleases, In my very humble submission, With the very greatest respect, my Lord" to some old fool no one has any respect for at all.'

'That's the point, Rumpole! You shouldn't have to stand up any more, or bow to anyone.'

'Those days are over, Hilda. Definitely over!'

'I *quite* agree.'

I was delighted to find her so easily persuaded. 'I shall let them go through their absurd rigmarole and then they can do their worst.'

'And you'll spend the rest of your days sitting,' Hilda said. I thought that was rather an odd way of putting it, but I was glad of her support and explained my present position in greater detail.

'So be it!' I told her. 'If that's all they have to say to me after a life-time of trying to see that some sort of justice is done to a long line of errant human beings, good luck to them. If that's my only reward for trying to open their eyes and understand that there are a great many people in this world who weren't at Winchester with them, and have no desire to take port with the benchers of the Outer Temple, let them get on with it. "From this time forth I never will speak word!" '

'I'm sure that's best, Rumpole, except for your summings-up.'

'My what?' I no longer followed her drift.

'Your summings-up to the jury, Rumpole. You can do those sit-ting down, can't you?'

'Hilda,' I asked patiently, 'what *are* you talking about?'

'I know what *you're* talking about. I had a word with Marigold Featherstone, in Harrods.'

'Does *she* know already?' News of Rumpole's disgrace had, of course, spread like wildfire.

'Well, not everything. But she was going to see Guthrie did some-thing about it.'

'Nothing he can do.' I had to shatter her hopes. 'Nothing anyone can do, now.'

'You mean, they told you?' She looked more delighted than ever.

'Told me what?'

'You're going to be a judge?'

'No, my dear old thing. I'm not going to be a judge. I'm not even going to be a barrister. I'm up before the disciplinary tribunal, Hilda. They're going to kick me out.'

She looked at me in silence and I steeled myself for the big bang, but to my amazement she asked, quite quietly, 'Rumpole, what is it? You've got yourself into some sort of trouble?'

'That's the understatement of the year.'

'Is it another woman?' Hilda's mind dwelt continually on sex.

'Not really. It's another man. A North Country comedian who gave me more of his down-to-earth common sense than I could put up with.'

'Sir Oliver Oliphant?' She knew her way round the judiciary. 'You weren't rude to him, were you, Rumpole?'

'In all the circumstances, I think I behaved with remarkable courtesy,' I assured her.

'That means you were rude to him.' She was not born yesterday. 'I once poured him a cup of tea at the Outer Temple garden party.'

'What made you forget the arsenic?'

'He's probably not so bad when you get to know him.'

'When you get to know him', I assured her, 'he's much, much worse.'

'What else have you done, Rumpole? You may as well tell me now.'

'They say I spoke to my client at lunchtime. I am alleged to have told him not to bore us all to death.'

'Was it a woman client?' She looked, for a moment, prepared to explode, but I reassured her.

'Decidedly not! It was a retired civil servant called Henry Sebastian Tong.'

'And when is this tribunal?' She was starting to sound determined, as though war had broken out and she was prepared to fight to the finish.

'Shortly. I shall treat it with the contempt it deserves,' I told her, 'and when it's all over I shall rest:

> *For the sword outwears its sheath,*
> *And the soul wears out the breast,*
> *And the heart must pause to breathe,*
> *And love itself have rest.'*

The sound of the words brought me some comfort, although I wasn't sure they were entirely appropriate. And then she brought back my worst fears by saying, 'I shall stand by you, Rumpole, at whatever cost. I shall stand by you, through thick and thin.'

Perhaps I should explain the obscure legal process that has to be gone through in the unfrocking, or should I say unwigging, of a barrister. The Bar Council may be said to be the guardian of our morality, there to see we don't indulge in serious crimes or conduct unbecoming to a legal hack, such as assaulting the officer in charge of the case, dealing in dangerous substances round the corridors of the Old Bailey or speaking to our clients in the lunch-hour. Mr Justice Ollie Oliphant had made a complaint to that body and a committee had decided to send me for trial before a High Court judge, three practising barristers and a lay assessor, one of the great and the good who could be relied upon to uphold the traditions of the Bar and not ask awkward questions or give any trouble to the presiding judge. It was the prospect of She Who Must Be Obeyed pleading my cause as a character witness before this august tribunal which made my blood run cold.

There was another offer of support which I thought was far more likely to do me harm than good. I was, a few weeks later, alone in Pommeroy's Wine Bar, contemplating the tail-end of a bottle of Château Fleet Street and putting off the moment when I would have to return home to Hilda's sighs of sympathy and the often-repeated, unanswerable question, 'How *could* you have done such a thing, Rumpole? After all your years of experience,' to which would no doubt be added the information that her Daddy would never have spoken to a client in the lunch-hour, or at any other time come to that, when I heard a familiar voice calling my name and I looked up to see my old friend Fred Timson, head of the great South London family of villains from which a large part of my income is derived. Naturally I asked him to pull up a chair, pour out a glass and was he in some sort of trouble?

'Not me. I heard you was, Mr Rumpole. I want you to regard me as your legal adviser.'

When I explained that the indispensable Mr Bernard was already filling that post at my trial he said, 'Bernard has put me entirely in the picture, he having called on my cousin Kevin's second-hand car lot as he was interested in a black Rover, only fifty thousand on the clock and the property of a late undertaker. We chewed the fat to a considerable extent over your case, Mr Rumpole, and I have to inform you, my own view is that you'll walk it. We'll get you out, sir, without a stain on your character.'

'Oh, really, Fred' – I already felt some foreboding – 'and how will you manage that?'

'It so happened' – he started on a long story – 'that Cary and Chas Timson, being interested spectators in the trial of Chas's brother-in-law Benny Panton on the Crockthorpe post office job, was in the Old Bailey on that very day! And they kept your client Tongue – or whatever his name was — '

'Tong.'

'Yes, they kept Mr Tong in view throughout the lunch-hour, both of them remaining in the precincts as, owing to a family celebration the night before, they didn't fancy their dinner. And they can say, with the utmost certainty, Mr Rumpole, that you did not speak one word to your client throughout the lunchtime adjournment! So the good news is, two cast-iron alibi witnesses. I have informed Mr Bernard accordingly, and you are bound to walk!'

I don't know what Fred expected but all I could do was to look at him in silent wonder and, at last, say, 'Very interesting.'

'We thought you'd be glad to know about it.' He seemed surprised at my not hugging him with delight.

'How did they recognise Mr Tong?'

'Oh, they asked who you was defending, being interested in your movements as the regular family brief. And the usher pointed this Tong out to the witnesses.'

'Really? And who was the judge in the robbery trial they were attending?'

'They told me that! Old Penal Parsloe, I'm sure that was him.'

'Mr Justice Parsloe is now Lord Justice Parsloe, sitting in the Court of Appeal,' I had to break the bad news to him. 'He hasn't been down the Bailey for at least two years. I'm afraid your ingenious defence wouldn't work, Fred, even if I intended to deny the charges.'

'Well, what judge was it, then, Mr Rumpole?'

'Never mind, Fred.' I had to discourage his talent for invention. 'It's the thought that counts.'

When I left Pommeroy's a good deal later, bound for Temple tube station, I had an even stranger encounter and a promise of further embarrassment at my trial. As I came down Middle Temple Lane on to the Embankment and turned right towards the station, I saw the figure of Claude Erskine-Brown approaching with his robe bag slung over his shoulder, no doubt whistling the big number from *Götterdämmerung*, perhaps kept late by some jury unable to make up its mind. Claude had been the cause of all my troubles and I had no desire to bandy words with the fellow, so I turned back and started to retrace my steps in an easterly direction. Who should I see then but Ollie Oliphant issuing from Middle Temple Lane, smoking a cigar and looking like a man who has been enjoying a good dinner. Quick as a shot I dived into such traffic as there was and crossed the road to the Embankment, where I stood, close to the wall, looking down into

the inky water of the Thames, with my back well turned to the two points of danger behind me.

I hadn't been standing there very long, sniffing the night air and hoping I had got shot of my two opponents, when an unwelcome hand grasped my arm and I heard a panic-stricken voice say, 'Don't do it, Rumpole!'

'Do what?'

'Take the easy way out.'

'Bollard!' I said, for it was our Head of Chambers behaving in this extraordinary fashion. 'Let go of me, will you?'

At this, Ballard did relax his grip and stood looking at me with deep and intolerable compassion as he intoned, 'However serious the crime, all sinners may be forgiven. And remember, there are those that are standing by you, your devoted wife – and me! I have taken up the burden of your defence.'

'Well, put it down, Bollard! I have nothing whatever to say to those ridiculous charges.'

'I mean, I am acting for you, at your trial.' I then felt a genuine, if momentary, desire to hurl myself into the river, but he was preaching on. 'I think I can save you, Rumpole, if you truly repent.'

'What *is* this?' I couldn't believe my ears. 'A legal conference or a prayer meeting?'

'Good question, Rumpole! The two are never far apart. You may achieve salvation, if you will say, after me, you have erred and strayed like a lost sheep.'

'*Me?* Say that to Ollie Oliphant?' Had Ballard taken complete leave of his few remaining senses?

'Repentance, Rumpole. It's the only way.'

'Never!'

'I don't ask it for myself, Rumpole, even though I'm standing by you.'

'Well, stop standing by me, will you? I'm on my way to the Underground.' And I started to move away from the man at a fairly brisk pace.

'I ask it for that fine woman who has devoted her life to you. A somewhat unworthy cause, perhaps. But she is devoted. Rumpole, I ask it for Hilda!'

What I didn't know at that point was that Hilda was being more active in my defence than I was. She had called at our Chambers and, while I was fulfilling a previous engagement in Snaresbrook Crown Court, she had burst into Ballard's room unannounced, rousing him from some solitary religious observance or an afternoon sleep brought on by over-indulgence in bean-shoot sandwiches at the vegetarian snack bar, and told him that I was in a little difficulty. Ballard's view, when he had recovered consciousness, was that I was in fact in deep trouble and he had prayed long and earnestly about the matter.

'I hope you're going to do something a little more practical than pray!' Hilda, as you may have noticed, can be quite sharp on occasions. She went on to tell Soapy Sam that she had called at the Bar Council, indeed there was no door she wouldn't open in my cause, and had been told that what Rumpole needed was a QC to defend him, and if he did his own case in the way he carried on down the Bailey 'he'd be sunk'.

'That seems to be sound advice, Mrs Rumpole.'

'I said there was no difficulty in getting a QC of standing and that Rumpole's Head of Chambers would be delighted to act for him.'

'You mean' – there was, I'm sure, a note of fear in Ballard's voice – 'you want me to take on Rumpole as a *client*?'

'I want you to stand by him, Sam, as I am doing, and as any decent Head of Chambers would for a tenant in trouble.'

'But he's got to apologise to Mr Justice Oliphant, fully and sincerely. How on earth am I going to persuade Rumpole to do that?' Ballard no doubt felt like someone called upon to cleanse the Augean stables, knowing perfectly well that he'd never be a Hercules.

'Leave that to me. I'll do the persuading. You just think of how you'd put it nice and politely to the judge.' Hilda was giving the instructions to counsel, but Ballard was still daunted.

'Rumpole as a client,' he muttered. 'God give me strength!'

'Don't worry, Sam. If God won't, I certainly will.'

After this encounter Ballard dined in his new-found splendour as a bencher and after dinner he found himself sitting next to none other than the complaining Judge Ollie Oliphant, who was in no hurry to return to his bachelor flat in Temple Gardens. Seeking to avoid a great deal of hard and thankless work before the Disciplinary Tribunal, Soapy Sam started to soften up his Lordship, who seemed astonished to hear that he was defending Rumpole.

'I am acting in the great tradition of the Bar, Judge,' Soapy Sam excused himself by saying. 'Of course we are bound to represent the most hopeless client, in the most disagreeable case.'

'Hopeless. I'm glad you see that. Shows you've got a bit of common sense.'

'Might you take' – Ballard was at his most obsequious – 'in your great wisdom and humanity, which is a byword at the Old Bailey; you are known, I believe, as the Quality of Mercy down there – a merciful view if there were to be a contrite apology?'

'Rumpole'd rather be disbarred than apologise to me.' Oliphant was probably right.

'But if he would?'

'If he would, it'd cause him more genuine pain and grief than anything else in the world.' And then the judge, thinking it over, was heard to make some sort of gurgling noise that might have passed for a chuckle. 'I'd enjoy seeing that, I really would. I'd love to see Horace Rumpole grovel. That might be punishment enough. It would be up to the tribunal, of course.'

'Of course. But your attitude, Judge, would have such an influence, given the great respect you're held in at the Bar. Well, thank you. Thank you very much.'

It was after that bit of crawling over the dessert that I spotted Oliphant coming out of Middle Temple Lane and Ballard imagined he'd saved me from ending my legal career in the cold and inhospitable waters of the Thames.

It soon became clear to me that my supporters expected me to appear as a penitent before Mr Justice Oliphant. This was the requirement of She Who Must Be Obeyed, who pointed out the awful consequences of my refusal to bow the knee. 'How could I bear it, Rumpole?' she said one evening when the nine o'clock news had failed to entertain us. 'I remember Daddy at the Bar and how everyone respected him. How could I bear to be the wife of a disbarred barrister? How could I meet any of the fellows in Chambers and hear them say, as I turned away, "Of course, you remember old Rumpole. Kicked out for unprofessional conduct." '

Of course I saw her point. I sighed heavily and asked her what she wanted me to do.

'Take Sam Ballard's advice. We've all told you, apologise to Sir Oliver Oliphant.'

'All right, Hilda, you win.' I hope I said it convincingly, but down towards the carpet, beside the arm of my chair, I had my fingers crossed.

Hilda and I were not the only couple whose views were not entirely at one in that uneasy period before my trial. During a quiet moment in the clerk's room, Henry came out with some startling news for Dot.

'Well, I told Eileen last night. It was an evening when she wasn't out at the drainage inquiry and I told my wife quite frankly what we decided.'

'What did we decide?' Dot asked nervously.

'Like, what you told me. I'm a big part of your life.'

'Did I say that?'

'You know you did. We can't hide it, can we, Dot? We're going to make a future together.'

'You told your wife that?' Dot was now seriously worried.

'She understood what I was on about. Eileen understands I have got to have this one chance of happiness, while I'm still young enough to enjoy it.'

'Did you say "young enough", Henry?'

'So, we're beginning a new life together. That all right, Dot?'

Before she could answer him, the telephone rang and the clerk's room began to fill with solicitors and learned friends in search of briefs. Henry seemed to regard the matter as closed and Dot didn't dare to reopen it, at least until after my trial was over and a historic meeting took place.

During the daytime, when the nuts and fruit and Madeira were put away and the tables were arranged in a more threatening and judicial manner, my trial began in the Outer Temple Parliament Room. It was all, I'm sure, intended to be pleasant and informal: I wasn't guarded in a dock but sat in a comfortable chair beside my legal advisers, Sam Ballard, QC, Liz Probert, his junior, and Mr Bernard, my instructing solicitor. However, all friendly feelings were banished by the look on the face of the presiding judge; I had drawn the short straw in the shape of Mr Justice Graves – or Gravestone, as I preferred to call him – who looked as though he was sick to the stomach at the thought of a barrister accused of such appalling crimes, but if someone had to be he was relieved, on the whole, that it was only Horace Rumpole.

Claude gave evidence in a highly embarrassed way of what he'd heard and I instructed Ballard not to ask him any questions. This came as a relief to him as he couldn't think of any questions to ask. And then Ollie Oliphant came puffing in, bald as an egg without his wig, wearing a dark suit and the artificial flower of some charity in his buttonhole. He was excused from taking the oath by Graves, who acted on the well-known theory that judges are incapable of fibbing, and he gave his account of all my sins and omissions to Montague Varian, QC, for the prosecution. As he did so, I examined the faces of my judges. Graves might have been carved out of yellowish marble; the lay assessor was Lady Mendip, the headmistress, and she looked as though she were hearing an account of disgusting words found chalked up on a blackboard. Of the three practising barristers sent to try me only Arthur Nottley smiled faintly, but then I had seen him smile through the most horrendous murder cases.

When Varian had finished, Ballard rose, with the greatest respect, to cross-examine. 'It's extremely courteous of you to agree to attend here in person, Judge.'

'And absolutely charming of you to lodge a complaint against me,' I murmured politely.

'Now my client wants you to know that he was suffering from a severe toothache on the day in question.' Ballard was wrong; I didn't particularly want the judge to know that. At any rate, Graves didn't think much of my temporary stopping as a defence.

'Mr Ballard,' he said, 'is toothache an excuse for speaking to a client during the luncheon-time adjournment? I should have thought Mr Rumpole would have been anxious to rest his mouth.'

'My Lord, I'm now dealing with the question of rudeness to the learned judge.'

'The boring old fart evidence,' I thought I heard Nottley whisper to his neighbouring barrister.

And then Ballard pulled a trick on me which I hadn't expected. 'I understand my client wishes to apologise to the learned judge in his own words,' he told the tribunal. No doubt he expected that, overcome by the solemnity of the occasion. I would run up the white flag and beg for mercy. He sat down and I did indeed rise to my feet and address Mr Justice Oliphant along these lines.

'My Lord,' I started formally, 'if it pleases your Lordship, I do realise there are certain things which should not be said or done in Court, things that are utterly inexcusable and no doubt amount to contempt.'

As I said this, Graves leant forward and I saw, as I had never in Court seen before, a faint smile on those gaunt features. 'Mr Rumpole, the tribunal is, I believe I can speak for us all, both surprised and gratified by this unusually apologetic attitude.' Here the quartet beside him nodded in agreement. 'I take it you're about to withdraw the inexcusable phrases.'

'Inexcusable, certainly,' I agreed. 'I was just about to put to Mr Justice Oliphant the inexcusable manner in which he sighs and rolls his eyes to heaven when he sums up the defence case.' And here I embarked on a mild imitation of Ollie Oliphant. ' "Of course you can believe that if you like, Members of the jury, but use your common sense, why don't you?" And what about describing my client's conduct as manslaughter during the evidence, which was the very fact the jury had to decide? If he's prepared to say sorry for that, then I'll apologise for pointing out his undoubted prejudice.'

Oliphant, who had slowly been coming to the boil, exploded at this point. 'Am I expected to sit here and endure a repetition of the quite intolerable . . .'

'No, no, my Lord!' Ballard fluttered to his feet. 'Of course not.

Please, Mr Rumpole. If it pleases your Lordship, may I take instructions?' And when Graves said, 'I think you'd better,' my defender turned to me with, 'You said you'd apologise.'

'I'm prepared to *swap* apologies,' I whispered back.

'I heard that, Mr Ballard.' Graves was triumphant. 'As I think your client knows perfectly well, my hearing is exceptionally keen. I wonder what Mr Rumpole's excuse is for his extraordinary behaviour today. He isn't suffering from toothache now, is he?'

'My Lord, I will take further instructions.' This time he whispered, 'Rumpole! Hadn't you better have toothache?'

'No, I had it out.'

'I'm afraid, my Lord' – Ballard turned to Graves, disappointed – 'the answer is no. He had it out during the trial.'

'So, on this occasion, Mr Ballard, you can't even plead toothache as a defence?'

'I'm afraid not, my Lord.'

'Had it out . . . during the trial.' Graves was making a careful note, then he screwed the top back on his pen with the greatest care and said, 'We shall continue with this unhappy case tomorrow morning.'

'My Lord' – I rose to my feet again – 'may I make an application?'

'What is it, Mr Rumpole?' Graves asked warily, as well he might.

'I'm getting tired of Mr Ballard's attempts to get me to apologise, unilaterally. Would you ask *him* not to speak to his client over the adjournment?'

Graves had made a note of the historic fact that I had had my tooth out during the trial, and Liz had noted it down also. As she wrote she started to speculate, as I had taught her to do in the distant days when she was my pupil. As soon as the tribunal packed up business for the day she went back to Chambers and persuaded Claude Erskine-Brown to take her down to the Old Bailey and show her the *locus in quo*, the scene where the ghastly crime of chattering to a client had been committed.

Bewildered, but no doubt filled with guilt at his treacherous behaviour to a fellow hack, Claude led her to the archway through which he had seen the tedious Tong listening to Rumpole's harangue.

'And where did you see Rumpole?'

'Well, he came out through the arch after he'd finished talking to his client.'

'But *while* he was speaking to his client.'

'Well, actually,' Claude had to admit, 'I didn't see him then, at all. I mean, I suppose he was hidden from my view, Liz.'

'I suppose he was.' At which she strode purposefully through the arch and saw what, perhaps, she had expected to find, a row of telephones on the wall, in a position which would also have been invisible to the earwigging Claude. They were half covered, it's true, with plastic hoods, but a man who didn't wish to crouch under these contrivances might stand freely with the connection pulled out to its full extent and speak to whoever he had chosen to abuse.

'So Rumpole might have been standing *here* when you were listening?' Liz had taken up her position by one of the phones.

'I suppose so.'

'And you heard him say words like, "Just get on with it. I've got enough trouble without you causing me all this agony. Get it out!"?'

'I told the tribunal that, don't you remember?' The true meaning of the words hadn't yet sunk into that vague repository of Wagnerian snatches and romantic longings, the Erskine-Brown mind. Liz, however, saw the truth in all its simplicity as she lifted a telephone, brushed it with her credit card in a way I could never manage, and was, in an instant, speaking to She Who Must Be Obeyed. Mizz Probert had two simple requests: could Hilda come down to the Temple tomorrow and what, please, was the name of Horace's dentist?

When the tribunal met next morning, my not so learned counsel announced that my case was to be placed in more competent hands. 'My learned junior Miss Probert,' Sam Ballard said, 'will call our next witness, but first she wishes to recall Mr Erskine-Brown.'

No one objected to this and Claude returned to the witness's chair to explain the position of the archway and the telephones, and the fact that he hadn't, indeed, seen me speaking to Tong. Montague Varian had no questions and my judges were left wondering what significance, if any, to attach to this new evidence. I was sure that it would make no difference to the result, but then Liz Probert uttered the dread words, 'I will now call Mr Lionel Leering.'

I had been at a crossroads; one way led on through a countryside too well known to me. I could journey on for ever round the Courts, arguing cases, winning some, losing more and more perhaps in my few remaining years. The other road was the way of escape, and once Mr Leering gave his evidence that, I knew, would be closed to me. 'Don't do it,' I whispered my instructions to Mizz Probert. 'I'm not fighting this case.'

'Oh, Rumpole!' She turned and leant down to my level, her face shining with enthusiasm. 'I'm going to win! It's what you taught me to do. Don't spoil it for me now.'

I thought then of all the bloody-minded clients who had wrecked the cases in which I was about to chalk up a victory. It was her big moment and who was I to snatch it from her? I was tired, too tired to win, but also too tired to lose, so I gave her her head. 'Go on, then,' I told her, 'if you *have* to.'

With her nostrils dilated and the light of battle in her eyes, Mizz Liz Probert turned on her dental witness and proceeded to demolish the prosecution case.

'Do you carry on your practice in Harley Street, in London?'

'That is so. And may I say, I have a most important bridge to insert this morning. The patient is very much in the public eye.'

'Then I'll try and make this as painless as possible,' Liz assured him. 'Did you treat Mr Rumpole on the morning of May the 16th?'

'I did. He came early because he told me he was in the middle of a case at the Old Bailey. I think he was defending in a manslaughter. I gave him a temporary stopping, which I thought would keep him going.'

'Did it?'

'Apparently not. He rang me around lunchtime. He told me that his tooth was causing him pain and he was extremely angry. He raised his voice at me.'

'Can you remember what he said?'

'So far as I can recall he said something like, "I've got enough trouble with the judge without you causing me all this agony. Get it out!" and, "Put us out of our misery!"'

'What do you think he meant?'

'He wanted his tooth extracted.'

'Did you do it for him?'

'Yes, I stayed on late especially. I saw him at seven thirty that evening. He was more cheerful then, but a little unsteady on his feet. I believe he'd been drinking brandy to give himself Dutch courage.'

'I think that may well have been so,' Liz agreed.

Now the members of the tribunal were whispering together. Then the whispering stopped and Mr Justice Gravestone turned an ancient and fish-like eye on my prosecutor. 'If this evidence is correct, Mr Varian, and we remember the admission made by Mr Claude Erskine-Brown and the position of the telephones, and the fact that he never saw Mr Rumpole, then this allegation about speaking to his client falls to the ground, does it not?'

'I must concede that, my Lord.'

'Then all that remains are the offensive remarks to Mr Justice Oliphant.'

'Yes, my Lord.'

'Yes, well, I'm much obliged.' The fishy beam was turned on to the defence. 'This case now turns solely on whether your client is prepared to make a proper, unilateral apology to my brother Oliphant.'

'Indeed, my Lord.'

'Then we'll consider that matter, after a short adjournment.'

So we all did a good deal of bowing to each other and as I came out of the Parliament Room, who should I see but She Who Must Be Obeyed, who, for a reason then unknown to me, made a most surprising U-turn. 'Rumpole,' she said, 'I've been thinking things over and I think Oliphant treated you abominably. My view of the matter is that you shouldn't apologise at all!'

'Is that your view, Hilda?'

'Of course it is. I'm sure nothing will make you stop work, unless you're disbarred, and think how wonderful that will be for our marriage.'

'What *do* you mean?' But I'd already guessed, with a sort of dread, what she was driving at.

'If you can't consort with all those criminals, I'll have you at home all day! There's so many little jobs for you to do. Re-paper the kitchen, get the parquet in the hallway polished. You'd be able to help me with the shopping every day. And we'd have my friends round to tea; Dodo Mackintosh complains she sees nothing of you.' There was considerably more in this vein, but Hilda had already said enough to make up my mind. When my judges were back, refreshed with coffee, biscuits and, in certain cases, a quick drag on a Silk Cut, Sam Ballard announced that I wished to make a statement, the die was cast and I tottered to my feet and spoke to the following effect.

'If your Lordship, and the Members of the tribunal, please. I have, I hope, some knowledge of the human race in general and the judicial race in particular. I do realise that some of those elevated to the Bench are more vulnerable, more easily offended than others. Over my years at the Old Bailey, before your Lordship and his brother judges, I have had to grow a skin like a rhinoceros. Mr Justice Oliphant, I acknowledge, is a more retiring, shy and sensitive plant, and if anything I have said may have wounded him, I do most humbly, most sincerely apologise.' At this I bowed and whispered to Mizz Liz Probert, 'Will that do?'

What went on behind closed doors between my judges I can't say. Were some of them, was even the sea-green incorruptible Graves, a little tired of Ollie's down-to-earth North Country common sense;

had they been sufficiently bored by him over port and walnuts to wish to deflate, just a little, that great self-satisfied balloon? Or did they stop short of depriving the Old Bailey monument of its few moments of worthwhile drama? Would they really have wanted to take all the fun out of the criminal law? I don't know the answer to these questions but in one rather athletic bound Rumpole was free, still to be audible in the Ludgate Circus *Palais de Justice*.

The next events of importance occurred at an ambitious Chambers party held as a delayed celebration of the fact that Mrs Phillida Erskine-Brown, our Portia, was now elegantly perched on the High Court Bench and her husband, Claude, had received the lesser honour of being swathed in silk. This beano took place in Ballard's room and all the characters in Equity Court were there, together with their partners, as Mizz Liz would call them, and I had taken the opportunity of issuing a few further invitations on my own account.

One of the most dramatic events on this occasion was an encounter, by a table loaded with bottles and various delicacies, between Dot and a pleasant-looking woman in her forties who, between rapid inroads into a plate of tuna-fish sandwiches, said that she was Henry's wife, Eileen, and wasn't Dot the new typist, because 'Henry's been telling me all about you'?

'I don't know why he does that. He has no call, really.' Dot was confused and embarrassed. 'Look, I'm sorry about what he told you.'

'Oh, don't be,' Eileen reassured her. 'It's a great relief to me. I was on this horrible slimming diet because I thought that's how Henry liked me, but now he says you want to make your life together. So, could you just whirl those cocktail sausages in my direction?'

'We're not going to make a life together and I don't know where he got the idea from at all. I mean, I like Henry. I think he's very sweet and serious, but in a boyfriend, I'd prefer something more muscular. Know what I mean?'

'You're not going to take him on?' Henry's wife sounded disappointed.

'I couldn't entertain the idea, with all due respect to your husband.'

'He'll have to stay where he is then.' Eileen lifted another small sausage on its toothpick. 'But I'm not going back on that horrible cottage cheese. Not for him, not for anyone.'

By now the party was starting to fill up and among the first to come was old Gravestone, to whom, I thought, I owed a very small debt of gratitude. I heard him tell Ballard how surprised he was that I'd invited him and he congratulated my so-called defender (and not my wife, who deserved all the credit) on having got me to apologise.

Ballard lied outrageously and said, 'As Head of these Chambers, of course, I do have a little influence on Rumpole.'

Shortly after this, another of my invitees came puffing up the stairs and Ballard, apparently in a state of shock, stammered, 'Judge! You're here!' to Mr Justice Oliphant.

'Of course I'm here,' Ollie rebuked him. 'Use your common sense. Made Rumpole squirm, having to apologise, did it? Good, very good. That was all I needed.'

Later Mr Justice Featherstone arrived with Marigold and among all these judicial stars Eileen, the ex-mayor, had the briefest of heart to hearts with her husband. 'She doesn't want you, Henry,' she told him.

'Please!' Our clerk looked nervously round for earwiggers. 'How on earth can you say that?'

'Oh, she told me. No doubt about it. She goes for something more muscular, and I know exactly what she means.'

Oblivious of this domestic drama, the party surged on around them. Ballard told Mr Justice Featherstone that it had been a most worrying case and Guthrie said things might be even more worrying now that I'd won, and Claude asked me why I hadn't told him that I was talking to my dentist.

'Your suggestion was beneath contempt, Erskine-Brown. Besides which I rather fancied being disbarred at the time.'

'Rumpole!' The man was shocked. 'Why ever should you want that?'

' "For the sword outwears its sheath," ' I explained, ' "And the soul wears out the breast, And the heart must pause to breathe." But not yet, Claude. Not quite yet.'

At last Henry managed to corner Dot, while Claude set off in a bee-line for the personable Eileen. The first thing Henry did was to apologise. 'I never wanted her to come, Dot, but she insisted. It must have been terribly embarrassing for you.'

'She's ever so nice, isn't she? You're a very lucky bloke, Henry.'

'Having you, you mean?' He still nursed a flicker of hope.

'No' – she blew out the flame – 'having a wife who's prepared to eat cottage cheese for you.'

Marigold said to Hilda, 'I hear Rumpole's not sitting as a judge. In fact I heard he was nearly made to sit at home permanently.' Marguerite Ballard, ex-matron down at the Old Bailey, told Mr Justice Oliphant that 'his naughty tummy was rather running away with him'. I told Liz that she had been utterly ruthless in pursuit of victory and she asked if I had forgiven her for saving my legal life.

'I think so. But who fed Hilda that line about having me at home all day?'

'What are you talking about, Rumpole?' She Who Must joined us.

'Oh, I was just saying to Liz, of course it'd be very nice if we could spend all day together, Hilda. I mean, *that* wasn't what led me to apologise.'

'That's the trouble with barristers.' She gave me one of her piercing looks. 'You can't believe a word they say.'

Before I could think of any convincing defence to Hilda's indictment, the last of my personally invited guests arrived. This was Fred Timson, wearing a dark suit with a striped tie and looking more than ever like a senior member of the old Serious Crimes Squad. I found him a drink, put it into his hand and told him how glad I was he could find time for us.

'What a do, eh?' He looked round appreciatively. 'Judges and sparkling wine! Here's to your very good health, Mr Rumpole.'

'No, Fred,' I told him, 'I'm going to drink to yours.' Whereupon I banged a glass against the table, called for silence and proposed a toast. 'Listen, everybody. I want to introduce you to Fred Timson, head of a noted family of South London villains, minor thieves and receivers of stolen property. No violence in his record. That right, Fred?'

'Quite right, Mr Rumpole.' Fred confirmed the absence of violence and then I made public what had long been my secret thoughts on the relationship between the Timsons and the law.

'This should appeal to you my Lords, Ladies and Gentlemen. Fred lives his life on strict monetarist principles. He doesn't believe in the closed shop; he thinks that shops should be open all night, preferably by jemmy. He believes firmly in the market-place, because that's where you can dispose of articles that dropped off the back of a lorry. But without Fred and his like, we should all be out of work. There would be no judges, none of Her Majesty's counsel, learned in the law, no coppers and no humble Old Bailey hacks. So charge your glasses, fill us up, Henry, and I would ask you to drink to Fred Timson and the criminals of England!'

I raised my glass but the faces around me registered varying degrees of disapproval and concern. Ballard bleated, 'Rumpole!', Hilda gave out a censorious 'Really, Rumpole!', Featherstone J. said, 'He's off again,' and Mr Justice Oliphant decided that if this wasn't unprofessional conduct he didn't know what was. Only Liz, flushed with her success in Court and a few quick glasses of the *Méthode Champenoise*, raised a fist and called out, 'Up the workers!'

'Oh, really!' Graves turned wearily to our Head of Chambers. 'Will Rumpole never learn?'

'I'm afraid never,' Ballard told him.

I was back at work again and life would continue much as ever at 3 Equity Court.